Gabrielle Lord is wi Australia's foremost logical thrillers are informed by a detailed knowledge of forensic procedures, combined with an unrivalled gift for story-telling. She is the author of twelve novels—*Death Delights, Bones, Tooth and Claw, Salt, Jumbo, The Sharp End, Feeding the Demons, Whipping Boy, Fortress, Baby Did a Bad Bad Thing, Lethal Factor* and most recently, *Spiking the Girl*. Her stories and articles have appeared widely in the national press and been published in anthologies. Winner of the 2002 Ned Kelly award for best crime novel *Death Delights* and joint winner of the 2003 Davitt crime fiction prize for *Baby Did a Bad Bad Thing*, Gabrielle has also written for film and TV. She lives in Sydney.

Other Jack McCain novels
Death Delights
Lethal Factor

DIRTY WEEKEND

GABRIELLE LORD

HODDER

To Ettie

HODDER AUSTRALIA

First published in Australia and New Zealand in 2005
by Hodder Australia
(An imprint of Hachette Livre Australia Pty Limited)
Level 17, 207 Kent Street, Sydney NSW 2000
Website: www.hachette.com.au

This edition published in 2006

Copyright © Gabrielle Lord 2005

This book is copyright. Apart from any fair dealing
for the purposes of private study, research, criticism
or review permitted under the *Copyright Act 1968*,
no part may be stored or reproduced by any process
without prior written permission. Enquiries should
be made to the publisher.

National Library of Australia
Cataloguing-in-Publication data

Lord, Gabrielle, 1946- .
  Dirty weekend: a Jack McCain thriller.

  ISBN-10 0 7336 2100 7.
  ISBN-13 9 780733 621000.

  1. Forensic scientists - Fiction. 2. Murder -
  Investigation - Fiction. I. Title.

A823.3

Text design and typesetting by Bookhouse, Sydney
Printed in Australia by Griffin Press, Adelaide

Hachette Livre Australia's policy is to use papers
that are natural, renewable and recyclable products
and made from wood grown in sustainable forests.
The logging and manufacturing processes are expected
to conform to the environmental regulations
of the country of origin.

ONE

I swung into the lane behind the Blackspot Nightclub, feeling almost nostalgic at the sight of crime scene tape sealing off the parking area and sections of the vacant land around it. As acting chief scientist of the Criminalistics section of the Australian Federal Police, it wasn't the usual thing for me to be attending a crime scene. Normally, I was taken up with more routine analyses and administration. But here I was, stuffed up with a bad head cold, attending a crime scene just as in the old days when I'd been a crime scene examiner with the New South Wales police.

Another fit of coughing interrupted my revery and I asked myself again why in hell I'd let the likes of bloody Earl Richardson talk me into getting up at sparrow fart on a frosty Canberra morning, leaving the warmth of the cottage and my bed, so much warmer these days for the presence of the woman who slept beside me. I'd planned to take a few days off work so as to spend some time with her but, instead of that, not only was I back on the job, but

I was also feeling bad about disappointing Iona—and that seemed to be happening a lot lately.

On the western side of the charcoal-grey exterior of the nightclub, I was waved down by a uniformed officer I didn't recognise. Handing over my ID, I looked up at the running lights spelling the club's name, now pallid in the dawn. Over the years, this building had undergone several transformations and name changes but I'd never visited it in any of its guises. Then again, I could say that about most clubs in the area. Since putting down the booze twelve years ago, I found I had little interest in places like nightclubs. I'd never liked them much even when I was a drinking man. Unless you were pissed, the noise was atrocious, the prices criminal and they didn't do a decent cup of tea.

The uniform logged my details and passed back my ID.

'Thanks, Dr McCain.'

I was right about not recognising him. No one who knew me ever called me by my honorific. He stepped back and waved me past the club, with its side wall plastered with layers of peeling posters of visiting rock bands, a hypnotist and an American evangelist.

I pulled up beside Harry Marshall's Riley, still angry with myself, yanking the handbrake harder than I'd intended. I didn't even *like* Earl Richardson—never had—he'd always been completely up himself in the days when we'd been colleagues in the New South Wales police; he was the sort of man who'd always got on my nerves with his pushiness and arrogance. I recalled the last time I'd talked to him, years ago, how we'd ended up blueing, and how he'd stormed off, me yelling after him. Not long after that, I heard he'd left the job, moved to Canberra and started his own security business. I'd never bothered to look him up and heard that he'd moved to Sydney last year.

My first instinct that morning, when I finally realised who was behind the hysterical voice, was to flick him off, fast, and right now I was wishing I'd done just that.

'*Please*, Jack,' he'd said, as I'd gathered myself, lurching awake, blinking and trying to clear my head, the luminescent green figures on the bedside clock showing 5.15. I hadn't been on call for years, but I still sprang awake, heart racing, at the first sound of the phone and it had taken me a moment to register the speaker. Red-eyed and still dopey with flu tablets, I tried to focus on what Richardson was saying.

'You've *got* to go out there! Tianna and me—just lately, I thought there was a real chance for us to get back together... Now I'm just the estranged husband and you *know* what the Homicide guys are going to think!'

'Calm down,' I'd said. 'Just slow down and tell me again what's going on.'

'For God's sake, Jack. I can't believe this is happening! Some female detective from Sydney crime scene has just left with my DNA in her kit! You've got to go out there and check it out.'

'Go where? Check what out?' I paused. 'Slow down and start from the beginning.'

I heard him take a deep breath. 'Right,' he said. 'I was woken up not long ago by a couple of youngsters in uniform.' His voice faltered before he continued. 'They said Tianna's been found dead in a car park somewhere down there—in Canberra.'

I stayed silent, thinking, as he paused to collect himself.

'Jack,' he whispered. 'Just when I was trying to reconcile with her—she's been murdered.'

That really took me aback. The few times I'd met Tianna—at conferences attended by both New South Wales police and Australian Federal Officers, or agents as they now term themselves—I'd warmed to the well-endowed brunette with a ready smile and a penchant for low-cut singlet tops.

'What happened?' I asked, then kicked myself for not sounding more compassionate.

'I don't *know*! That's why I want you to go out there and check things out. She was just left lying in the car park of some nightclub.'

'Where?'

'I don't know!' His voice broke completely then.

'I'm so sorry, Earl,' I said, and waited until he composed himself.

'Then this kid from the forensic unit wanted a buccal scrape from me!'

'You know it's standard practice to get a DNA sample,' I said, trying to calm him down. 'It's for elimination purposes too.'

'Yeah, so they said. But you know what that means. They'll be matching it against crime scene samples. Shit! I was only down there a week ago, trying to sort things out with her. *And* she was listening to me. My DNA is all through the bloody house. Please don't let them draw the wrong conclusions!' His distress was distorting his voice, making it hard for me to hear him.

'There's a big difference in the deposition of historical DNA compared with the amount deposited on the body during violent physical contact. Scientists *can* read the difference; that's our job. Surely you realise that,' I said, though I wasn't as confident as I sounded. This sort of case could make things very hard for investigators, unless there has been a violent struggle with the offender shedding a lot. But despite my feelings about Earl Richardson, his plight had touched me. How would I feel, I asked myself, if the cops had come knocking on *my* door with the same news about Genevieve? Wouldn't I be shit-scared too?

'I've been to hell and back over the last couple of years,' Earl was saying. 'I just don't think I can take any more stress. Just when I thought we might make it... You've gotta make sure things are done right. I was here alone! I've got no alibi! You've got to help me!'

'Earl, there are very competent crime scene crews here in Canberra. Besides, it's just not part of my brief. I'm a bench analyst in a lab. Not a crime scene examiner.'

'You tell him, Jack,' Iona whispered, snuggling up to me. 'Don't you dare go out at this hour!'

I kissed the top of her head, glancing at my watch as I pulled her closer. It wasn't even five thirty.

'I know the best people here, I'll talk to them and—'

'Please, Jack,' he cut in. 'I'm *begging* you. I remember what they used to say about you in Sydney. You were the *best*.'

And that's when I knew the man was really desperate. No way in the world would someone like Earl Richardson say something like that about me, about anyone.

'Look,' I said reluctantly, 'I'll go out there and check it out but I'm not promising anything.'

'God bless you, Jack.'

'You must be despairing,' I said, 'God blessing me like that.'

He sounded hurt. 'I'm a Catholic now, Jack,' he said. 'In fact, I'm a daily communicant.'

God preserve me from converts.

'You were my second call, after Father Basil. I need your prayers, Jack.'

'Give me a break,' I muttered, as I put the phone down. I'd forgotten what a daily communicant was.

'Jack, you're not going?' Iona rolled closer to me, a warm hand on my bare shoulder, and I cursed Earl Richardson afresh.

'I won't be away long,' I said. 'Promise.'

She sat up in bed, pulling the doona close, watching me as I dressed in the dark, finally tucking my shirt in and clipping my Black Commandos bikies' buckle on the belt to my denim jeans. A skull with a dagger through the eye socket over the Harley insignia, it had been given to me by my son Greg last Christmas and was a sure-fire conversation starter.

'Who was it?' Iona leaned over and switched on the bedside lamp.

I groped around for a jumper, feeling the autumnal chill in the air.

'You look real good in my bed,' I said, admiring her tousled early morning languor, her skin warmly pale in the lamplight. 'I'd like to paint you stretched over like that. I'd call it *Iona, Early Canberra Morning*.'

But she wasn't playing. 'Who was it?' she repeated.

'A bloke I used to work with in the police,' I said, still trying to recall what Earl Richardson and I had argued about that last day I saw him.

'Jack, you have to start saying *no* to people like him. You're not supposed to be on call like this.'

I watched a frown darkening her fine brows and shadowed eyes and I saw her go to say something, then change her mind.

Before we'd moved in together, we'd laid our cards on the table—we were grown-ups, we each had strong, independent lives, and now we were living what Charlie sometimes referred to as 'the Great Experiment', a relationship of equals built on mutual respect, honesty and self-awareness. Well, that was the theory at least. The reality was that I was in love with this woman—a true equal in every way—and I hadn't felt such powerful feelings since I'd been a young man. Sometimes it scared me stiff.

'Sweetheart, you know how busy I've been. You know we're understaffed. You know what my workload is like,' I said, sitting on the edge of the bed, taking her hand.

She didn't pull away but she didn't respond either. 'But we'd made plans for today,' she said, disappointment shadowing her eyes. 'To have the picnic we were supposed to have last week except you had to go haring off somewhere else instead.'

'I'll be back in plenty of time for lunch,' I said, glancing at my watch. 'Why don't you go out there whenever you want and I'll join you later in the day.'

We had a favourite spot not far from here, where the river curved around the roots of a huge willow tree whose green shade covered a perfect spot for rugs and cushions, books, magazines, cold chicken and salad and Iona's chilled crème caramels. So far, I think we'd managed to get out there once since Iona came to live with me.

'Last time you said that, you were away until dark,' she said, climbing out of bed, pushing hair away from her face, throwing her dressing-gown around her so that her strong body and her breasts with the terrible scar above them were hidden.

'You're beautiful,' I said, unable to take my eyes off her. I never tired of watching her.

'You're impossible.'

'It's cold. Get back into bed and I'll bring you a cup of coffee before I go,' I said.

But she didn't stop so I followed her down the hall and through the living room, still warm from last night's open fire, and into the kitchen. On the way, I crouched down in front of the fireplace and kick-started the fire with kindling, stirring the glowing coals, enjoying the scent of eucalypt and the snap and crackle as the bits of bark and twigs flamed up.

Because of my job in Canberra, I'd taken over a colleague's weekender, situated about nine kilometres out of town along the Woden Road. Very much a work in progress, the old-fashioned cottage had some modern areas—like the flash new kitchen, which delighted my brother—but the bathroom was still pretty dismal, with an old iron tub and ancient toilet with a noisy overhead cistern. Despite a bad leak in the ceiling, which I'd been meaning to fix for months during this dry spell, the lounge room was very comfortable and as there hadn't been any rain for ages, we hadn't been troubled by drips. Already, the cottage was reflecting the woman who now graced it. Like me, Iona was an amateur painter and her *Blue Monkey* a strange work that had once hung on the staircase of her Annandale house, now hung on our lounge room wall. She'd brought cushions and woollen rugs to throw over the old club lounge and chairs and she always managed to find something in the garden so that the rooms were brightened with fresh flowers. Often, I'd catch myself looking round with a silly smile, noting the beauty she'd brought into my life and, even now, after six months together, I still couldn't quite believe it. Iona was a woman full of grace and I swore to myself I'd make time for her—somehow.

After toast and coffee, I pulled on my old leather jacket and prepared to leave, checking that I had everything I needed packed in the back of my wagon, my breath steaming in the early morning chill, my footsteps crunching through one of the first frosts. Even the birds weren't saying too much just yet.

When I came back inside, Iona was already dressed and sitting near the fire, her long legs in brown corduroy slacks and my favourite soft fawn jumper with the sleeves rolled back, marking her students' music theory books. She'd dusted off her Australian Music Examination Board qualifications to teach keyboard practice and theory and walked into a full term's teaching at a leading girls college in Braddon while the permanent teacher was off on maternity leave.

'You look like you mean business,' I said.

'I do, Jack,' she said, looking up at me with her deep-set eyes, putting her pen down. 'We really need to talk about this.'

Whenever a woman said that, I got worried.

'We seem to be having this conversation too often lately,' said Iona, frowning. 'What do I have to do to convince you that if you want a relationship with me—with *anyone*—you have to put *time* into it? It's important to spend time with the person.' She pointed at me. 'You, me, together. Doing things. Talking, laughing. Making love. Time to let ideas and thoughts arise and be discussed. Above all, letting me in to you. Not shutting me out.'

'I don't shut you out,' I said.

'You do,' she countered. 'You're always in a hurry. Our relating has become—well—superficial over the last few months.'

'You're right,' I said, coming over and kissing her. 'I have been hard to catch lately. Always running from one thing to the next.'

'Jacinta rang me yesterday because she couldn't even reach you on the mobile,' she said.

'Did she say what she wanted?' I asked. My daughter would sometimes ring to grizzle when her boyfriend Andy was being—according to her—'a total dickhead'.

'That's not the point I'm trying to make,' she said.

'We've had all that extra work—lots of people away,' I said, trying to explain. 'Samples from the Indonesian police. I've had to pitch in with everyone else *and* manage the administration side of it as well. If I didn't switch the mobile off occasionally, I'd never get anything done—and with some assays, it's critical to work without interruption.'

I could see she wasn't convinced.

'What did Jacinta want?' I repeated after a pause.

'She's worried about Shaz. Said she turned up to yesterday's lectures with a black eye.'

One of Jacinta's friends from rehab days was involved with a violent man and Jacinta had spoken to me already of her concern.

In the firelight, I could see the love and concern in Iona's eyes and I put my arms around her. I didn't want to stuff up with this woman. My life span was reducing every day; I didn't want to go to my grave without experiencing real love and, with Iona, this was possible. It had taken both of us so long to find the other and I'd lived long enough to know that a woman like her was a rare gem. We were financially independent of each other and had no small children, so the usual grounds for conflict were not in place. Neither of us viewed the other as a means to an end, nor wished to derive any benefit from the other apart from mutual happiness and growth. My marriage—ill-judged and hormone-driven—had quite quickly turned into a war zone and I was determined to do things differently this time, and was very hopeful that I could.

'I really will do better,' I said, trying to lighten her mood, leaning to kiss her solemn face. 'Charlie and Greg will be down sometime today. I promise I'll be around for the next few days.'

Maybe I overdid the enthusiasm a bit.

'Practically a lifetime,' she said, turning back to her books with the hint of a smile on her full lips.

I went to kiss her properly but she fended me off with a cheek.

'You're pissed off at me,' I said.

'You can redeem yourself this time,' she said, smiling. 'Just remember the extra milk and bread and other basics for our visitors.'

I promised I wouldn't forget.

As I left the cottage, she kissed me goodbye on the doorstep then stepped back to regard me with her sombre, smoky eyes. 'I love you,' she said, steadily regarding me. 'But I can only do fifty per cent of our relationship.'

'I'd better go,' I said.

TWO

I was still thinking of Iona's words as I slammed my car door shut in the area behind the Blackspot Nightclub, in an outer suburb of Canberra. Signs of the terrible bushfires of a couple of years before were still visible, but rebuilding and the growth of new vegetation had softened the scars.

Iona was right. Not only did we need to spend more time together, but I needed to examine what it was that sabotaged the plans I made to do exactly this. I knew as few others can how easily and quickly a couple can start to grow apart, living separate lives, becoming estranged. It was partly what had happened in my marriage. The routine set in, the job, the shopping, the housekeeping, the taxi service for the kids. Too tired to make love at the end of a difficult day, physical intimacy fell away. And although my marriage had fallen apart inevitably because of the emotional immaturity of both parties, I was only too aware that my alcoholism had played a large part in its destruction. I knew how important it was for a couple to spend unhurried time together and Iona needed me to make that time for her.

I wasn't too sure I understood what she meant about me shutting her out. But it was true that too often lately she'd had to eat dinner alone because I'd been catching up on urgent work at Forensic Services. Or she'd have a couple of late evening music lessons to teach and would eat in town, coming back to the cottage later to find me crashed out with exhaustion. My kids, although both now studying at university, still needed the emotional support and occasional financial help of a father and I wasn't spending as much time with them as I wanted either. I needed to make more time for my kids, time for my woman and time for myself. Even forensic analysts have souls, I'd joked to my brother, Charlie, not so long ago. And it had been too long since I'd taken out my paintbrushes and completed the watercolour of Boora Point, the sandstone headland that butted out in the ocean at Malabar. Yet no matter how much I told myself that I wanted to do these things, something always seemed to be getting in the way. A talk with Charlie might help clarify things—if I could bring myself to do it.

I decided to give my brain a break by surveying the landscape for a while before I headed to the crime scene proper. I spent a moment taking in the place—dull, heavy skies that threatened rain, a bird of prey high above, circling on a thermal, the stink of cars and asphalt.

During the year, the isolated storms that had brought rain were over far too quickly, wetting only the surface, turning dirt roads into skidding traps, not delivering any real moisture, merely settling the dust awhile. I looked down, then cursed when I realised I'd just trodden in dog shit and tried to rid myself of it by scraping my shoe up and down in the burnt-off grass.

I walked over to the far side of the parking area, towards a small group of people, noticing beyond them the figure of a space-suited young woman working by herself, taking soil samples. Wisps of fair hair escaped the plastic covering her head and the outstanding features of her slender body were not entirely hidden by the rustling, impermeable fabric. There'd never seemed to be such attractive women working crime scene when I'd been in the job in Sydney. Curious, I diverted from my course to join the group to check her out. She straightened up as I neared, waiting for me to reach her. At closer quarters, her face reminded me of those overbred dogs whose eye sockets seem too small for their large eyes.

'What are you doing here?' she snapped. 'Who are you?'

Was it my belt buckle or the fact that I hadn't shaved? I could've replied that when I'd started out in this work, she'd been blowing bubbles in her milk.

She crinkled her nose in a grimace. 'What's that stink?'

Guiltily, I looked down at my sneaker. I couldn't smell anything. I pulled out a handkerchief and blew my nose.

'What's in there?' I countered, pointing to the small plastic collection jar in her hand.

In response, she turned to one of the locals in the group behind us. 'Brian!' she called. 'Can you get this fellow out of here? He won't identify himself and he's contaminating my samples.'

Brian Kruger, with whom I'd worked quite closely on a previous case, straightened up from where he'd been squatting, his frown gabling his thick eyebrows. Then, as he recognised me, his expression of aggravated surprise switched to a grin.

'You heard the lady, pal,' he said, standing up and coming over to join us. 'Stop contaminating her samples.'

The young woman looked from one of us to the other, trying to read the situation, her face betraying nothing. This was a very cool customer.

'Sofia,' Brian said. 'Meet your boss. Dr Jack McCain.'

So this was the latest member of the team, I thought, remembering the name from the very impressive application she'd forwarded. After the disastrous events of the previous year, including the loss of two of our most senior scientists and the relocation of another two to Indonesia, several vacancies had been advertised, including that of chief scientist. A couple of less senior positions had been filled, but, increasingly, it looked as if I was pretty well stuck with the acting position until the right applicant turned up. The early selection process and interviews had been held at Sydney headquarters, and I'd been away in Sydney during the recent final interviews in Canberra. The palynology lab was housed separately from the main complex, linked by a covered walkway, otherwise Sofia and I would have met sooner.

Sofia didn't bat an eyelid. Instead, she stared at me, her eyes moving down towards the Black Commandos buckle and back again, before saying, 'And how was I supposed to know that?'

Brian's grin widened as he inclined his head in her direction. 'And this,' he said, 'is Sofia Verstoek. Sofia's new on the block. She's been helping us out over the last few weeks.'

Sofia Verstoek had still barely acknowledged me, nor did she seem to notice the irony in Brian's voice. Ordinarily, I'd have welcomed someone like her on board, but she'd got me on a bad day and I was still feeling pissed off.

'I want to know what you're collecting,' I repeated, again indicating the collection jar she was holding.

'Soil samples. From a series of locations around the scene.'

I noticed how mask-like her face seemed, as if it were stretched too tight across the bones of her face.

'Samples I need to examine,' she said. 'And from what I hear,' she looked around at the others, 'things in Canberra are still somewhat backward.

I believe I'm the first palynologist employed here full-time.'

I couldn't help thinking that if they were all like her, she'd probably be the last.

'Okay. Carry on,' I said and watched while she went back to work, confident she'd won that round. I actually knew something of her discipline, but I didn't intend to play ego games with her. And, to be fair, as a particle man myself, the forensic evidence Sofia Verstoek might discover could be of great help to this investigation.

'She can't help it,' said Brian, before I could say anything. 'You've heard the definition of a well-balanced New Zealander.'

I hadn't.

'A chip on both shoulders.'

It certainly seemed apt in this case.

'Apparently, they've been using forensic palynology in New Zealand for twenty-five years, but until I met her ladyship, I'd never heard of it.'

I went to my car and pulled on a sterile suit and gloves from the collection I keep in the back in a plastic fishing container. I had to admit Sofia Verstoek had a point—I *should* have suited up before approaching. As I was about to pull the plastic covers over my shoes, I bent and sniffed. Damned if I could smell anything.

I collected my video camera, grabbed the smaller tackle box that I used to house my bits and pieces and made my way towards the small group of people who stood around the body of Tianna Richardson.

Even from a slight distance, the body on the tarmac, left arm flung out at shoulder height, legs sprawled, head turned away, could never be mistaken for someone who was merely sleeping. Or even unconscious. I'd been to the crime scenes of a lot of violent, fatal sexual assaults and this had all the trademarks—legs outflung, skirt bunched up, panties tugged down, abrasions down one side of the leg, dried blood smearing the thighs.

Tianna still had her curvaceous figure, perhaps a little heavier than I recalled, and the lurex thread on her jacket glittered as I approached. The spangled top she was wearing revealed a strip of tanned belly just above her waist and her long dark skirt was bunched up across her thighs and belly, barely keeping her decent. Her panties, a black lace figure-of-eight, were twisted round her right ankle above a high-heeled sandalled foot, the shoe half pulled off. The other sandal was missing.

'Ah, Jack,' said Harry Marshall, nodding to me. 'I thought it was you getting out of that wagon, but then I remembered that you're supposed to be keeping decent hours these days.'

Insomniac clinical director and senior pathologist at the Canberra morgue, Harry was an old friend and we went back a very long way—I counted him as a personal friend as well as a colleague. The good humour in his lively eyes was unmistakeable but he was looking tireder and older than when we last met.

'I wish we didn't always have to meet like this,' I said, 'over half-naked women.'

'It's our fatal charm, Doctor,' Harry said, looking more closely at the woman who lay near my plastic-covered shoes. 'Someone's charm was certainly fatal for this one,' he continued, gently lifting and turning the dead woman's head to reveal a matted, bloody area at the back. 'Nasty,' he said. 'Looks like she's been bashed with a weapon of some sort.'

'We haven't found any weapon,' said Brian, who'd been directing the search around the immediate area. 'This place,' he continued, gesturing back towards the nightclub building, 'is one of those grab-a-granny joints. Some of the guys from work come here towards the end of the week. They reckon you're guaranteed a sure thing. Reckon the old chicks are really into it. Some hot bodies, too. Monday night was a special singles night.'

'Got lucky, did you, Brian?' I asked. 'What do the grannies think?'

'Modesty prevents me from saying,' he said.

'Never prevented you before,' I said, recalling a couple of conversations I'd had with Brian over the years. 'Who found her?'

'The guys on the drunk patrol,' he said. 'They called me around 2 a.m. I'd only been down for a few hours.'

I remembered that life well and was happy to be out of it. Why, then, was I buying back in like this?

'So what's your take on this?' I asked.

'I heard she liked a bit of rough. Maybe things got out of hand.'

'Who told you that?' I said, immediately interested.

'Can't remember.' Brian shrugged, then got up and walked around the other side of the woman's body.

'Try. It's important,' I persisted.

'Sorry, Doc, Can't help you. It was just one of those things. People talking.'

Rumours, I thought. This place lived on them. If Brian didn't remember, maybe someone else might.

I took out my video camera and began recording, starting with a slow pan around the area, establishing the place and surrounding conditions. While I did this, Brian took a lot of stills of the same area. Later, if the need arose, I could get copies from him.

After I'd filmed the surrounding areas, I focused my attention on the dead woman on the ground. My job here was to record, collect, collate and later analyse any traces that might be helpful to the investigation. I panned down, recording the woman's body, the scratches and abrasions on her arms and legs. I thought wearily of the hundreds of scenes like this I'd attended over the years, documenting a human being's last struggle. Knowing Tianna, even slightly as I did, made me feel that much worse. With my sodden head, aching face and sweaty space-suited body, I suddenly felt old and unaccountably sad. I needed a holiday. I tried to focus on the bright side. At least here I didn't have to deal with decomposition.

There was something about the presence of a dead body, especially a murdered one, that still touched me. Despite its silence, a dead body posed an immense question. A murdered body even more so.

Why did your life end like this? I silently asked. Who did this to you, Tianna? And why?

Gilded flies already clustered around her staring eyes and open mouth, disappearing then reappearing from the shadowed area covered by the bunched-up skirt. One species of fly arrived within four minutes of death and they'd had quite a few hours already to get busy.

While Harry waved the flies away, I focused in on a dark, extensive bruise covering one side of her face, the dried matter gathered on the lower side of her mouth. Had she been attacked and taken by surprise in the dark while getting into her car to go home? Or had she danced the night away with someone who'd later turned nasty in the car park? Moving down, I filmed a reddish mark just visible in the declivity between her left shoulder and the swelling of the breast and I wondered what it was, noticing another similar mark just visible on her jaw, near her left ear. After filming them and asking Brian to take some stills, I turned back to my examination.

'What's that stuff?' I asked, my attention taken by something I could see through the magnifying glass. Brian came closer and leaned over my shoulder. On the blood-matted hair, coarse grains of greyish sand could be seen adhering to the wounds and their edges, and I could see more of them, some as big as sugar crystals, embedded in the reflected scalp tissue now shrinking and drying around the seat of the major damage. As Harry held the head, I used a small brush to sweep the grey particles into a specimen jar, taking as much as I could gather.

Before getting up, I carefully checked over the ground around and beneath the dead woman. Then I straightened, frowning. The car park was made of old asphalt, strewn with debris from the trees and the fine dry soil that surrounded it. I took samples of this soil in another jar for comparison back at the laboratory. Curious, I thought, that I couldn't see any of those larger grains. Maybe closer examination would reveal more.

'How long has she been dead?' I asked Harry as he stood up, knowing it would only be an estimation. The cool of the early hours of the morning would be tempered by the stored warmth of the previous day in the asphalt.

Harry considered. 'Six or eight hours, maybe longer.'

I glanced at my watch, calculating. That would make time of death somewhere around or between ten p.m. and midnight. I heard voices behind me and turned to see a police officer letting people in and out of the back door of the nightclub, taking down the details of the staff who'd been working last night. Meanwhile, Brian set about securing the exhibits from this particular crime scene—scrapes and lifts from clothes and flesh—most of which would end up in the locked fridges at Weston.

A perfectionist, Harry discouraged questions before he'd had a chance to go over a body with his usual fastidious attention to detail. Still, it wouldn't hurt to press him a little.

'Those marks?' I asked, pointing to the discolourations on the thigh. 'What do you make of them?'

Harry took off his gloves. 'Call me later on today and I'll tell you what I *know*, Jack.'

Chastened, I went back to checking the area. Looking around the car park, I realised which vehicle had belonged to the dead woman from the people gathered around it. I videotaped the car, a dark blue Ford Laser, knowing it would be taken away to a secure parking area and checked out thoroughly. Then I looked at the two garbage bins near the club's back door. 'What are you going to do about those?' I asked Brian. 'And all this?' I indicated the scattered rubbish lying around the parking area.

'We'll get the piglets from the Academy,' said Brian. 'Nothing they love more than a nice long fingertip search. If they find anything, it'll end up on your table.'

'Speaking of piglets,' I said, aware of the unfortunate memory cue, 'I seem to remember the Richardsons had at least one kid.'

'Yeah. There's a son somewhere,' said Brian, checking his notes. 'Jason Richardson. According to the Sydney police who informed the ex-husband, he hasn't spoken to his mother or his father for some time.'

Jason was going to feel bad about this, I thought. But I'd been a copper too long not to move on quickly to the next thought. Murder was a family affair. Wherever there was a relationship, there was potential for murder. We needed to find Jason.

I frowned, seeing a faint impression in the dust. 'There's a bootprint over there,' I called to Brian. 'Or at least a partial. Could be important.'

Brian brought his camera for still shots while I filmed it. Though it might turn out to be nothing, the fact that it was within the perimeters of the disturbed area gave me a little hope. After we'd finished our respective shots, Brian sprayed the print to fix it—a large, clear front sole imprint and a partial of the heel impression.

Sofia Verstoek approached. 'You should have let me take samples from that bootprint. *Before* you fixed it. You could have lost valuable evidence,' she said. 'I should always get priority before other procedures.'

Brian's thick brows formed an ominous line. 'Ma'am,' he said, with pointed courtesy, 'I've been getting convictions for years without your birds and bees stuff.'

'I want a section of that print,' she snapped. 'I only need very small amounts.' I wondered why she didn't do the female thing and try to wrap Brian round her little finger. God knows he's an easy enough mark. We all were.

Brian stared her down without answering. I felt mean because inside I was silently cheering him. I had to remind myself that I was a man of science and shouldn't let personal animosity get in the way.

'Is anyone going to turn her over?' Sofia asked. 'I want to take samples from right underneath the body.'

We'd finished recording the body in situ, so Brian and I lifted the body, carefully, so as not to miss anything. That's when we saw the half-smoked reefer that had been lying just under her stiff right hand. I stood back while Brian took a few close-up shots of it, noting the lipstick stains on one end. Once he was out of the way, I used the video to shoot this new angle, then I carefully tweezered it up and bagged and labelled it aware of Sofia watching every move. If Tianna had shared a joint with her assailant, there might be valuable traces of him captured on the thin paper of the joint.

'Has anyone had a look in there?' she asked, her attention moving to the small beaded evening bag lying near the body.

'How do you think we knew who she was?' Brian said, picking up the bag and showing her the contents—a small wallet with driver's licence, a key ring with several keys and a squashed twenty-dollar bill.

'That's odd,' Sofia said, peering inside the small bag, then touching the gleaming silver and black beads that decorated it.

'What's odd?' said Brian. 'No one's nicked anything.'

Sofia glared at him then turned back to the body on the ground. With a puzzled frown, she unscrewed the lid from another sterile container and took more samples from beside the handbag. 'Hasn't anyone noticed what's truly weird about the way this woman's dressed?'

'Truly weird?' I repeated, hearing her New Zealand accent more clearly. 'You tell me what's truly weird.'

'You're a man,' she said, the sneer obvious. 'Typical of you not to notice.' She pointed to the sprawled body. 'Look at her jacket. Then look at her top.'

I did and was none the wiser.

'Look at her shoes. *And* her bag,' Sofia went on. 'Then take a look at her earrings.'

Tianna Richardson had worn narrow silver and black high-heeled sandals on her last outing. They matched the silver spangles on her cropped top and the flashy diamanté flower on her jacket.

'Now look at that daggy skirt,' said Sofia, 'and tell me there's nothing weird about what she's wearing.'

Women's fashion was not my forte. With my brain fogged up and the spacesuit becoming oppressive, I was in no mood to play clever dick with the likes of Sofia Verstoek.

'Truly weird is your territory, Miss Verstoek,' I replied, and continued my business with all of my usual caution, bagging the dead woman's hands, leaving the clipping and cleaning of her fingernails to Harry Marshall, who'd send what he found over to me for analysis. Then, even though Brian had already done this, I collected samples from her clothing, face, hair and shoes, using whatever method suited the surface best, lifting, scraping and collecting fibres and particles with the small hand vacuum and tape from my box of tricks. I'd been in the job too long not to take duplicate samples for myself. Exhibits have been known to walk from even the best-secured areas.

I was finalising the last of my list of samples, when, sensing someone approaching, I looked up to see Sofia Verstoek back again.

'In future, I insist on first go at the pollen traps,' she said. 'And I want Harry Marshall to let me have the clothes as soon as he's finished with them.'

I bridled, and thought of Genevieve saying 'what's the magic word?' all those years ago to our children. For one childish moment myself I wanted to say: *Stuff you, you're not getting hold of my samples.*

'You'll have to ask him that yourself,' I said, knowing Harry was more than capable of putting someone like Sofia Verstoek in her place. 'Clothing goes to Vic or Florence first, so they can examine for trace evidence.'

'And what do you think pollen is?' she said. 'It's *my* trace evidence. I don't want you washing out clothes or doing other procedures that might compromise *my* findings.'

It was time to let her have one barrel. 'You know as well as I do that pollen is extremely tough and resistant,' I said. 'Washing's not going to dislodge all of it and, even if it did, I'd find it in the filters.'

She didn't look impressed enough, so I fired the second barrel. 'And if I do happen to find any palynomorphs, you'll be the first to know.' I couldn't resist continuing: 'Or any acritarchs or phytoliths.'

She blinked.

'I'll centrifuge the whole damn lot to concentrate the pollen assemblage and send it on to you. Okay?'

I was going to have to invite Sofia Verstoek into my office soon for a chief scientist 'we all work as a team here' chat. I reminded myself that this applied to me too, and stopped myself from any further escalation.

If my saying my bit had impressed her, Sofia gave no indication. She pointed a pen at the body on the ground. 'I heard she's the wife of a New South Wales police officer.'

'Ex-police,' I said. 'He's been running his own business for some years.'

'No doubt he thinks he'll get special treatment.'

There was no missing the contempt in her voice and something in her manner again reminded me of Genevieve. Before I could stop myself, and despite my earlier intentions, I let my irritation get the better of me. 'What is it with you?' I said. 'Are you always this difficult?'

The large brown eyes widened and her face paled. I noticed her gloved hands clench and for an unbelievable split-second I thought she might hit me. Then, suddenly, sun lighting the fine hair of her brows created a golden aura over her cheekbones and I found myself speculating how I could best capture it in paint. You look like a honey bee, I thought, fuzzy gold, and you'll sting anyone who comes near.

Sofia Verstoek stood uncertain a moment longer, then turned on her heel and strode away.

'Hey,' I called after her. 'You haven't told me about the earrings. Or the skirt.'

She turned and gave me a look. *As if*, it said. As I stared after her departing back, I regretted my words but this woman riled me and I no longer had the patience to remain professional every minute of the day and night. According to my brother Charlie, I was heading for burnout.

Turning my attention back to my work, I decided I'd do a more thorough examination of Tianna Richardson's clothing back at Forensic Services before passing on anything interesting to the relevant experts, including the latest ungracious addition to our staff.

I was sealing and documenting packages back near my wagon when my mobile rang.

'I can't talk to you, Earl,' I said as soon as I recognised his voice, wishing like crazy I'd never let him talk me into this. I could still be in bed with Iona, looking forward to a relaxing day together instead of logging endless crime scene items and dealing with an uppity young scientist.

'Now you're doing it too,' he said. 'Treating me like a suspect.'

'You know the ropes, Earl,' I said, irritated. '*Everyone* close to the victim is potentially a suspect in this sort of thing. I can't have any contact with you.' I didn't add 'of all people', which was better left unsaid. I paused in my lecture, feeling sorry for the poor bastard. Now that he *was* on the line, I might as well put it to good use. 'We're going to have to talk to your son, Jason. How can we get in touch with him?'

'That little bastard,' said his father. 'No idea.'

'That's a hard line for a daily communicant to take.'

'You don't know what he's like,' said Earl. 'I've washed my hands of him.'

'Like Pilate?' I said, unable to resist.

'He drives around Australia in a shaggin' wagon—wouldn't work in an iron lung. Bludges off his grandmother. Smokes dope and God knows what other drugs. Swore at my spiritual director. Father Basil was a gent about it, but I was ropeable. Thinks he can just lob up at my mother's place or my place any time and sleep on the floor,' said Earl, his tone becoming more and more heated. 'You know I've had to leave my nice house down there and live in a rented place?'

I took down the details out of habit. Glebe Point Road was a major thoroughfare these days and must be noisy, I thought, compared to the bungalow in Kincaid Street, Deakin.

'I wouldn't know how to contact Jason, anyway,' Earl added.

'Okay,' I said. 'Brian Kruger will be in touch then to get further details. And you must *not* call me again. Everything's being done according to the book. I was there myself and I can assure you of that. So from now on, no more contact, okay?'

'But I'm really scared they're going to come after me. You've got to make sure the scene and the expert analysis is handled properly. My bloody life could depend on it! Jack, we were friends!'

'We were *what*?'

That did it. Despite Earl Richardson's delusions about the state of the past relationship between us, I had done what he'd asked. Getting religion must have softened his brain worse than I'd believed and the bad head cold I had must have softened mine even more. 'I've gotta go,' I said, and tucked my mobile back on my belt.

I waved at Harry who was also about to leave. 'Will you do something for me?' I asked. 'Get those earrings over to Cec Peabody, the jeweller, before they're returned to the family? I want to know what he says about them.'

I'd been piqued, more than I was prepared to admit, by the blonde palynologist's observations.

Harry gave me a long stare. 'You don't look too well, Jack. How long since you had a check-up?'

I laughed and brushed off his concern. '*You* should talk.'

I'd packed my wagon, bundled everything up for disposal and was about to start the drive to work when I remembered something. I walked over to Brian.

'That comment you made about Tianna Richardson liking a bit of rough? Was it recent?' I asked.

Brian's eyebrows reached their highest altitude. 'I can't remember.'

'Think.'

Brian shook his head. 'I think it was at a conference. Or in the meal room.'

'Why was Tianna Richardson the subject of gossip in a police meal room?' I asked.

'Search me,' said Brian. 'Crime scene people don't get to have meals.'

Back in my wagon, I wondered if the rumour had any substance and puzzled about why a woman might seek out rough handling. One for my brother Charlie, the clinical psychologist, I decided.

THREE

On the drive out to Weston, I thought about Earl Richardson and whether he was capable of killing Tianna in a fit of jealousy or anger. Finding myself on this mental trajectory about men and their estranged wives, I realised it had been a while since I'd heard from Genevieve. I'd spoken to her a couple of times a few months ago, about the kids. Greg, now twenty-one, was living in a communal house in Stanmore while studying for a Communications degree at the University of Technology Sydney. Despite the bad times she'd endured, nineteen-year-old Jacinta had begun her first year of a science degree this year. At fifteen she'd run away and lived on the streets of Kings Cross. I'd eventually tracked her down and she'd finally come home and got clean and sober shortly after, going on to spend time at a rural rehabilitation establishment in Queensland where, between milking cows and putting in fence strainers, she'd begun to learn how to get on with other human beings, starting the long road home towards healing mind, body and soul. It was much the same journey I'd been forced to undertake years before, when I'd faced up to my alcoholism and stopped drinking. Now she lived at Malabar, in the house I'd bought after the divorce.

My ex-wife was very suspicious about how I'd been able to afford to buy something so soon after the divorce and I'd told her my father had helped me. The last thing I ever wanted Genevieve to find out—the last thing I ever wanted *anyone* to find out—was that I'd used dealer's money. Jacinta had come back into my life after a year and a half on the streets of Sydney, with hundreds of thousands of dollars in cash in her carrybag, smacked off her face and on the run from the dangerous dealer she'd robbed. So far, only my children, my brother and my old partner in the New South Wales police, Bob Edwards, knew about this money. Malabar, with its mix of housing commission, modest old-fashioned cottages and brand new faux-Tuscan villas was just the right suburb for me, far away enough from the demanding city, close to the ocean and the sandstone cliffs.

Lately, Jacinta was managing her academic load and her relationship with her boyfriend Andy well. I could always tell how things were going between them by keeping an eye on the velour and velcro toy lemurs Andy had given her for her last birthday. If the lemurs were twined together somewhere, all was well. Occasionally, I'd find the male lemur in disgrace, head first in the wastepaper basket. Only last week, when I'd spent a couple of days at Malabar, Jacinta had returned from a visit to

Andy's place, raced inside, ignored me, grabbed the lemurs from where they were hanging in a tangle from the light fitting, pulled their velcroed paws apart and hurled the black and white one out the window by his striped tail.

I felt relieved and happy that, despite the shenanigans of Genevieve and me, both our kids were travelling better than a lot of young people I knew about. Genevieve, a difficult woman, had been resentful that both kids had elected to live with me after we'd separated, but we'd finally come to an agreement for us both to give some financial help to the kids while they were students.

On the way back to work, I picked up a hamburger. As I munched it in the car, my eyes taking in the dry countryside, I thought about the crime scene I'd just left. Considering the half-smoked reefer I'd tweezered into an evidence bag, Brian Kruger's reconstruction of the scuff marks could well prove to be correct. Tianna Richardson and her companion had probably slipped outside into the relative privacy of the parking area to share a joint. Maybe then the other party had decided that the invitation to share a joint extended to a more intimate exchange of body fluids. If we found traces of both people's DNA on the reefer stub, and Harry Marshall found something similar when he took vaginal swabs, we might be well on the way to tracking down the other person. If the other party had form, we might already have him filed away on CrimTrak's database. In my experience, murder was the last stage of a journey of violence that began in the offender's babyhood with violent parental assaults. Children learned violence—if violence was the language at home—as thoroughly as they learned speech. Violence became the automatic tool for conflict resolution—the first resort. Proceeding through a series of escalating assaults, the violent offender—because invariably that was what he'd become by now, and almost always he was male—arrived at the inevitable assault where someone died.

I was reasonably sure that whoever killed Tianna Richardson had either killed prior to this or, at the very least, had been involved in a serious assault or two. I felt sure he would have already served time for crimes of violence and that we'd have his genetic material on record to match against. And if it turned out that he owned a pair of boots that had made the print I'd noticed, we could lock him up and throw away the key. If, on the other hand, he hadn't served time, he had the luck of the devil. And the investigators would have their work cut out for them.

By the time I'd arrived at Weston and disposed of my used gear, the threatening skies were flashing distant lightning. I still didn't hold much hope for more rain; we'd seen this light show too often lately for my hopes to rise. My head had cleared a little and I hoped that my defences were winning against the virus.

Swiping myself into the building with my security ID, I logged and stowed the various bags and jars of physical evidence into the secure refrigerator where they would remain until analysis.

On the way down the corridor to my office, I saw Dr Florence Horsefall, who heads up Biological Criminalistics, coming out of one of the examination rooms, pulling off her white coat and shaking her bushy hair free of the cap that had restrained it. 'Jack,' she said, surprised. 'I heard you went out to that crime scene at the nightclub. I thought you were supposed to be having some time off.'

Florence and I have a long history, some of it a little embarrassing due to a misunderstanding on my part. On the whole, however, we had a good working relationship and she was one of the best—fastidious, reliable and utterly trustworthy.

'I know. But I couldn't really get out of this one.' It sounded pathetic. 'I wrap one job up and then I find another one coming in the door.'

'You've got to learn not to pick the phone up,' said Florence. 'Just let it ring while you walk out.' She sighed. 'Now that you've found someone like Iona, you mustn't neglect her.' Florence had met Iona in the meal room and the two of them had hit it off immediately.

Recalling Iona's face that morning, her disappointment, I nodded. 'You're right. I should have let it ring this morning.'

I looked more closely at Florence. Under her thick hair, her face showed tiredness and strain. I suspected mine would be the same. We were all overworked and understaffed, trying to straddle two, sometimes three people's jobs—the disease of our age. The worst thing was, we were all adapting to this, as if it were acceptable, partly because if we said too often and too loudly that it wasn't, our own jobs could be in danger. And I was about to add to Florence's load.

'Florence, I'll be putting some items through your lab today or tomorrow. And you can expect more when Harry sends the victim's clothing over here.' I visualised the outflung body of Tianna Richardson, her dainty earrings and rumpled skirt. 'I want samples cut and processed then sent on to CrimTrak for matching.'

'Where am I going to find the time to do all this? You know I'm snowed under already—we *all* are.' She gave me a look to emphasise her point. 'And if you go on leave, it'll be impossible. I'm behind with so many cases, and two new urgents came through last week. I'm supposed to be supervising junior staff as well as do my own work. Vic Agnew told me last week he's thinking of taking a fortnight off—'

I interrupted her, not wanting to get into a long argument about staffing levels and work overload.

'I'll ask Vic to help out,' I said quickly. 'Make sure Miss Verstoek takes delivery of the victim's clothing before any other procedures are carried out.'

Florence's face reddened with fury. '*Miss* Verstoek? Don't get me started on *her*,' she said, getting well and truly started. 'I've never seen anything like it before! In my day, the junior scientists showed some respect for the older, experienced people. She's already tried to tell me how to do my job and she hasn't been here five minutes! We'll be signing petitions soon to have her removed, understaffed and all.'

'Surely she's not that bad,' I said, trying to make light of it. I didn't need this right now.

'I'm not joking, Jack. She's a nightmare. No one can work with her. She's hardly been here five minutes and she's demoralising the whole team.' She paused. 'What's left of it.'

The team at Weston worked in state-of-the-art laboratories and with automated procedures using the latest techniques. There were separate rooms for the processing of known and questioned samples and completely different areas in the laboratory building for pre- and post-amplification material. But no matter how refined the analysing techniques, these systems were still run by human beings with all their passions, conceits and failings—and the current acting chief was one of these.

Florence's eyes narrowed and she looked closely at me. 'You *have* met her. So you know what I'm talking about. You'll have to do something about her, Jack. As acting chief, you're responsible for talking to people—whatever they call it these days—*human resource deployment*?' She paused, running out of puff. 'If you were chief scientist you might be able to get rid of her somehow. Or at least get her shifted to another area. Surely the Ag Station needs botanists? So why don't you apply for the top job?'

If I did, I thought, I'd be having conversations like this all day every day. Just *acting* in the position was already giving me blisters. I shrugged and spread my hands, saying something about my love for hands-on science and bench analysis.

'You'd be a much better contender,' I said.

'I'll bet Little Miss Nightmare was out at the nightclub scene, bossing everyone around,' said Florence, but I could see she was pleased by my comment.

I didn't want to become involved in office bitching so I made some sort of soothing remark and hurried away. I reached the relative safety of my office with relief, closed the door and made for the classy leather lounge the previous chief scientist had ordered for this spacious corner room. The office was equipped so that I could make tea and coffee here if I didn't want to go down to one of the common room areas. There was even a small glass-fronted cabinet containing a bottle of scotch and a bottle of brandy for visitors.

I picked up the phone and rang Sydney to speak to my old friend and erstwhile crime scene colleague, Bob Edwards. We often swapped intelligence and I told him about the murder of Tianna Richardson. Bob, now team leader of the Physical Evidence Unit, was pleased to hear from me and we talked for a few minutes about the crime scene. Like me, he remembered meeting Tianna once or twice.

While talking to Bob, I started sorting through the formidable pile of mail on my desk: invoices, staff claims for interstate travel and accommodation, inter-agency accounts that I'd have to examine, debtor invoices from different case officers, incident reports, government circulars and additions to the *Public Service Act* that would have to be filed in the right places, as well as orders needing to be checked.

'How come you're involved with the Richardson case?' Bob asked.

'Bloody Earl Richardson rang me from Sydney at some ungodly hour this morning. He was a mess,' I said, wishing again I'd never got involved. 'Asked me to make sure things were done properly.'

'That prick,' said Bob. 'He's been ringing around like a blue-arsed fly, leaning on everyone he knows. He deserves to be locked up just for being a pain in the backside. Best thing that ever happened was when he left the job. But this morning he was back on the phone, bothering us.'

'What do you know about his private life?' I asked.

'He's gone religious,' said Bob, in exactly the same way he might have said 'he's gone mad'. 'His first wife left him a couple of years after they were married. Can't say I blame her. When we heard he was getting married again to Tianna, we took bets in the meal room on how long *that* would last.'

I'd never heard Bob quite so hostile about an ex-colleague. Over the years a cop could attract a lot of bad feelings—not only from colleagues. I thought of the gangland killings in Melbourne and how, more and more, the sentimental bullshit of not harming women and children was being disregarded.

'I wonder if her death is connected to Richardson.'

'The man's a complete dill, but it's unlikely anyone would take it out on his missus. Especially since they separated.'

'But they'd recently reconciled,' I said.

'He thought so,' said Bob.

'One of the young fellows here had heard she liked a bit of rough,' I said.

'I'll keep my ears peeled.'

'Thanks. What's new down your way?'

'Too bloody much,' said Bob. 'I've just been seconded to the commissioner's new baby, the Unsolved Homicide Unit. I've spent a couple of days going through the bone room with the forensic anthropologist, sorting through the boxes. We're making a list of anything with any physical evidence attached, noting it down for possible DNA testing or other analyses that weren't available in the past. Remnants of clothing, wallets. Shoes. You know how much things have improved. You'll probably end up getting samples if DAL can't handle them all.' The Division of Analytical Laboratories covered almost every field of forensic testing using modern instrumental techniques.

I recalled the bone room at the morgue, where tiers of shelves held large brown boxes, sometimes two deep, containing the unidentified skeletal remains found in shallow graves around the state, revealed in crawl-spaces during renovations, partly buried in caves, upturned in excavations, along with any remnants of shoes, wallets, rotted clothing or personal effects. I liked bones and I knew Bob did too. It was the living who created problems.

I wished Bob luck with it all and rang off, looking with dismay at the pile of mail I'd been trying to sort. After being away in Sydney for a few days with Jacinta and barely back in the building, already staff bitching and work overload were coming straight at me. At the bottom of the pile of things I had to do was the almost forgotten outline of the presentation I was supposed to be giving to George Abernathy's senior chemistry students in a few weeks. Somehow, I would have to make time to do that. Worse was the finished brochure for the three-day conference we were hosting here for police personnel from all over Australia, due to start happening all too soon. Fortunately, I hadn't had to organise that, but it was yet one more piece of business that needed attention and would take up people's time and energy. I glanced over the contents: 'Increasing the probability of finding clandestine graves', 'Comparative investigative technology over the last twenty years' and 'On-site detection systems for accelerants', and a presentation by Peter McGrath, one of our team working on the Australian Embassy bombing in Jakarta. I stood a few moments, reading down the list. Despite the remarkable improvements in technology, Newton's laws were still fundamental to the physicist; we were still building on foundations laid down in earlier times. I put the brochure down, remembering

I'd promised George Abernathy that I'd do a paper for the conference as well.

The more urgent items of mail had already been processed by the secretary but this still left me with a pile that needed my personal attention. I skimmed through it, making diary notes about conferences and fancy new equipment that I already knew our budget for this year couldn't allow.

My mobile rang and I hoped it wouldn't be Earl Richardson again. When I heard the voice, I smiled. One of my two favourite people.

'Dad!' Greg said. 'We're in town! Me and Charlie.'

'Where are you?' I asked.

'Here. At the cottage. Charlie brought heaps of food.'

'Shouldn't you be at uni?' I scolded.

'I've only got two lectures and a tute this week. Ellie's doing my lecture notes for me and this tutor never marks the roll.'

I'd met Greg's spike-haired girlfriend a couple of times and hoped she would be a good influence on him. He'd been finding it hard to settle down after a year away, travelling around Europe as the spirit—and his bank balance—took him.

'Ellie spoils you,' I said. 'And you shouldn't be skipping lectures like that.'

'What time do you think you'll be back?' Greg asked, giving no indication he'd heard my last remark, let alone been affected by it.

I looked at my watch. 'I promised Iona I'd be back in time for a picnic lunch on the river. Give me an hour or two,' I said, glancing at the horror pile of mail. 'I should be there by about one.'

My spirits lifted after hearing my son's voice and I looked at the beautifully coloured Venetian glass paperweight that sat on a small wooden stand on my desk, a gift from Iona. It was a good feeling. Almost all the people I loved most in the world close by and Jacinta only a phone call away in Sydney. Thinking of Iona's complaint, I rang my daughter but the call went straight to voicemail.

I turned to the paperwork with renewed enthusiasm, making a priority pile. Next I checked the internal phone book and called Sofia Verstoek.

'The clothes from this morning's case are in the exhibit storage area. You indicated you wanted them first,' I said, quoting the case number.

If I'd been expecting that this concession might soften her approach to me, I was sadly mistaken.

'Did you think I wouldn't notice them?' she snapped.

'If you can't manage your workload,' I said, deciding to ignore her belligerence, 'someone else can do it. Vic Agnew has expressed interest.' It wasn't quite true.

'Okay,' she finally said. 'I'll take them.'

I rang off.

An hour later I was preparing to go home, my hand on the door, when the desk phone rang. Recalling Florence's earlier words, I hesitated. If I didn't pick it up, I could walk out right now. Someone else would hear it or it would go back to the switch and be redirected. Or, even if I did pick it up, I could always delegate it. I stood, irresolute, thinking of lying back on a blanket in the autumn sunshine, replete with ham, chicken and crème caramel, reading something unrelated to my job, my head in Iona's lap, Charlie and Greg beside us, listening to the sounds along the river and the distant lowing of cattle.

But the ringing of the phone summoned me in a way I couldn't explain and I strode back to the desk and picked up the receiver.

'Jack,' said Dallas Baxter, chief scientist at the Agricultural Research Station a little out of town, attached to the university. 'Thank goodness you're there. I was told you were away.'

'I'm trying to be,' I said.

'We've got a problem out here,' he said.

'Okay. I'll make sure someone competent follows it up for you,' I said, not even wanting to know what the problem was.

'You don't understand,' said Dallas. 'I want *you* to come out. You'll realise why once you've heard what's happened. We've got a sealed lab situation and I don't want anyone else in on it at this stage. There's been an incident.'

'What sort of incident?' I asked. Agricultural scientists can be working with pesticides, toxicides, disease pathogens and every biohazard imaginable—all of them reasons to seal off a lab in the event of a spill or contamination incident.

'That's just it,' he said. 'We don't know what we've got. And until we do, I've sealed everything right off. I can't keep this under wraps much longer. That's why I want you over here right now. Can you come? I don't want to say too much over the phone. But you'd better bring full protection gear.'

I didn't get the chance to get a word in as Dallas hurried on. 'I heard you were called out to a death near the Blackspot Nightclub earlier today?'

'That's right,' I said, wondering how he'd heard this news so quickly.

'Anyone we know?' asked Dallas after a slight hesitation.

'Do you mean someone from the academic world?' I asked.

'I just wondered—you know—if it was anyone I might know.'

'She *was* a local,' I said.

'Jack, you've got to come here personally,' Dallas said, changing the subject abruptly. Suddenly, I was everyone's favourite scientist. 'With this sort of situation the scientists have to go in first. It's in the protocols.'

He was right. I put the phone down. Why the hell had I picked it up?

My daydream of the riverbank had been pulled out from under me. No, I corrected myself, *I'd* pulled it out from under me by picking up the damn phone in the first place.

I locked up the office, gathered up the equipment I might need from a storeroom, including full self-contained breathing apparatus, and packed it all into the car. Then I headed for the Agricultural Station.

FOUR

Twenty minutes later, I turned off the highway and drove through a raised boom gate before continuing up a dirt driveway and pulling up near the clearing in front of the main entrance to the Agricultural Research Station. Set well back from the road, its several buildings were surrounded by both native eucalypts and acacias as well as ripening exotics, their leaves a mixture of reds and golds among the green. As I looked at the splendid foliage, I realised I'd never much liked Dallas Baxter. I distrusted his pink and gold *smoothness*.

From some distance away, a plume of steam arose in the cool air. The autoclave must be working, I thought.

I pressed the security door and was let into the foyer carrying my gear, video camera and notebook. Challenged at the security desk by a man with a huge belly and a lot of metal hanging off his belt, I told him why I was there and was directed towards the reception counter, a little way down the corridor, where I filled in the visitors' book. I took a clip-on tag to identify myself and glanced around at the pale grey walls and matching non-slip, easy-clean floor covering. Gone forever was the freedom of movement we'd all once enjoyed, moving around government and private institutions with relatively few restrictions. Individual acts of bastardry and the international menace of pathological religio–politics had changed all that.

Almost before I'd finished reading the one-page sheet concerning visitors' behaviour, and before I could ask for Associate Professor Baxter, I looked up to see Dallas himself, impeccably suited, striding towards me, gleaming blond hair brushed back from his fleshy face, his slightly protuberant eyes even wider than usual above his blue shirt and pink tie. He always looked spick and span, even when tending his famous garden at Airlie House. Dallas Baxter was the sort of man who wore ironed khaki shirts and trousers and matching hat outdoors.

I hurried to join him and, as we shook hands, I thought I saw something else behind the expression of professional concern on his face. We set off along the narrow corridor, where offices with half-closed doors revealed staff members sitting in front of computer screens or scribbling at desks.

Dallas pushed open the double doors that divided the offices from the working laboratories. 'No one really noticed anything amiss,' he said as we walked along an enclosed verandah then into another building, passing various airconditioned laboratories with banks of cages and radios tuned into the local ABC station for the lab animals' benefit. Outside again, and into another smaller building where the dedicated labs were: Susceptible Culture, Resistant Culture, a wash-up room and the scullery.

'It wasn't until my secretary, Pauline, called me to say that Dr Dimitriou—Claire—wasn't taking any of the calls she'd been trying to put through all morning and that Peter Yu hadn't turned up for work either today, that I started to get worried. Then Pauline went out to the car park and noticed that Claire's car had condensation rivulets over the roof and bonnet, indicating it had been there all night. When I checked her office computer, I found she hadn't logged off from our internal security website.' He paused. 'That's when I really knew something serious was amiss. Look, Jack,' he said, eyes flickering away from mine, 'it may be nothing. She might have got a lift with Peter yesterday—I don't know. Or she might be lying in there ill. Or anything. But with the two of them not accounted for like this—'

'You've tried to contact Dr Yu?' I interrupted.

'Of course. He had an important meeting with a scientist from the CSIRO today. I can't believe he'd miss that. The man was on his way down from Sydney. It was very embarrassing. But Peter's not answering his mobile. And his car's not at his place either. I asked Pauline to check.'

'Maybe they're together somewhere,' I suggested. 'He and Claire.'

'But Claire's married to another scientist!'

'So?' I asked, surprised. Until he'd said this, I hadn't considered anything but a professional association. Now I immediately suspected something more. 'Are they romantically linked?' I asked.

'Certainly not,' Dallas hurried on, as if aware he'd given something away by his remark. 'Like I said, Claire's married to another scientist—Anthony Dimitriou—a lecturer at the University of Canberra.' He paused a moment before continuing: 'Pauline tells me he's away at the moment, attending an ANZFSS conference in New Zealand.'

'I'll need his details,' I said, noting down the name and remembering that Gavin Samways, one of our junior chemists, had also attended. I could check up on Anthony Dimitriou's attendance with him, if necessary.

'Dallas,' I said when I'd finished writing, 'if you know something about the two missing people in the way of a personal relationship, you must tell me.' I indicated the general direction of the laboratory. 'The more I know beforehand, the better position I'm in to go inside.'

Dallas picked at a spot on his cuff. I waited. Sometimes silence does the trick.

'It's only rumours,' he said finally.

'So you have heard something about a romance?'

Dallas shook his head too emphatically. 'Just tea-room gossip.'

'And?'

'I'm giving the wrong impression. It was just innuendoes, jokes. That silly nudge-nudge, wink-wink business. You know how people like to carry on.'

I looked at him squarely. 'If you've heard anything, you'd better tell me now. If you're concerned about Claire's reputation, or the reputation of the institution, it's essential that we get to the truth.' I paused. 'It's easier to put the fire out when it's only small,' I added.

Dallas spread his hands in a helpless gesture, and a large ruby winked on his little finger. 'You know the way people talk in these small, intense communities.' He waved an arm around to indicate all of the research buildings.

'Yes,' I said curtly, his prevarications starting to irritate me.

'And there was something else.' His demeanour changed as he moved to surer ground. 'One of the maintenance staff overheard Peter and Claire having words in her office yesterday.'

I made another entry in my notebook. 'What sort of words?'

'He didn't tell me. Pauline mentioned it to me this morning, when we started to wonder about where Claire might be. You must understand that it wasn't an issue until this.' He made an open gesture with his hands. 'Some sort of argument, I believe. But then scientists are always arguing. Especially when there's a joint project between them. Different ways of procedure, of moving down the decision tree.'

'But taken in context,' I said, 'with all the other things you've heard...'

'It's still only workplace gossip,' he said, uneasy. 'And it couldn't possibly have anything to do with this business.'

'How in hell can you say something like that—' I began, wondering who or what Dallas Baxter was protecting.

'Dallas?' A woman in a dark maroon suit approached, high heels clicking on the vinyl floor.

'Pauline,' said Dallas, clearly relieved by the interruption. 'Pauline Lamb, this is Dr Jack McCain who's going to take a first look inside the lab.'

We shook hands, but Pauline, despite her polite smile, was preoccupied. 'Yvonne Abernathy on the line for you,' she said. 'And no, she *won't* tell me what it's about. She insists on speaking to you. Now.'

'Yvonne?' Dallas looked at me, the worry lines on his face deepening. 'What does *she* want?'

Yvonne was the wife of George Abernathy, head of the school of chemistry at the university.

'Tell her I'll call back,' said Dallas, shooting an embarrassed glance at me. 'She must have heard about Claire.'

'Heard what about Claire?' I asked. 'You told me you'd kept this under wraps.'

Dallas blinked. 'I simply meant the fact that her car's been here all night,' he stuttered.

We both knew straightaway that his answer didn't make sense.

'She wants to talk to you,' said Pauline. 'Personally. I've been running round all over the place trying to find you.'

'I want to know what Yvonne could have heard about Claire,' I persisted. I was also interested in why she'd be ringing Dallas Baxter.

Dallas frowned. 'Peter might have said something to someone.'

'But he's not here. You just said so yourself.' I looked from one to the other.

'I called his parents in Sydney, Dallas, just in case he'd made a quick visit,' said Pauline. 'No one seems to know where he is.'

'Tell me about Peter Yu,' I said, notebook at the ready.

'Peter is a very bright, up-and-coming researcher,' said Dallas. 'University medallist. Got his doctorate three years ago and he's been working with Claire for about two years now.'

'Girlfriend?' I asked.

Dallas shrugged. 'I believe there's a girlfriend somewhere.'

'There's always a girlfriend,' said Pauline with a tolerant smile. 'Dr Yu has the reputation of being a bit of a heartbreaker,' she said, then suddenly turned around and wrinkled up her nose. 'Can you smell something off in here?'

I shuffled my feet. Surely it couldn't be that goddamn shoe again.

'It's probably something from one of the pens,' she concluded.

'What's this nonsense about being a heartbreaker?' Dallas said, his face becoming pinker.

'You *must* have noticed, Dallas,' Pauline insisted.

One of the most common motives for crime—sex—was already becoming a possibility. The crime scene I'd visited earlier came back vividly. Tianna Richardson had almost certainly died because of sex.

I refocused my attention on the present situation.

'Were there rumours of something going on between Claire Dimitriou and Peter Yu?' I asked again, looking from one to the other.

Pauline looked at Dallas. Secretaries generally knew everything going on in a department. She gave me an arch look and shrugged again. 'It's quite possible,' she said. 'This place is a hotbed of intrigue.'

'Don't exaggerate!' Dallas scolded.

Pauline rolled her eyes. 'What's to exaggerate?'

I made a mental note to get Pauline aside for a chat.

'What were Claire and Peter Yu working on?' I asked.

Instead of answering, Pauline tapped her boss on the sleeve. 'Are you going to take that call?' she insisted.

'Tell Yvonne I'm in the middle of something,' said Dallas, looking irritated. 'Can't you see I'm tied up here?'

Pauline looked at Dallas uncertainly and then turned and walked away in her clicking heels.

Sometimes government scientists, sworn to secrecy under the Official Secrets Act, undertake work for the Department of Defence. I wanted to know as much as I could about what had been going on in the sealed-up laboratory before I went in.

'You're sure they weren't involved in some sort of secret Defence project?' I said.

'Not unless the Army's taken to using rabbits and mice as WMDs,' Dallas joked, standing back to allow me through a security door.

'So what were they working on?'

'Straightforward, non-secret, agricultural research on rabbit control,' he said. 'Claire and Peter started their Faithful Bunnies project about two years ago.'

'Faithful Bunnies?'

'It started as an experiment to alter the mating habits of rabbits.'

'And all the research is open and available to scrutiny?' I asked.

'Of course. It's a supervised project. Dr Leonie Pringle was signing it off every month.'

Immediately, the project rose in my esteem. Leonie Pringle was Emeritus Professor in the science department at our premier state university, not to mention an international legend in the world of molecular biology. She was *the* expert in lagomorphs—gnawing animals with large incisors top *and* bottom, unlike rodents—as well as leporids: rabbits and hares.

'I know from my own experience that researchers can be very protective of their projects,' I said, thinking of the other big motive. 'Especially if it involves something that has the potential to make a lot of money down the track. Like rabbit eradication.'

'I guess it could be a goldmine one day,' Dallas said, after a pause. 'But you could say that about any of our research. *If* the project is successful. And it's always a pretty big "if".'

I knew there were a hell of a lot of steps between doing research and then attracting the big money. Most scientific research was underfunded, so researchers had to scratch for money all the time. Until the events in Bali and Jakarta had opened the funding purse more generously, research labs had not had big budgets.

'They might have been using potentially dangerous pathogens,' I said.

'Like myxomatosis and the *calicivirus*?' Dallas's voice was derisive. 'They're only dangerous if you're a leporid. Claire and Peter were working at the cutting edge of molecular design, shuffling receptors and genetic markers, encoding proteins, that kind of thing. No pathogens dangerous to humans were involved.'

'But they were arguing,' I reminded him, glancing down at my notebook.

'That's hardly a revelation. As I said, scientists are always arguing.'

I made a note to get back to that one later.

We'd stopped at a large, secured biohazard door with a warning about unauthorised entry and a sheet of Hazchem protocols affixed to it. Tanks of oxygen and fire extinguishers stood nearby, adjacent to a cleaning station where gumboots, buckets and sophisticated cleaning and antibacterial agents sat on a shelf.

'Beyond this door is the clean room, where you can gear up, and then an airlock and a negative pressure chamber, then the lab,' said Dallas.

'There seems to be a great deal of security for an innocuous research project,' I said. 'You're talking about a set-up demanding high levels of safety. There must have been *some* concern about what they were working on.'

'Highly infectious material is handled here,' Dallas said, 'but it's only dangerous if you're a rabbit. We're still using these old Level Four labs even though we now have the new additions—you saw the ones we walked through. We've got state-of-the-art Levels Three and Four safety rooms in the new wing, so the old hot suites in this building are used for routine work. We can't afford to have any of our facilities lying idle.'

'Anyone else use this lab?' I asked.

'Claire and Peter have had exclusive use of it for the last two years. Apart from Claire's PhD student who's sometimes here.' He pulled out a photocopied building map. 'This is the layout inside the lab,' he said, passing it to me. 'You might find it helpful when you go in.'

'I'd better have the name of Dr Dimitriou's student.'

'I can't think of it just now. I'll look it up and let you know.'

'Tell me more about the change in mating habits,' I said, taking the plan from him before unpacking the respirator and checking it. 'What were they hoping to achieve?'

'They were working on the receptors for vasopressin.'

'Isn't that a hormone?' I asked, trying to remember.

Dallas nodded. 'They'd based their original project on an experiment with field voles and mountain voles in the USA.'

'Voles?' I wasn't even sure what a vole *was*.

'The American scientists induced behavioural changes in voles with hormonal tweaking,' said Dallas. 'From being promiscuous, they became faithful to one mate.'

I considered that. Restricting a male rabbit to only one mate could have a big impact on rabbit populations. 'You said the project started out that way,' I reminded him. 'Did it change?'

'The original Faithful Bunnies series was not successful,' said Dallas. 'Consequently, over the last few months, they've been working on another angle—a double-edged sword. They called it Terminator Rabbit. Working with rabbit pox in a double-barrelled way. Increasing lethality as well as tweaking the virus genetically to carry a sterilising payload.'

I tried to keep up but Dallas must have sensed my bemusement.

'You know there's always this arms race going on between the virus and its host,' he explained. 'The virus getting weaker over the generations, the host animal developing immunity. The idea is that any females who survive the initial infection—and that's generally around five to ten per cent of the population—will eventually breed themselves out of existence because the sterility will be passed on to the next generation as part of the maternal DNA material. So that, one day, the last litter will be born and, after those individuals have all died without issue, that's the end of the rabbits in Australia.'

And the end of Thomas Austin, Esquire's experiment, I thought. The wealthy Geelong grazier had imported rabbits to Australia from England in 1859 so as to have a little hunting and shooting.

'Of course,' Dallas was saying, 'it's still in the developmental stage.'

It had been estimated that rabbits caused trillions of dollars of damage per year to farmers and, in the long run, to the economy. Many countries are plagued by them and a scientific solution to their infestation would certainly be lucrative.

'So how close were they to delivery?' I asked.

'Years away. It was a very long-range project.'

I couldn't make up my mind about Dallas Baxter. Though he was expansive, almost boasting, about his scientists' work now, he had been evasive previously and I wanted to know why.

'I want you to go in there, Jack, and find out what the hell is going on. I'm hoping there's been some malfunction with Claire's mobile or even that they *have* eloped...' He paused.

'Get Hazchem on standby,' I said. 'I can't go in until you do that.'

He seemed reluctant and again I wondered why. But I stood, waiting, until he made the phone call, turning away into a corner as he talked to the chief of the local Fire Investigation Unit.

Eventually he rang off and came back. 'Ewan Purcell confirmed the protocols state that in the case of a possible biohazard, you're to go in first.'

'I'll bet he did,' I said. 'You've just spent some time assuring me nothing toxic could be involved. Now you're behaving as if there's a risk of contamination.'

'There's no risk to humans at all,' said Dallas, sounding annoyed. 'I might have been an administrator a long time, but I *am*, first and foremost, a scientist. I'm simply being ultra-cautious. Until I'm sure in my mind that it's safe in there, I'd rather be too careful than not careful enough. But I can assure you, there's nothing in the Terminator Rabbit program nor the earlier project that could cause any concern to a human being.'

At this stage, I had to keep my suspicions to myself, but if I'd been a betting man I'd have taken odds-on that Dallas Baxter knew a great deal more about all of this than he was revealing. His unease was obvious as he strode over to the first door.

Once I'd made a last check of my gear—including the respirator, which I was using in case the air was contaminated—Dallas swiped the door free of its locks. I stepped into the clean room, past the shelves of white lab coats, boxes of shoe protectors and face masks. The next door had a cartoon pasted on it—a fierce-looking, AK47-swinging Terminator Rabbit.

Not since my last investigation, involving *Bacillus anthracis*—better known as anthrax—had I worn a full respirator suit on the job. Yet despite Dallas Baxter's reassurances, I would take no chances. Staying on the side of caution kept investigators alive longer. Accidents in labs were not uncommon and, excluding suicide, every year there was a workplace fatality in a lab in Australia.

I opened the door and stood a moment, taking in the scene. Somewhere a radio was playing. My first impression was how extremely *clean* everything appeared and, for the briefest of moments, I envied Claire Dimitriou and Peter Yu's neat habits. But hard on the back of that thought came another. *This is not natural.* This didn't look like a working research lab—or indeed any working lab I'd ever been in. Stepping carefully, I moved further inside.

I couldn't hear the hum of the airconditioner over the soft hissing in my ears as I breathed, but I could see it was on. Every surface was sparkling clean, the sinks shone as if brand new, the glassware sparkled. The walls, bench spaces, fridges and feed bins, apparatus covers, enamelled technical equipment all gleamed white and chrome, bright as the day they'd been delivered. The frosted glass of the windows, the light fittings and vinyl floors were spotless. On the bench to my left, an ELISA—enzyme-linked-immunosorbent-assay—machine sat, lights on, ready to go, linked up to the colour monitor and printer. But no assay was in progress—the machine was not loaded with test material. The lab looked as if it had been cleaned by a team of detailers. Then I saw why. Standing near a large stereoscopic light microscope was the portable generator and handgear of an industrial-strength steam-cleaner. The whole lab had been steam-cleaned.

I inhaled deeply, the sound of my breath rushing like surf through the respirator, and relaxed a little, not realising till then how tense I'd been. Somewhere, I considered, there must be test animals. Where were the bunnies faithful or terminating? If Claire and Peter had been working on encoding proteins and receptors, surely they would have animals here?

The answer to this question came as I saw another door right at the end of the L-shaped laboratory. Large red letters commanded NO ADMITTANCE. HIGHLY INFECTIOUS AREA. I was about to return to Dallas and ask him to let me have the electronic swipe card when closer inspection revealed the door was slightly ajar. Cautiously, I pushed it open.

There should have been the sound of negative pressure but there was no need in this room. It was empty. Only a row of benches and several empty food containers indicated it had once been in use. Along the bench on my right, a heavy vinyl hood covered what looked like more lab equipment.

With my gloved hand I lifted the corner to reveal a series of cages, the sort used to house lab animals, stacked on top of each other almost to the ceiling. They too shone spick and span, water bottles and food trays spotlessly clean, nothing written on the whiteboard tags at the front.

I stepped back into the main area and started videoing the laboratory, slowly taking in the ultra-clean equipment and surfaces until I approached the small office annexe glassed-off at the far wall of the laboratory. Inside, lab books and records were housed above a small desk and a filing cabinet.

As I got closer, some sixth sense sent my hackles rising.

FIVE

Claire Dimitriou hadn't run off with anyone. Her white-coated body lay face-down halfway into the small office annexe, white coat bunched up around her left shoulder. Putting the video camera down, I rushed over to see if there was anything I could do. There wasn't. Until a proper examination, it wasn't possible to determine why she'd died like this, in the doorway of the office where the log book and other paperwork would be, one hand reaching towards the desk, the other hidden somewhere under her body.

I stood a moment, memories of other death scenes I'd attended crowding in yet again—suicides, accidents, murders. Claire Dimitriou may have died accidentally or from sudden illness, but there were enough oddities in the surrounds of the laboratory to make me very uneasy. Someone had cleaned this lab as if their life depended on it. It was the sort of job that I'd seen after a toxic spill, or a Level 4 pathogen incident.

Until I had some idea of what had made Claire Dimitriou stop breathing, I needed to keep my face mask and respirator in place. Squatting down beside her body, I hoped there'd be something left in the clothes and hair despite the steam-cleaning.

Gently, and keenly aware of the cold hardness I was touching, I rolled Claire over. Her arm maintained the angle it had been lying in, so that her double-gloved hand remained stiffly raised, as if in protest. The sight of a mass of congealed blood put paid to any notion of accidental death. She would once have been a pretty woman, with fine dark hair and brows, but now her face was distorted from lying squashed on the floor. Her mouth gaped half open and her eyes were dull and drying behind half-closed lids, yet she still had the same expression of surprise that I'd noticed once on a suicide's face.

I could see from the lividity surrounding the areas of skin that had pressed against the floor that she'd been dead for some time. The front of her white coat had set with blood, crumpled and stiff. When I rolled her over again, I could see a small neat hole that had been hidden at first by the darkening folds of her once-white coat. I peered closer. The entry hole surrounds were discoloured by gunshot residue. Someone had shot her in the back at close range. I couldn't see the injuries to the front of the body because of the bloody folds in the bunched-up clothing and lab coat, but where it gaped was a dark knitted fabric.

I gently lowered the body back down and it resumed its previous position. I examined the floor area carefully. There had probably been a great deal more blood before the clean-up. Just under the desk and still on its clip lay a plastic ID card with a small photo of Claire Dimitriou smiling. I picked it up and stowed it in a small bag.

In the sink in the office, a few drops of pinkish water remained but there was no sign of any dishcloth or towel. I opened the cupboard marked 'Cleaning/Disinfection Station' but apart from large containers of bleaches, solvents and a bottle of antibacterial liquid soap, there were no cloths there. Whoever had cleaned up had taken everything away. Crime scene would have to dismantle the drains to see if they could find any helpful residues. Killers often mopped up after themselves in an attempt to reduce evidence, so maybe this was nothing more than that. But did such thoroughness point to another scientist? Either way, two women dead in suspicious circumstances in one day had to be some sort of record for the nation's capital.

Making my way carefully back to the crash doors, I opened them and retraced my footsteps. I had to push the door closed against the negative pressure to get to the small area where Dallas was waiting for me.

'Well?' he asked as soon as he saw me.

I switched off my air supply and unfastened my mask. Then, smoothing the small plastic bag that held the ID card, I held it up to him. 'Is this Claire Dimitriou?'

He peered through the plastic and nodded, his face showing raw fear. Every instinct in me said the man was withholding something. Something big. And important.

'Then I'm afraid it's bad news,' I said, lowering the bag.

'What is it?' he asked, his face turning white. 'Did someone—is she dead?'

Wondering at the change of direction mid-question, I replied carefully. 'I'm no pathologist, but I'd guess she's been dead for quite some hours.'

'How? What killed her?'

'Looks like a gunshot injury but I'll need a pathologist to confirm that.'

Dallas stared at me. 'You mean she's been shot? Someone's *shot* her?'

Though his questions were typical of the things people say when they're shocked, not wanting to believe the worst has happened, there was always the possibility it was feigned.

'That's what it looks like,' I said, pulling off my gloves. 'And the whole area is very clean. Someone's gone to a lot of trouble.'

Dallas looked away, blinking with apparent bewilderment. 'I don't understand how something like this could have happened.'

'This place must be kept sealed until the local detectives arrive. I take it they're on their way?' I said, brusquely.

'I haven't called them, yet.'

'Do it now,' I ordered. 'The first twenty-four hours of a case are vital. We've already lost too much time.' Claire Dimitriou could have been dead since yesterday.

'But, Jack, that's the reason I called you in. I want *you* to do the whole thing from start to finish. Gathering any physical evidence.'

'Not on your life,' I said, wondering if he was aware of the significance of what he'd just said. 'The local detectives must handle this. Any trace evidence they find will be sent back to our lab and we'll deal with it there, as usual.'

This was the closest involvement I wanted with the incident. So far today, I'd been running from one job to the next, like in the old days. Now I was anxious to get back to the cottage. I was already in strife with Iona and I wanted to spend some time with her, Greg and Charlie before sundown. Once, obsession with a local case like this one would have closed down all thoughts of family, but now, with Iona in my life, things were different.

'It would be so much better if we could keep this quiet,' said Dallas.

I stared at him, wondering if he could possibly be serious. A murdered scientist in a laboratory under his administration kept quiet? Even the current tory government wouldn't be able to manage that. Seeing the look on my face, he rushed to clarify.

'Of course there must be a full investigation. But if the media could be kept at bay—'

'I'll call Brian Kruger,' I interrupted. 'Maybe you should sit down,' I added, aware of his pallor.

'It's nothing,' he said, and made as if to head back the way we'd come. 'I'm shocked. Not thinking straight.'

Dallas Baxter had been rocked right down to his designer socks, I knew. But he was also behaving like a man with a secret and I was determined to find out what it was.

In the small change room I discarded the suit and placed the respirator tackle in the relevant bin, ready for sterilisation.

'Better organise for Harry Marshall to come ASAP,' I said. 'Give him the chance to take a look at the body *in situ* while everything's still quiet.'

Despite Dallas's wishes, it would only be a matter of time before the press got wind of this second violent death and we'd be reading headlines about a crime wave. I looked at my watch. It was already after two. Although I'd missed lunch on the river bank, there was still a chance I might redeem myself if I picked up afternoon tea from the French patisserie.

I rang Harry and gave a brief description of what I'd found.

'I'm going to need some names, Dallas,' I said, after ringing off. 'And no one must leave these premises until the police have arrived. Understood?'

Dallas nodded, promising to find the details of the maintenance worker who'd heard Claire Dimitriou arguing with her research partner, as well as Claire's doctoral student.

•

Back near the main front desk, Dallas Baxter hovered around like an anxious plover guarding its young as I spoke to Pauline. Aware of him listening, I suggested to Pauline that we step into her office.

She took me into a tiny room adjacent to the reception counter with just enough room for a swivel chair and desk.

'Is everything all right?' she asked, her eyes searching my face, her anxious tone betraying concern.

'How easy is it to get in here after hours?' I asked.

'As long as someone's inside, they can let you in.'

'So Claire could have buzzed someone in after hours?' I asked.

'Oh yes. She often worked back alone. Please tell me what's happening. Is she all right?'

I assured her I'd give her some information just as soon as I could, thinking all the while of the hours I'd spent alone in deserted buildings late at night, writing up overdue reports and certificates. 'What are the protocols surrounding security for people working back?'

'There's an arrangement whereby anyone staying back alone logs out from the internal website when they leave. The security panel resets itself after they've keyed themselves out.'

I looked around. 'Any other exits?' I asked.

'Everyone arrives and leaves this way. There's no other exit except the boom gate over there,' she said, pointing through the glass doors.

'What if the person working back late is expecting someone, or someone buzzes the door?' I asked.

'Then the alarm can be switched off at the main switch near the front door. It automatically resets itself after they've let the person in.'

I thought of the glass doors of the main entrance area. A visual check would reveal the identity of the newcomer. Claire Dimitriou would have been able to see the identity of any visitor.

'So there should be a digital trail showing who was in the building?'

Pauline nodded. 'Normally. But if someone were let in by a scientist working late, there wouldn't be a record of that person. As long as the scientist kept keying in their code every hour or so, the alarm wouldn't go off.'

'So there are no electronic records that show who's in or out or what time they came or went?' I queried. At Forensic Services, the system recorded all individuals' movements at all times.

'We're due for an upgrade. At the moment, we're still just the country cousins. But I guess you've got to wonder who'd want to steal records concerning off-shears mortality and fly-strike?'

She had a point.

I took the number of the Ag Station's security company, to check up on Claire Dimitriou's movements, then I asked Pauline to print out a list of all the people who'd been at work the day before and those who'd arrived today. I caught myself wondering why I was taking over the Homicide detectives' work like this, especially after telling Dallas that I wouldn't, *couldn't*, do such a thing.

'I can arrange that. There's also this,' Pauline said, passing a book to me.

'What is it?' I asked.

'The Work Alone Register,' she replied.

I flipped through some of the pages and saw columns with recorded names, dates and the times signed off when people left. Claire Dimitriou's name had been scrawled down on Monday evening, but the last column, the sign-off, was blank.

'I'll be wanting the details of Peter Yu's girlfriend and his address and telephone number,' I said.

'Her name's Annette Sommers,' said Pauline. 'She runs an arts and crafts gallery in town—Galleria Rustica. But she hasn't rung here for a while. She might not be current.'

I made a note of Peter Yu's details and of Annette's name and place of work, thinking I could pass it on to Brian.

'Please tell me about Claire,' Pauline said. 'It's bad news, isn't it?'

Her hand flew to her mouth before I could say anything, my expression giving it away.

'Oh, poor Anthony,' she said.

On my way out through the glass doors I saw Dallas Baxter coming out of his office.

'You're going, Jack?'

'Is there anything else you need to tell me before I do?' I asked, using a technique that sometimes caught people off guard.

He shook his head.

Like hell, I thought.

I sat in my wagon looking back at the Ag Station, then I rang the cottage again. The clouds had lifted and there was no answer so I hoped they were all down at the river, having fun in spite of my absence. I tried Iona's mobile, and left a voicemail message saying that if they weren't back by the time I got home, I'd drive down to the river and see if I could catch them. Then I rang Brian and passed on the information about Annette Sommers, telling him I'd already started the ball rolling for him out here.

Driving away from the research station, I took in the stunted feed crops and patches of cracked soil. There was something amiss in what I'd just witnessed, something wrong about Dallas Baxter's reactions. *An unusual situation*, he'd said, in breathtaking understatement. Claire Dimitriou dead in her lab from a gunshot wound and her work partner missing—more than unusual. How long would it take, I wondered, before we knew what sort of firearm had been used? Because of the fatal triangle created by the weapon, the killer and the victim, tracing the movements of the weapon used in a homicide was just as important as tracing those of the people involved.

After cleaning up and stowing my gear at Forensic Services, I off-loaded the video camera for processing, thinking all the time of the new widower, Anthony Dimitriou, into whose private life I'd unavoidably intruded—and in the most intimate and horrible way. It was awful to think I'd knelt by the body of his dead wife while he was completely unaware of what had happened.

I mentally compared the two murders. The circumstances surrounding Tianna Richardson's crime scene suggested a random incident of terrifying bad fortune—a woman in the wrong place with the wrong man at the wrong time. Claire Dimitriou's death, on the other hand, appeared coldly premeditated; someone had deliberately sought her out in her laboratory.

I was about to leave my office when a knock at the door interrupted me. Vic Agnew, my smart young scientist colleague, whose receding hairline made his forehead formidably high, stood in the doorway with a package in his hand. I could see he wasn't happy.

'Florence just told me I'm supposed to help her with some of the analysis work for this,' he said, holding up the package. I could see the Tianna Richardson case number. 'She said I'm to just drop my work and help her straightaway. Is that right? I'm still only halfway through those two Sydney cases, not to mention that Northern Territory job.'

The joys of staff management, I thought. Who would have guessed this job would involve so much playing referee among overworked colleagues.

'I'm sorry Florence saw you before I could tell you what was going on. My apologies.'

Vic frowned.

'There've been two local murders,' I explained. 'Which means twice as much work for everyone. Including you, unfortunately.'

'Two? I heard about the murder at the nightclub,' said Vic. 'What was the other one?'

'I can't reveal much until all the relatives have been informed. Like I say, I'll need you to work with Florence. And to take on a few of the things I might do otherwise.'

'Okay,' said Vic, sounding resigned. 'I'll talk to Florence and get the precise details of what she wants me to start on.'

'There's something you could do right now,' I suggested, and indicated he should follow me down to the exhibit fridge. Unlocking it, I took out the bag with the half-smoked reefer inside.

'See what you can get off it,' I said, handing Vic the small packet. 'You'll need to call Harry Marshall for a swab from Tianna Richardson, so you can eliminate her and see who else might be present.'

'I've got a backlog that you wouldn't believe,' said Vic. 'The job turnaround is three times what it was this time last year. And even then we were always months behind.'

'Jane can give you a hand. Just do what you can,' I said, trying to sound patient.

Vic peeled off to open the door to his office, then hesitated. I braced myself for another grizzle.

'What's that stink?' he asked, sniffing. 'I can smell something bad.'

'I can't smell anything,' I said. 'Cold's too bad.'

'Dog shit,' he said. 'I can smell it.'

I waved him away and went into my office. I pulled off my right shoe. Damned if I could smell a thing. I put it back on, making a mental note to give it a good scrubbing the minute I got home—which should be in under half an hour if there were no more interruptions.

Prior to locking my office, I checked my mobile to find I'd missed a message from Dallas Baxter. 'The place is already swarming with crime scene personnel,' he said. 'They're upsetting my staff.'

Life's tough, I thought, still listening. He'd found out the details of the maintenance man who'd overheard the argument so I grabbed a pen and jotted down the name: Kevin Waites.

'And the PhD student's name is Jerri Quill,' the message continued.

I noted her address and phone number as well and ended the call. I'd hand this information over to Brian Kruger and that would be the end of it, I thought, switching off my mobile. I planned to do this a lot more often.

Finally, the coast was clear and I hurried to the car park, hoping that no one would stop me with more complaints or work problems. But I couldn't stop my thoughts focusing on this latest crime. I wanted to speak with Pauline Lamb on her own. Click-clacking down the corridors in her neat leather heels, she clearly covered a lot of ground. I knew from my own experience that women like her become almost invisible because of their efficiency. They ran departments, administered rosters and timetables, connected people and effortlessly gathered information. The brilliant capabilities they brought to bear on their work tended to disappear into the background. A woman like Pauline shouldn't be overlooked, either as a potential source of information or as a possible suspect. Maybe she hadn't told me everything she knew.

But that was all for tomorrow. And in any case, hadn't I determined to leave this case to Homicide? My job now would be limited to reporting on anything I might find in the examination room, or passing on expert analysis to the relevant departments. Relieved with my plan, I got into my car.

Just for the moment, I was free of the job and its demands and if I drove straight to the bend in the river near Seven Oaks, where the huge willow waved its now yellowing leaves, I might just be in time to join the party and help them pack up. My heart started to lift as I drove too fast and the deaths of the two women, sad though they were, almost faded from my mind. These days, instead of turning the key and entering a cold and empty cottage, I came home to Iona's warmth.

But some little devil of curiosity kept at me. I wanted to know more about Claire Dimitriou and why she'd ended up dead. Switching my phone back on to see if I could get Greg on his mobile, I saw I'd missed two calls, both from Earl Richardson. Even though I understood his desperation and his grief, it wasn't right that he should be contacting me again.

The phone rang and I snatched it up, steering off the road and coming to a halt near a large eucalyptus stump that sprouted tender new leaves in bunches.

'My name is Kevin Waites,' said the caller. 'Dallas Baxter gave me your number.'

'Kevin Waites. You're the maintenance man at the Ag Station.' I wound the window up as a truck went past.

'I have to talk to someone,' he said, the urgency clear in his voice.

'I'm listening,' I said.

'It's worrying me sick,' he said. 'I should've done something.'

'You heard an argument,' I prompted, 'between Claire Dimitriou and Peter Yu.'

'I couldn't tell that deadshit Baxter,' said Kevin. 'You just can't talk to him.'

'Let's meet,' I suggested. 'You can take your time and tell me the whole thing. What about tomorrow? You name a place.'

'The Cat and Castle. You know it?'

I did and we made a time for the next day.

Great work, Jack, I said to myself as I switched the damned mobile off again. Now I'd gone and put myself right back into it. Iona would not be happy. Curiosity killed the bloody cat. Curiosity might have killed the cat, but it also made a good scientist—a good investigator.

I started the car again and swerved back onto the road, heading for the bend in the river. But when I got to the clearing there was no one there. I parked and walked down the path to the river bank, where there was just a couple of grazing steers that must have got through a fence. Low afternoon sun streamed through the gold-green ribbons of willow leaves and the autumn bees went about their business in the late-flowering eucalypts. It seemed impossible in this golden, autumn afternoon that anything malignant could happen, yet two women who yesterday had lived and breathed now lay still and cold.

Sitting down on the dry grass, I pondered how police were always interested in the first person who alerted them to a murder. I pulled out my notebook. In Tianna Richardson's case, a police patrol had found her. Claire Dimitriou's death had been revealed after two people became worried: Pauline at the front desk and Dallas Baxter the boss—and there was no doubt he was hiding something. I scribbled down his name, then the rest of the usual suspects: husband Anthony Dimitriou and missing co-worker Peter Yu. I started making a mental list of the people who would need to be interviewed—workmates, neighbours and friends.

Then, almost without conscious thought, I drew up a list next to Tianna Richardson's name. Her Earl was obviously the primary suspect and he knew it. But he'd been almost a four-hour drive away and was woken by police, whereas Tianna, a woman who was rumoured to like a bit of rough, was out partying at a local dive. Had she picked up someone who took the idea of rough sex to its terminal conclusion, I wondered, as I jotted down the name of her son. I was making another mental note about talking to neighbours and friends when I suddenly stopped. It struck me that sitting here, in this little piece of heaven, a place where other people relaxed and enjoyed themselves, I was spending time doing the Homicide detectives' work for them.

This was what Iona had been trying to tell me for the last six months. I had to stop this sort of behaviour. I put my pen away.

I sat there a moment longer but found that without something to do I quickly became restless and uneasy. I walked back up to my wagon.

SIX

It wasn't long till I was turning into the dirt driveway to the cottage. I put out a hand to stop the white roses I'd bought for Iona falling from the passenger seat as my wagon bumped over the corrugations. Immediately, it became clear that everyone was home again—both Charlie's car and Iona's were parked near the cottage. It was heading to dusk and the sun was behind the hills.

From high above, a butcherbird sang and smaller birds fled the garden, warned by his melodies. As soon as I got out of my car I could hear Greg's infectious laugh and I found myself smiling as I walked through the doorway and into his bear hug. Charlie came out of the living room and hugged me too. If Jacinta had been here, I thought, as I slapped my brother on the back, everyone I loved would have been in this cottage.

'Where's Iona?' I asked.

'Here,' she said, coming out of the bedroom, pulling on a dark green cardigan. 'We missed you.'

I spread my hands in an apology and went to her, kissing her. 'I tried to get there,' I said. 'I thought of you all down there, sprawled on rugs in the sun, talking about me behind my back and getting silly on champagne.'

She disengaged her hands from mine. 'Are the roses for me?'

Before I could answer, the house phone rang and Greg picked it up. 'It's for you,' he said, pushing the phone my way. 'Brian Kruger.'

'Your mobile's switched off,' said Brian.

'That's right,' I said. 'I'm not at work.'

'In your dreams,' said Brian. 'Peter Yu's place is clean as a whistle. There's nothing there.'

Just like the laboratory, I thought.

'Nothing about work, nothing about his personal life. Just clothes in neat piles,' Brian continued. 'And a Bible.'

'A Bible?' That surprised me.

'Lot of underlining in places. Stuff I can't understand. Thought you might like to take a look at it.'

'Why me? Bibles aren't my thing.'

'And there's that girlfriend,' Brian said. 'I've got a couple of guys checking up on all known friends and acquaintances of both of them. Might get something off the dead woman's mobile phone. When we find it. And her email. When we can get into it. Right now, we're still trying to locate the husband. He's already left the conference accommodation.'

'Just in case no one tells you,' I said, recalling Dallas Baxter's evasive manner, 'there's something called a lab book.'

'What's that?'

'A record of what's been done. We don't keep them in our labs because all the techniques we use are set in concrete and not to be changed. But my guess is it's probably a detailed description of procedures—something like a mixture of casenotes and exhibit book. Make sure you get hold of it. I should have checked it out when I was in there. It'll be in the office annexe. Every step a research scientist takes is recorded.'

'How the hell would I make any sense out of it? I'm just an average cop.'

That wasn't quite true, I thought. 'If you get hold of the lab book,' I said, 'I'll take a look at it for you. But then it'll have to go to an expert.'

Brian and I discussed things a little further and I told him what I'd found out about Jerri Quill. Then I hung off and took off my jacket, throwing it on the lounge. More and more, it was looking as if Claire Dimitriou's murderer was another scientist. Only another scientist would know the significance of steam-clean and the removal of all items that might be tested for trace evidence.

I realised I was hungry and that the cottage was suddenly quiet. Greg had gone to one of the two little back bedrooms he and Charlie shared, and from the bathroom I could hear the sound of Iona singing in the shower. Charlie was still unloading picnic things from his car so I went outside to help him.

After I'd showered, changed into a tracksuit and chewed my way through a chicken roll, the world seemed perfect for a moment: my son and brother close by, Jacinta doing well at university, my ex-wife and her new boyfriend several hundred kilometres away and, best of all, Iona's laugh pealing from the kitchen as she helped my brother.

Later, I pulled the big table out from against the wall in the lounge room and set four places, so we could eat in the warmth of the crackling fire. In the crowded kitchen, we worked out a routine to serve out the pasta and sauce Charlie and Iona had made, while Greg organised a salad.

My head cold had become heavier and wetter, as they seem to do at the end of the day, and I suddenly remembered Iona had asked me to bring bread rolls and extra milk from town. Fortunately, Charlie and Greg had brought supplies with them so I was off the hook. But as I sat down with the others, feeling more relaxed than I had in days, I was assailed by a wave of tiredness. If I didn't take some leave, experience told me, the odds were I'd make an error of judgement that might prove disastrous. I'd seen it happen before to acquaintances when their workload became crushing and they didn't take a holiday. The greatest tool a scientist has at his or her disposal is his mind, his clear interpretation of the facts leading to a final conclusion. I'd seen careers destroyed by just one error. The scientific community never forgets. Not to mention the fact that I'd promised Iona I'd take the next few days off. I'd meant it when I said it—but I hadn't counted on *two* murders.

'A guy's been ringing for you,' said Iona, as we cleared the table and carried plates into the kitchen. 'Someone called Earl Richardson? Poor man sounded desperate.'

I frowned. How had he found out where I was living?

'Said he'd ring back,' she added. 'Said you were doing a favour for him?' She turned enquiring eyes towards me.

I didn't like the sound of 'doing a favour' one bit. It's not the way I operate. And yet what else could he call it? I scoured the pasta saucepan, scraping off cooked-on cheese, angry that I'd ever agreed to help him.

'You doing favours for some crim, old man?' Greg asked and I chased him out of the kitchen, grabbing one of the old tapestry cushions and whacking him with it. In turn, he pounced on me and we wrestled together, like we hadn't done for a long time. Eventually I won with a tricky wristlock, taking him down and straddling his back.

'The old man can still beat you, young whippersnapper,' I puffed.

'Only by using dirty cop tricks,' said Greg, rolling over and sitting up as I released him.

'What else is an old fellow supposed to do? Look at you! You're taller than I am.'

'Talk about the heavy hand of the law,' he countered, rubbing his wrist where I'd pinned it.

'The law is only heavy when you resist,' I said and laughed, helping him up. 'And I've got to keep something up my sleeve. You'd beat me hands down in a fair fight.' It was true. Greg was developing into a powerfully built young man, starting to fill out his previously rangy adolescent frame.

'Hey,' said my son. 'I can smell dog shit.'

I took the offending shoes outside and left them on the back step, intending to give them a good clean later, then padded back to the bedroom where I found some very old tan leather slip-ons.

Pressed by the others, who weren't going to leave the subject alone, I gave a brief outline of Earl Richardson's predicament, his belief he'd be the prime suspect and why I'd become involved.

'Statistically, he's the most likely suspect,' Iona remarked on her way to make coffee.

'Hey!' I grabbed her wrist as she passed by and kissed the inside, delighting in her sudden smile. 'We don't charge people on statistics, but on evidence.'

'Can't say I blame him for worrying,' said Charlie. 'In his place, I'd be worried too.'

From the kitchen drifted the very welcome fragrance of coffee.

'I don't think in this case the husband needs to be too concerned,' I said, walking over to join Iona and finding mugs in the cupboards for all of us. 'He was in Sydney at the time. The cops had to wake him in the early morning to tell him what had happened. And it's hardly likely Tianna Richardson would get all dressed up to go dancing with her estranged husband. Brian's questioning the locals who were at the club. We would have heard if he'd been there.'

'So if it wasn't the husband or another close rellie, it's one of the six per centers,' said Charlie, using his name for the random stranger or sociopath that Tianna Richardson might have encountered.

'Or some other acquaintance,' I reminded him. 'She was an attractive woman and we already know there are boyfriends.'

Iona poured the coffee and passed a mug to me. I took another of the mugs for Charlie. Never one for convention, he was happy to take it as well as still sitting with two different wines, a red and a white. Greg's mobile rang and, looking down to see who it was, he headed off into the hallway.

'Talking of rellies,' I said to Iona and Charlie, 'there's an estranged son. But I don't expect to be involved in the investigation any longer. I've acquitted myself.'

'That's good to hear,' said Iona, kissing the top of my head before sitting down on the floor near the fire. She leaned her back against one of the big club armchairs that sat either side of the hearth. I plonked down in the same armchair and Charlie sat on the other, lining up his three drinks carefully on the wide armrest.

From the spare bedroom, I could hear the low murmur of my son's voice on his mobile. He's talking to Ellie, I thought.

'So,' said Charlie. 'We get the chance to see a bit more of you, bro. Is that right?' He looked at me more closely. 'You don't look too good right now,' he added.

'I'm tired, Charlie,' I said. 'I've been trying to organise a decent holiday, but with every passing moment it seems less likely.' I thought of Florence, Vic and the others trying to carry the workload without me. 'I've managed to swing a couple of days,' I added. 'Everyone's snowed under with too much work and there are still unfilled positions. I talked to Bob Edwards last week and he's been lumbered with heading up this new Unsolved Homicide Unit. As well as running Physical Evidence at Surry Hills. These days everyone's doing two—sometimes three—jobs.'

Then I had to explain how the police commissioner had recently announced that nearly four hundred cold cases, some dating back to the late seventies and early eighties, were being reopened and reinvestigated in the light of the latest scientific procedures—any case, for instance, where the physical evidence lifts and samples collected at the crime scene were still packed away with the investigating detectives' briefs. Already, a couple of suspects had been charged over two separate murders.

'You've got to slow down, bro,' Charlie insisted, turning his attention to Iona. 'My brother's very lucky to have you, Iona. He's starting to *look* like our father with those lines in his forehead.'

Frowning, I put my hand to my head, feeling for the lines.

'*And* you're always frowning. Just like the old man.'

'For Christ's sake, I hope not,' I said, awkward as I always was when Charlie got personal with me, and thinking of the sour old man in his shed.

'Ask him when he last had a holiday,' Charlie said.

Iona cocked her head and looked back at me, eyebrow raised. 'Well?'

I searched my memory.

'See? You can't remember, can you?' She gave me a gentle smack and I seized her hand, imprisoning it with both of mine.

'How *is* Dad?' I asked, changing tack.

'Same as he ever was.'

Charlie kept in touch with our father far more than I did. By the time I was fifteen, the old man had pretty well moved out of the marital home and into the increasingly furnished garage. Even after the death of our mother some years later, he'd never moved back into that house. Couldn't say I blamed him.

Charlie was able to be more compassionate about the old bastard. He was younger and didn't seem to remember what I couldn't seem to forget. We were abandoned in that house; we raised ourselves, with a father who never came inside and a mother who had usually passed out by the time I'd got home from school. Somewhere in me was a hard ridge of anger, dense and dark—with my father and mother fixed in the middle of it, like corpses locked in ice. I was aware of it sometimes and it concerned me. Over the years, I'd noticed other recovered alcoholics' behaviours, seen their clenched smiles, their hot, aggressive reactions to things that weren't their business. I sensed their anger, cemented over with a denial that did nothing to release it, only locking it down deeper. To my way of thinking, far too many recovered alcoholics died much too early of cancer, angry down to the marrow of their bones.

'Grandad's the same as he ever was,' said Greg, coming back into the room, 'only more so.' Neither of the kids had been able to make much of a relationship with the old curmudgeon.

'He propositioned the community nurse last time she visited,' Charlie laughed.

'There goes the inheritance,' said Greg.

I couldn't smile at the joke. Whenever I thought of my father and that house in the mountains, with its dripping gardens in the winter and almost no sunshine in summer, it brought back memories that were still too painful to entertain very long. The place had been rented out for the many years since our mother's death.

'He told the nurse she had great legs and that it was a pity she didn't have a husband,' Charlie said.

'I can't imagine anyone marrying *him*.' My son's face was a picture.

One woman had married him. Our mother. Maybe only a drunk could do it.

Iona went to bed after *Lateline* and Greg disappeared with his laptop, either to work on an assignment, or, more likely, to tie up the landline, leaving Charlie and me sprawled opposite each other on the two big chairs.

'I went to a crime scene today and it had been steam-cleaned,' I said. 'What do you make of that?'

'Sounds like a very particular person,' said my brother. 'Someone who's fastidious in their habits. Someone who very much wants to cover their tracks.' He poked the fire and tiny red-gold sparks flew up the chimney. 'Or,' he added, 'it might indicate a scientist.'

'I'd arrived at much the same conclusion,' I said, smiling. 'Without all the hassle of a Master's degree in psychology.'

'Ah, but you don't have the required psychologist's concerned expression,' he said, bunging it on, frowning and pursing his lips. 'Only someone halfway through a doctorate gets to look like this.'

I hurled a cushion at him.

'I'm a scientist,' I said, 'but I don't think I'd steam-clean after I'd murdered you. Perhaps our killer's watched one too many episodes of *CSI*.'

Charlie grinned. 'Let's hope.'

'Why?'

'Because, in *CSI* the killer *always* fucks up,' Charlie said, deadpan, hurling the cushion back.

'You didn't make it to the picnic,' he said then. 'The riverside was unbelievably beautiful.'

'I did, but everyone had already gone.' I thought about how I'd sat there working. 'Charlie,' I started, wanting to ask my brother about this, but not finding the words easily.

'Yes?' he drawled, taking a drink from his second wine glass, observing my struggle.

'I *want* to spend time with Iona, I make plans to do it. But something always comes up and I end up disappointing her. She's been very patient. But I can tell she's starting to get fed up with me. She's given up her life in Sydney to be with me and all I have to do is make some time for her—for us—on the weekends, in the evenings, like other couples do. I found myself sitting on the river bank earlier and I was automatically in working mode. I don't understand myself. Charlie, I love this woman. I love spending time with her.'

'Are you sure about that?' asked Charlie, leaning back further in the old chair, as if to examine me from a more distant perspective.

'Of course I am!' I said, irritated by his challenge, my fingers picking at the worn velvet of the armrest. 'Why do you doubt it?'

Charlie pulled a face and shrugged. 'Oh, I seem to remember a man with a history of choosing difficult women. What about that woman down here you were involved with?'

I thought of Alix, who I used to refer to as 'the convenient association', and how badly that had ended.

'That wasn't the best, I have to admit,' I said. 'But I wasn't in love with her.'

'And what about the woman you married?'

'Fair go, Charlie! Genevieve is a self-centred sociopath who picked a drunk for a lifetime partner!' I said.

'Granted. But why did the drunk pick her as his wife?' Charlie challenged.

I mumbled something about physical attraction.

'And what about the first woman you spent time with—the first woman in your life?' he continued.

'What's Kerry-Anne Cooper got to do with this?' I asked, puzzled. 'I'm amazed you even remember her!'

'I'm not talking about your first girlfriend. I'm talking about the *first* woman in your life. In any man's life. The woman who helps set up the woman template in a man's unconscious.'

'You know what I think about all that unconscious stuff,' I protested. 'You make too much of it.'

'Hang on, Jack! You admit it in other areas. You seek it at crime scenes!'

'I'm not a goddamn crime scene,' I said. But Charlie only raised an eyebrow before continuing.

'Your hero, Edmund Locard, says whatever the offender leaves consciously or *unconsciously* is just as important as any other physical evidence. You're smart as paint when it comes to *offenders* and the unconscious.'

'That's different,' I said, irritated. What could a nineteenth-century criminologist have to do with Iona and me?

'But what about *investigators* and the unconscious? You pick up things other people don't notice. What about *this* investigator sitting opposite me?' he said. 'What about the unconscious influences of the first woman in *his* life and how it affects his present?'

Hell, I thought. The mother. *Our* mother. 'You think I should see someone, don't you? A professional, I mean,' I said.

'Wouldn't hurt,' said Charlie in his non-directive fashion.

'But what would that do? How would that help?'

Charlie stood up. 'It would make you focus on your behaviour and its motivators for an hour or so every week. That in itself would create some space for you. Solutions might have the chance to arise then. The way you're living now doesn't permit any time for quiet reflection.'

'I think while I'm driving,' I said, then wished I hadn't because it sounded pathetic.

'Plus it's more about *feeling*, bro, than thinking. Either way, you've got a big job ahead of you,' said Charlie.

'What big job ahead of me? What do you mean?'

Charlie looked down at me in his kindly way. Sometimes it seems as if he's so much older than me, despite his chronological age.

'Think about what it means to spend time with a woman. What does that mean to you?' he said.

I frowned. 'Doing things together,' I said. 'Spending time together.'

'Doing what?'

'Reading books, going to the movies. Talking,' I added, more irritated by the minute.

'You can do all those things with me,' said Charlie. 'Or with a colleague.'

'Making love.'

Charlie nodded.

'So what are you getting at, Charlie?'

'Iona wants you to spend intimate time with her. That means opening up. Talking about your hopes and fears. Especially your fears. Revealing who you are. That's what intimacy *is*—self-revelation. But to be truly intimate with another person, you've got to know yourself. And while ever you're living in your defence system, you're never going to be able to do it.'

I didn't much like the sound of any of that, especially the self-revelation part. Even when I was invited to speak at AA, I didn't ever say much about that sort of thing. Just told my story about what it was like, what happened and how it was now—in terms of my relations with my kids and my work life—immeasurably better.

'But that's not me,' I said, finally. 'That's not my style.'

'You might have to do something about that. And then you've got to factor in the other part of your behaviour,' Charlie said. 'What happens when you are inactive? Do you know?'

'I start to feel restless,' I said, remembering the moment on the river bank.

'And where do you suppose that restlessness might take you?' Charlie asked.

'Hell, Charlie, what is this?'

'A simple question. Requiring only a very simple experiment to discover the answer. And now, I'm going to bed,' Charlie announced.

He paused at the doorway on his way to the back room. 'You'd better find out a bit more about yourself, Jack, otherwise...' His words trailed off.

'Otherwise what?'

'I think you already know the answer to that,' he said. 'Goodnight.'

SEVEN

Charlie's comments were still in my mind when I woke. I'd had strange dreams of trying to intervene in a violent disagreement between my mother and Iona but I couldn't remember what the struggle had been about. Beside me, Iona stirred and I gathered her into my arms, snuggling into her warm body. I thought of the other things Charlie had said last night, that the first woman in my life had somehow set me on some dangerous trajectory when it came to affairs of the heart.

Her eyes opened and she smiled up at me.

'What are you thinking?' she asked.

'That you're nothing like my mother,' I said.

'Thanks a lot! I should hope not!'

My heart melted and I held her as she burrowed into my chest. I felt my body respond to her proximity and realised it had been a while since we'd made love. I resolved to change that very soon, but unfortunately Charlie's remarks and the business of the day dominated my mind and thoughts of lovemaking slipped away. I started to throw the bedclothes aside.

'Hey,' she said. 'What's your hurry? We've got all day.'

I fell back on the pillows. 'Sweetheart,' I said.

'Don't "sweetheart" me in that tone!' she said, her smile fading. 'You're about to tell me something I don't want to hear.'

'Iona, I've just got a couple of things to do today but I swear I'll come home early,' I said, sliding out of bed, shivering, and dressing quickly.

The silence in the room was deafening.

'I'll make you coffee before you go,' she said finally, starting to get out of bed.

'No. Stay there. I'll grab a coffee from the Cretan's café.'

I went outside to bring in some more firewood from the sheltered stack near the old laundry shed. It had rained during the night, not enough to penetrate the deeper soil layers, but enough to turn the driveway into mud. A soft mist hung over the garden, staining the air in pastel tones around the drooping roses. I could capture that, I thought, with watercolours. If I had time.

Nothing moved in the paddocks, not even the odd rabbit. I guessed the stock had been sold some time ago, soon after the drought began to bite. If this was how it was at the end of summer, God help the landscape over winter and the next hot season.

A flock of gang-gangs screeched overhead and I went inside, unloading the wood in the chest beside the open fireplace in the lounge room. I scribbled a note and put it under the butter dish on the kitchen table, envying my son and brother their leisurely day in the company of Iona. I went into the bedroom to say goodbye, but Iona was sound asleep again. I leaned over and kissed her hair and she stirred and even smiled.

Heading towards the front door, I passed the photograph of my sister Rosie and remembered how Jacinta had called her a guardian angel. Show me, Rosie, I prayed. Teach me about how to slow down so I can be with Iona.

Then I picked up my leather jacket from the hall table, together with my briefcase, and set off for Weston, rolling the car slowly down the dirt drive because of the sleeping household behind me, only starting it near the gates.

My feelings for Iona Seymour were very powerful. We'd talked about it like adults and her acceptance of my proposition had filled me with wonder and gratitude. And yet...I had to face the fact that I was sometimes made very uneasy by her. Also, only a day or two earlier I'd had several days' leave ruled off on the calendar, yet somehow I had become involved with two major new cases. These thoughts and the *Light Cavalry Overture* on the car radio were interrupted by the sharp tones of my mobile.

'Yes?' I said, more sharply than I'd intended.

'Am I interrupting anything important?' Harry Marshall asked.

'I was thinking about men and women,' I admitted, 'and what my chances of domestic harmony might be. What do you think, Doc?'

'You'd have to ask my wife,' said Harry. 'That's her area of expertise.'

I swerved to miss the carcase of a large wallaby on the roadway.

'When you can,' Harry continued, 'come over and have a look at Tianna Richardson's body. I want to show you something.'

Harry greeted me at the front desk of the morgue and took me through the building which had recently been recarpeted and smelled of new, slightly damp wool. The door of the pathology lab was open and I caught a glimpse of the exhibits as we passed. Diseased or poisoned tissues hung in formaldehyde for the education of student pathologists, and I also spied the exquisite skull of a baby with its pearly milk and permanent teeth arranged in double rows like tiny shark's jaws.

'You're busier than usual,' I said to Harry, thinking that in the nearby refrigerated room lay the bodies of the two women whose crime scenes I'd attended.

'I like being busy,' said Harry, as we stepped inside his office. 'I was in here before five this morning,' he continued, 'catching up with some paperwork. No rest for the wicked.' He laughed.

'Tell me something, Harry. What does your wife think of the hours you keep?'

We had stopped in a small cul-de-sac lined with cupboards and shelves.

'She knows that I'm an overworked, under-appreciated pathologist. Sometimes when I go home she points to the door and shouts at me, "Out! You stink of the morgue. Don't come inside until you've had another shower and dumped those clothes!"'

'But what about your life away from here?' I persisted. 'Your private life.'

'I don't have one of those according to my wife. And she thinks I should.'

'Are you going to do something about that?' I asked.

'Maybe,' Harry said. 'But sitting around idle doesn't suit me.'

He passed me a gown from one of the cupboards and I pulled disposable gloves and plastic booties from a dispenser before following him into the brightness of the large post-mortem room with its several tables. Sitting around idle wouldn't suit me either, I thought.

My mobile rang and I fumbled under the light blue gown to unhook it. Brian Kruger was on the other end of the line.

'I'm calling from Tianna Richardson's place,' he said. 'I thought you might like to have a look around. Also, her boyfriend's agreed to an informal chat.'

'Give me the address. I'll get there once I'm finished with Harry.'

I scribbled down the details, aware that Harry had gone ahead and that a morgue attendant was wheeling in the body of Tianna Richardson, her blue bag zipped up to her chest.

'In a few years you'll be retiring, Harry,' I said, joining him near the trolley.

'That's right,' said Harry. 'My wife is leaning on me to take up bowls.'

'Make a change from bowels,' I said, unable to resist. In the harsh white light, I clearly saw the tiredness and strain on his face but turned my attention to his words.

'You can see these marks on her much better today,' Harry said, unzipping the rest of the bag. 'I know you got them on video and Brian took the stills, but we could need more shots.'

Beside the restitched dark incision in Tianna Richardson's chest cavity, Harry's probe pointed to the odd marks I'd noticed near her left breast and jaw line. They were no longer the reddish colour of yesterday, but had taken on a grey-purple colour. I looked more closely at the small, semi-circular bruises.

'What are they?' I asked.

'Take a good look,' said Harry. 'Tell me what you think they look like.'

Under a hand-glass, I could see that there were two faint rows of marks, a top and bottom layer. 'I'd say they were bite marks, except—'

'Except what?'

'They just don't look right somehow.'

'That's exactly what I was thinking. They're not quite like any bite marks I've seen before,' said Harry, tracing the marks with the thin probe. 'Superficially, it *looks* like the impression of teeth. But, generally speaking, the underbite should leave a stronger impression than the top row of teeth. In this case,' I followed the tapping probe, 'both upper and lower "jaws"—I'll call them that for the moment—are identical. And the upper and lower jaws don't overlap properly. They seem out of whack.'

Harry turned away and came back with a plastic packet containing black and white photos. He passed it to me. 'Take a look at those. That's what a human bite looks like.'

I studied the series of photographs, seeing the familiar oval shape in all of them—upper and lower jaw impressions joining up, the underbite showing more darkly.

'And it isn't an animal,' I said, peering as Harry revealed the similar marks on the skin of the jaw near the ear, 'because animal jaws are far more acutely shaped than human jaws.'

'Whoever or whatever did them, they were made *ante*-mortem,' said Harry. 'I'll have to wait for the histology report to be a hundred per cent sure, but I'm prepared to bet on it.'

'Someone with badly made false teeth?' I asked.

Harry shrugged. 'You're the investigator. I was hoping you might be able to cast a little light on the matter. I'm just telling you what I've found.'

'Stop being so modest, Harry,' I said. 'Tell me what *you* think made these marks.'

'I can't think of anything that would make those double rows,' he said. 'Unless it's the bite marks of someone with some facial deformity.'

'Why don't you send these over to the forensic dentist,' I said. 'See what he makes of them.'

'That's exactly what my next step was going to be.'

I noticed that the earrings had gone from the woman's ears and remembered Sofia's remarks. *Hasn't anyone noticed what's truly weird about the way this woman's dressed?*

'Did you find out about those earrings?' I asked, remembering my request concerning Cec Peabody, the jeweller.

'Nineteenth-century Victorian rose gold in a distinctive design of interlinked hearts set with seed pearl and peridots, is what the man said. I have the report in my office.'

'Peridots?' I queried. 'What are they?'

'Semi-precious stones,' he replied. 'A yellowy-green form of olivine, according to Cec.'

We left the post-mortem room, dumped our gowns and booties and walked back to Harry's office.

'Have you looked at the gunshot case yet?' I asked. 'The scientist from the Ag Station?'

'She's next. It's been a busy day.'

'Tell me about it,' I said. 'Getting a quarter of our annual murder allocation in one twenty-four-hour period.' Generally speaking, homicide rates in the Australian Capital Territory hovered around eight victims per year.

'Find out what made those marks on Tianna's body and you'll be moving in the right direction,' said Harry as I made to leave.

'So, what was the cause of death?' I asked. 'Those head injuries?'

Harry sat behind his desk. 'My report hasn't been typed up yet but I can tell you the main points. Cause of death was due to injuries on the back of the head. I found eggshell fracturing of the skull and severe injuries at the frontal lobes too. The result was a lot of venous damage and bleeding in the subdural space resulting in a very large clot. This would have raised the pressure in the cranial cavity until it eventually exceeded the arterial blood pressure.'

I thought of Tianna Richardson lying unconscious while her own blood filled the narrow space between the lining of her brain and the curved bone of her skull. 'And that stopped the blood flow to the brain?' I asked.

'Correct,' said Harry. 'Deadly, unless you get to an ICU pretty smart and have the pressure relieved.'

'You said impact injuries. Any idea what made them?'

'That's the odd part,' said Harry. 'It doesn't look like a bashing to me. I'm thinking contre coup.'

I frowned. 'I've heard that term before. But I've forgotten it.'

'There's still a lot of argy-bargy about contrecoup injuries,' Harry explained. 'And how and why they occur. Some scientists reckon they're caused by rotational force or shearing effects.'

'I don't get it,' I said.

'I don't either, to be honest. But one thing is pretty clear. The presence of this sort of injury almost always implies that the person's head was moving fast when it suddenly hit something hard and unyielding.'

I imagined Tianna Richardson being hurled violently to the ground of the car park. But hard enough to cause those deep wounds? It would be difficult for even a very strong offender to muster the speed necessary from a standing position.

'At first I thought she might have been thrown from a moving vehicle, because of these abrasions and scratches,' said Harry.

'And hit the ground on the back of her head at speed?' I asked. 'But why do it there, in the car park? There could be witnesses. There'd be cars coming and going as well as parked around. How could he get up enough speed under those conditions?'

Harry nodded. 'That's right. Then I thought maybe, as she was pushed out of the vehicle, one of the doors swung back at speed and hit the back of her head. Or she was hit by another vehicle.'

'But, Harry, there's no suggestion of any car being involved. Not at the crime scene.'

'Yes, and I haven't found anything on her that would indicate the involvement of a vehicle,' Harry said. 'No flakes of paint. No other abrasions consistent with that interpretation. You know how it is, a bit of car on the person and a bit of person on the car.'

Locard's theory of the transference of particle evidence formed the basis of my trace evidence work. Except in this case, there *was* no evidence of such an exchange.

'You said at *first* you thought all this,' I said, remembering Harry's words. 'What do you think now?'

There was a silence as Harry stared off into the middle distance. I could almost hear the machinery of his formidable mind. But whatever he was thinking, I had the sense he wasn't quite ready to share it with me just now.

'I took swabs of the injury at the back of her head—they're waiting for you. Maybe you'll find things at the trace level,' he said as he passed a bagged sample in a specimen container to me. 'I found these sandy particles on the wound site.'

'Yes.' I recalled the large grains I'd brushed into a container from the matted hair. 'I collected identical particles.'

There was another silence, broken only by the entrance of a morgue attendant wheeling in a body at the other end of the post-mortem room, a young woman wearing expensive European riding jodhpurs smeared with mud and filth.

'I'm mystified, Jack,' Harry said after a while. 'The injuries she's sustained are consistent with the head striking a hard surface at speed. But I can't make any sense of how that might have happened.'

He gave a little grimace. 'Maybe you can do better. I'm going to have a closer look at that bruise on her face.'

I'd worked with Harry for many years and I'd never seen him as puzzled as this. 'Your wife's right, Harry. You do need a break,' I said. 'All those early mornings and late nights. Not enough conversation down here with the dead.'

He looked up at me and for a second I thought there were tears in his eyes, but it could have been the light or the way his spectacles reflected. 'It's not the dead who worry me,' he said.

I knew what he meant. For a split second I wondered if I could talk to him about what Charlie had said last night, but I just couldn't do it so I silently signed for the bagged specimen Harry had given me and put it in my briefcase.

'You might as well take these back with you too,' he said. 'Save me sending for the courier. The swabs from body cavities—there were signs of recent sexual activity.'

Considering the facts of the case, that didn't surprise me.

'You should get a DNA profile from the semen.'

EIGHT

My next stop was outside the neat, double-fronted brick veneer cottage of the late Tianna Richardson on Kincaid Street. I pulled up behind Brian Kruger's crime scene wagon and walked up the cement pathway past several weatherbeaten garden gnomes huddled around a small declivity that might once have been a little fishpond before the big dry. Now, only grass grew in it. Apart from a vermilion geranium in a pot near the front door and a wide-branched pepper tree, the garden was bare. Just as I was about to knock on the front door, Brian called out.

'Who's that?'

'It's me. Jack.'

'Give it a shove. It's not locked.'

Brian appeared as I pushed open the door, hesitating because I wasn't wearing protective gear. 'It's okay,' he said. 'We've finished with the physical evidence sweep. Take a look.'

'We?' I asked, looking round.

'Debbie was here but she's gone out to get some eats.'

I walked into a large living room furnished with fawns and timbers, an old-fashioned floral carpet on the floor, framed family photographs standing on the mantelpiece and sideboard and lots of ornaments and knick-knacks. Genevieve had loved this sort of thing too, and our house had been infested with collections of coy shepherdesses, little donkeys and carts, draught horses and Toby jugs.

'Have you had a chance to talk to Harry Marshall?' Brian asked.

'I have,' I answered. 'He says he knows what killed her but he can't work out how. Except to say that her head was moving fast when it hit something stationary.'

'That sounds like a fall,' said Brian. 'But where we found her, there was nowhere she could have fallen from.'

I told Brian about the odd marks on the dead woman's body before looking around. 'Find anything?' I asked.

'Nothing obvious. No sign of anything amiss here. It's all neat and tidy. We've talked to her nearest and dearest and they all say the same thing. She was a popular girl. No enemies. Sure, she had boyfriends, but doesn't everyone. She liked dancing and partying.'

From outside came the sound of a vehicle pulling up. I looked out the window to see a Holden ute, its hotted-up engine burbling before it was cut.

'That'll be the boyfriend,' said Brian. 'Damien Henshaw, local resident. Painter by trade. He's agreed to an informal chat. You can help me do a search of the place.'

'Hey!' I remonstrated. 'You said you were finished.'

'I lied.' Brian smiled. 'I meant we'd finished the fancy stuff.'

A young fellow, long blond hair in a ponytail, swung out of the car, shoved his hands deep into his padded chequered shirt and approached the house. As far as I could see, there was absolutely nothing wrong with his teeth or jaw line. In fact, he was a strikingly handsome young man. Tianna Richardson, I recalled, must have been in her early forties; this youth couldn't have been much older than my own son. Or hers.

Brian met him at the door and held it open while Henshaw came inside, scared eyes darting from Brian to me. 'This is Jack McCain, Damien,' said Brian. 'He's part of the investigation into Mrs Richardson's death. He's a scientist.'

Damien nodded at me, hands still firmly in his pockets, slightly stooped, standing awkwardly until Brian ushered him into the living room. He relaxed a little in the familiar surroundings and sat down on one of the lounge chairs.

Brian had his notebook out, ready to take a statement and I wandered around, leafing through the photo album that lay open on the coffee table, listening, while Brian took down the details.

Damien was twenty-four and had known Mrs Richardson for about four months.

'I did some painting for her,' he explained.

'That's not all you did for her,' said Brian. 'Tell me about that.'

'Yes,' I interrupted. 'How did that come about?' I looked up from the photograph I'd been studying of Tianna out for dinner with a group of people. 'Who made the first move?'

Damien Henshaw looked around the room, his gaze fixing on a shopping bag and scarf thrown over the back of the other lounge chair. He shrugged. 'She came out of the shower when I was doing the hallway. She put it right on me. Asked me how about it.'

'And?' I prompted.

'It started from there.'

'What sort of relationship was it?' I asked. 'How often did you see each other?'

'I can't believe it,' Damien said, ignoring my question, 'I can't believe she's dead like that.' His words sounded strained and unnatural and his head suddenly slumped down.

'Please answer my question,' I said. 'Can you describe what sort of a relationship you had with Mrs Richardson?'

Damien shifted in his seat and looked accusingly at Brian. 'You told me this was just going to be a chat.'

'It is,' said Brian, reassuring him. 'We will need you to drop down to the station sometime, though.

And do a proper statement. No need to be worried. It's standard procedure with a case like this. Okay?'

Damien was still uneasy but he straightened himself on the chair.

'So tell us,' I prompted.

'I'd drop by a couple of times a week, usually in the evenings, and we'd have sex.'

Couple of times a week, I thought. If I was his age, with a woman so obliging and attractive, I'd have been dropping in a couple of times a *day*.

'I just want to get an idea of what happened the night before last,' said Brian. 'Monday—when Mrs Richardson went to the nightclub. Did you see her that day?'

Damien nodded. 'I dropped round after work finished and she wanted me to stay in and watch a video. That's the other thing she was always wanting me to do.'

'And the first thing?' I asked.

I thought he'd blush, but his answer wasn't what I was expecting. 'Bloody dancing,' he said. 'She loved going to nightclubs with bands and *dancing*.'

Shocking behaviour, I thought.

'But you wanted to go to the pub with your mates?' I suggested.

'Right. Then she started saying she wanted to come with me. To the pub.' There was a long pause. 'But I didn't want her to come. I didn't want her hanging round me when I was with my mates.'

'What did she think of that?' I queried.

'Not much.'

A long silence.

'So you argued?' I asked.

Damien nodded. 'We had a fight. It ended up with her calling it off. I told her I didn't care and I walked out. She came after me, screaming at me.' His expression changed as he suddenly realised the implications of what he was saying. 'Look, I didn't touch her! I mean, she was upset at me. Yelling. But I didn't do anything!'

I could see he was scared now and I decided to lean on him a bit.

'You and Tianna had had this fight before?' I asked. 'You never wanted her to come to the pub with you because you've got a girlfriend, haven't you? Someone your own age.'

I saw his face change and soften. 'Yes. We're getting married at Christmas time.'

'Name?' Brian asked.

'Kylie McGovern.'

'And you didn't want them to know about each other,' I said.

Damien Henshaw's eyes flickered between Brian and me.

'Is that what the fight with Tianna was about? Is that why she called it off? Because she'd found out about your girlfriend?'

'She's not just a girlfriend!' There was energy and enthusiasm in his voice. 'She's my *fiancée*.'

'Did Mrs Richardson find out about your fiancée?' Brian asked.

'No! I've just told you. She was pissed off about not coming to the pub.'

'So why didn't you tell us this in the first place?'

I saw the red flush rising from his neck. 'Because it's none of your bloody business, that's why!'

I stood up and walked to the chair where the shopping bag and scarf hung. 'Let's get something straight, Damien,' I said, gripping the back of the chair, facing him. 'Tianna Richardson was murdered the night before last and it's my business to talk to everyone who knew her. That includes you. And the people *you* know. People like your fiancée, Kylie.' I came closer, standing over him but remaining as polite as possible. 'We want to know about them too. In fact, *everyone* who knew Mrs Richardson is our business in a murder investigation.'

The red flush in his face subsided, although his lips were set in a thin white line. This was a very different character from the casual knockabout image he'd first presented. Now I had the sense of someone maintaining tight control.

'So what happened that night?'

'You're getting this all wrong. I don't have to talk to you.'

Although we'd rattled his cage, I didn't like the way things were going. We didn't want to get him offside at this stage. Much easier for everyone if he cooperated.

'You're quite right,' I said, glancing over at Brian who got the message.

'But it makes our job easier,' said Brian, 'if we've got an idea of what happened that night.'

'We understand that couples argue all the time,' I continued in the same tone as Brian. 'You should have heard me and my ex.'

'We weren't a couple,' he said. 'You're not listening!'

Brian spread his hands in appeal. 'I know this is tough for you, but we have to ask these questions.'

The moment passed and I saw Damien relax.

'So just tell us,' I said, 'in your own words. Your own time.'

'Like I said, I went to the pub, then I went to Kylie's place. I stayed there all night.'

Further down the track, all this would have to be checked. But I didn't want to mention that just now. 'See?' I said, with a friendly smile. 'You've got nothing to worry about. We appreciate your cooperation.'

'We'll get you downtown at a convenient time over the next couple of days and you can make a statement. I'll need to talk to your fiancée too. Okay?' said Brian.

'No way,' said Damien. 'Don't drag her into this!'

'Hey, take it easy,' said Brian. 'We won't mention your extra business with Mrs Richardson. We just need her to alibi you.'

Damien stood up, still wary. 'I've left a bit of gear here. I need to pick it up.'

'I'm afraid that's not possible for a little while,' said Brian. 'We're required to keep the house intact just for the moment. I'm sure you understand.'

Damien looked alarmed. 'But it's gear that I need. Work gear.'

'We'll get it back to you as soon as possible.'

Damien anxiously looked from one of us to the other. 'When? When can I get them back?'

I noticed the change in language. 'What have you left here?' I asked.

'My boots. I need them for work.'

'We'll make sure you get them back as soon as possible,' said Brian. 'And we'll need to get a sample from you, for DNA testing.'

He didn't like that. 'Why? I haven't done anything wrong. What do you want to test me for?'

'Cops and doctors have their fingerprints on record,' I said. 'Mine are on the database. It's for elimination purposes only.' I gave him a reassuring pat. He wasn't much older than my son and for a moment I felt sorry for him. 'Because of your association with the deceased, there are legitimate reasons for your genetic material to be around this house.' I leaned on the word 'legitimate'.

'Don't worry, the samples are routinely destroyed once they've served their purpose,' I added. 'You have no reason for concern. It's normal procedure.'

While Brian took down Damien's details and made a time for him to come down to the station at Heronvale for a statement, I studied the young man, thinking again of how he was young enough to have been Tianna's son. Which reminded me.

'Did Mrs Richardson ever talk about someone called Jason?' I asked.

Damien nodded. 'I knew about him. She mentioned he was travelling around Australia. He's a surfer. Follows the surf.' He shrugged. 'She said I reminded her of him.'

He glanced at his watch. 'I have to go,' he said.

'No worries,' said Brian. 'We'll be in touch.'

Brian took him to the door and saw him out. Outside, the ute revved up and took off.

Brian returned, closing the front door behind him. 'What do you make of him?' he asked.

'Your average opportunistic young bloke,' I said, wandering around the living room, looking for items of interest. 'Steady relationship, older woman on the side.'

'Half his bloody luck,' Brian muttered as I followed him into a small room, fresh and light with white-painted furniture and pale pink and white curtains billowing from the window behind the double bed.

Tianna Richardson might have liked low-cut tank tops and high-heeled shoes, but her bedroom resembled that of a little girl.

'We need to find Jason Richardson,' said Brian, looking around. 'And talk to Damien Henshaw's fiancée.'

'What about the neighbours?' I asked.

'We've already had a chat to number seventeen,' said Brian, indicating the neighbour on the right.

'And the other side?'

Brian shrugged. 'The woman's away, apparently. But I'm told she's the street watchdog and knows everything that goes on. I've got her name here somewhere.' He flipped through his notebook. 'Vera Hastings.'

Unlike the rest of the house Tianna Richardson's bedroom was untidy, with shopping bags on the floor and swathes of tissue paper issuing from empty boxes. She'd opened those boxes like a whirlwind. Shopping frenzy?

I surveyed the scene, trying to work out what this room revealed about the woman, what was important to her and where she put her energy. Except for the dark brown bedspread, everything was pink and white and very feminine. It was a little too frilly and had too many bunches of artificial flowers for my taste, but it was still a pleasant room.

'You can see how pissed off she was,' said Brian, following my gaze to the shopping. 'The place is really tidy except for this room and the parcels. She's just ripped things open, put the gear on, left the mess where it was and driven straight to the Blackspot.'

'And somehow, between doing all that and us finding her, she goes and gets herself murdered,' I said. Brian stooped to lift the corner of a square of tissue paper and squinted under it.

'Tell me what you think about young Damien's story,' I said.

'I think it probably happened like he said it did,' said Brian. 'Mrs Richardson gets the dirts because her young boyfriend prefers to go off to the pub alone and drink with his mates rather than go dancing with her.' Brian lifted up another piece of tissue paper and peered under it. 'My problem with him as a suspect is that I can't see he really has a motive.'

'That we know about,' I added. 'Have you checked to see if he's got a record?'

'I'll do that next.' Brian made a face. 'But, Jack, you've got to *care* to kill someone. This was just a casual root with an available woman. He just dropped around now and then.'

'That's what he's told us. He admitted that they fought and he was pretty protective of the girlfriend. What if Tianna had threatened to tell her that Damien was playing out of school? People have died for less than that.' I knew that the best way to lie was to tell the truth, but leave out the last part. 'What if the fight wasn't about staying in and watching a video but about going dancing? Let's say they *did* go to the nightclub but kept on fighting and she threatened to tell Kylie, and late at night, when all is quiet, he takes her out to the car park, smokes a joint with her, then kills her? That take-it-or-leave-it attitude might change dramatically if he felt threatened.'

I recalled some of the people I'd spoken with in the aftermath of a violent death, with the body lying in another room, the ghost of a just-dead lover, spouse, or friend hovering around the edges of our dialogue. I'd witnessed the range of human emotions: rage, grief, despair, hatred, terror, numbness, denial, and shock to the point of hysteria. But the carelessness I'd witnessed in Damien Henshaw—apart from one expression of disbelief—made me wonder.

I looked up at Brian, who was lost in his own inner discourse. Not wanting to interrupt him, I pulled on a pair of gloves I always carried and picked up a framed photo from the bedside table. In it, Tianna was cuddling up to a fair-haired man who was neither Earl Richardson nor Damien Henshaw. The entwined lovers sat with a group of people gathered around a table on which glasses and wine bottles stood. Behind them, the timber of the banquette they were sitting in was carved in fake Jacobean twists. Some bar or hotel, I thought. Tianna seemed to have been a very busy, sociable girl.

Brian must have broken from his trance because he moved over and looked at the framed photo too. 'We need to know who this guy is,' he said.

'We sure do,' I replied. 'She's keeping him in the bedroom, for private display only, not out in the living room with the family and the friends.'

'Maybe the family and friends didn't know they were an item,' Brian suggested.

I checked the frame of the photograph, prising it open in case Tianna had further secrets locked behind it, but found nothing. I passed it to Brian who bagged and labelled it then went over to study the dressing-table.

It looked to be just as Tianna had left it—hairbrush lying on its side, three different perfume bottles standing in a row and a Cecil Peabody jewellery bag. I peered inside to see a smaller, maroon velour jewellery pouch and a receipt. First I opened the drawstring of the little pouch. A pair of earrings winked up at me, fancy dangly things, silver sprays dripping with black crystals of some sort. I hooked one out and stared at it for a moment before examining the receipt.

'Look at these,' I said, turning to show Brian.

'Nice,' he said. 'They'd really suit you.'

'She didn't wear them that night,' I said. 'Yet they would have gone perfectly with her outfit.' Sofia Verstoek's taunt came back to me, yet again.

Brian shrugged dismissively. 'She probably just liked those little green and gold numbers with the pearls.'

I picked up a docket lying on the floor near an open cardboard box and read the details of the purchase. 'She bought this gear only the day before she died,' I said. 'Stewart Chambray cocktail suit, $489. That's a lot of money for a doctor's receptionist.' I put the docket back in the empty box.

'What are you suggesting?' Brian asked, puzzled. 'That she's a working girl?'

'Not that,' I said, recalling the spangled black and silver top I'd seen on Tianna Richardson's body, under the black and silver jacket. The black and silver shoes, the beaded handbag. Black and silver. I looked again at the docket and over to the smart black and silver skirt I'd noticed lying over the back of the bedroom chair. I picked it up and checked the label—it was the bottom half of the Stewart Chambray cocktail suit.

'I don't know much about women's clothing,' I said, turning around to Brian, 'but I'll swear this is the skirt that goes with the jacket she was wearing at the Blackspot. Same fabric. This is the skirt from that suit.'

'But she was wearing a long winter skirt,' said Brian.

'That's right.' I recalled the charcoal woollen skirt bunched up mid-thigh.

'It's hot work dancing at a nightclub's disco,' said Brian. 'So who'd wear a long woollen skirt like the one she had on when she could've worn this?'

'Usually I don't ask questions about what women wear,' I said, remembering how my daughter and her mother had dressed on occasions. 'Yet I can't stop wondering why the hell she didn't wear the matching skirt and the matching earrings she'd just bought. Everything else she had on her was black or silver. And judging from this room, she seemed to be into matching colour schemes.'

'You're an artist,' Brian said, frowning. 'Isn't there something called contrast?'

I nodded, considering this.

'Well, she wanted some of that,' Brian added.

'But remember what Sofia Verstoek said. If a woman draws attention to something odd in another woman's clothing, it's usually just bitching. But it's a different sort of comment at a crime scene.'

'Yeah, but the Kiwi Krait is in a league of her own, she's so poisonous,' said Brian. 'But even if what she decided to wear *is* weird, what the hell does it mean?'

I tried to imagine Tianna Richardson, alive and well, dressing for what would turn out to be the last night of her life. I saw her taking the new clothes out of their boxes, angry and hurt by her young lover's rejection, pulling them on, enjoying their newness like women do. *Damn you,* she might have been thinking. *I'm going out dancing by myself. I'm an attractive woman even if you don't think so. I'm going to wear my cute new outfit and damn you.* Then I tried to imagine her rejecting the sexy matching skirt and digging out a heavy dark woollen one that came down almost to her ankles. Then doing the same with the black and silver earrings, choosing the antique interlinked gold filigree hearts with the peridots and pearls instead.

I held the docket out to Brian, indicating the skirt hanging over the chair. 'So why didn't she wear the skirt of her new suit, or her earrings?'

'I don't think we're qualified to even think about those questions,' said Brian. 'I wouldn't dare question anything about women's fashions.'

'The palynologist did. She questioned and she's a woman,' I said.

Brian was deep in thought. 'Tianna decides to go out dancing by herself,' he said. 'She puts on her smart new gladrags—'

'—not all of her new suit,' I corrected. 'Her new shoes and *half* a new suit. She doesn't wear the skirt of her brand new outfit. Or the earrings that match.'

'Maybe the skirt was too small, so she's grabbed something else that fitted better,' said Brian, coming over to check out the earrings more closely. 'My girlfriend put three different outfits on the other night before we went out and asked me which one looked best. I told her they all looked great, so she decided not to wear any of them. Then she got really pissed off with me.'

I knew what he meant. I went to the painted wardrobe and opened it, leafing through the hanging clothes. 'There are two black skirts here and even I can see that either of these would be a better match than the woollen one she wore,' I said, pulling them out and swishing them around near the unworn skirt, then holding the waistbands against each other. 'They're all the same size. Why would she pay almost five hundred bucks for a skirt that she couldn't fit into?'

'My girlfriend does it all the time,' said Brian. 'She calls it motivation.'

'And at the nightclub, decked out in half a suit and a woollen skirt, she meets a stranger—'

'Or someone she knows,' interrupted Brian.

'Right,' I said, thinking of Damien Henshaw. 'And he goes outside with her, drops her on her head. At speed.

'And after he's dropped her, he gets down and bites her with his deformed jaws.'

Brian's eyebrows hit maximum altitude. 'Mate,' he said dryly, 'there's something we're missing.'

We continued our search, going through the wardrobe and the chest of drawers, but didn't find anything that could throw any light on either the mystery of the spurned new skirt or the unknown fair man.

Under the lining of the underwear drawer—a favourite place for women to hide their love letters and other secret things, as I'd discovered over the years—I dug out an envelope of polaroids. Tianna Richardson keeping company with the fair mystery man again, this time naked and doing all sorts of fun and interesting things.

'Athletic, isn't she? I wish my girlfriend would do that,' said Brian, bagging them while I blew my nose. My head cold seemed to be getting worse.

'We definitely need to find this fellow. I've seen more of him than I need to.'

'Already we've got four potential suspects,' I said. 'Damien Henshaw; her husband, Earl; her son, Jason. And the mystery man in the photographs. You'll be busy checking all of them out.'

It wasn't long before we found some things that were not Tianna Richardson's—a pair of men's underpants and overalls.

'These must belong to Earl,' said Brian.

'Or Damien. Or the other one,' I said. 'Or someone else we don't even know about.'

We went over the living room again, opening drawers, looking through the photo albums.

'I spent a while with the staff at the Blackspot,' Brian said as we flipped through the photographs. 'We've only got one person who remembers Tianna Richardson. And she couldn't tell us much. The doorman says he doesn't recall what time she arrived, but said she could easily have just walked into the place without him noticing. It was one of their busiest nights and he had a couple of fights to deal with.'

'What's the name of the person who remembers seeing her?' I asked.

Brian pulled out his notebook and scrolled pages until he came to it. 'Here she is,' he said. 'Danby. Michelle Danby.'

I took the details, deciding I'd have a quiet chat with this witness. Sometimes people remembered things after an interview and never got round to contacting the police again.

I checked outside in case there was a hungry, thirsty animal languishing forgotten on a chain—a situation I'd come across more than once at a murder victim's house. On the way back inside, I noticed a pair of work boots standing near the back door. I could see at once that, although they were far from new, they'd been recently cleaned. Carefully, I picked one of them up with my gloved fingers, turning it upside down. These could be the work boots young Damien was so keen to recover.

'We need to check these against that partial bootprint you fixed in the nightclub car park,' I said to Brian as he joined me outside.

Brian turned the boots over. 'Sure looks similar,' he said before bagging them.

Similar wasn't good enough. We would need an exact match and fit. I watched Brian label and log the boots before he was interrupted by a phone call. It sounded as if there'd been a delay with the food, but Debbie was now on her way.

I looked around the neat backyard; it was surrounded by a fence with double gates opening onto a quiet lane. I hauled myself up and looked over, seeing only other fences and garages and garbage bins that hadn't been collected. I dropped down again. On the clothes line, jeans, shirts and pretty underwear waved in the light breeze, a load of washing that would never be brought in by its owner. I stood staring at Tianna's clothing for a few moments.

Brian's intermittent grunts into the phone were punctuated by the shrieks of a plover. If CrimTrak didn't have tabs on the semen depositor, this could turn out to be a very complex job, I thought, especially now we'd turned up a third man. I glanced over the fence and saw the plover running with its wings outstretched towards something that had either disturbed it or stepped too close to its eggs or young.

Just as I was glancing at my watch, Brian hung up. 'Thank God, Deb'll be here in a sec with pizza. Want some?' he asked.

'I keep thinking of that damned skirt,' I said. 'It reminds me of her bedroom.'

'How's that?' asked Brian, following me back for a last look at Tianna Richardson's bedroom. I focused on the decor, ignoring the distraction of the boxes and shopping bags spread around.

'Everything matches in here, except that dark brown bedspread,' I said.

A few moments later, we were done. I walked out with Brian and waited as he locked the door.

He was on his way down the steps when he turned. 'Do people still have cocktails?' he asked.

'I'd be the last person to ask about that,' I said as we parted.

NINE

I was still thinking about Tianna when I walked into the bar of the Cat and Castle and looked for a quiet corner where I could wait for Kevin Waites to arrive.

The smell of beer, disinfectant, stale cigarettes and humanity made me think of Starro, my informant of many years, now a guest of Her Majesty at the Long Bay Hilton. All thoughts of Starro stopped when I noticed the fake Jacobean carving on the first banquette along the wall and recognised it as the background to one of the photographs of Tianna and the unknown man. I got a buzz of adrenaline as a piece of information, no matter how inconsequential, fell into place.

I ordered a lemon, lime and bitters from the barman and, as he returned with my chaste drink, flashed my ID at him, making sure I did it too fast for him to notice that I wasn't a police officer any more.

'Tell me,' I said, as he put my drink in front of me, 'know of a woman called Tianna Richardson? She used to drink here.'

He frowned.

'The woman whose body was found outside the Blackspot Nightclub,' I prompted. 'Maybe you haven't heard? I'm involved with that investigation.'

'Oh, yeah. That one. She was often in here. Different guy every time,' he said, his face taking on a sour, disapproving expression.

Tianna Richardson, I thought, I wish you'd stayed home. You're making life more difficult for me.

'The people from the Ag Station also drink here, I believe,' I continued.

The barman's sour expression worsened. Had I come across the only Calvinist working in a pub?

'That lot,' he muttered. 'They're dickheads.'

'Dickheads?'

'I could tell you a thing or two.'

'I'm sure you could,' I said.

'Those people from the Ag Station, they're worse than Tianna Richardson ever was.'

'Tell me more,' I said, interested.

'I hear things from over here,' he said. 'I see things going on.'

'Like what?' This vagueness wasn't promising; maybe he was just being self-important. I looked around, keeping an eye out for Kevin Waites.

The barman leaned closer, conspiratorial. 'You've heard of *swinging*?' he asked.

The old-fashioned term took me by surprise. 'Swinging' belonged back with Formica table tops, red ceramic bulls and the famous print of the green-faced Chinese beauty. It hailed from days when people spoke of flower power and free love. These days, people just had sex.

'People from the Ag Station swing?' I asked, affecting astonishment.

'You bet,' he sniffed. 'I didn't know scientists behaved like that! They come in here for drinks and then they play up.'

In a flash, the murders of Tianna Richardson and Claire Dimitriou fused together, heightening my adrenaline buzz. This hotel was common ground for both women. It could be a coincidence or it could be very important. In any case, I knew from long experience to always take note of connections. Claire Dimitriou could have been involved in a swinging group.

'They think they're being real discreet but I know what's going on,' the barman was grizzling. 'Different partner every week.'

'Tell me more about that,' I said, looking stern and disapproving.

I waited while he served a local lout who'd clearly had more than his share and was staring, bleary-eyed and belligerent, at his reflection in the mirror behind the rows of bottles of spirits.

'They played this game,' said the barman, returning. 'Like a lucky dip.' He leered. 'Lucky *dip* all right.'

'It's not making much sense to me,' I admitted.

'Listen, mate,' he said. 'I can't stand around answering your bloody questions all day.'

I put a twenty dollar note on the bar. 'Let me buy you a drink.'

At that point, the morose lout started a topple that would have ended up with him on the floor, but at the last moment he overcorrected and fell on the other side instead. There was a lot of scraping and sliding and swearing near my feet as he got himself upright again.

'Some bastard's got dog shit on his shoes,' he yelled.

I realised I'd put the wrong shoes on this morning and moved away from him.

The bartender whipped the twenty dollars into his pocket. 'I don't drink while serving,' he said.

'The lucky dip? You were going to tell me more about it,' I said.

'I want a head job with no ice and sex on the beach for my friend,' came a female voice from behind me, addressing the barman.

I watched while he made up the two drinks, a pink foaming thing with a little umbrella and its twin in green with an olive. Yes, Brian, I thought, people do still have cocktails, although only very dedicated drinkers would be ordering such drinks at this hour of the day.

'Okay,' said the barman, leaning closer as the girl carried her drinks away. 'This is how it goes. After everyone has a few rounds, these two envelopes come out. I couldn't see what was in them—looked like white paper in one and coloured paper in the other. You know that coloured paper we used to cut up in school?'

I remembered the squares of brilliantly coloured flint paper—red, crimson, orange, turquoise, blue, yellow, green, black and white—that Sister Celestine and Miss Ogilvie had handed out in kindergarten and first grade for our infant craft works. I recalled those particular colours vividly. This could be very good information—if it were true. Sometimes you got things on a plate like this, without having to lift a finger. But not often.

'So how did the lucky dip work?' I asked.

'How would I know?' said the barman. 'I can only tell you what I saw.'

The drunk was insisting on another beer but the barman wasn't playing. 'Go home, Tiger. It's the law. I'm not permitted to serve you any more.'

'So what did you see?' I persisted.

Ignoring some slurred invective from the lout, the barman hunched over. 'They'd take a white card out of the first envelope and then pass it on to the next person. When that envelope had gone round the group, they'd do the same with the second envelope.'

'The one with the coloured paper?' I asked. 'And?'

He shrugged. 'That's all I can tell you. That was it. I don't know how it worked.'

I deeply regretted losing my twenty bucks.

'That was their favourite spot,' he said, pointing to the banquette across from the bar. 'They always sat there. One of the women asked *me* one night if I wanted to join in. She'd been checking me out all night. Moll,' he growled.

I was intrigued by the game and wondered what the different pieces of paper meant. If Tianna were a player with this group, it was possible she had met her killer as part of the lucky dip game. She may not have picked up a stranger that night at the Blackspot. She could have known him from here.

'When does the group usually come in?' I asked.

The barman glanced at his watch. 'Towards the end of the week. Sometimes as early as Wednesday.'

I wondered if they'd come in this week or would lie low? I pulled out my card and circled my mobile number. 'If they come in, no matter what time it is, I want to know. I'll make it worth your while,' I added.

I didn't think I'd be hearing from him in the next little while. The group would surely be in shock and, conceivably, even in hiding after what had happened to one or possibly two of their number.

I was leaving a message on Brian's mobile, informing him that the unknown man in the photograph with Tianna Richardson drank here, when the double doors from the street were flung open. I felt sure the approaching man in a tight-fitting, buttoned jacket was Kevin Waites. After years of stakeouts and clandestine meetings, I'd identified something like a current that seemed to run between the investigator and the target.

Waites breasted the bar a little distance from me, looking around, checking out the people standing drinking and those clustered in the alcoves around the room. I wondered why he didn't undo a few buttons on his too-tight jacket.

He reminded me of Mo, from the long ago days of my childhood and black and white television and the Three Stooges.

I picked up my drink and went over to him. 'Kevin?' I asked, putting out my hand. 'Jack McCain.'

We shook and I asked him what sort of drink he wanted.

'I'll have a double Scotch,' he said.

Interesting choice, I thought as I bought it for him, along with another fizzy drink for myself, then together we made our way to a quieter spot, sliding into the seats, resting our drinks on the oak veneer surface.

'I appreciate you taking the time to meet me,' I said and explained where I fitted in the investigation. When I mentioned a couple of other local investigations I'd been involved with, he visibly relaxed.

'I'm not the police,' I explained. 'And you'll need to do a statement for them.'

He nodded, throwing back some Scotch.

'Anything you can tell me about that argument you overheard on Monday afternoon?' I asked. 'Between Dr Dimitriou and Peter Yu.'

'Dr Dimitriou was a real nice lady. I used to clean her lab most days—the areas she'd let me touch anyway. Often she'd still be there, late, and say hello. She wasn't up herself like some of those people. She'd ask me how I was. Have a chat.' He paused, rattling the ice in the Scotch.

'Tell me everything you can recall about the last time you saw—or heard—Claire Dimitriou.'

Kevin took a pull on his drink and looked around. 'Have you got a cigarette on you?'

'Sorry. Can't help you. I don't smoke these days,' I said.

I waited while he went back to the counter and made his purchase, then we took our drinks outside to the desolate beer garden, a narrow strip of paving between two wings of the hotel, so he could smoke. Several miserable pot plants stood around, their soil poisoned by the many cigarette stubs half buried in them.

Kevin Waites stared at the wall as he began to speak. 'I was outside Dr Dimitriou's office. I was having a bit of trouble getting the dead fluoro tube out of its housing and it broke,' he said, lighting up and inhaling deeply.

'Where exactly?' I asked.

'Her office is in the administration wing of the Ag building. It runs off to the right of the main entrance some distance away from the old laboratory.'

The direction Dallas Baxter had been hurrying from, I recalled, when he'd rushed over to meet me yesterday.

'I put my stepladder against the wall and started cleaning up the mess,' Waites continued. 'That Asian fellow—'

'Dr Peter Yu?'

Waites nodded, sucking on the cigarette, his other hand fiddling with the cellophane on the packet. 'He came running down the hall from the laboratory wing. Just about knocked me over—I don't think he even saw me. He went straight into her office and they started talking. I wasn't especially listening. No point, really. I never understand a bloody word they say. Not when they're talking shop. And he's got a bit of an accent.'

'Go on.'

'Their voices just got louder and louder,' he said, wiping his fingers free of the condensation from the glass, using his handkerchief. 'See, it was the tone of their voices that made me take notice.' He paused. 'Distressed. Dr Dimitriou was really upset. That's what made me sort of stop and—I didn't mean to be deliberately listening in to a private conversation, you know. But I couldn't help it. They were so loud.'

He paused and I nodded encouragingly, willing him to continue. 'I didn't know what to do,' he said finally. 'Dr Dimitriou was crying. She kept saying "She saw, she saw! She saw sixteen blue!"'

I was suddenly riveted, thinking of what the barman had told me about coloured paper. 'You're sure she said "sixteen blue"?' I asked.

'I'm sure, all right. There might have been another word after that, but I'm positive that's what I heard. I keep hearing her voice. She's dead and I still keep hearing her voice.'

I touched him briefly on the arm. 'Please continue.'

'She was always kind to me. Some of the scientists don't even see me. I'm just the maintenance man, invisible. Not important like them. But Dr

Dimitriou was different. She used to answer my questions, tell me about her work. And she understood that I'd sometimes get sad when one of the animals died.' He glanced at me to take in my reaction. 'You probably think that's stupid—that a grown man could care when a lab sheep dies.'

'I don't think it's stupid at all,' I said.

'I like all the animals, even the sheep. They all have little stalls with their name on and whatever disease they have. You get to like them. They don't know it, but they're doing something very important for their brothers and sisters, they lay down their lives for the betterment of their friends.'

'I suppose they do,' I said. 'Somewhere there's a monument dedicated to all the experimental animals.'

'Is there?' he said, pleased. 'They become like friends. Especially when you're lonely. Dr Dimitriou used to say, "Don't worry, Kevin. None of my rabbits are going to die. My work is to stop them breeding, not breathing."'

I saw his expression soften further and I noted down Claire's words thinking, yes, Dr Dimitriou did sound like a kind woman. Her research didn't involve lethal experimentation.

'Anything else you want to tell me?' I asked.

'That's it really. That's how it went. Him saying "We can't! You mustn't!" And her saying "Don't you see now we have to!" She kept saying that over and over. "Peter, we have to!" And he kept begging her not to—"No, no, we can't! We mustn't!"'

I pulled out my notebook and wrote the words down, underlining 'sixteen blue' and adding three dots after the last word.

Kevin Waites jerked his cigarette at it. 'You're not recording what I'm saying, are you?'

'It's just for my own use,' I explained. 'Did you hear anything else?'

He paused to knock off the last of his drink. 'They might have gone on a bit longer. But it was all the same stuff. Arguing. Her crying. I'm still upset about it. Maybe if I'd done something, she'd be alive now.'

'You weren't to know,' I reassured him and we sat in silence awhile.

'I wish I hadn't been there,' he finally said.

Thank God you were, I thought, because this was the only information we'd had so far about the scientist's state of mind and that of her colleague shortly before her death.

'Kevin,' I said, 'I'd like you to accompany me through Dr Dimitriou's laboratory, do a walk-through with me. You'd be very familiar with that laboratory. I've only seen it once. You might notice something I didn't.'

'But I don't work there any more,' he said. 'Dallas Baxter finished me up last night. Said he'd got some new contractors.'

Interesting, I thought, then said, 'I'll sort something out and let you know when to meet me.'

His face brightened. 'I have to drop over there on Friday to pick up my severance pay.'

'I'll be in touch about when is best for both of us,' I said.

I went to the bar for another double Scotch. 'Was there anything else?' I asked, sitting down with him again. 'Anything else that might help find Dr Dimitriou's killer?'

'Look,' he said, 'I *want* to help. But my memory isn't too good. Especially for scientific things.'

I pulled out one of my business cards and passed it over. 'If you remember anything else, I don't care if it's the middle of the night, you ring me. Okay?' I said, standing up.

'I will,' he said. 'Sure you don't want me to buy you a proper drink?'

I shook my head. 'I'm sure.'

TEN

Before heading back to Weston, I bought a newspaper and sat down in the arcade with a cappuccino. MURDER CITY! blared the headlines followed by: SITTING MEMBER PROMISES INQUIRY. The press loved murder. Murder sold newspapers. And media exposure puts lots of pressure on Sitting Members and public officials generally. I wondered how long it would be before someone in turn leaned on me—on all of us at Forensic Services.

I folded the newspaper, paid for the coffee and rang directory assistance to get the address for Galleria Rustica, curious as hell to find out more about Peter Yu.

I walked the three blocks until I came to the gallery, tucked away in an arcade, with fierce primitive-style carvings dominating the front window. Before going inside, I rang Brian again to bring him up to date with the Kevin Waites discussion while silently debating whether or not to share my information about the partner-swapping group just now. But my call rang out and switched to divert so I left a message.

Surrounded by local craft and artefacts, I browsed, picking up dot-painted clap sticks or silk batik scarves. A beautiful red and blue one took my attention and I imagined how good it would look on Iona, contrasting with her fine skin and soft dark hair. On the walls hung landscapes by local artists and I walked slowly along, sizing them up. Two in particular stood out, both obviously executed by the same hand, one a bush shack in the dry hills under a glaring sky, the other a shimmering expanse of Lake George, in silvers, mauves and turquoises. The rest were a mixture of the just okay down to the barely competent.

I studied the woman behind the short counter in more detail as she talked with a customer, wrapping his purchase. She was sleek in a long jersey dress, dark hair twisted up on the top of her head and held with some sort of arty comb. Her gold hoop earrings swung as the purchaser left with his package and she flashed a dark-eyed smile across at me.

'Can I help you?' she said.

I came straight to the point, flashing my dodgy ID and explaining the reason for my visit and my need to talk to Annette Sommers. 'I'm a scientist with the Australian Federal Police.'

She worked it out straightaway. 'You're here about Peter. I really don't want to talk about him.'

'He could be in big trouble,' I said.

'I'm not surprised,' she said. 'He sure was heading that way.'

'It's just an informal chat,' I said. 'I don't want to frighten the customers away. Is there somewhere we can talk? You'll have to talk to the local detectives at some stage so why not practise on me?'

She gave the slightest smile then frowned, glancing at her watch. 'Let's go over there,' she said, pointing to the coffee lounge opposite. 'I'm ready for a coffee and lunch.'

'I'll buy you a sandwich,' I said. 'But first I want to make a purchase.'

She wrapped up the silk scarf in red and gold paper, tying it expertly with a flourish of red ribbon, and I paid for it and slipped it into my pocket.

I waited while she locked the cash drawer and as I walked across to the coffee shop with her a tiny question formed in my mind: why aren't you leaving this to Brian and his crew? Charlie's words of the night before came back to me and I pushed them aside—knowing they'd rise up and haunt me later.

We made small talk as we waited for what turned out to be very bad coffee. I leaned back, stirring sugar in, leaving a silence into which Annette eventually spoke.

'Actually, it's a relief to talk to someone—someone like you, I mean. Official.'

I nodded, pulling out my notebook. 'Like I say, I'm only here in a very informal way. Brian Kruger will have to take a full statement.' I flinched at the sip of coffee and put it down. 'It's very good of you to agree to talk to me at all.'

Annette threw her head back, pulled out the arty comb, rewound her hair and repinned it. 'I only met him five months ago. And now…'

She picked up a paper tube of sugar and tore the end off. 'Does anyone know where he is?'

'No.'

'He certainly hasn't contacted me, if that's what you're thinking.'

'I wasn't,' I said, watching her closely. 'Do you know who he was seeing before you met him?'

Annette's gaze flickered away. 'Yes. As soon as I heard about the murder, I went straight round to her place. I was sure he'd gone back to her. Instead…' She shrugged. 'I find I'm the eighth in a series. That's when I got really angry. He'd left a lot of stuff at my place… I was furious, I…' Annette's expression belied her tough words and she covered her face with both hands. 'Sorry,' she said, taking a paper napkin from the metal holder in the centre of the table. 'I thought I was about to burst into tears. I've been so unhappy lately.' She blew her nose on the paper napkin and the gesture touched me. 'I hardly know a soul in this town,' she said. 'I got this job through a friend at the university, then soon after she left for Sydney. I haven't had anyone to talk to.'

'That's hard,' I said.

'That's why you're copping it,' she said. 'And after being really good, things were going so awfully with Peter. And now this.' She screwed up the crushed napkin and pushed it away.

After being really good, things went bad. A chill went through me as I thought of Iona and me.

Annette told me in more detail about getting the job at the gallery through the friend, of meeting Peter at a university function hosted by the Ag Station. 'He seemed so keen. He used to spend most of his time at my place—and we were talking about him moving in officially.' She paused, sniffed and wiped her eyes again. 'I thought he was great. Funny, sexy. Spiritual. Brilliant. We had this fantastic connection.'

I had no reason to doubt that and nodded.

'But within a few months he seemed to lose all interest in me.' She put her head down.

'In what way?' I asked.

'In every way,' she said. 'He was never available. We stopped making love, he was always out. He said it was the pressure of work.'

Again, the chill went through me. I'd recently heard something very similar to this from the woman I loved. Quickly, I recovered myself and focused on Annette.

'What did you think?' I asked.

Annette took a deep breath. 'At first I thought he was still involved with his ex. A couple of times in the last day or so before he vanished, I walked in on him when he was on the phone and he just terminated the call like that.' She snapped her fingers. 'I even challenged him about it. He said I was being absurd. That it was just work. That the Terminator Rabbit project was taking up all his time and energy.'

I made a note of that. 'It's quite possible that he was telling the truth. It's hard sometimes to explain to someone who hasn't been involved in an absorbing research project.'

'Now you're sounding like him,' she said. 'I didn't buy it then and I don't buy it now. When someone works like he was working, I knew he was avoiding me. Us.'

My blood ran cold. A dart of ice pierced a part of myself I didn't know existed until now. I shifted uncomfortably in my seat, glad of the distraction of the waitress bringing us our sandwiches.

'You used the word "spiritual" in your description of Peter. What do you mean by that?' From my experience, the word could mean anything from trekking in Nepal to getting wasted on grass instead of alcohol.

'Peter developed some strange ideas. From having a scientific, rationalist approach to religion, like mine, he had become a *believer*.'

'In God?' I asked. She nodded. Sometimes I was, too.

The seats at the next table were taken by an enormously fat man and his small wife. We both tried not to stare and I wondered how she survived sexual intercourse without full breathing apparatus.

'You were saying that Peter seemed to change,' I prompted.

'I feel foolish mentioning this. In a way, it was my fault. We'd gone to hear this American evangelist. Dr Chuck Hackett.'

You've gotta love those American names, I thought, recalling the poster I'd seen unfurling on the wall of the Blackspot Nightclub.

'As I said, I actually talked Peter into it. I thought it would be a hoot.' She paused. 'Peter was a hardline rationalist.'

'So what happened at Dr Chuck's turnout?' I asked.

Annette looked away from me. 'You've heard the saying "He went to mock but stayed to pray"?'

I hadn't, but it didn't take Einstein to work it out.

'That's what happened. Peter was really quiet on the way home and I asked him what was up. "I've been living in the dark. Everything I thought I knew is part of that darkness," he kept saying. At first, I thought he was joking. But he was deadly serious. He explained he'd had a revelation during the meeting. That while Dr Hackett was preaching, something had opened in his mind and this big ray had shone in.' She paused. 'At that stage, I still couldn't quite believe he wasn't pulling my leg and I said, "Death ray or stingray?" It was when he got really angry with me that I realised he wasn't teasing, that something *had* happened to him. He said he'd had this moment of brilliant clarity and the truth of everything had been revealed to him.'

Once, I would've been astonished by this, but at my age I'd seen a lot of peculiar behaviours, and scientists were just as susceptible. I recalled some friends of Charlie, a charming psychiatrist and his smart molecular biologist wife, who'd fallen under the spell of an entity channelled by a Californian housewife. Despite his two medical degrees and everything rational Charlie could throw at him, the psychiatrist and his wife sold his Sydney practice and their house before buying a house at Mount Victoria because the entity had prophesied a huge tsunami would hit the east coast in 2000, demolishing and flattening everything and everyone from Wollongong to Gosford right out to the foothills of the Great Dividing Range.

'He kept trying to make me understand the nature of the revelation,' Annette was saying, 'that when the ray shone into his mind he understood everything and that God was like some huge morphic resonating field, constantly extruding or projecting in all dimensions and at all times, building like a multidimensional crystal, forming the universe and creation, tumbling out billions of worlds. He said he'd seen it, been given the understanding of it.'

I frowned, trying to keep up with her.

'Peter kept saying the nature of God was cocreative, but he likened it to the nature of a virus, combining with everything and reshaping it and creating new combinations of proteins.'

I'd heard lots of interesting ideas about the nature of God, but this one took the cake. 'Dr Chuck certainly has a refreshingly different take on God,' I said.

'No, no.' She shook her head. 'That's just it. Dr Chuck wasn't saying anything of the sort. He was serving up the usual evangelical repent-and-turn-to-righteousness-and-be-saved stuff, in that high-octane American way. There was nothing remotely like giant morphic resonating crystal viruses.'

'So what did you make of Peter's behaviour?' I asked.

'I was really confused at first. Now, I think it was symptomatic of some sort of psychotic state. He'd been under too much strain and the high emotionalism in the hall that night tipped him over the edge.' She pushed a tendril of hair back behind an ear. 'I think this so-called revelation he had was actually a breakdown of some sort. He'd stay up all night. He kept telling me that humans had been interfering in the work of God and bringing about climate changes and diseases like AIDS. He'd rave on about how humankind had become hostile to the work of God, behaving like antibodies or something, interfering with the rightful growth of the multi-universal process.' She stopped. 'God, it sounds so stupid! If anyone had asked me, I'd have said Peter was the last person in the world to get religion.'

'It's okay,' I said, patting her hand. 'All sorts of people believe all sorts of strange things. But what about his own research the Faithful Bunnies project? And the Terminator program? Surely that's interfering. Trying to change the mating habits of rabbits.'

'That was before his conversion.' She sighed. 'Peter thought he had some direct line to the great morphic process. According to him, selected people were chosen by God to work as co-creators. That's why he'd been granted the vision.'

Of course he'd believe that, I thought.

'He told me he'd been reviewing his life,' Annette was saying, 'and now he could see the hand of God had directed him to science. He went to tech but then found he'd been in the wrong class for nearly a month. By that time, he knew he wanted to do science.' She made a little face. 'He thought that was the hand of God. I suggested he have a medical check-up.' Her face became grave. 'That was one hundred per cent the wrong thing to say. He hit the roof. He attacked me, called me part of the forces of darkness, interfering with the multi-universal process. We had a terrible fight.' She spread her hands on the table before picking up one of the neglected sandwiches. 'I told him I'd had enough of his giant morphic crystal, and that not only did I think he was going crazy, I was almost certain he was seeing someone else.'

She blew her nose on another paper napkin and crushed it in the ashtray. 'I even wondered for a time if the giant crystal business might have been some elaborate diversion hiding his infidelity.' She made a sharp, contemptuous sound. 'Now I realise that Peter Yu doesn't bother with secrecy.'

'So who did you think the other party might be?' I asked.

Annette Sommers stared incredulously at me, as if I should have known. 'Claire Dimitriou,' she said and I heard the pain and anger. 'Doctor Claire Dimitriou, long-time married woman. Who else?'

'You sound very sure,' I said.

'I checked his mobile records.' She put her empty cup down. 'And the amount of calls he'd made to her over the weekend you wouldn't believe! Besides, Peter made a habit of sleeping with his research colleagues.'

She slumped back in her seat and I noticed the bitter downturn of her pretty mouth.

'Tell me more,' I said, now on high alert.

'I'm surprised no one mentioned it at the Ag Station. When he first worked on Faithful Bunnies, it was with another partner, Cheryl somebody. Anyway, according to Peter, she just wasn't up to his standard.'

'You mean academically or romantically?' I asked, writing down the woman's name.

Annette laughed, an expression of contempt. 'I didn't ask him. Probably both.'

'So,' I said, after noting this down, 'do you know what happened to her?'

'I should,' she said. 'Discarded, just like me. Replaced with Claire Dimitriou. At least I wasn't considered a professional failure like poor Cheryl. I believe she's teaching somewhere in the district. You know, "those who can't, teach".'

'Where do you think Peter might go?'

Annette Sommers raised her eyes to mine. 'I have no idea,' she said. 'I just wish I'd never met him.'

I held her hard gaze and she didn't blink. I didn't know what to make of this and wondered if what I was seeing was hatred.

The hard glare softened, the moment passed and her face relaxed. 'I wish I did know where he might go. He owes me a lot of explanations.'

'Did Peter ever speak to you about an open sexual arrangement? What they used to call "swinging" in the seventies?' I asked, wondering if Cheryl had also been part of this.

Annette shifted in her seat. 'No,' she said. 'Why? Is this important?'

'I'm involved in the investigation of a murder and a disappearance,' I said. 'Two murders, in fact, that may be related. A partner-swapping group has been mentioned in connection with some of those involved. It's important.'

'Means nothing to me. Although,' she said slowly, putting down her half-eaten sandwich as if recalling a forgotten conversation, 'I do remember Peter pulling the conversation round to sexual experimentation several times very early in our relationship, asking me what my thoughts were. But it never went very far.' She tossed her hair back from her face. 'I was in love with the man! I wasn't interested in swapping.'

My mobile rang and I excused myself, moving away from the table. It was Brian.

'Cop this,' he said. 'Anthony Dimitriou's in Woden Hospital. In the ICU.'

'What happened?'

'Looks like an overdose. Some sort of narcotic. They don't know yet.'

'When did this happen?'

'Not sure,' he said. 'I've only just heard the news.'

Was the man so grief-stricken that he couldn't face life without his partner? Or was he one of the third of all murderers who killed themselves?

'And that's not all. Jerri Quill's sunk without trace,' Brian continued. 'Her flatmate said she's gone away up the coast for a few days with a girlfriend. She'll probably ring in the next day or two.'

'Let me know when she does,' I said, thinking I'd like to interview the postgrad student myself at some stage.

Then I thought of the dozens of phone calls from Peter Yu. 'Any sign of Claire Dimitriou's mobile yet?'

'Not yet,' said Brian. 'Nothing at the marital home either. Her laptop's nowhere to be found.'

I recalled the steam-cleaned laboratory; such care didn't entirely surprise me. 'Did you know there was an earlier research assistant who worked with Peter Yu? Called Cheryl somebody. But she wasn't up to scratch scientifically, and Claire Dimitriou got the job,' I said.

'I'll chase that up. Who told you?'

'Annette Sommers. I'm here with her now, having lunch.'

'Scientists. They're a bunch of weirdos,' said Brian.

'Steady on,' I warned, ringing off.

'I'd better get back to the shop,' said Annette, finishing her coffee and glancing across the arcade.

I paid and we walked across to the gallery door.

'You said Peter Yu had left some things at your place,' I said. 'What sort of things?'

She shrugged. 'Papers and gear. I threw them all in a carton and dumped them on the front verandah. I rang him and said if he didn't come and pick them up by the end of the month, I'd have to dispose of them.'

'Don't,' I said. 'The police will be interested in that.'

'With my blessing,' she said. 'I don't want anything there to remind me of that man.' She gave me her address and then excused herself as she noticed a customer carrying a statuette waiting at her deserted counter.

Forty minutes later, I was driving while Brian stuffed his hamburger lunch down his throat with one hand and with the other found Annette Sommers' address in Kingston in the street directory.

We climbed the steep path past a low granite retaining wall, then mounted the steps leading up to the verandah. At the top of the steps, we paused to look around. A waist-high masonry wall ran along the front of the house, forming an L-shape around the left-hand side. A pile of cardboard cartons were stacked at the end. It didn't take long for us to transfer them into the back of my wagon.

'We might find something about Cheryl in all this,' I said. 'It would be a hard blow for a scientist to be dismissed like that. Especially when there's also been a personal relationship.'

I watched, back at the police station, as Brian and Debbie sorted through the contents of Peter Yu's gear. There were several expensive shirts, casual clothes, socks, Calvin Klein underwear and piles of papers, receipts, bills and letters.

'What's this stuff?' Brian asked, passing me a thick wad of typed pages. I assumed it was drafts of Peter Yu's doctoral thesis, way over my head. I noticed the name of Willem 'Pim' Stemmer, one of the founders of a well-known biotech company in the USA, and a quick glance through a few more pages confirmed it as I noticed references to Stemmer's work with *E. coli*.

'I'd say these are notes for his thesis,' I said. 'I can't tell you anything more than that. Except that it's about gene-shuffling and the maximisation of genetic diversity.'

Something rattled at the bottom of the box and I fished out a set of keys hanging from a plaited red and white plastic thong, one of them an old-fashioned iron key of the sort not seen in modern locks for decades, the other an ordinary Lockwood.

'Looks like the key to a pirate's treasure chest,' said Debbie, pointing to the old-fashioned one.

'Sign these over to me, Brian,' I said. 'I'll check if they're keys to his flat.'

Once that was done and Brian had given me the missing man's address in Manuka, I left them to it and continued on my way, unable to stay for the time it might take for them to find a lead, a name, a telephone number, something, out of that pile.

On the way to work, I stopped at Peter Yu's address, a flat in a block of six. The doors downstairs were unlocked but the Lockwood didn't fit and a glance was sufficient to tell that the old key wouldn't fit either. Peter Yu's flat on the second floor had a Yale lock. Perhaps these keys belonged to a now discarded girlfriend's flat, I thought.

Short of trying the door of every place in Canberra, there was little chance of finding out what these keys opened. The day was more than half gone and I still hadn't got to the office so I hurried back to my wagon.

Finally at my desk, I wrote up in longhand my notes about my meeting with Annette Sommers. As I put my pen down, I wondered if the hurt and anger I'd seen in her eyes was fierce enough for homicide. Then I considered the dismissed Cheryl. Could she have been burning with resentment and jealousy the last two years until it festered into murder?

I rang Pauline and told her what I'd heard from Annette.

'Cheryl Tobin?' she responded and I wrote the surname down. 'I remember her well. She was on the Faithful Bunnies project for a short time with Peter a couple of years ago, but it didn't work out.'

'Do you know where she is now?' I asked.

'I'd have to go through old records—but they've been archived. It could take a while, Dr McCain. Do you think she might know something about what happened to Claire?'

'If we don't track her down,' I said, 'we'll never know.'

Pauline assured me she'd do everything she could. After I'd rung off, I finally forced myself to write up the abstract for the presentation I was due to make at our own forensic conference. When I was satisfied with my outline, I printed it out, put it in a folder and shoved it into my top drawer. Noticing the time, I realised hours had gone past. The building was quiet—most people had left for the day so the examination rooms and the laboratories would be virtually empty by now—and in the silence I could almost hear the breaking of my promise to Iona to be home early.

Maybe if I left now, I thought, and brought something swish for dessert tonight, I might redeem myself a little. But I was keen to examine the samples of coarse grey particles both Harry Marshall and myself had noticed on Tianna Richardson's body and compare them against the swabs I'd taken from the surrounding asphalt. I sat a moment, irresolute, until my curiosity won.

Despite the late hour, I geared up and went into the lab. I prepared several slides from the swabbing Harry had taken from the wound on the back of Tianna Richardson's head. Then I did the same with the sample I'd taken from her hair. After that, I made a series of slides from the third source, the surrounding car park grounds. These larger coarse particles could have blown or been walked across from bushland or roadways nearby.

Starting off with low-level magnification, I peered down the stereoscopic lens, examining Harry's sample first. Apart from the large particles, the fluid contained mostly blood cells and other microscopic floaters as well as botanical fragments and the occasional grass seed. I also found the same large grey particles in the sample I'd taken from Tianna's hair. But when I examined the sample from the asphalt of the parking area, the assemblage was quite different. Although rich in debris such as soil particles, botanical fragments and the usual floaters, there was absolutely no sign of the large grey particles. Curious.

I examined the three samples again under higher magnification, focusing the colour monitor linked up to the microscope. At this magnification, the particles looked like rocks and I took notes of their distinctive shapes and distribution. This examination only confirmed my initial findings—the large particles were only to be found in the samples from Tianna Richardson's head, either the wound site itself or the hair around it.

At a higher level of magnification still, I could see the delicate tracery of various palynomorphs—the pollen that Sofia Verstoek would examine. Under the scanning electron microscope, these would reveal themselves to be as delicate and detailed as snowflakes. I hoped Sofia Verstoek would prove her worth by telling us from which variety of tree, shrub or grass they'd come. She had taken multiple samples from near the body so it would be interesting to match my samples against hers and see if any of the mysterious sandy particles showed up for her. If the particles hadn't come from the surrounds, they must have been introduced by the killer. But what were they and where did they come from? I moved back from the eyepieces and printed off copies of the magnification on the screen.

I knew two experts on sand. One, Ellis Smith, had retired. The other, staff member Nigel Slater, was in the USA, working at Quantico with the FBI. In one case, Ellis had been able to differentiate sand from the northern and southern ends of a beach from the way the grains had been worn by the tides and this blew holes in the suspect's story of where he found the body.

Weary now, I cleaned up and cleared away before discarding my gear to go back to my office and write up what I'd done in my casenotes.

As I wrote, I thought again of the coarse grey particles and the way they only appeared in the wound sites. An idea that had been circling for a few hours started to land. The question posed by the particle examinations I'd just completed demanded an answer and, as I thought about all the facts of the killing, I realised we'd been barking up the wrong tree. Well, that wasn't quite the right metaphor—we'd been at the *right* tree, but the dog who'd been barking up it was the wrong dog.

I picked up my phone to call Harry Marshall.

ELEVEN

'Funny,' said Harry. 'I was just about to call you.'

'The car park at the Blackspot,' I blurted. 'I'm pretty sure it's a secondary crime scene. I think Tianna Richardson was killed somewhere else and dumped there.'

'Exactly what I was thinking,' said Harry. 'When I had a look at the histology slides of that large area of bruising on her face and some of the superficial cuts and abrasions on her knees and arms, I couldn't find any signs at all of vital reactions. They're all post-mortem injuries.'

'So he's killed her somewhere else and then gone to all the trouble of loading her up and dumping her back at the car park?' I said. 'But, Harry, it just doesn't make sense.'

'Sense or no sense, the fact is we found Tianna Richardson at a secondary crime scene.'

We both considered this a moment.

'And we've found evidence of another man in Tianna's life,' I said, briefly detailing the few facts I knew about the man in the photograph.

'She's not making it easy for us, is she?'

'I thought you liked a challenge, Harry.'

'I'm getting too old for challenges. I just want a nice quiet life. Pottering in my shed. Reading all the books I've shelved for three decades.'

'That's not what you were saying earlier,' I said, not believing a word of it.

Harry grunted.

'Those coarse particles of grey material. You didn't find them anywhere except embedded in the wound site?' I asked.

'That's right.'

'I took extensive reference samples from the area around the body and I compared it with the samples we swabbed from the wounds,' I said, then paused, thinking of Locard's caveat that 'Only human failure to comprehend physical evidence can negate its value'. And that was what I'd done. It had taken me too long to see the obvious.

'Wherever she was killed is where we'll find those particles. At the primary crime scene,' I said. 'We all made the wrong assumption. Thinking she'd been murdered at the nightclub.'

'But she was definitely there,' said Harry. 'I heard a woman identified her from photographs.'

'She might have *been* there,' I said, 'but she wasn't killed there.' I remembered the half-smoked joint on the ground near the body and made a mental note to check if Vic or Jane had found DNA from Tianna and anyone else. 'She probably spent time with her killer sharing the smoke. And then, after bringing her back when she was dead, he does that biting routine,' I added.

I recalled how Brian's eyebrows had risen to maximum altitude when I'd made this suggestion and, echoing Brian's ironic statement of the obvious said, 'We're missing something. Have you still got Tianna Richardson's body with you?'

'Yes,' said Harry. 'She's waiting to be released.'

'I'll be over as soon as I can.'

Half an hour later I stood with Harry as he unzipped the long blue bag, revealing Tianna's cleaned-up body lying on a trolley.

'Give us a hand, Harry,' I said, pulling the Stewart Chambray cocktail skirt out of its tissue.

It was an awkward job, even with the two of us, getting the skirt onto the dead woman. Undertakers were experienced in dressing the dead, but we certainly weren't. Finally, we did the button up at the waist and jerked the zipper closed.

I stood back to get a better view. 'So,' I asked Harry, who'd turned away to grab a handful of cotton waste to mop up some spillage, 'how do you think that looks?'

'Perfect fit,' he replied.

The brand new skirt hugged the body's contours in a way that should have made any wearer wanting to look sexy delighted with it. I looked down at Tianna's pale, dead face, her sunken cheeks and dry white lips. 'Why, Tianna?' I asked, patting her hip with a gloved hand. 'Why wear that daggy woollen thing instead of this?'

Harry and I looked at each other across the inert body, the question hanging between us.

I was still musing on this mystery as I left the morgue but a call on my mobile interrupted.

'I don't want to sound like I'm nagging,' Iona began.

'You couldn't,' I said. 'I know I promised I'd be home early today. I'm on my way. Is there anything you need?'

'Just you, Jack,' she said and rang off.

I got into my car and was clipping my seatbelt on when my mobile rang again. It was Brian.

'Where are you?' I asked.

'Back at Tianna Richardson's place. Just some checking. Tell you later. Listen, can you do me a favour?'

'What exactly?' I asked, wary. No way was I going to get involved in anything new right now.

'We've just had a call from a woman who lives near Ginninderra who's worried about her neighbour. She hasn't seen him for a day or so and wants someone to go round and make sure he's okay. It's on your way home and it'd take me ages to do the round trip from here.'

'Okay,' I said, resigned. 'But that's all I'm doing. Then I'll ring police, ambos or the undertaker, if required. But that's it. Okay?'

In a weak moment, I'd already been roped in to check out Michelle Danby, the woman who'd seen Tianna Richardson at the Blackspot, as soon as I could.

I took the details of the concerned neighbour and, from Brian's description, realised I knew the place—one of a few houses on the outskirts of a small hamlet on the way out to my cottage. I'd sometimes stopped there in the past to pick up free-range eggs and seasonal vegetables from a rickety roadside stall that ran on an honesty system.

Before I could tell him about my latest discussion with Harry, Brian started talking quickly. 'I think I've worked it out. Tianna and Damien Henshaw have this fight, she nags and nags him, puts on her new clothes and says, "You take me dancing or I tell Kylie we've been playing hide the sausage." *He* says, "Okay okay", because he's shit-scared of losing his fiancée. They go to the Blackspot. He's saying, "You wanted to go to the fucking nightclub, well here you are, bitch." Then he kills her. Drives away knowing that we'll think Tianna was picked up by some stranger.'

I waited till he finished. 'Nice story, Brian. But Tianna wasn't killed at the Blackspot,' I said, then explained how we'd arrived at that.

'But where's the primary crime scene? We've gone over her house and grounds and found nothing. So where does he kill her?'

'That's the big question,' I replied. 'Some place with coarse grey particles. Maybe at Damien Henshaw's place. You've got a big job ahead of you, Brian. You're going to have to check obvious possibilities like that first before casting a wider net.'

'You sound like you're bowing out of this,' he said.

'I never really bowed in. Earl Richardson talked me into attending the crime scene—much against my better judgement.'

And that was where I should have drawn the line. But my natural curiosity and some sense of obligation to the murdered woman had taken me a bit further.

'Look,' I heard myself say, 'I'll do what I can. But you'll have to get more assistance from the local guys.'

There was a silence. The virus or whatever bug had me in its grip was seriously moving in now, and trying not to think of all the diseases my aching head could be heralding kept my mind occupied and away from the fact that I didn't seem to be able to walk away from either investigation just yet.

'Let me know if you find anything interesting on those work boots belonging to Damien,' said Brian.

I thought of the careless, handsome young painter with his long blond ponytail and his two women. Maybe he was about to run out of luck.

'See,' Brian continued, 'I've got a feeling about this bloke Henshaw.'

'And if it's not him we have a very wide field to examine. Like the husband,' I said.

'He's got an alibi,' said Brian. 'Like supposedly being asleep in Sydney at the time.'

'Anyone checked that out further?' I asked. 'But even if he was, a lot of men get a third party to do their dirty work. Then there's the son, Jason. Not to mention the man in the photographs. Plus our old mate Stranger-danger.'

'My money's on young Damien,' Brian insisted. 'We come up with evidence against him, bury Tianna Richardson, case closed and lots of kudos.'

'Kudos doesn't do it for me.'
'What else is there?'
'I'll have to think about that,' I said.

I drove out to the address Brian had given me, one of several widely spaced timber houses at the edges of Mill Hill, the tiny hamlet along the Ginninderra Road.

At this time of day, the vegetable stall, little more than a trailer with an old beach umbrella over it, had neither vegetables nor the honesty box. But behind it I could see lights on in the house and I made my way through the gathering gloom and knocked on the door.

'Mrs Allen?' I asked the elderly woman who cautiously opened the door. 'You rang Heronvale Police Station? About your neighbour?'

I waved my ID and introduced myself.

'It's Albert,' she said when I'd finished, indicating the house some distance away from hers. 'I went over to give him a letter that had been delivered here by mistake, but he didn't answer when I knocked on the door earlier and the house seems to be full of blowflies.'

Mrs Allen knew already, I realised.

'I didn't want to go in there alone,' she added.

'Albert's full name?' I asked.

'Vaughan. Please,' she went on, 'I'm forgetting my manners. Come in.'

'I should take a look next door first,' I said. 'Do you have a key?'

She shook her head. 'Albert's a cranky old fellow these days. Doesn't go out much now that his asthma's got so bad. Although he reckoned it was a lot worse when he lived in town.'

I took my torch and, out of habit, a pair of disposable gloves from the glove box and, aware of Mrs Allen standing at her front door, made my way across a fallen wire fence and past some straggly shrubs until I came to the house. It was all in darkness.

I went up to the front door and banged loudly. 'Mr Vaughan?' I called.

I tried the door to see what sort of lock it was and found to my surprise that it turned and opened. Mercifully, at this hour, the blowies were absent and I shone the torch down the hallway, continuing to call his name. I didn't have to go too far into the house. I could see the body lying at the other end of the short hall, face down and sprawled away from the front door so that I could see his boots. An asthma attack, I thought, walking up to see if there was anything I could do. Then I saw the bloody dark red mess at the back of his head and the brown pool around his neck and shoulders. I backed away and out, slammed the door shut and called Brian.

By rights, I should have stayed on the dead man's property but I kept an eye on it from Mrs Allen's place while having a cup of tea with her.

I rang Iona once more, apologising, and suggested she and the others have dinner and leave something for me. I could tell from the tone of her voice that she wasn't impressed with this arrangement, but when I told her why I'd been held up, she sounded resigned.

Force of habit caused me to ask questions and I discovered that Mrs Allen thought she'd heard a car sometime Monday night. 'It woke me, but I went back to sleep,' she said, explaining that sometimes motorists used her or Albert's driveway as a place to turn their cars and so it may not have been significant.

By the time Debbie arrived with her crime scene gear it was getting on for nine, and it was well after by the time I arrived back at the cottage, but not before Debbie had organised me to make a statement first thing next morning.

'Thanks for being so patient,' I said to Iona as she sat with me while I tucked into one of the dishes Charlie had cooked, frozen and brought with him—a lasagna, by now somewhat dried out but still tasty. She'd eaten earlier and Charlie and Greg were in town taking in a movie Greg wanted to see.

'I had to stay until the police arrived,' I explained. 'And it took them nearly an hour. Otherwise I'd have been home in time to eat dinner with you.'

'You could have told Brian to get someone else to go to the house,' she said. 'What is it with you that people assume they can call you out like this? Why do you feel so responsible for everyone?' She paused. 'Well, not quite everyone,' she added. 'Everyone else seems to take priority before your family. Before me.'

I dropped my fork. 'Don't say that,' I said, seizing her hand. 'You lot are my priority! Especially you.'

'Jack, I came to Canberra to *be* with you,' she said, the sadness in her eyes going straight to my heart. 'To live with *you*. Not share a cottage with you like some flatmate. I left my life in Sydney, my music students, my job at the radio station, my friends, to come down here because I believed that you and I could live a loving and honest life with each other. I'm not some foolish girl—expecting you to make a life for me—but I *was* expecting that you'd be a whole lot more available than you are. I keep wondering when we're going to start *being* together.'

I picked up my fork but I'd lost my appetite. From a decade ago, I heard my ex-wife voicing something similar and a familiar sinking feeling accompanied my words. 'It's the nature of my work, Iona. It's very demanding. It takes me away. It requires me to work late. Often.'

I groped for words to explain. It was necessary. The dead have no voice. They *need* me, I wanted to say. But somewhere, another small voice was saying, Bullshit, Jack. That's not the whole story. There's some part of you that makes choices that take you away.

'Darling, Iona. Living with you is so good. I didn't know a man and a woman could live together in this peaceful way. Come on,' I said, standing up. 'Come to bed. The house is nice and quiet.'

She shook her head. 'You're changing the subject,' she accused, levelling her gaze straight into mine. 'Just tell me this. How is it different from last year—having me living here? Apart from us sleeping in the same bed every night. I want you to tell me what changes you've made to include me in your life here.'

She walked past me while I considered her question, watching her as she went into the kitchen to get herself a glass of wine and returned to sit with me again.

'It's made a huge difference,' I said. How could I explain that the very cottage was scented with her, that it *felt* different in every way, that my heart lifted every time I saw one of her belongings on a chair or smelled the fragrance of the coffee she was making. That even the *light* seemed different now that she was here. 'I *love* having you here,' I said finally.

'Why?'

'*Why?*' I repeated. 'Because I love you. I want you to be here with me.'

I saw one of her fine eyebrows lift. 'I think you're living in exactly the same way as you did before I came. Me being here has made no difference to you—apart from you having more regular sex,' she said. 'You want me here, but you don't seem able—or is it willing?—to make any of the changes necessary to accommodate me in a *life lived together*.' She stressed the last three words. 'I've seen it in a couple of my girlfriends. So often I hear them say they want a man in their lives, but when they get down to it, they're actually not willing to make even the slightest change to accommodate this. They don't want their nice tidy lives and houses mucked up by a man. As if the man should somehow be able to squeeze himself to fit any convenient little empty crack in all their busyness. Like a book or a piece of sewing that you have lying around and just pick up when there's nothing else to do.' She looked straight into my eyes. 'My sense is you're doing exactly the same thing with me.'

Her words stung me. Women could do this. They seemed to be able to feel and say things that I didn't seem to know about until I heard them. Then I recognised the truth of them.

In the first few months that Iona had come to live with me, I'd been working very long hours, trying to catch up on everything the outgoing chief scientist had been dealing with; some projects barely started, others needing my input to oversee and sign off, others still ongoing. All of it demanding. Some nights, I hadn't been able to get away till very late at night. And now, just as I'd almost got on top of things, I had somehow become entangled in two demanding murder investigations.

'I'll have to think about this. You could have a point,' I said.

She stood up.

'Where are you going?' I said, suddenly fearful.

'To have a bath,' she said. 'Before the boys get back.'

I took her hand again.

'Tomorrow night, I'll make dinner. We'll have a family night, a proper meal around the table, all of us,' I said, still holding her hand.

'That would be nice,' she said. 'And a good start at least. I'll be late tomorrow—staff meeting. I may as well work if you are.'

Later, before we went to bed, I took her in my arms and kissed her, pulling out the blue and red silk scarf I'd bought, concerned that my behaviour had hurt her. 'See?' I said, handing it to her. 'I'm always thinking of you.'

She took it from me and opened it out, floating it onto the bed. 'It's beautiful, Jack,' she said, picking it up and holding it near her cheek.

'It's been a long time since I lived with a woman. It might take me a little while to get back into the rhythm of it.'

When we got into bed, she leaned up on an elbow, dark hair around her neck, her nightgown slipping from a shoulder, regarding me. 'You're a good man, Jack, otherwise I wouldn't be here. You say you want me and yet almost every time we've planned to do something together over the last few months, you've taken on something that prevents you doing so. Are you aware of that?'

She paused, lying back down again, staring up at the ceiling while I thought about what she'd just said.

'I look at you and think of your history. I'm frightened, Jack.'

'Of *me*?' I said, surprised.

'Your mother. Your ex-wife.'

'Iona, I don't understand.'

'You have great relationships with your kids,' she said. 'What about your women?'

I thought of Genevieve's self-centredness, my late mother's addiction and the eerie way Iona's comments reflected not only some of the things Charlie had said to me but also the failure of the relationship between Annette Sommers and Peter Yu.

'There's something in you that holds back from me,' she concluded.

'Not true,' I said, running my hands over her warmth and softness. 'I can't remember when I've wanted a woman as much.'

'I wasn't talking about sex,' she replied smartly.

'Neither was I,' I said, suddenly very tired.

I cuddled her into me as she settled down to sleep and lay awake, my mind filled with Iona's considered words but mixed with images of Tianna Richardson lying sprawled on the asphalt of the car park, Dr Claire Dimitriou's squashed, cold face on the smooth vinyl of the Faithful Bunnies lab. Now they were joined by the figure of an old, asthmatic man, brutally murdered in his own hall. Maybe I'd worked with the dead for too long and forgotten how to exist with the living.

Unable to sleep, my mind played around with the murders of the two women, putting them together, teasing them apart, trying to make them fit some sort of pattern. The two women could be connected via the Cat and Castle. Despite my tiredness, my brain wouldn't rest, recycling the possibilities. The killer of Tianna Richardson could be an outsider, a random pick-up gone wrong. Or, equally, someone she knew. Despite the evidence we were gathering against Damien Henshaw, it was essential to find the unknown man in the photograph. Maybe he was part of the partner-swapping group? The killer of Claire Dimitriou could have been her missing work partner, either of two women he'd been involved with or another party, perhaps someone connected to the partner-swapping group. All the participants of that particular club would have to be interviewed. But if we came down hard, people would close ranks, duck and run. We needed a soft approach. Then I caught myself. After all that Iona had said earlier, I was doing it again, planning more investigative work on cases that could be dealt with by other people. None of us were indispensable, I knew.

Finally, listening to Iona's steady breathing, I slept.

TWELVE

By daylight, the Mill Hill house where Albert Vaughan lived looked depressing, badly in need of a coat of paint. Putting Iona's comments and questions of last night out of my mind for the moment, I pulled up beside the forensic unit wagon, listening to the thornbills and weebills twitching in the thickly overgrown hedge, feeling the cold morning breeze moving over the dry hills where a pair of wedge-tails marked out their skyway in lazy arcs.

Brian had called as Iona was getting ready for work and, because I'd been first on the scene, I couldn't avoid meeting him and Debbie at the house to describe what I'd found and make my statement.

I was stepping into a spacesuit when Brian came out of the front door.

'I've gotta go to another call-out, but take these with you when you talk to Michelle Danby,' said Brian, handing me a plastic sleeve with copies of two photographs, both head shots, one of Damien Henshaw and the other of the fair man cropped from one of Tianna's hidden stash of intimate pics.

I frowned. 'Where did you get the shot of young Henshaw? Is that from a mugshot?' I said, slipping the pictures into my pocket.

'Yep. Deb's back there,' he said, jerking his head in the direction of the house. Before I could question him further, he'd jumped into his car and was on his way.

Before going inside, I took a look around the area I'd navigated the night before with my torch—patches of long grass surrounded by dusty earth and a scrappy low hedge separating the house from the roadside.

The flies that Mrs Allen had heard humming in the house the day before were still around, but the body had been removed and only the large blackening stain at the end of the hall, the stench and the blood-splash patterns on the surrounding walls and ceiling reflected what had happened. Debbie was seated on the lounge in her stiff new blue police overall, writing something in her laptop while it balanced on her knees.

'Come and have a look,' she said. 'Then I'll write up your statement.'

Reminding myself I was here only to tell of what I'd seen and done the night before, and not to get involved in a case, I followed Debbie around Albert Vaughan's neat, dull house. A bloodstained white paper bag lay stuck to the carpet and Debbie prised it up in her gloved fingers. 'Brian was just about to write this up when he was called out,' she said. She peered inside the bloody bag and, frowning, lifted out a brand new asthma inhaler together with its box and a cash register docket...

'This was purchased from O'Halloran's 24-hour Pharmacy at 11.40 p.m. on Monday night,' she said, studying the docket. 'We found the old one on the floor near his bed. It was empty.'

I knew O'Halloran's Pharmacy. It was a big corner shop near the city centre, and just about the only place—apart from the hospital and the police station—open at that hour on a weeknight.

I wondered if Albert had woken up fighting an asthma attack, grabbed his inhaler, found it empty, and managed to get to the all-night pharmacy where he'd purchased a new one, used it, then shoved it back into the paper bag, gone home, parked the car and let himself into his house. Perhaps the killer was waiting for him. Or had he followed him home?

Poor old fellow hadn't even had time to put his package down.

'Robbery?' Debbie asked, squatting back on her heels. 'His wallet and watch are missing.'

The smell of stale blood, like the stench from old kidneys, was in my nostrils as I walked through the rooms of the house, which clearly hadn't been changed since the sixties. Beige walls, fawn shag carpet and brown furnishings were relieved only by some faded orange cushions on the lounge and a clump of creamy-pink flower orchid spikes in a large pot.

'Has anyone had a talk to whoever served him at O'Halloran's?' I asked.

'The locum chemist said he remembers the old man coming in, wheezing badly,' said Debbie, nodding. 'He sat him down with the new inhaler until he could breathe better. Then he assumed he went home.'

If someone had followed Albert Vaughan into his house, that person just might have been hanging round in the street near the pharmacy and there was a chance a security camera might have captured something useful. Might be worth dropping round and checking out what sort of security cameras were operating in the area. Also, it would be good to get Sofia Verstoek in to take soil samples from the garden and check them against lifts from the carpet in the hall. I recalled a case in the UK where police had caught a killer with pollen traipsed in on his shoes from a rare plant growing in his backyard.

'Any photos of the deceased?' I asked Debbie, curious as to what the old man had looked like.

She passed me a framed picture of a couple. 'That was taken some years ago, according to Mrs Allen.'

I checked the photo out. Vaughan's face reminded me of an El Greco icon, gaunt and shadowed, his frailty clear to see.

'He's only got a daughter and a couple of grandchildren and Mrs Allen says they don't visit often. Once a week he liked to go into the city centre and do some shopping. Sometimes he had a bet. According to her,' Debbie continued, 'Mr Vaughan had been quite ill the last couple of months and occasionally she'd done some shopping for him, but he tended to keep to himself.'

Debbie looked around at the sparse furnishings. 'From what we've noticed here,' she said, 'and from what Mrs Allen and the people across the road say, Mr Vaughan was living the life of a semi-invalid.'

I followed her to the bedroom door and peered in. On the surfaces and tables of the old-fashioned dark veneer furniture, a clutter of prescription medicines, bottles and boxes of pharmaceutical mysteries looked as if they'd been building up since about 1958.

'Mrs Allen told us that the deceased has lived here for the last year or two, since his wife died. Before that he lived closer to town.'

Finally, I sat down with Debbie and gave her my official account of exactly what time I'd arrived here last night and my subsequent actions. I left her still making notes and taking photographs.

Another senseless brutal act, I thought, as I stashed the used spacesuit in the back of my wagon, transferring the photos Brian had given me to my briefcase. A harmless old man killed for a few bucks and the proceeds probably already up some terminal junkie's arm.

I rang the number Brian had given me for Michelle Danby, the woman who'd seen Tianna at the Blackspot Nightclub, and told her I was on my way to her place—if it was convenient.

Half an hour later, Michelle Danby, a pretty woman with hair pulled back from her face and gold hoops swinging in her ears, let me into her townhouse.

Declining her offer of tea or coffee, I said, 'Tianna Richardson, the woman who was murdered, may have been with a man. I've got some photos here. It would be helpful if you could look at them.'

She frowned at the two photographs for a long half minute then shook her head, passing them back, her gold hoops swinging. 'I've never seen either of them before.'

I put my notebook and the photos back in my briefcase and was about to take my leave when Michelle stopped me near the front door. 'You know, I've been having second thoughts. I might have made a mistake,' she said.

I waited.

'I'm actually wondering now if the woman I saw really was Tianna Richardson,' she added.

'My colleague said you seemed very sure earlier.'

She shrugged. 'It's not very nice, getting mixed up in a murder investigation.'

It's not very nice being murdered, I thought but didn't say.

'And it's real dark in there. The lights do funny things. Maybe I saw Tianna Richardson. Maybe I didn't. You know.' She gave a little shrug. 'I'd hate to give information that was wrong.' We continued heading for the door and she stepped in front of me and opened it. 'I hope I haven't wasted your time.'

She had, but there was little point in telling her that. Instead I thanked her for trying and stepped de, going back to the wagon to think about at I should do next.

After ringing Brian with the bad news that the positive identification of Tianna's presence at the Blackspot was now seriously in doubt, I had a question. 'We know now that there's a prior, unidentified crime scene,' I said. 'What if Tianna was never at the nightclub at all? Just dumped there?'

'To make us suppose she was there?' said Brian.

'Right. And who was in a position to do just that? Who knew she wanted to go dancing that night?'

'It's a no-brainer,' said Brian. 'Damien Henshaw. And I'm on my way to see the magistrate to get a warrant to search his place. Wish me luck.'

'You have it,' I said, ringing off.

Next I drove to O'Halloran's 24-hour Pharmacy, where I found Brian had already taken delivery of the relevant security tapes. I asked after the pharmacist who was on duty during the night and was given his phone number.

I sat back in my wagon, feeling a headache starting. I reached into the glove box and found a couple of old aspirins that I chewed up, flinching at their bitterness. If I was smart, I could do the next thing I'd undertaken to do for Brian and then go to work. Sort that mail. Find out what new samples needed urgent examination. Just do *my* work. That way, I could go home at five and spend a happy, relaxed evening with Iona. Spend time with the people I loved.

But I couldn't stop thinking about the vicious way Tianna Richardson had been murdered and dumped and I wanted to know—I *had* to know—whether she'd died at the hands of the likes of Damien Henshaw or the unknown man in the photographs, or if being in the partner-swapping mob had created the conditions that led to her murder. Nor could I walk away from the cold-blooded shooting of a fellow scientist. How could I leave Claire Dimitriou and her peculiar cry, 'She saw, she saw sixteen blue!' Was it possible that these two women were linked to the partner-swapping group that the Calvinist had told me about? I needed to find out. Dallas Baxter had been forthcoming with information about the Terminator Rabbit project, but very evasive, I recalled, when the subject changed to that of sex. This could be the result of natural or conditioned reticence but I was keen to explore another—and much more likely—possibility. Almost on automatic, I checked to make sure I had Baxter's phone number. I already knew his address. Finally, I had been touched by the killing of an old man in his house. It wasn't in me to simply walk away from these people. It wasn't just that I was as consumed with curiosity as a kid who's spotted interesting parcels hidden on top of a tall cupboard a week before Christmas; my very humanity demanded that the persons who'd murdered these three people be brought to trial. And if I could help bring this about, I was going to do everything in my power.

●

After ringing Sofia Verstoek and having an almost civil conversation with her in which she assured me she was on her way to the crime scene on the Ginninderra Road, I gave her the address of Damien Henshaw's current painting job, a house in Kingston.

'I want soil samples from there,' I said, thinking of the coarse sandy particles.

Sofia acceded in a surly tone, but I thanked her heartily before heading for the Cretan's café and grabbing some takeaway souvlaki and salad for lunch later. Then I called the nightshift pharmacist and introduced myself.

'He was in a pretty distressed way,' he said. 'Said he'd woken up with a bad attack only to find his inhaler empty. I gave him an immediate dose from his new inhaler and then put it back in its box for him. His breathing improved within a minute or so.'

'Did you talk to him?'

'Oh yes, once he could speak. He said something about it being a small world—that he'd just seen someone he knew while he was waiting at the red light.'

I felt myself tense with anticipation. 'Did he say who?'

'Unfortunately, I had to answer the phone. Woden Hospital rang and by the time I'd finished the call, Mr Vaughan had gone.'

I wasn't going to get any more than that. Maybe Harry's post-mortem would yield further information.

●

Ringing the secretary at Forensic Services, I told her I was out on fieldwork and would be in my office later in the day.

'Is Sammy Samways back yet?' I asked her, using Gavin's more usual nickname.

I held a moment while she checked. 'Not yet. He's on the roster for tomorrow,' she said.

'Please ask him to pop in and say hello when he gets back,' I said.

She promised she would and then I called Dallas Baxter at the Ag Station. Every instinct told me that this man was withholding something important and I was determined to winkle it out of him. I got through to Pauline and she told me he was having a flex day so I turned my wagon round and drove to his home.

Airlie House, one of the best addresses in town was on a slight rise just on the other side of the city. An elegant Victorian mansion set in wide gardens, it had a three-storey tower and turret, verandahs running around two sides and wrought-iron lace everywhere. Despite the drought, both Dallas Baxter and his wife were passionate about restoring the grounds of Airlie House to their former glory. The old stables-turned-garage housed two cars and, when I looked over at the house, I noticed one of the French doors onto the marble tiles of the wide verandah stood slightly open. I hurried up the steps, passing the nymphs surrounded by falling late red roses, and pressed the brass doorbell on the imposing front door.

'Yes?' came Dallas's voice from inside.

'Jack McCain. I need to talk to you, Dallas.'

Dallas's anxious face peered out at me through the half-opened French door. He was clearly not keen on my idea. Nevertheless, he stepped back, allowing me through into a front room dominated by a huge chandelier, with a magnificent equestrian painting of a thoroughbred and its rider over the marble fireplace.

'This *is* a surprise,' Dallas said, looking more uneasy every moment as he ushered me towards some chairs. Even though the newspaper near one of the club chairs was upside down, I could see it was opened at the report of Claire Dimitriou's death.

'You'd better sit down then,' he said, indicating a stiff brocade lounge opposite the cushiony club chair from which he'd clearly just risen.

'I would have rung,' I lied, ignoring the offer and moving further into the room, 'but I didn't have your home number.' Getting straight to the point, I said, 'I'm concerned about a number of things, Dallas. All the time I was at your laboratories on Tuesday, I had the distinct impression you weren't being straight with me.'

I paused, but he remained silent.

'And you did a curious thing,' I continued.

He looked even more uneasy.

'We were talking about a problem at the Ag Station,' I said, watching him intently, 'and in the same breath you asked if the death at the Blackspot was anyone we knew.'

I waited, letting the pressure of silence grow.

'Why did you think you'd know this person?'

Dallas picked up the newspaper, closed it, folded it and put it down.

I took it up again and found the story about Claire Dimitriou's death with its accompanying photo of a pretty, vibrant woman, which contrasted sharply with the lifeless corpse I'd turned over in the old Level 4 lab.

'Why do I have this very strong sense that there's something you're not telling me?' I said, tapping the report in the paper.

Dallas shoved his hands in his pockets, walked over to the marble mantelpiece and fixed his attention on the fox-hunting English gentleman. When he turned, his expression was miserable and I saw he was looking past me, through one of the tall windows that ran along the northern side of the room. I followed his gaze to the end of the garden, where a figure was visible near the round summerhouse, through the lattices of autumn roses.

'This is a murder investigation,' I said. 'A woman—two women—have lost their lives. I've been conducting a line of inquiry that has resulted in some very specific information. I know a lot more than I did when I came to see you. Now I'll ask you again: is there anything else you should be telling me?'

A long silence ensued during which Dallas Baxter continued to stare out into the garden.

'There was...' he finally started, his face looking grey. 'I mean there is... a group of people, from the department and the university...'

I stood unmoving and silent, my back to the French doors, waiting.

'...who enjoy a fairly liberal interpretation of marriage.'

Exactly what the bartender from the Cat and Castle had said, in his own way.

'The swingers?' I asked. 'The partner-swapping group?'

Dallas looked shocked. 'Who told you?'

'Was Claire Dimitriou one of them?'

'How did you know that?'

'In a place as small as this, people notice things, Dallas. Various staff and patrons of the Cat and Castle have been helpful. I've been told by more than one source about a group of people from the university and the Ag Station who played a certain game involving envelopes and coloured paper.'

Dallas shoved his hands deeper into his pockets, looking even more miserable. 'Oh, dear. I've been dreading something like this.' He looked up at me. 'It's all consensual, adult business, you know. And we prefer to call it share-mating.'

The term sounded like something in animal husbandry. 'Was Tianna Richardson also a member of the group?' I asked.

'The woman who was murdered at the nightclub? I don't know. There have been locals involved over the years. She could have been one of them,' he said.

'I think you suspected that and that's why you asked me if she was anyone we knew. Isn't that so?'

His silence was the answer I sought.

'Was Cheryl Tobin part of the group?'

Dallas blinked. 'Cheryl Tobin?' he repeated. 'What's she got to do with it?'

'That's something I'd really like to know,' I said. 'I didn't even know she existed until I'd spoken to Annette Sommers. Was she one of the share-mates?'

'But that was over two years ago,' he protested.

'Was she one of the share-mates?' I repeated.

'No, as far as I know. I'm surprised you're interested in her.'

'Peter Yu put her off from the laboratory and possibly also out of his bed. Then he took on Claire Dimitriou. Don't you think that might create a motive to murder?'

I could see the idea shocked him. 'But Cheryl was only a little thing,' he said.

'When it comes to handling firearms, Dallas, size really doesn't matter. And furthermore,' I continued, 'the reason you know so much about the group is pretty clear too.'

A movement from the garden took my attention and I watched his wife, hatted and wearing gumboots, appear from behind the summerhouse, pushing a wheelbarrow of grass cuttings over to a compost pile near the fence.

'You'd better tell me everything,' I said finally.

He walked away and I moved to block him, thinking he was going to leave. But all he did was pick up his jacket from the back of a chair.

'I'll tell you,' he said. 'But not here.'

THIRTEEN

Not long after we were back at the Ag Station in Dallas's office. A stiff brandy had helped him regain some of his gloss. I declined his offer of one and watched as he put the bottle back on the shelf above his desk.

'You're not really on duty,' he said. 'Not like a police officer.'

'It's not that. I don't drink.'

'I'm not sure where to start,' he said, ignoring my comment.

'Try the beginning,' I answered.

'There were about half a dozen of us originally,' he said, standing by the window looking out at the the nearby holding paddock. 'Not Ellen, of course. My wife is very straight-laced about that sort of thing. She doesn't like sex much at all.' He looked at the remaining brandy in his glass, swirled it around and then tossed the lot down. 'Or, at least, sex with me.'

Genevieve had discovered the same disinclination towards me.

'I don't know about you, but as far as some things go, I've found marriage unsatisfactory,' he stated, putting the empty glass on the windowsill. 'And from asking around, I find that a lot of people—men and women—have the same problem.'

Memories of Genevieve surfaced like a rolling shark. I would have used something stronger than unsatisfactory myself. The word 'impossible' came to mind. 'Intolerable' and 'unbearable' were more like it.

'So tell me how it worked and who was involved,' I said.

'There was me,' he said, then paused, picking up his glass and going back for a refill. 'Are you sure you won't have one?' he asked.

'Very sure,' I answered. I'd never forgotten where bottles like this one had once taken me.

'Like I said, there was me and Anthony Dimitriou and Claire. Although, as I recall, Claire wasn't as keen as the others. It started up about three years ago,' Dallas continued. 'Peter Yu was a pretty active member, together with whatever girlfriend he might have had at the time. If she was willing. I guess you could say that we were the founding members.' He looked up at me and his distress was palpable. 'There's still been no word on Peter?'

'I want to know how it worked,' I said, not letting him get off the hook, thinking of the small white envelopes and the coloured flint paper the bartender had mentioned.

'Did you write names down on bits of paper?' I asked.

Dallas shook his head. 'No. No names. Not in writing. I was paranoid about Ellen ever finding out and a couple of the others were just as cautious. I never went to the hotel meetings for that reason. The younger ones didn't worry about that sort of thing.'

'You said there were six of you originally, but you've only mentioned three men and two women.'

'Yvonne Abernathy was also a member,' said Dallas. 'She was *particularly* concerned about secrecy.'

'She rang you the morning I found Claire's body,' I said, remembering Dallas's evasive manner. 'She must have heard something about Claire already.'

'I'd actually rung her first,' Dallas confessed. 'I'd asked her if she knew anything about any extra involvement Claire might have had.'

'The coloured paper? Was that part of the code?'

'Yvonne's idea. She's a primary school teacher and she was the one who brought the flint paper along. She chose red, I was white and Anthony was purple. I only remember his colour because he hated it. I can't remember Claire's colour because she used to pull out more often than not.'

'Who was blue?' I asked.

Dallas shook his head. 'Sorry. It was a while ago.'

Someone had seen Blue. Someone had seen him or her at a place he or she shouldn't have been—perhaps a motel or a hotel. At last, Claire

Dimitriou's cryptic cry was making some sense. Was that why she'd had to die?

'What about the other envelope? With the plain cards?' I asked.

'They each had a number written on it and each number stood for a motel or hotel. We tried to use places a bit off the beaten track. But it was still risky.' He paused. 'That was part of the excitement. You'd pick a number to see where you'd go that night. And a colour.'

So much for Canberra being dull.

'We used lots of motels and hotels in the district—some as far as Queanbeyan. Then, as other people became involved, we used even more colours. Lime, aqua, orange, gold—I forget now. But everyone had a different colour or shade.' He paused and his voice when he spoke sounded tired. 'It sounds pathetic now, like kids playing cloak-and-dagger games. But at the time it somehow made everything feel more exciting, pulling out a number and a colour. Riskier.'

I recalled the old board game, Cluedo—Mrs Plum in the library with the candlestick, Miss Prim in the dining room with the revolver. 'So you'd get a colour and a number. You might pull out number four and then the red?'

Dallas nodded again. 'Red meant you met Yvonne Abernathy and I can't quite recall where four was—could have been the motel off the highway near Collector.' He looked away into the distance.

'You said you *used* to be part of the group,' I said, considering his earlier words. 'What happened?'

'One of Peter's girlfriends got a crush on me,' he said, not sounding too displeased about this. 'Suzie started ringing me at work, wanting to see me. Then she started ringing the house and hanging up if Ellen answered. My wife suspected something was going on. She started asking questions. I told her it was one of my Hong Kong postgrad students, having a hard time away from home, seeing me as a father figure—which was largely the truth.'

I saw him look at the brandy bottle again, consider another drink, then think better of it. Thinking better of it was something I'd never been able to do.

'I started to panic,' Dallas was saying. 'I couldn't afford any scandal. It was getting too dangerous for me. I'd never intended to put my marriage in jeopardy.' He took a deep breath. 'I'm very fond of my wife. You get used to a person. We've got along very well for a quarter of a century now. I know my wife—she's a proud woman. If I made a fool of her, played up on her—especially with a student from the university—she'd divorce me in a flash. And I couldn't afford that. It'd ruin me. Airlie House means a lot to me. It's listed among the ten most famous colonial residences in Australia in private hands. And it all belongs to Ellen. If she divorced me, I'd lose my beautiful home. The children would never forgive me. After the Hong Kong student, I got scared. So I pulled out of the group. That was last year. I don't really know how things stand these days.'

I wondered what he did for sex now. Probably what most men did, with a stash of pornography hidden somewhere. The only magazines I could see in the room were some journals on genetic improvements in merino sheep.

'It was only ever supposed to be a bit of fun,' said Dallas, 'with willing people who would be as discreet as I was. It was just meant to be a bit of sex on the side.'

A bit of sex on the side. The phrase made it sound so harmless, like a green salad or a bowl of chips with the main meal.

'So Tianna Richardson *could* have become a member of the group after you left?' I asked.

'It's quite possible. I knew that people from town joined even when I was still active in the group. She could easily have become part of it.'

'That's why you sacked Kevin Waites,' I said, suddenly understanding.

'When he told me what he'd overheard, I immediately imagined Claire's words referred to the colour code. I didn't want him repeating that anywhere. He's getting too old for the job, anyway,' he said. Dallas spread his beautifully manicured hands and the ruby winked on the little finger of his left hand.

'The words Claire used were "Sixteen blue",' I said.

'Perhaps Claire *was* alluding to someone in the group then... Although we usually put the colour first. She could have meant Blue Sixteen. Like I told you,' Dallas said, 'I haven't been involved for nearly a year now. If it had come out that I was involved with a student, anything could have happened. You don't know what it's like these days. A complaint from a student about harassment can end an academic's life. There are plenty of hungry young associate professors coming up through the system ready to take my place.'

Outside, kookaburras were laughing raucously.

'Dallas, you're hardly like an academic in a position of trust with a student. It's not like that. This girl joined the group as an equal player.'

'Even so, I got scared.'

Scared that the good life you've made for yourself might all start to unravel, I thought. 'That's why you didn't find it very funny when I suggested earlier that Claire Dimitriou and Peter Yu might have eloped.'

'It *wasn't* funny. A couple of people got a bit too serious once before,' he said. 'That was one of the things we discussed at the beginning. It was all meant to stay light-hearted, not end up in the bloody divorce courts.'

The phone rang and Dallas picked it up while I made a mental note to talk to Jerri Quill, Claire Dimitriou's postgrad student.

'Yes, dear,' Dallas was saying. 'No, I remembered later and didn't want to disturb you. I'll be home soon.'

He put the phone down and stood up. 'I've got to go. Please God, I can't have a scandal, Jack,' he said.

I felt sorry for the poor sod. I must have been getting soft in my middle years. First Earl bloody Richardson and now this fellow. Men of my vintage were starting to get to me. Did I see myself reflected back in them? It was not a comfortable thought. Maybe once I'd had a break, I'd be back to my usual self. Spending time with Iona could only do me good.

'My interest in your personal life is purely professional. If it's possible, I'm happy to be discreet,' I said. 'But you must get the names that go with the colours for me. That's non-negotiable. And the corresponding numbers for the venues. It's essential that I know who Blue Sixteen is. Or was.'

'It's been a long time,' he said. 'They'll think it's strange if I start asking questions like that.'

'I don't give a rat's arse what they think, Dallas. I'm sure you can get that information somehow. Otherwise I'll lean on you and blow the whole group wide open.'

He flashed me an angry glance then pulled out a very large handkerchief and wiped his glistening brow. I wondered if his agitation was simply the result of anxiety or whether he was still withholding something important.

He shoved the handkerchief back into a pocket. 'I'll do what I can.'

'You get me that information. All of it.'

'Jack, I only just hung onto my job in the most recent reshuffle. Ever since the amalgamation of the Agriculture Department with Fisheries and Primary Industry, things have felt tenuous at work. If I lose this position, I'm finished. Men of my age aren't being hired anywhere. And then if Ellen divorced me...'

He didn't have to tell me. After my divorce, I'd had to start again, like a young man in his twenties. If it hadn't been for the windfall from the dealer, I wouldn't have been able to buy a house.

'So I've been wondering,' said Dallas, interrupting my thoughts 'if...you know... now that I've told you everything... you might be able to see your way clear to ruling a line under the information about my part in it.' His voice faltered. 'I can't see how I could be related to anything that might be going on now. Surely my name can be left out of it?'

I didn't envy him his beautiful house or his head-of-department salary package right this minute. Right this minute, Dallas Baxter was just a sad, frightened middle-aged man trying to wring out a favour.

'Dallas, this is a murder investigation. Nothing and no one can be left out of it. Surely you realise that.'

Dallas went a paler shade of grey. 'I just hoped, you know... I never thought that the share-mate business would end up becoming involved in something like murder. What's happened is horrible.'

Millions of women have died at the hands of jealous men, I thought. And women, too, have wreaked vengeance on men they considered faithless.

'You've lived too long in your academic ivory tower. You're out of touch with reality,' I said as I pulled out my notebook. 'Okay. If someone wanted to join the group, what would they have to do?'

'They need to be nominated by a member.'

'Like joining a club?'

'That's right. And the first time someone *partakes* of a partner...' He hesitated.

'Go on,' I said.

'It's like an initiation—they don't know who they're meeting. They have to go to the nominated place and see who's there.'

The lucky dip game, I thought. 'How do they know what the nominated place is?'

'They meet up with the group and take their chances by picking a number and a colour at the pub, or if they don't want to go out, someone does the selection for them and then rings through with the information,' said Dallas. 'It's always up to the lady to leave a message at Reception so that her visitor can find her.'

I thought about that a moment and got up. 'Okay, Dallas. I'll do what I can to keep your name out of this.'

'That's good of you, Jack.'

'You can do something for me.'

'If I can...'

'Give Kevin Waites his job back. You said yourself how hard it is for men of your age—his age—to get another job.'

'If I do, you'll keep quiet about this business?'

'I'll do my level best,' I said. 'And as to the swingers group...'

'Yes?' he said.

'Get me those names and place numbers.'

'Yes, yes.'

'And one more thing?'

'Anything I can do, Jack. I swear.'

'Get someone who's still a member to nominate me.'

FOURTEEN

I left Dallas Baxter in his office, probably succumbing to a third brandy, while I hurried back to my car and rang Brian. I told him about the partner-swapping group and also stressed that I didn't want any dickhead detectives charging in and frightening the horses. I didn't tell him my plan to infiltrate the group and I had to bargain extremely hard to buy a little time from him. I asked him about Vera Hastings, the street gossip who lived next to Tianna Richardson's place.

'I've contacted her,' said Brian. 'She's expecting someone to call round. Let's hope she's the busybody she's supposed to be.'

'They can be goldmines,' I said.

I drove a little distance until I came to a pleasant roadside spot with a cement table and two cement benches on two sides. I pulled out the souvlaki and salad containers and sat down to have some lunch, noticing a 'missed call' on my mobile. It was my daughter, asking me to call her about something important, but before I had the chance, a call from Harry interrupted me.

'Come over,' he said. 'I've got something to show you. I want you to take a look at what I've found on Albert Vaughan.'

It didn't take me long to get to the morgue where the receptionist called through to Harry.

'He's being cleaned up now,' Harry said, arriving a few minutes later and leading me through the secured door. 'I need to leave here quite soon but I wanted to give you this in person.'

Harry passed me one of the two gowns he'd picked up and I entered the main post-mortem area, following him down to the table where the pale body lay, waiting to be bagged. On the counter behind it, the samples Harry had taken and weighed stood in labelled specimen jars.

'What did you find?' I asked. In death, all Albert Vaughan's fragility was visible; the skin on his face and neck translucent as an embryonic bird's.

Harry pulled gloves on and checked one of the specimen jars, then put it down again, before turning to me.

'Very strange,' he said, rolling the head over to one side to reveal the damage at the back. 'I found something here that will interest you,' He pointed with a pair of long-nosed scissors. Then he looked about, frowning. 'Now where is that bucket?'

He was looking for the brain, which he'd previously removed and weighed and which was now hardening in solution before it could be sliced and examined by the neurologist.

'It's okay, Harry,' I said, raising a hand. 'I'll take your word for it.' Just at this moment, with my head aching and stuffed up, brains in buckets weren't my cup of tea.

'A severe wound to the back of the head.' He turned and waved his gloved hand over the body. 'I'd say it was made by some blunt instrument—maybe a piece of timber or metal. Delivered from behind, as your crime scene people found. I found evidence of three separate events.'

'Whack, whack and whack,' I said.

'And I found coarse sandy particles embedded in the wounds. I think you'll be very interested in these,' he said, frowning over his bifocals. 'You're going to have to take soil samples from around Albert Vaughan's place and Tianna Richardson's.'

'I'll get our palynologist on the job,' I said, making a note.

I pulled gloves on and took the specimen jar Harry passed to me. 'I took two samples of these particles from the head wounds one for me and this one for you. I knew you'd want your own,' he explained.

I looked down at the fluid in the tightly sealed specimen jar, gently shook it, then held it up close to my eye, watching the large particles swirl around in the fluid. Then I refocused to see Harry's intelligent eyes magnified through the container.

'Of course,' I said, 'I'll need to analyse them officially. But I'd put the rent on this being the same material we found in Tianna Richardson's wounds.'

Somehow, an elderly man living on the outskirts of a small hamlet north of Canberra and Tianna Richardson, murdered in a suburb over thirty kilometres away, seemed to be connected.

After getting rid of our sterile gear, I walked back to Harry's office with him, double-bagging the specimen jar and then slipping it into a thick envelope. I could feel myself being drawn further into this investigation. Now that their deaths were linked by unique evidence, I had to know everything I could glean about the last hours of Tianna Richardson and Albert Vaughan.

'So who's going to do the fine work on this?' said Harry, interrupting my thoughts.

'I'll try to woo Ellis Smith out of retirement for it,' I said. 'I think he lives somewhere in Sydney these days.'

'Good idea,' said Harry, pushing open the door for me. 'We'll need the best man for this.'

Back in my car, I found the number of Ryan Holbrook, a smart, young detective I'd met on an earlier case in Sydney, and asked him to track down Dr Ellis Smith. Ryan promised he'd ask around and get back to me.

All the way to Tianna Richardson's street, I wondered about how these two murders might be connected. Was it conceivable that Albert Vaughan was a member of the partner-swapping group? I dismissed the notion smartly as I tried to imagine him throwing a leg over Tianna. He looked so frail in death that I couldn't imagine life would have made much difference.

Vera Hastings, a fair woman with her hair pulled tightly back from her forehead in a high bun near the top of her head, had two grey, tadpole-shaped lines drawn above her eyes instead of eyebrows. After I'd identified myself, she walked ahead of me in a bright purple tracksuit, showing me through into her living room. Several striking orchids displayed their floral spikes in pots and containers around the room.

'It's good of you to help us, Mrs Hastings,' I said, looking around past the orchids. Too much heavy dark furniture cluttered the room so that when I sat opposite her, I felt too close.

'Please, call me Vera. My late husband was in the job,' she said, turning to a portrait of a chubby man in uniform hanging on the wall, 'so I know how important it is to get as much information as possible. It's a terrible thing to have a neighbour murdered.'

I made sympathetic noises and she lowered her voice. 'I know I shouldn't speak ill of the dead, but just between you and me, I'm not so surprised about Tianna coming to such an awful end.'

'Why is that?' I said, as if surprised.

'Since Earl left, Tianna's been out with quite a few different men. I feel sorry for him. He wanted her back, you know. Came up just a week or two ago,' she said, offering me a ginger snap. I declined and she took a couple herself. 'She wasn't a bad girl, you know. But she was left on her own a lot.'

I had a sudden vision of a woman eating her evening meal alone and it wasn't Tianna Richardson.

'And Tianna liked to party,' Vera Hastings was saying. 'Loved dressing up and going clubbing and dancing. That sort of thing. She asked me if I was interested once, but I'm a bit beyond that.'

I took out the photograph Brian had removed from Tianna Richardson's bedroom of Tianna with the unknown man. 'We were wondering if you might have seen this man?' I said, passing it to her.

She studied the photograph a few seconds, frowned and then I saw recognition dawn on her face. 'Oh yes,' she said, nodding. 'That good-looking fellow. He dropped by from time to time. Always parked his car way down the street and then walked to the house. But he didn't fool me.' She looked up from the photograph. 'He was here not so long ago.'

'What sort of car did this man drive?' I asked, taking the photograph back from her.

'A white one,' she said. 'Ford, Holden, I don't know. An ordinary sort of big white car.'

'Sedan?'

'No,' she said. 'It was a station wagon, like yours.'

'And you never heard his name?'

She shook her head. 'Tianna and I didn't talk all that much, just a nod hello from time to time. Or we'd bump into each other in the Plaza shopping.'

'Mrs Richardson had a son that we're trying to locate,' I said.

'The surfer?' she asked. 'Jason?'

I nodded.

'Oh dear, oh dear. He visited once.'

I nodded again, encouragingly. This woman clearly kept the entire street under constant surveillance.

'You're wondering how I know?' said Vera Hastings, reading my mind. 'The whole street knew! There was a terrible row. Ended up with him storming out of the house. Everyone was screaming and carrying on.'

Interesting, I thought, and made a note of it. 'When was that?'

Vera shrugged. 'Can't really say. Sometime last year. July, August.'

'Did you hear what they were arguing about?'

'Can't really say.' She frowned. 'And by the way, he was her stepson, not her own blood.'

I made another note, more interested than ever in finding Jason Richardson. He might have had more than a filial interest in his father's wife. 'Any idea where Jason might be now?'

'Who can say? He follows the surf, I heard. Lives all over the place apparently.'

'What does he drive?' I asked.

She gave me a vague description of a van with a board on top. It wasn't much. Clearly, her nosey-parkering didn't include cars. 'If you think of anything else,' I said, handing her my card.

'Thanks,' she said, propping it up against a pot plant.

As soon as I'd taken my leave, I rang Brian, passing on the information about Jason Richardson and agreeing he should now alert the police in other states too. Sometimes this worked. Jason Richardson was certainly shaping up as a potential suspect. Then there was the mystery man. If he was part of the partner-swapping group, he might very well have visited their favoured pub. I pulled the photograph out of my pocket again and studied it. The know-all barman at the Cat and Castle might be helpful.

On the way into town, I made a quick diversion, calling at the address of Claire's doctoral student, Jerri Quill, who lived in one of the apartment buildings along Northbourne Avenue.

It was her flatmate who answered my knock—a sweet-faced Asian youngster, glossy hair pulled back, no make-up, wearing a man's cardigan over her crop-top and jeans so low on her hips that I held my breath.

I explained who I was and how I'd come to talk to her flatmate.

'Forgive me for not shaking hands,' Wendy Chen said after I'd introduced myself. She held up fingers dusty with what looked like plaster or clay. 'I'm working on something.'

'I'm sorry to interrupt.'

'Don't be,' she said. 'Just let me wash my hands. Jerri's not here. She left Monday night.'

'Business or pleasure?' I asked.

'Definitely not pleasure,' said Wendy. 'I need a coffee. Want one?' She poured herself a cup from a nearby percolator, then vanished a few moments.

'What are you doing?' I asked on her return.

'Anthropology,' she said. 'Doing my thesis, like Jerri.'

I followed her into a bright room where a tall pot stand supported the sculpture of a human head, its back to us.

'You're a sculptor as well?' I asked, walking round so as to view the head face-on.

'Sort of. This is part of my doctorate. It's not so widely used now that electronic reconstructions are cheaper and quicker. But it's a skill that's still needed.'

Wendy was working on a facial and cranial skull reconstruction, building up thicknesses of 'flesh' using soft clay. I studied the young face forming in the soft fawn clay. This head was almost finished, awaiting the final touches of colouring, hair and eyebrows. It was an eerie sensation. Because this wasn't an imagined face—it had been built up on a plaster cast of a human skull according to anatomical statistics, tissue depth, nose length, eye orbits. This was the face of a real person. Someone no one had missed. No one had noticed that she'd vanished.

'Where did you get her?'

'I was able to get a cast taken from the skull of one of the cold cases the New South Wales police have reopened. I'm hoping it'll assist someone to put a loved one to rest. It would be wonderful if I could get a result from her.'

'A friend of mine is involved with those cold cases,' I said, thinking of Bob. 'I'll let him know that this face is on its way.'

'Not sure exactly when that will be,' she said.

I walked around the young face. Lashes hadn't yet been put around the blue glass eyes, nor did she have any hair yet. But with the addition of these refinements, someone, somewhere, might say, 'That looks like my daughter.'

'So why did Jerri go away?' I asked, turning my attention away from the facial reconstruction on the stand and noticing a vase of very early violets on the windowsill. 'I thought she was a doctoral candidate too.'

Wendy shrugged. 'She had a big fight with her supervisor.'

'Dr Dimitriou?'

Wendy nodded. 'Yes. Well, actually not a fight, but some huge blow-up between them. Now Dr Dimitriou's dead. *Murdered*. Jerri might not even know.' Her voice was almost a whisper.

I leaned forward so close I could feel the warmth rising from her; if I'd had clear sinuses, I could have smelled her. 'The fight,' I said. 'What do you know about it?'

'She was really upset when she came in after being out at the research lab last Monday. She came home very shaken and said she was going up the coast with a friend and then she was going back to

Sydney. To her parents' place. She'd had enough. She was even talking about giving up uni for good.'

I noted all this down. 'Tell me, Wendy,' I said. 'What was the blow-up with Dr Dimitriou about?'

Wendy tipped up her coffee and emptied it in a couple of long swallows.

'That's just it,' she said, shaking her head and putting her cup down. 'Jerri said she'd done absolutely nothing to warrant such behaviour. Even if she *had* made a mistake, no one would tell her what it was. And she said Claire had always been so kind before.'

I knew about 'mistakes' in the world of science, knew all about a year's work being wiped by a bumbling neophyte, or painstakingly gathered notes being shredded by mistake. The sorts of mistakes that even old hands sometimes still made. I had to admit to a couple myself over the years.

'What she really couldn't understand,' Wendy continued, 'was why Dr Dimitriou was so unhinged about it. I mean, Jerri was really distressed. I was quite shocked at her appearance. She was almost hysterical when she came home.'

'Did she say what she'd done?'

'She said she'd done exactly what she always did, but that Dr Dimitriou implied she'd done something terrible—used the wrong thing.'

'What wrong thing?'

She frowned, trying to remember. 'She didn't say.' She spread her hands. 'Sorry.'

Could be a lot of things, I thought. Glassware of some sort, the wrong assay plate, the wrong reagent.

Wendy wandered over to the young girl's sculpted head, eyeing it critically from the side. 'And it wasn't just the mistake, Jerri said. What really upset her was the way Dr Dimitriou behaved afterwards, the way she'd questioned her. Jerri said she felt she was being interrogated by the secret police!'

I couldn't imagine a journeyman mistake creating the need for close questioning. But I already knew Claire Dimitriou had been under a great deal of stress—a woman straining under the weight of a huge decision, a burden she couldn't deal with. A burden that was making her act out of control. A burden she felt she had to *do* something about.

'Did Jerri ever talk about anything between Dr Dimitriou and her colleague Peter Yu?'

'Like what?'

'Something that would indicate they were more than just workmates?'

Wendy considered. 'I can't really say. I'm not even sure Jerri would have told me if she'd seen anything interesting like that! She's a quiet type. Doesn't gossip. Bit like me, really. We're happiest when we're just working quietly by ourselves. That's why we're such successful flatmates.' She paused and the smile left her face. 'But, boy was she upset. I'd never seen her cry before. She said Dr Dimitriou attacked her as if she'd done something absolutely dreadful—unforgivable!'

Wendy sat back on her heels. 'And Jerri didn't deal with it at all well. It's the sort of thing you need to take up with your supervisor when things calm down. But Jerri didn't go back to the university or the Ag Station after that. I was worried about her. And then she up and left. She's been really hurt by this.'

'Do you have the address where she's staying?'

Wendy came back with her address book and gave me the details of Jerri's parents in Lane Cove. I finished my coffee, stood up and made my farewells, taking one last look at the young, half-completed anonymous girl.

'She's shaping up to be such a lovely creature,' Wendy said. 'Hard to believe that no one loved her.'

We walked together towards the door and Wendy passed me her card. 'Give Jerri my love,' she said, opening the door for me. 'And if you ever need a facial reconstruction done…'

'I think it's too late for that,' I said.

On the way to the Cat and Castle, I rang the Quills at Lane Cove only to discover that Jerri had gone bushwalking with a girlfriend and wasn't expected back for a couple of days. Her mother promised to leave a message with my details on her daughter's voicemail. But she couldn't promise Jerri would use her mobile.

The Calvinist barman wasn't working at the Cat and Castle that afternoon. In his place was a golden girl with wide grey eyes, whose accent revealed her as a visitor from England. I introduced myself, showed her my ID, ordered a lemon, lime and bitters and we chatted a while. She worked there most weekends, I learned, as part of a six-month savings stint to get enough money together to move west to Adelaide and then on to Broome and Perth.

'Sounds great,' I said. 'But no hitchhiking.'

I pulled out the photograph of the mystery man and showed it to her.

'That was taken here!' she said. 'You can see the timber fittings. Are these your friends?'

'Not exactly. In fact, I was wondering if *you* knew who they were, and him in particular,' I said, pointing to the mystery man.

'You should know him,' she said. 'I thought all you coppers knew each other.'

'I'm not police,' I said. 'I work with the police. You say he's in the job?'

'I've seen his warrant card,' she said. 'He was trying to get free drinks.'

'You sure about that?' I wondered why Brian hadn't recognised him.

'He's been in here a couple of times. He always gives me a dirty look now. Knows he can't get around me.'

'Can you tell me anything about him?'

She shook her head. 'Just that he's a New South Wales copper,' she said, sounding like an extra from *The Bill* and revealing why Brian hadn't known the man.

'It's men like him who give the police a bad name,' she said, turning to lift a tray of washed glasses up onto the counter behind her.

I took the photograph back with me to Forensic Services and rang Bob Edwards, telling him I was about to fax a photograph of a man thought to be a police officer. 'He flashed a New South Wales warrant card to a bar attendant,' I said.

'If it was genuine, we could have a name for you in twenty-four hours,' said Bob.

On the way back to the office, I dropped in on Heronvale Police Station and found Brian on the verge of leaving. He looked exhausted.

My mobile rang and when I heard Sofia Verstoek's voice I signalled Brian to hang on a moment, in case she had something he should know about.

'I've just completed a long series of pollen assemblages and soil profiles,' she said. 'From both the Kincaid Street address and the Ginninderra Road house. Then I went on to that house at Kingston where your suspect has been working. I've got a negative result from all three places. None of them reveal any of the large grey particles you gave me as reference samples. Those particles look to me like some sort of granite and the soil around the other three properties has a completely different composition. I then took the analysis a step further and had another look at the samples taken from Tianna Richardson's head wounds. I *did* find something unusual there. A rare native orchid pollen.'

The phrase 'rare native orchid pollen' found a hit somewhere in my memory, but failed to surface.

'Thanks, Sofia. That could be very helpful if and when we ever locate the primary scene.'

'Just doing my job,' she said. 'Pity about some people. And as for your mate Brian Kruger—' she started but I cut her off.

'He's right here with me,' I said. 'Do you want to talk to him?'

'No way! I'm not overly impressed with the samples he sent. I've told him I should be given priority. He didn't let me know about the Ginninderra Road scene until his lot had tramped all over it.'

'Sofia, you just wouldn't know what it's like working crime scene, night and day on call, reports backing up behind you, new work coming in every few hours and—'

The line clicked. The little bugger had hung up on me.

'What's she on about?' Brian asked.

'She's done some soil profiles and hasn't found any trace of those grey particles anywhere at either Kincaid Street, the Ginninderra Road crime scene or Damien Henshaw's place of work,' I said. 'Almost certainly they've been brought in from somewhere else. And so has some rare native orchid pollen. That's the main news.'

'That's not news. It's fucking heartbreak,' cursed Brian. 'It reminds me all over again of the time and energy we've wasted.'

'Not entirely,' I said, trying to cheer him up. 'If we find a site with the grey particles and the rare orchid, we could have the place Tianna met her death. Or at least a link via the killer to the primary scene. That's got to be very helpful. Could be our killer's backyard.'

The phrase 'rare native orchid pollen' was still worrying at my memory. I frowned, trying to remember. Was it just that I'd seen orchids recently at Vera Hasting's place, I asked myself. I didn't think so. I remembered a conversation at the Sydney morgue and someone remarking about pollen evidence. I racked my brains trying to remember which case it was but could not dislodge the memory. Bob had been there too.

'It's puzzling that the same coarse sandy particles showed up in the head wounds of Albert Vaughan,' said Brian, interrupting my thoughts. 'Could be the same killer.'

'It's a connection,' I said. 'I've also discovered there's a Blue in the partner-sharing group.'

'That's it. I'm going to have to move on that lot,' said Brian.

'Just give me a couple of days,' I begged. 'I'm working on a way in. I'm hopeful I can get what you want without you blowing the whistle on the group. This is a far more intelligent way to do it,' I argued.

'I'll give you till midday tomorrow. Then it becomes a police matter,' he said. 'Maybe,' he went on, taking his car keys out of his pocket and thinking aloud, 'some woman who's not in the group, sees *her* man, Sixteen Blue, at a place he shouldn't be. Or the other way round—a man sees his woman somewhere she shouldn't be. How would you feel if you saw your woman coming out of a motel room with some strange man?'

'I wouldn't like it,' I said.

'Hey, Jack, I've got it,' he said, his voice becoming animated. 'Claire Dimitriou has been somewhere having sex with Blue whoever he is, and the two of them are spotted coming from somewhere they shouldn't. And whichever woman it is who sprung them, she goes home, gets the Browning she's put away for a special occasion, buzzes Claire out at the lab that night, goes down to the lab with her and shoots her.'

'Then does a huge steam-clean of the whole lab,' I said, 'and gets rid of the laptop, the mobile and the lab book? Why do all that?'

My mind turned to the earlier researcher. 'Any news on Cheryl Tobin?' I asked.

'Nothing so far,' said Brian.

There was a silence. Then Brian's voice, angry and frustrated: 'What else have we got?'

I passed on the contact information for Jerri Quill and Brian said he'd talk to her as soon as he could get a few hours free to drive to Sydney. I told him she'd been so upset by the fight with her supervisor in the Faithful Bunnies lab that she was thinking of leaving university. We conjectured what the dispute in the lab might have been about. We didn't get very far.

'She could have been the party who saw Blue,' Brian said. 'Maybe she's in love with Blue and pissed off that her boss is rooting him. That's why she's left town.'

I thought about that. There were just too many possibilities, too many ways to stack the deck. We needed more evidence.

'Maybe we'll have a better chance to work it out once we know who Blue is,' I said. 'I'm trying to track down Ellis Smith. And I'll be sending him samples of the coarse grey sand as soon as I can. If anyone can discover where that comes from, it's him.'

'What about that rare orchid?' Brian asked. 'If it's that rare, it might suggest some places to start looking.'

'I believe the palynologist is on the job,' I said, voice deliberately neutral. 'Do you remember a case involving a native orchid?' I asked him. 'Unidentified skeletal remains found some years back?'

'It's ringing a bell,' he said. 'But I've got a feeling it was New South Wales jurisdiction anyway. Why?'

'I'm curious, that's all.'

'You think there might be a connection with one of these murders?'

'Doesn't seem likely,' I said. 'The case I'm thinking about had been dead about twenty years.'

'I've spent most of the day trying to find a murder weapon out at Ginninderra Road,' said Brian. 'No luck.'

I glanced at my watch. It was getting late. I reminded myself that I was on a promise—and I'd better deliver. All I had to do was catch up with my notes and I could go home and cook dinner for Iona—and my family.

FIFTEEN

Back at Forensic Services, I secured the trace evidence Harry had given me from the wounds of Albert Vaughan, wondering how long it might take to track down Ellis Smith. I'd certainly take a look myself as well.

Then, while the information I'd gathered recently from Harry, Kevin Waites and Jerri Quill's flatmate Wendy was still fresh in my mind, I hurried to my office and started writing up fuller notes from the jottings in my notebook.

I drew up a list of the prime movers in the murder of Dr Claire Dimitriou. I conjectured all sorts of possibilities trying to link the flight of Jerri Quill with the Blue Sixteen incident. This code could cover any amount of people, male or female. Was Blue Claire's lover? Like Brian, I tried out a variety of different ways to fit the jigsaw pieces together. Cheryl Tobin, the rage she'd contained for over two years finally exploding, making her way to the laboratory, killing the woman who'd replaced her and the man who had betrayed her then using her skill as a scientist to make sure no trace evidence of her presence would ever be found. But how did she dispose of Peter Yu's body? And where? Maybe the killing was carried out by a twosome and not an individual?

Then I considered the idea of Jerri Quill stumbling onto something she shouldn't have seen—Claire Dimitriou and Dr Peter Yu, clothing in disorder, writhing in passion, going hell for leather on the easy-clean vinyl of the old Level 4 lab. But it didn't work. Surely, these days, anyone walking in on something like that would just discreetly back out again. It was inconceivable, then, that Jerri would tell Anthony Dimitriou. In my experience of suburban adultery, the partner is the *last* person to be told by anyone. And if all of the players were involved in the colour-coded sex group, a discovery like that shouldn't have been an issue anyway. Consensus infidelity. And then there was the husband. Was it only grief that made Anthony Dimitriou OD? I stood up, restlessly walking around the office. I had no reason to link the flight of Jerri Quill with the Blue Sixteen incident. She may not have been the 'she' who 'saw' at all. Had Cheryl visited after hours and seen something she shouldn't have?

My mind juggled different reasons for Peter Yu's desperate pleas and Claire Dimitriou's passionate insistence. Had she been saying that because Blue Sixteen had been seen they *had* to go public? Was she wanting to leave Anthony? Had Peter Yu, whose pattern of serial girlfriends reminded me of my brother Charlie's, finally met the woman he really wanted only to find her thoroughly married?

Whatever the disagreement had been about, Dr Claire Dimitriou was now dead and I would have to talk to Anthony Dimitriou soon. I wanted to get a sense of the man myself. Was he the sort of man who might ask around for a contract killer and then make sure he was obviously attending an overseas conference? Discovering that your woman wanted to leave you, that she loved someone else—that could gut a man.

Dallas Baxter's fears of casual sex becoming something else were well grounded. A fling was one thing, a marriage bust-up quite another. Safe sex, said the billboard. There was no such thing.

I made diagrammatic notes of my various dramas—Claire saying of Peter's current girlfriend, 'We *have* to tell her we're in love', the urgency in their argument suggesting that a secret could no longer be contained by the two of them. Then I drew up a new triangle. In this one, Peter Yu walked in on Jerri Quill and Claire Dimitriou doing the writhing on the easy-wipe surface. But I wasn't sure that walking in on your woman with another woman triggered quite the same homicidal place in the male brain. Finally, I wrote 'Cheryl' in large letters and drew a line and a question mark beside my love triangle. Science had never been like this when I was a student.

'Come in,' I called as someone knocked. Gavin Samways, who'd taken some leave to go to New Zealand, peered around the door then came in.

'Welcome back, Sammy. How was the conference?'

Gavin ambled over to a chair, pulled it close and sat on it back to front, eyes smiling behind rimless glasses that, combined with his grey moustache and small beard, gave him a Victorian gravitas.

'Not bad. There were some good speakers. I was mostly interested in the computer programs, especially the improved facial reconstructions. But the guy from Quantico did a great job on drug-assisted sexual assault.'

'Can't beat the Yanks,' I said.

'I don't know about that,' said Sammy. 'The presentation on DVI by Guy Cavanough from Sydney police was just as good. The first team to hit the ground in Thailand after the tsunami was Team Australia.'

Disaster Victim Identification, often a problem in multiple violent death, required expertise as well as patience—and often a sense of mission, which helped make the difficult work more bearable. Currently, we had around eighty of our Federal people in Banda Aceh alone.

After we'd chatted a little more, I asked Sammy the question I had been building towards. 'Anthony Dimitriou from the university was at the conference, I believe?'

'I heard about his wife. Terrible. He must feel even worse being away like that when it happened.'

'So he was there all the time?' I queried, pulling my notebook out and finding his name.

'He attended every session,' said Sammy.

We talked a little more about a new technique that had impressed him—the chronological sequencing of indented impressions on questioned documents—until he glanced at his watch and decided it was time to go home.

Now that Anthony Dimitriou's alibi had been checked, I ticked his name on my notes, then, to give myself a break from the contingencies circling my mind, I switched on the small radio. Peggy Lee came breathing her classic number through the speakers. *Fever*, she sang. Her voice reminded me of Iona's pinot noir voice and my cock stirred. I felt a smile move my lips as I thought of tonight.

On the way back to the cottage in time to cook dinner, I made another unsuccessful attempt to call Jacinta. I hoped she was okay and that the lemurs were snuggled up nicely together in a furry cuddle. I wondered what it was that she wanted to talk about and made a mental note to buy plenty of the nut and chocolate bars she loved when I next went back to Sydney.

I was delighted as I pulled up at the cottage, to see Jacinta's car parked on the brown grass where Charlie's had been. Now we could all be together for dinner. I knew Iona would be late this evening, so decided to greet my daughter and then take off again to the nearest supermarket for supplies.

I hurried inside. As I approached the kitchen, I could hear low voices.

'Jass?' I called out.

Walking through the living room, I noticed the lemurs had come along on the trip and lay tightly curled together on one of the big club armchairs in front of the fire. Maybe Andy had come too. Not wanting to walk in on a tender moment, I called out again as I approached.

'We're in the kitchen,' answered Jacinta.

But the person sitting at the kitchen table wasn't Andy Kelly. It was Jacinta's friend Shaz, her face swollen from crying, with Jacinta hunched forwards on the kitchen chair beside her.

I kissed Jacinta on the top of her head. 'Hullo, Shaz. What's going on?'

Shaz lifted her head to nod to me in response and that's when I saw that the swelling on her face wasn't only from weeping.

'Shaz, what's happened to your mouth?' I said.

'He hit her, Dad,' said Jacinta. 'The bastard punched her. I'm trying to talk some sense into her.' She smoothed her friend's hair back from her flushed face. 'You've got to piss him off, Shaz. You must.'

Shaz leaned forward, pulling a handful of tissues out of her pocket, blew her nose. 'I'm scared of what he'll do. He says if I leave him, he'll kill himself.'

'Perfect!' said Jacinta. 'One less bully.'

'But, before he does that, he says he'll kill me first,' added Shaz.

'I've been leaving messages for you,' said Jacinta, turning her mother's eyes on me. 'And then I keep missing your calls when you do ring. Then I thought it would be nice just to kidnap Shaz and bring her down here for a day or two of fresh air anyway.'

She must have seen the look on my face. 'We're only missing one lecture, Dad. Shaz needs a break.'

'You're very welcome for a day or two, Shaz,' I said, patting her on the shoulder. 'But Jacinta's right. You're going to have to get rid of a man who behaves violently towards you.' But even as I said the words, sounding a bit like a police lecture, I knew the potential realities of the situation—staying or going. Either way, Shaz could be in real strife. Her violent lover had threatened this already.

'Let's talk about this later, Shaz,' I said. 'You might need a plan of action to deal with him. Right now, I'm nipping back to town to do a bit of basic shopping. If Iona arrives before I get back, will you tell her I'm on my way?'

'I'm sorry for intruding, Dr McCain,' said Shaz.

'You're not intruding at all,' I said. 'You're very welcome. Especially if you call me Jack. You girls can sort out sleeping arrangements?'

'Sure can,' said my daughter, throwing me a look of gratitude.

I leaned down and kissed the top of her head again before turning to Shaz. 'And we'll talk further about this,' I added. 'Okay, Shaz?'

Shaz stared up at me with wide, frightened eyes. If I'd been her father, I'd have hugged her tight.

I drove to the nearest supermarket, where I bought good quantities of the basics, the frozen mango yoghurt and the nut and chocolate bars that I knew Jacinta loved, plus a Greek-style takeaway chicken. That was cheating a bit, but it'd been a helluva day.

It was almost an hour later when I got back to the cottage, lugging shopping bags, my heart lifting at the sight of Iona's car. I was fumbling with keys and shopping at the front door when it was suddenly opened and there she was, a wide smile on her face.

'You're actually here! And it's not even eight o'clock yet. Or is this a hologram?'

I put the shopping down, grabbed and kissed her.

'*Not* a hologram,' she said. 'But just to make sure, do it again.'

'I've missed you,' I said.

'Liar,' she replied.

'Where are the girls? And Charlie? And Greg?' I asked, picking up the shopping bags and taking them out to the kitchen, Iona following.

'The girls are in the spare bedroom having a heart to heart, I think. Charlie's in town using the library. And Greg is somewhere,' she said, putting groceries away.

'That smells good, Dad,' said Jacinta, appearing at the doorway and noticing the Greek chicken in its foil bag. 'Yum. I'll do some olive oil and oregano potatoes and anything else I can find.'

Anticipating my next question, she said, 'Shaz has crashed out on the sleeping bag. Iona made her this herbal tea. Smelled pretty drastic but it really calmed her down.'

'Camomile and skullcap,' Iona said.

'Sounds like something the Medicis might use,' Jacinta called as she went outside to pick oregano from the straggly herb garden.

'Go and put your feet up,' I ordered Iona. 'Jass and I'll do dinner.'

'I'm really pleased now that I bought the largest lemon meringue pie from the patisserie,' said Iona, coming over to me. 'I must have known we'd have a full house.'

One of the best things about Iona was her height so that our eyes were almost level. When she was close, I could see into the deep world behind her eyes and I held her a moment, kissing her full lips, filled with love and gratitude. 'Tonight,' I whispered, 'you'd better watch out.'

I felt her shiver at my words and press herself closer, before breaking away to look at me with her shadowed eyes. I couldn't quite read their expression but it was hard to let her go.

'Doesn't Shaz want to get away from this guy?' I asked Jacinta a little while later, as we chopped vegetables together.

'It's not as straightforward as that, Dad. She reckons she loves him.'

'*Loves* him? He bashes her!'

'Dad, you don't get it.'

'Too right I don't!'

My daughter turned her hands outwards, a graceful gesture of helplessness. 'Talk to Charlie when he comes back. He'll explain.' Sometimes my daughter sounds like a wise old grandmother. 'And ask Shaz to tell you about her father sometime. She doesn't know what love *feels* like. She believes in the words people *say*. She doesn't seem to be aware of what people *do*. Her father is a basher, too. So for Shaz, that sort of behaviour is normal and familiar. Probably feels like home.'

'You're starting to sound like Charlie,' I said.

'What's the matter with that? Charlie would understand straightaway.'

'He would, would he? Well, if he doesn't get here soon, he's going to miss out on a great dinner,' I said. 'What's the name of the boyfriend?'

'Karl. Karl Docker. He works at the university. He's one of the security blokes.'

I'll remember that name, I thought, as I asked, 'Is Greg around?'

'He saw how things were with Shaz and kindly retired to the back bedroom to give us some privacy. Said he was going to study. Most likely he's napping. Or talking to Ellie.' She paused. 'That reminds me, I've brought some of my work to show you. But I'll leave it till later,' she added, pushing the trays of potatoes and other vegetables into the oven.

'No. Wash your hands and get it now. I'd love to see it,' I said. 'Those potatoes aren't going anywhere for a while.'

I watched as Jacinta returned to the kitchen, placed a science assignment on the table in front of me, then smiled and signalled for me to open it. Turning the cover page of the assignment I saw her mark: 89 per cent, High Distinction, and felt something sting my eyes. This was the girl who'd run away at fifteen, lived on the streets of Sydney, developed a heroin habit and nearly died out there. I'd always felt so guilty that the conflicted relationship I'd had with her mother had been part of the mess Jacinta had fled. But now, after rehab and matriculating through tech, my daughter was doing first-class academic work. I flicked through the pages. 'Congratulations, Jass,' I said, leaning over and kissing her. 'You really are something.'

'Come on, Dad,' she said. 'You've *got* to say that. You're my father.'

'You couldn't stay with someone who bashed you?' I asked. 'You're not blinded by what a man might say to you. You watch what people do. Not just listen to what they say. Don't you?'

'I do now,' she said, after a pause, holding my gaze.

I thought of her mother, who had still not learned this wisdom.

Jacinta picked up the assignment, suddenly serious. 'Shaz hasn't got the sort of family where you can show a good assignment. In Shaz's family, nobody cares.'

I made a salad to go with the meal while Jacinta set the table and we sat together in the kitchen, listening to the spuds in the oven.

'Shaz could go to the police and get an AVO,' I said. 'That way, he'd have to stay away from her.'

'She doesn't want to do that. Says he'd find that too provocative. It'd make him worse.' She looked in the fridge. 'Have you seen the lemon meringue pie Iona brought for dessert? Hey, I nearly forgot.' She straightened up from the fridge. 'Some Sydney cop rang for you.'

She went over to the kitchen bench and checked the scribbled note she'd written near the phone. 'Someone called Ryan Holbrook. He left a phone number for you—some guy you'd wanted to contact?'

I glanced at the scribbled name and number. Ryan Holbrook had tracked down Ellis Smith. I hoped we'd be as quickly successful with tracking down the unknown male in Tianna's intimate photographs.

The long dining table set up in the big lounge room looked inviting with its white tablecloth, and Iona and Jacinta had hunted out the last late roses and interwoven them around several candles along the centre. A bottle of white wine sat in a ring of sparkling glasses and even the humble kitchenware seemed more elegant by candlelight.

Jacinta and Shaz, looking almost happy, proudly carried out the trays of baked vegetables and the salad. I followed them, making a grand entrance with the Greek chicken, decorated with some ethnically incorrect bacon slices.

'Delicious, Jacinta,' said Iona, tucking into her potatoes. 'These are done to perfection.'

I picked up a chicken leg and bit into it, thinking of Tianna Richardson and the odd bite marks on her body, the rumour surrounding her, and I put the leg down. 'Charlie, why do you think a woman would deliberately seek out men who treat her roughly?' I asked. Before he could answer, I felt a kick under the table.

'What?' I said, looking across at my daughter. She was mutely indicating Shaz next to her, who, with head bowed, was poking at a potato. It hadn't occurred to me that Shaz might identify with my question—might find it pointed.

'It's a case I'm on,' I said. 'Without mentioning any names, I'm really curious as to why a woman would seek out men who hurt her.'

Jacinta glared at me and I held her gaze. So much the better, I thought, if young Shaz could pick up a few tips from this discussion. Why tippy-toe round the subject?

Charlie, who had no idea of the underground discussion between me and Jacinta, finished chewing and took a good swig of wine.

'Could be a few reasons,' said Charlie. 'Why?'

I told him, aware that Shaz had put her fork down and was now watching Charlie, wide-eyed.

Charlie considered. 'Some women feel guilty about being sexual,' he said. 'Being pushed around makes it seem like it's not their idea. Absolves them of any sexual guilt. That way, it's *his* doing, not hers.'

'I think it's also because that's what they *expect*,' said Iona. 'If you've been pushed around all the time while you were growing up, you get to think that's how it is. That's how people behave with each other.' She picked up her wine glass.

'That's certainly part of it,' said Charlie. 'And maybe it's exciting for them in some way—creates some high drama in an otherwise drab and boring life. Violence can make people feel that something big and important is happening here. Being the focus of negative attention is better than being ignored—ask any kid that.'

'Hey!' Greg objected. 'Why were you looking at me when you said that?'

Charlie laughed. 'You were a shocker, mate. I remember.'

'And you know, there are some people—especially women,' Iona said in her thoughtful way, 'who believe that they have to put up with violence. That nobody else would want them.' She paused. 'That what they had was the best they could expect. I used to believe that. That no one could possibly love me.'

In the silence following Iona's sad confession, Jacinta flashed her a look of love that melted my heart. I was about to say something to Iona but at that moment Shaz, tears spilling from her eyes, jumped up and ran from the table. After a startled hesitation, Jacinta got up and hurried after her.

'Well,' said Charlie. 'That certainly hit the spot.'

'Poor kid,' Iona murmured. 'Maybe I should go and see how she is.'

Charlie put a hand on her arm. 'Jass is with her and knows her. What you said is the best help you could ever give.'

'Maybe I shouldn't have raised the issue at the table,' I said. 'What do people talk about at dinner parties?'

'At my dinner parties, we mostly talk about bands and cars,' said Greg. 'Oh, and girls.'

Charlie helped himself to some more chicken. 'Then there are some people who seem to want to feel even *more* victimised—too many people, not only women, enjoy being martyrs. Makes them feel special and different. "Look at me, how much I can suffer."'

He finished his glass of wine with relish. 'But masochism is not really my thing, Jack. You'd have to talk to one of the experts.'

Jacinta returned and we all looked at her, expectantly.

'She wants me to drive her to the station,' she said. 'I can't talk her out of it. Honestly, Dad. Why did you have to start on that?'

'Now just a minute,' I said. 'You want me to censor conversation in this family? It wasn't even about Shaz!'

'Try and tell her that,' said Jacinta.

'I wouldn't,' said Charlie. 'She wouldn't believe it. People in pain are extremely self-obsessed. They feel *everything* is pointed at them.'

'What Iona said could be very helpful to Shaz,' I said. 'Someone who's been in a similar position and now thinks well of herself is a powerful teacher.'

Jacinta sat back down, looking up at me from under her brows—her 'little bull' look that I hadn't seen for years. My mobile rang and I cursed, wishing I'd switched it off.

'Leave it,' said Iona as I twisted to unhook it. 'You're not at work now.'

'Maybe I should have a word with Shaz?' Charlie said.

Jacinta shook her head. 'No. She said she doesn't want to talk, she just wants to go home. I'm going to finish dinner and take her into town so she can get a train or a bus back to Sydney.'

'Are you going to answer that bloody phone or not, Dad?' Greg asked. 'Kill it, can't you?'

'Leave it, please,' pleaded Iona.

'It might be important,' I said, standing up with the mobile in my hand.

'So is this, Jack,' she said, indicating the family feast, the diners settling down after Shaz's sudden exit.

'Come on, Dad. Give the bad guys a break for a while, eh?' said Greg, patting the seat beside him. I stood there a moment, immobilised by indecision, watching Jacinta eat too quickly. Then, to my great relief, the mobile suddenly stopped ringing and when I checked, there was no message.

'See?' said Iona. 'They rang off. Couldn't have been very important.'

I sat down and added some carved chicken breast to my plate.

'Jacinta, don't bolt your food like that,' I said. 'And I think it's crazy of Shaz to expect you to run her into town now. And crazy of you to let her do it. Tell her you'll do it in the morning.'

Jacinta threw her fork down. 'Jesus, Dad! Will you get off my case? She's my friend, not yours. And I'll make my own decisions about my friend without you telling me how I should do it!'

I heard her muttering something about no wonder people used drugs and ignored it. Family dinners, I thought. What a bloody minefield. The mobile started ringing again and I put the fork down, defeated. 'I have to answer it. Someone ringing my mobile after hours like this means someone really needs me...' I trailed off as I unhooked it again.

'Yes?' I said.

'That matter we spoke about earlier,' said Dallas Baxter. 'I've organised your introduction. You've got a meeting tonight.'

I knew straightaway what he was talking about and now, with all eyes on me at the dinner table, I was not keen. 'Let's make it another time. I'm busy tonight,' I stalled.

'Too damn busy,' Jacinta muttered.

'No, you're not,' came Dallas's sharp reply. 'You don't know how hard it's been for me to set this up after being out of the scene so long. I've had someone nominate you. Your first engagement is *tonight*. That was part of the deal.'

My mouth was suddenly dry. I hadn't expected this to happen so soon—and with such bad timing.

'Knock this back and you're on your own,' Dallas said in the face of my continuing silence. 'This has been very awkward for me. I've had to call in every favour for you.'

'Where do I go?' I said finally, capitulating.

'That hasn't been organised yet. I'll call you back when I know the other party and the place.'

'Dallas, getting me the colours and the numbers is the most important thing. I don't have to actually go and—' I suddenly realised the silence around me. Everyone was listening so I hastily changed what I was about to say. 'I don't feel so well. I don't want to have to go out again,' I said, truthfully. But he'd rung off before I could finish what I was saying.

Greg, who'd stopped chewing while I was speaking, nodded vigorous approval. Iona reached over and put her hand on mine as I put the mobile away.

'You're not having a bet, are you?' Greg asked. 'What's with the colours and numbers?'

I couldn't look Iona in the eyes, knowing that any time tonight, the damn thing would ring again and then I'd have to make some excuse and leave the cottage to go out to meet some unknown woman waiting in an anonymous hotel or motel, ready to have sex with a stranger. With me. This idea was disturbingly arousing. I reminded myself that I was living with the woman I loved and was gathering intelligence, not embarking on a sexual liaison. My cold and headache would stand me in good stead as an excuse to avoid sex.

'Are you okay?' Iona asked, frowning.

I cleared my throat again. 'I think I'm coming down with a cold,' I mumbled.

'Dad! You've already got a cold!' Jacinta pointed out, restored to better humour.

'It's got worse then,' I said lamely.

My daughter regarded me with a particularly hard look. 'You're up to something. What's going on, Dad?'

'Nothing,' I said.

'You *are* having a bet! Look, everyone! Dad's actually *blushing*!'

'Jack, it's true! You are blushing!' said Iona, delightedly.

'Don't *you* gang up on me too!' I pleaded.

'Okay. Anyone know where the nearest Gamblers Anonymous meeting is round here?' Greg joked.

'You should come too, son,' I said. 'The way you've been studying it's a bloody gamble whether you'll pass this year or not.'

In Greg's roar of mock outrage at my remark, I almost didn't hear the mobile ring again. I grabbed it and this time a text message flashed onto the tiny screen. I jumped up, excusing myself. *Olims at Braddon = 9 with colour Blue. Suite 12. 21.30 hrs. BE THERE.*

Quickly, I switched the mobile off and glanced at my watch—not much more than half an hour to get there. Somehow, Dallas had lined up Blue. Excitement mixing with guilt made it hard as hell to play it cool. I knew now that Blue was a woman.

'I'm terribly sorry,' I said, turning to everyone at the table. 'I have to go out. Something really urgent has come up.'

No one said anything. I looked around at four pairs of eyes, all of them disbelieving. Then, in the silence, Iona, who had stopped eating and crossed her knife and fork neatly, stood up, threw her table napkin down, pushed her chair back into the table and left the room.

Everyone else was silent as I followed her down the hall into our room. Feeling like an absolute bastard I closed the door behind us.

'Iona, sweetheart. Please,' I said.

She turned to face me. All traces of the melting woman who'd been in my arms in the kitchen had vanished.

'This can't go on, Jack,' she said, tears shining in her eyes. 'You have to make a decision about us. Otherwise there's no point in me being here.'

'Iona, I *have* to go out. I wouldn't do it if it wasn't absolutely essential. You must know that.'

'I don't know any such thing.'

'It's very important to me that I follow every lead I get—if it will get me closer to bringing Claire Dimitriou's killer to justice. Tonight's meeting will hopefully bring me face to face with someone whose identity could be crucial to this investigation.'

'And tomorrow night, will you be out meeting someone else who's crucial to another investigation? And someone else the night after that? And the night after that? When is this going to stop?'

'Once these cases are over—'

'There'll be new ones! More and more cases,' she interrupted angrily. 'I've been here long enough now to see your pattern.'

'What pattern?'

'You're still behaving as if you're an investigating detective on call! You're not! You're an analyst—a scientist with a nine-to-five job, plus overtime. A nine-to-five worker with a commitment to a woman he claims to love!'

'It's not just a claim, Iona.'

'I'll bet Florence and the others go home at five o'clock!'

'Iona, these murdered women can't tell us what happened. They need me. I feel I *owe* them.'

'What about *this* woman?' she said, pointing to herself. 'Don't you "owe" me something too? We have a pledge, an understanding!'

'Of course I—'

'What are you running from? Why do you avoid being with me? Didn't you say in Sydney that you'd been searching for a lifetime for a woman like me?'

'I did, and it's true!'

'Then why do you continue to make choices that keep you so busy? So that you have no time for me? For us?' The distress in her voice cut me.

'Iona, please. Once these two cases have been wrapped—'

'I don't know what to say, Jack. I don't know how else to put it so that you can *hear* it—hear what I'm saying. We continue to come to this place in our conversations. Over and over I hear myself saying the same things. You too.'

Even while she was talking, I was looking around, making sure I had everything necessary, money, keys, wallet.

'You're not even listening now, are you? You've already gone.'

'Iona, I—'

'I don't want to hear it, Jack. Just go.' She turned away from me and went to the window, staring out into the night, breathing hard as she contained her anger.

'I'll be back as soon as I can.'

She didn't move. Nor did she speak as I left the room. I called a 'goodbye' to the group and hurried outside to the car.

SIXTEEN

Concentrating on the drive to Braddon was difficult. I felt torn in two and the knowledge that I'd left Iona hurt and disappointed was hard for me to live with. Yet it was essential that I honour my duty to the murdered scientist Claire Dimitriou. The sense that I owed her my time and my talents seemed overwhelming and, for a moment, I caught myself wondering why this was so. The things Iona had said to me, I'd heard from another woman, my ex-wife. I'd heard the same complaints from Annette Sommers about Peter Yu. As far as I knew, no one else on the staff, except perhaps the grim little palynologist, seemed to take on the sort of extra workload that I did. Why did I behave like this? Especially now, when I had so much to lose? Iona's questions blazed in my mind and, somewhere, I knew they were legitimate and demanded answers. The thought of Iona changing her mind about me and going back to Sydney filled me with anguish and yet here I was, walking out on a festive dinner she'd been looking forward to so much, one that I'd *promised* her. What was going on here? *In* here, I thought. In me?

There were plenty of car spaces in the gracious grounds of Olims but I parked my wagon across the road from it, just in case. I glanced at my watch. It was just past nine-thirty.

Blood pounded in my ears and again I had to remind myself that I was attending to business, gathering essential intelligence and not meeting a woman for an illicit assignation. For a second, I wondered what the hell I was doing, visiting a stranger in a hotel instead of being with Iona, but after sussing out that Suite 12 was on the second floor, I nodded to the receptionist as if I owned the place and hurried upstairs.

I had to walk the length of the hall before I came to the room. I knocked and waited, heart pumping hard. Nothing. Maybe, after all this, I'd been stood up. This was a double blind date after all. But, faintly, I could hear music coming from behind the door and with it a subtle fragrance, the sort that Jacinta sometimes liked around her— floral essences in an oil-burner. I knocked again and this time I heard a woman's voice. 'It's not locked. Come in.'

Maybe she was in bed already. This thought gave me a shock because I'd assumed there'd be a getting-to-know-you chat first. And in that chat, I'd hoped to gain further knowledge of the workings of the group. If she was in bed, there were two ways I could go. Either risk humiliating her and getting her badly offside by saying I had a bad cold—true enough—and suggesting she get dressed so we could talk. Or climb in with her and hope we could talk before. That way, I could claim a headache. Yeah, right, Jack, I heard myself say. Who was I kidding? But that would mean crossing a boundary. It was the sort of dangerous engagement that could throw a future prosecution right out the window.

'Don't be shy. It's okay,' she repeated through the closed door. 'Come in.'

I should have walked away right then. But I didn't. Instead, I opened the door and went in. Then I stood still. Staring.

If only she *had* been in bed.

What I saw shot straight to my brain, activating nerve paths long hidden under civilised niceties, flash-flooding circuitry with energy. I stood transfixed, unable to move, to speak. Immobilised by the sight of her magnificent, naked arse raised high in the air, exposing her Brazilian; the rosy slit and, above it, the cute brown button of her anus. It was all I could do to stand my ground. My body was powered by an almost unbearable urge to leap on top of the crouching woman on the bed and screw the arse off her.

Then came her low laugh as she twisted her head round to see me, peering past her raised haunches. Our eyes locked and I recognised her. As I did, the sexual energy stiffening my cock, increasing my heart rate, started to drop away. Reason screamed: this is impossible. Get out. Now.

I backed away and felt for the door behind me, watching her as she slowly lowered her body, rolling over to face me, fair hair draping her naked shoulders, pink nipples jiggling on her breasts, the smile on her lips fading.

'Not staying to play, Dr Jack?' she whispered, her voice mocking.

I grabbed the door and wrenched it open, stepping outside, blinded with shock and lust, almost tripping on the stairs. I walked back to my car as fast as I could while trying to maintain some dignity. I scrambled in, heart racing, slammed the door, sat in the dark, getting my breath and my balance. Realigning myself.

Not till then did I realise I was shaking all over.

In a few moments, I was steady enough to drive. I somehow managed to get back to the cottage on autopilot. I didn't see the road; my mind was filled with the primal vision I'd just witnessed.

When I pulled up outside the cottage, I sat there a moment. I couldn't go inside like this so I got out of the car and walked around a bit, recalling now the fight with Iona, looking up at the icy stars, shivering.

It was after ten thirty when I quietly opened the front door and crept past the closed door of our bedroom, going through to the lounge room where warm firelight flickered and Charlie sat, listening to some orchestral piece on the radio and working on his laptop.

I went straight through to the bathroom, calling out something vague to Charlie's enquiries, and had a shower. Eventually, the shaking in my legs subsided and I got out.

Charlie looked up from closing the lid of his laptop.

'You came in fast, bro. On the run?'

I muttered something. 'Is Iona in bed?'

'Yes,' he said.

'Where are the kids?'

Charlie looked at his watch. 'Jacinta should be back any time now.'

'She's got to get away from that guy,' I said, relieved to be talking about Shaz and not myself. 'He sounds like a real mongrel. Maybe the dinner conversation will give her a different perspective. Even though Jacinta was pissed off with me. Shaz must get out of that scene.'

'She's not ready to leave him yet,' said Charlie. 'Like the poet said, human beings can only bear so much reality.'

I removed the cuddling lemurs from the chair and sat opposite him, waiting for my brain and body to resume their normal settings.

'I gave Shaz my card when she was leaving,' said Charlie. 'Told her I'd be happy to see her on discount rates if she wanted to sort something out. It helps to talk about it with an objective stranger.'

'The girl's in big trouble,' I said.

'So are you, bro.'

I was suddenly exhausted with it all, the shock of Olims, the way things were between Iona and me.

'Yes, I am,' I admitted.

'I'm having a drink. Want some fruit juice?' Charlie asked.

I shook my head and Charlie poured himself a brandy. Lurching into the kitchen, still feeling shocked and shaken, I tried to remember how to make coffee.

'You better tell me what's going on,' Charlie called.

'Hell, Charlie, I wish I knew,' I said as I came back into the living room with my hot drink.

'You look a little better than when you first arrived,' he said, leaning back in the old armchair. Outside, a forlorn calf wailed in the distance, emphasising my silence in the face of my brother's intense scrutiny.

'You want to talk about it?' Charlie asked.

'Not really.'

Charlie settled back even further in his chair, put his drink down and comfortably crossed his legs and arms. 'I think you'd better,' he said.

'I don't quite know where to begin,' I said, after a long silence.

'You could begin with the problem that's developing between Iona and you,' he suggested.

'But something else just happened—'

'Let's take them one at a time? First, what do *you* think the problem is?'

I cast about, trying to find a concise definition. 'Iona thinks that I'm on the run from her—that I avoid time with her by working too hard,' I blurted out eventually. 'She says I keep taking on responsibilities that aren't really mine.'

'And is it a fair comment?'

I considered. 'Maybe that's what it looks like to someone else,' I said finally. 'The way I see it is different. I'd never thought about it until you mentioned it and she started complaining about it. It was just what I *did*. But now, I've had to examine why it is, and it's because I feel deeply *obligated* to do whatever is in my power to help the dead. This might sound peculiar but that's the feeling—that I have a duty, that I owe it to these victims.'

Charlie nodded. 'At least you've got an idea of what's driving you.'

'*Motivating* me,' I corrected.

'You prefer that word?' Charlie asked, raising one of his dark eyebrows.

'"Driving" makes it sound like I'm not in control of the process,' I said.

'That's right,' said Charlie. 'That's why I used it.'

'What do you mean?' I asked, irritated.

'And this behaviour of yours is hurting Iona,' said Charlie, ignoring my question.

I stood up and walked around the room, restless and angry. 'What am I supposed to do, Charlie?'

'What is it you want, Jack?'

'You know that. I want Iona. I want to live with her and make a good life together.'

'And how exactly are you going to do that? What action are you going to take? What plans are in place for that to happen?'

'Well, I asked her to come and live here,' I said.

'And?' Charlie prompted.

'And what? She got a job in the first month. She said she was happy living here. She goes to Sydney once or twice a month to catch up with friends and an old uncle.'

'So Iona's obviously made plans to live here with you but I was asking what *you're* doing,' said Charlie.

'It shits me when you go sphinx-like,' I said. 'Going on with questions like this. I'm asking you for your help, not a bloody interrogation!'

'Jack, you've got to know what you want and how to get it before you can achieve anything.'

'I know that,' I said.

'I don't think you do—not when it comes to relationships. You know it in your work life very well.'

'What am I supposed to do?' I said, capitulating. 'Give me a hand.'

'Think about it for a while,' said Charlie. 'But not for too long. I've got a feeling Iona has had enough of you—or rather, she's had enough of not having enough of you, if you get my drift.'

'She says I shut her out,' I said.

'And do you?'

I poked the fire and found a good-sized log to put on for the night, then raked the coals around it, watching the flickering tongues of flame emerge underneath and wrap around the wood.

'I suppose I do. I never seem to have the sort of unhurried time for pottering around that Iona wants.'

'That would be too dangerous,' said Charlie.

'What do you mean?' I asked, irritated by his remark and knowing exactly what he was doing.

'Just what I'm saying. You don't want to open up to her so you keep busy. That way, the moment never comes. You should ask yourself one day why it is you're so scared of opening up to a woman.'

I'd had enough of this conversation. 'Something happened. Just a while ago,' I began.

We both turned as we heard the front door being unlocked and Jacinta's footsteps coming down the hall. She threw herself on the old lounge, pulling a knitted scarf from around her shoulders and flinging it wildly behind her. 'Shaz is crazy! I did everything I could to persuade her but she said she had to get back. That means to *him*. It's like she's under some evil spell.'

'Jazza, she's not ready to leave him,' Charlie repeated. 'It'll take time. But let's hope this evening we've started a process with that discussion—even though she found it so confronting. There could be a very good outcome a little further down the track.'

'You sound like a clinical psych,' she said. Charlie shrugged and I could see Jacinta's feathers settling down again.

Finally, she stood up and kissed Charlie then me goodnight. 'Dad, I think I overreacted earlier. Shaz *should* hear other people's experience and ideas.'

'How else do we learn to change?' I said.

'You tell him, Jass,' said Charlie. 'I've been trying to influence your father and getting nowhere.'

Jacinta rolled her eyes in a way reminiscent of Genevieve's mad-horse look. 'It's an impossible job,' she said. 'I've been trying for years.'

'Hey,' I protested. 'What is this? Get Jack week?'

'Dad. I know it's none of my business and you two have to sort things out, but I really like Iona. She's a terrific woman. I was really sad at what happened tonight.'

'I'm sorry, Jass. I'm not so good at some things.'

'You look sick or something,' she said, staring closer. 'You okay?'

'Sure I am. Go to bed.'

She gave me another concerned look, picked up the lemurs, draping them over her shoulders, and went to her room.

'Okay,' said Charlie, when he heard the sound of the spare bedroom door closing. 'Where were we?'

I took another deep breath and told him about the partner-swapping sex group, the colour and numerical codes favoured by the group and, finally, my own trip to Olim's to meet Blue as I tried to gather intelligence on the group. I stopped for a moment at the point where I'd opened the door of Suite 12, my mind filled again with the overwhelming vision of complete sexual availability.

'Go on,' Charlie prompted.

I cleared my throat, then continued, describing exactly what I'd encountered there, right down to the golden stubble surrounding Sofia Verstoek's Brazilian.

'That sure would break the ice!' Charlie leaned forward. 'Great way to meet. So?'

'So, what?' I asked.

'So what did you do?'

'What do you think I did? I backed right out of there, fast as I could.'

There was a silence.

'Spoilsport,' Charlie said after a long silence.

'For Christ's sake, Charlie, she's a colleague! *And* a subordinate.'

'So? From what you've just told me, no one else seems to have worried about that sort of nicety. I didn't think that sort of thing mattered any more.'

'Bloody oath it does,' I said. 'To me, anyway. Not to mention the fact that I'm deeply involved with a woman—'

'*Deeply* involved?'

'You heard me. I'm deeply involved with a woman I love very much,' I repeated. 'I'm not interested in playing up. Plus I'm acting chief and the woman at Olims is someone I might pass in the corridors a couple of times a week. She's also someone I don't consider to be particularly stable emotionally.'

Charlie chuckled. 'Could make for some interesting moments in the lunch room.'

He was right. I sat and considered the possible consequences of my visit to Suite 12.

Now that Sofia Verstoek had recognised me, I realised, unless I made sure I was seen as a genuine member, the group would close ranks. If I wanted to get in, I'd have to leave my investigator's hat right out of it.

I recalled other, classic unsolved cases concerning suspicious deaths where scientists and doctors had been involved: of lovers poisoned on a riverside bank celebrating New Year's Eve, a doctor bashed to death by an unknown intruder while garaging his car late one night.

'You missed your chance, bro,' said Charlie. 'You could have got laid *and* gathered intelligence.' He stood up and went to the small bar I kept, pouring himself another brandy.

'I can't seem to get her image out of my head, Charlie. Every time I close my eyes, it's all I can see.'

'I'm not surprised,' he said. 'My guess is that it's hardwired in the male brain. Earlier even than *Australopithecus.*'

'Australo-*what-icus*?'

'Early hominids,' said Charlie. 'Our primitive forebears back millions of years. Female squats and presents, male pounces and penetrates. Simple, beastly copulation. Easy.' He sat down with his brandy, grinning like a chimpanzee. 'And somewhere, hidden under layers of repression and civilisation, it's still to be found in the modern male consciousness.'

'Give it a rest, Charlie.'

'But *my* brother is unique,' Charlie teased, going out to the kitchen. 'He's given this great chance to do the manly thing. The *natural* thing! Talk about an investigator's dream.'

'Nightmare,' I corrected him. How was I going to manage this at work? Pretend it hadn't happened? Take her aside and tell her that, as far as I was concerned, the incident was closed and no further communication would be entered into? Get her shifted to another laboratory like Florence and the others wanted? At least that way, my dignity could remain reasonably intact. The idea was very tempting.

'What are you doing out there?' I called. 'Come back and help me.'

'I'm getting you something to eat. There's no chicken left.'

'I don't need food. I need some advice! Do the psychologist thing. Make a helpful suggestion, for Christ's sake.'

But he kept fiddling out there and I could smell bread toasting. He returned some minutes later with buttered toast and still-warm baked potatoes.

'I haven't mentioned that the female involved in all this is completely obnoxious,' I said, taking a piece of toast.

'With a fantastic arse!' laughed Charlie.

'It's no laughing matter. What am I going to do about this woman?'

'Don't you think there's a much more urgent matter involving a woman that you should be considering?' said Charlie, suddenly serious.

Charlie had this ability to switch from mirth to gravity and I'd always found it disconcerting.

'If you don't do something about your relationship with Iona, you will lose her,' he continued.

That shocked me and I put my toast down. 'Did she say something to you?'

'She didn't have to,' said Charlie. 'I saw how distressed she was. But yes, I did talk to her.'

'And?'

Charlie raised his hands. 'You know I don't do that—tell tales. *You* need to talk to *her* about this. About what you're going to do.'

He came back to the chair opposite, sipping his brandy. 'The males in our family are a pretty sad lot when it comes to making good relationships with women,' he said. 'Take me, for starters. I seem unable to get properly serious about a woman. They call me the playboy in my supervision group and it's not entirely a joke.'

'But you're only a youngster,' I said, taking a potato. For me, Charlie always feels perennially young.

'I'm only twelve years younger than you,' said Charlie. 'And it's high time I found a possible woman and became a father. But I have difficulties with intimate relating which we won't go into right now. So that's me; our father had a dreadful marriage with an impossible woman; your first marriage was to a borderline personality disorder—'

Charlie and Genevieve had never seen eye to eye, to put it mildly.

'Who had no capacity whatsoever to grasp that there are other points of view than hers. So what I'm saying is, you have to face the fact that now you've been fortunate enough to have found a possible woman—'

I interrupted him. 'That's the second time you've used that term. What do you mean "possible woman"?'

'A woman who is not so emotionally and psychologically disfigured by the events of her childhood that she's able to connect in a reasonable and mature way, with compassion and understanding. A woman who can be part of a shared experience—a couple—without trying to dominate the other. Iona Seymour *is* possible. So don't bugger up this wonderful chance—the Great Experiment—because of *your* character defects.'

'Exactly which character defects do you mean?' I said, knowing I had quite a few, although I thought I was continuing to deal with them. 'Tell me.'

'There's really only one to be concerned about. Your persistent inability to slow down—to stop and just be.'

'Be what, for Christ's sake? What am I supposed to be?'

'That's such a typical workaholic's response!' Charlie laughed. 'You don't have to be anything. Just *be*.'

I stared at my brother. At least the stunning incident of earlier in the evening had receded from my memory as I considered Charlie's words and proceeded to defend myself.

'I know how to do that. What about when I just lie on a blanket on the river bank and look up at the willow leaves and the sky? Isn't that just being?' I countered.

'It certainly is,' Charlie said. 'So tell me, how often do you do that?'

'Come on, Charlie. You know how busy I've been lately.'

'How often do you do it, Jack? Honest answer now, please.'

I cast my mind back. I remembered a time last year when I'd waited for Jacinta and Iona to meet me for a picnic at the river bend and how the air had been filled with drifting white blossoms that turned out to be tiny butterflies. Then there'd been another occasion with just Iona and me, not long after she arrived here. I told Charlie about these.

'So there you are, Jack. You can do it once a year. That's about it, isn't it?' He stood up and stretched. 'The rest of the time you're racing around like a hairy-nosed wombat.'

'Wombats don't race,' I reminded him.

'You need to think very seriously about what your priorities are, Jack. Presumably, you want this woman in your life?'

'Of course I do!' I said, pissed off that he should question me.

'Then you've got to *make* space and time for her. You've got to learn to open up to her, to let her in. Show her who you really are. You can't wait until things quieten down at work. It's that simple. When was the last time you had any quiet time at work?'

I tried to think of some quiet time in the last few years, but there'd been none. Every time we thought we were getting across the workload, another homicidal martyr, with his head full of hell, would detonate something somewhere and half my staff would vanish for weeks, only to return with more work and their backlog to catch up with as well.

Greg bumped into the lounge room lugging his overloaded backpack and a long batik carry bag. 'I'm heading off tomorrow morning,' he said. 'I'll get a lift with Jass.'

'Is she going?' I asked, disappointed. 'What happened to the time we were going to have?'

Greg pulled his head back, looking at me. 'Are you serious?' he asked. 'You're never here. I'll come back when *you've* got some time.'

'Okay,' I said, chastened. 'Did you open any of those?' I gestured to the books.

'Who's asking, old man?' And Greg, grabbing me in a bear hug and lifting me out of the chair I was sitting in, would have taken me down straightaway except that I remembered a piece of fancy footwork designed to interfere with any plans a superior attacker might employ. Eventually, we tussled to the floor and this time, when Greg won, it wasn't because I'd let him.

As he helped me up, I felt every year of my age.

When at last I slid in beside Iona's warm body, I lay listening to her gentle breathing, pondering Charlie's words. He was right. It *was* that simple and somewhere I knew it. Then why, I asked myself, did I constantly take on more and more work? Why did I feel so responsible?

I couldn't find the answer and so I turned my mind to my other concern. The thought of Sofia

Verstoek making herself sexually available to any man who walked through the door of Suite 12, then donning her scientific white spacesuit and frowning around a crime scene, would give me no peace. How could I ever look at the blonde down of her eyebrows again without thinking of her shaved mound? Then I tried to imagine her seeing something at venue sixteen, something that made her so angry she could murder a scientist at the Ag Station. Jealousy was a common human emotion. Claire could have let her in and Sofia would know how to leave no trace evidence. But although I could imagine Sofia as a murderer, I couldn't see how she'd give a damn about anyone except herself.

Finally, at about 3 a.m., around the same time as a storm broke overhead and heavy rain suddenly started to pelt down, I slept.

SEVENTEEN

When I woke up alone, I felt sad that Iona had already left for work, but somewhat relieved that I didn't have to talk about last night. It would take time, I knew, for the previous night's scene to settle down in my mind and I really needed to think about Charlie's words.

I breakfasted alone—neither Charlie nor the kids had emerged yet—and, after I'd cleaned up, I sat at the desk Iona used near the window of the lounge room and wrote a note. *Please forgive me for taking so long to learn a few simple truths. Let's talk soon. I love you.* I signed it, left it propped up in an envelope where she'd find it, locked up and climbed into my wagon, thinking of the busy day ahead of me. I'd decided to try and arrange a meeting at the Ag Station with Kevin Waites as well as everything else.

As I drove to work, a couple of grey kangaroos bounded away, startled from their feeding on the roadside grass, vanishing into the scrub. Even they were doing it hard in this long drought, trying to find feed so close to the dangerous road.

Focusing tightly in on work was a survival mechanism that had kept me going through my darkest hours. But now, the searing vision of Sofia Verstoek presenting herself for sexual action kept flashing into my mind. As well, the conflict with Iona underlay everything and Charlie's questioning of the previous night only served to destabilise me further. I'd heard lots of old cops talk about post-traumatic stress disorder and how flashback scenes appeared in their minds, unbidden, to torment them. I'd witnessed awful murder scenes, crash scenes, bodies fused in incinerated automobiles, children dead in toilets, but things I pushed out of my mind generally stayed put, in some underground archive where they could not trouble me. Not this time, and it was adding to my unbalanced state; as if the crowded contents of that archive had been tipped out of their accustomed places and then just tossed back in again. I didn't know how long it would take for things to settle back into the usual patterns. Blue's bold manner of greeting me had created a psychological Trojan horse, penetrating and undermining my domain of focused reason. I needed all my energy for Iona and me and I cursed Sofia Verstoek out loud as I drove, willing her to get back in her box.

It wasn't until I was sitting at work, sifting through the internal and external mail trays, that I remembered Tianna Richardson's funeral was that day and would be starting soon. I arranged for the particle samples to be sent express courier to Ellis Smith and then grabbed my jacket, hastily leaving a message with the secretary. I wanted to put in an appearance at the funeral, not only because I had known Tianna, or because of my professional connection with her, but also because the life of this woman and the manner of her death had touched me. I had helped her put on her brand new skirt, the one she'd not been wearing when she met her chilling fate. There was another reason, too.

I got to the church just in time to see the pallbearers carrying the coffin out to the hearse.

'Jason Richardson's here,' Brian said as I joined him near his car and he indicated a battered Holden panel van with a surfboard on racks on the roof. 'I'm going to the cemetery for the burial and, after that, I'll bring him back with me,' he continued. 'Meet me at the station in an hour or so?'

He walked over to the wide entrance with its Norman doors and I followed as he made his way past the people flowing out in the other direction. Earl Richardson, in a dark suit and black tie, was accompanied by a brown-robed and sandalled Franciscan—Father Basil, I imagined. As they came closer, I realised Earl's tie wasn't black but dark purple. The man had no taste. Trailing behind him was the youth who had to be his son Jason, awkward in a black suit, white-blond hair and dark tanned features, eyes squinting against the glare of the skies. Earl saw me and his eyes lit up. Damn, I thought.

'Jack!' Earl said, stepping forward with his hand out to shake mine. 'How kind of you to come to this sad occasion.'

I took his hand and, while Brian busied himself with the Franciscan, Earl introduced me to a woman nearby.

'Deirdre Delaney, meet Jack McCain, one of my oldest friends. Deirdre is a bereavement counsellor—she's been a tower of strength to me in all this.'

'Earl is so brave,' said Deirdre, shaking my hand then imprisoning it with her other hand. Looking at her black lace mantilla over her yellow hair, her brows wrinkling in professional concern, I found I'd taken an instant dislike to her. 'I simply don't know how he's managing to stay so calm and centred despite his loss,' she said.

I retrieved my hand and she reached up to brush dandruff off Earl's black shoulder. I excused myself, watching Earl as he shook hands with other members of the funeral, while Brian took Jason aside, leaving the bereavement counsellor and the Franciscan to each other.

Little more than an hour later, I was at Heronvale Police Station, sitting at a table with a bad coffee in front of me, watching on a colour monitor the proceedings in the next room where Brian was taking a formal statement from young Jason. Except for his long, narrow face and nose, something like an anteater, Jason reminded me of Damien Henshaw. He was a similar age, with the same blond hair and rangy, tall physique. I tuned out as Brian went through the formalities with the young man and wandered over to the window. From there, I could see Jason's van. I stepped outside and went over to the vehicle. It was a Holden, about eight years old and due for registration. I walked right round it and then noticed that the passenger door was unlocked. I couldn't resist.

Pulling on a pair of gloves, I opened it and looked inside, picking over the assorted mess on the floor—girlie and surfing magazines, takeaway food containers, the odd beer can, an empty plastic sandwich envelope which I sniffed. The scent of dope was unmistakeable. I pulled open the glove box and several items fell out onto the mess on the floor, including a fancy and well-used bong, packets of cigarette papers and a circular tin of tobacco, almost empty. It was the last item to slide out that mesmerised me. Carefully, I picked it up and slipped it into an envelope, then closed the door and went back inside, making a call to Brian in the next room as I did.

'Come outside a minute. I've got something you might want to use in your interview,' I said. 'I found it in young Jason's car.'

'Jack,' Brian started to say, his tone a warning.

'It's okay. It was unlocked.'

I watched Brian on the monitor as he excused himself and, moments later, he was with me.

'Look,' I said, fishing out what I'd found, letting it hang from my still-gloved fingers.

Brian frowned for a moment before light dawned. He hooked it closer with his pen and studied it. 'This necklace goes with those earrings,' he said.

'Nineteenth-century Victorian rose gold in a distinctive design of interlinked hearts set with green peridots and seed pearls,' I quoted, remembering the gist of the jeweller's certificate. 'Just like this necklace.'

'She must have had a matching set,' said Brian as I dropped it back into the plastic bag and handed it to him. 'How come Jason's got this?'

'Good question,' I answered.

A few moments later, I watched on the monitor while Brian presented the necklace in its packet and laid it on the table. I studied Jason Richardson as closely as I could under the circumstances. He stiffened, clearly shocked.

'You've got no right!' he cried. 'You've been going through my things!'

'Not *your* things, Jason,' said Brian. 'This doesn't belong to you, does it?'

Jason, who'd been leaning forward against the table that stood between him and Brian, pushed himself away.

'Just relax, Jason,' I heard Brian say. 'And tell me about how this comes to be in your glove box.'

Tianna had been wearing the matching earrings when her body was found and, unless we had a coincidence of the greatest magnitude, Jason Richardson must have taken this necklace from his stepmother.

I watched as he twisted awkwardly in his chair. 'Can I have a coffee or something?' he asked.

'Sure,' said Brian. 'I'll go and get one, and while I'm gone I want you to think about this: your stepmother's just been murdered and in your glove box we've found a gold and pearl necklace that matches the pair of earrings she was wearing when she was killed. You can see what people might think.'

'Shit! I never touched her! I wasn't even in the bloody state! Gran gave me that necklace.'

Brian's face was a picture. 'Gran? Your grandmother gave you that necklace?' he said, all eyebrows. 'What? To wear to impress your mates?'

Again, I watched the monitor closely, but Jason's face was half-hidden by the way he was sitting.

'You just wait here and think about what you're telling us, Jason.' Brian stood up and went out the door and I watched Jason sitting there, hunched over, staring at the wall while Brian left him to stew.

Brian was back a few minutes later with two steaming styrofoam cups.

From somewhere I could hear a butcherbird carolling his call sign and another, more distant bird answering.

'Tell me about the necklace, Jason.'

Jason sipped his coffee and grimaced. 'I usually have sugar,' he said.

'We're all out,' Brian said. 'Sorry.'

'You ask Gran,' Jason said.

'I will,' said Brian. 'In the meantime, we need a little cheek scrape from you. A DNA sample.'

Jason spluttered in his coffee.

'Just to put you in the clear,' added Brian.

After Jason had provided his sample, I accompanied him and Brian back into the interview room.

'So how do you spend your time, Jason?' I asked.
He shrugged. 'Work a bit. Surf a bit. Travel a bit.'
'Bit of a nomad, are you?' Brian asked.

Jason didn't answer so I decided to engage him a little. 'Nice sort of life,' I said. 'I've got two kids—not much younger than you. I'd love to be able to do that. No bosses. Just work when I need to and keep driving all round Australia.'

'Not just Australia. I've been to England too,' he said proudly. He hadn't achieved much else in his life so far, I thought.

'Not much surf there,' said Brian. 'Why England?'

'I was trying to trace someone,' Jason said, his voice wavering. I remembered Earl Richardson's first wife had, quite wisely, I thought, gone back to the UK. Must have been hard for Jason—feeling dumped by his mother when he was just a youngster.

'Your grandmother bring you up?' I asked.

He nodded.

'That must have been hard sometimes.'

The grunt he answered with might have covered a lot of ground. It could have meant my mother didn't want me, nor did my father or his new wife.

We sat in silence for a while.

'So did you trace your mother?' I asked.

Jason looked away and shook his head. 'She didn't want to be found,' he said, voice sad, muted. 'At least, not by me.'

'How do you know that?'

'I just know it. Okay? She didn't answer any of my letters. I found an old aunt who said she'd had a letter from her and that she'd run off with some man. She was entitled to a new life,' he added.

'And a baby is entitled to his mother,' I said. 'You must have resented Tianna Richardson for replacing your mother.'

He shrugged again, either with bravado or genuine indifference. 'I did okay.'

'So how were your relations with Tianna?' Brian asked.

'They were fine. How often do I have to tell you?'

'Okay,' I said. 'We'll have to have a chat to your grandmother.'

Jason sat back and looked at me. 'That necklace,' he said. 'I should tell you. Actually, Gran didn't exactly give it to me.'

'You pinched it?' I asked.

'It's not like that.'

'Then how is it?' Brian said.

'Gran was going to give it away anyway. It's not like she wanted it.'

'You still haven't answered me,' I reminded him. 'Did you pinch it?'

'Tianna loved that set. She was always on about it.' Another of his shrugs. 'I took it. I thought it might have been valuable if she was after it.' He looked at me. 'It was my mum's.'

I frowned. 'Why would your mother give it to her mother-in-law?'

'How would I know? I took the necklace last time I visited Gran's. From the drawer.'

'We still need to talk to your grandmother, Jason,' said Brian. 'We need to confirm if you're telling the truth now.'

'She's not here at the moment,' he said.

'Let's check that out, shall we?'

Brian left the room to make a call and came back a few minutes later. 'No one's answering at her number, but I'll be sending someone over later to check it out,' he said.

'See? I told you. She's away for a few days. Visiting a friend. She's often away.'

'Okay, Jason,' said Brian. 'You've already tried some bullshit story on me. We'll be checking to make sure if the necklace was in the possession of your grandmother. What if you didn't get it from her at all? What if Tianna already had the stuff? And you had a big fight with your stepmother? Or maybe you were pinching it from your stepmother except she returned unexpectedly and you killed her. Is that what happened?'

'No way! Like I told you, I pinched it from Gran's place!'

'We have a witness who recalls you having a terrible fight with your stepmother,' Brian said. 'And your father too. You didn't get on with either of them, did you? You better stay in town, Jason. Until we've checked that what you've been telling us is true—that the necklace came from your grandmother's place,' he added.

'How's your father?' I asked.

Again the shrug.

'You don't get along with him, do you?' I said.

He didn't answer me, remaining silent.

Brian told him he could go. 'But don't leave town, son, until we've spoken to your grandmother,' he said.

Jason got up and hurried outside and over to his van. I watched through the window as he jumped in and slammed the door shut, long blond hair shining. I felt sorry for the kid, abandoned by his mother, neglected by his father, lost and wandering around surfing.

I stayed with Brian and had an instant coffee with him in the meal room while he organised notes into various folders. I flipped one open and glanced at the contents: photographs, print-outs of statements signed by those who'd made them. I pulled out Earl Richardson's and glanced at it. *I spent the evening watching television until about ten o'clock then I went to bed. I did not know anything about my wife's death until I was woken by the police at four-thirty in the morning.*

Pulling the Richardson folder closer, I leafed through it, pausing at a clipping from a recent edition of *Police News* complete with candid photo taken at a Christmas party. I read how Earl Richardson had thrown a shindig at Balmain Leagues Club for some of his erstwhile colleagues in the police; the close-up shot of Earl showed him as a jovial host, holding a schooner of beer aloft.

'I used that photo in the first twenty-four hours or so,' said Brian, 'until I had a better shot. Showed it round the street but no one had seen him the day Tianna was murdered.'

I looked closer at a blonde woman behind Earl in the picture and recognised her. 'That's the bereavement counsellor,' I said, pointing her out to Brian.

He nodded. 'I remember her. She was at the funeral.'

'I wonder why you'd need a bereavement counsellor *before* your wife's death,' I said.

'She's associated with the Glebe morgue,' Brian said, flipping through his notes on Jason Richardson, sorting them into some sort of order. 'What do *you* make of young Jason?' he asked.

'He's a lost soul leading an aimless life,' I said, leaning back in my chair as I considered the young man who'd just left.

'Do you think he's a killer?'

'You should be asking my brother that, not me,' I replied.

'Come on, Jack. You've been around longer than me. What's your gut feeling?'

'Jason's the sort of kid who often ends up involved in criminal matters,' I said, looking through the crime scene photographs. 'Raised by a grandparent, few ties to the community, no girlfriend, a loner, on the road a lot, unemployed—he's not on a good trajectory. You'd have to ask how he supports himself moving around like that.'

'He reckons he's on an extended working holiday,' said Brian, 'but he was very vague on names and places. Bit of bar work, fruit-picking, that sort of thing.'

'He could hate Tianna for taking his mother's place,' I said. 'I'd like to talk to the grandmother, find out a bit about his background.' I wrote down her address on Sparrows Ridge Road some fifty kilometres from Heronvale out in the high country that surrounds the nation's capital. Then I stood up to leave. Brian accompanied me, grabbing a drink of water from a cooler near the foyer.

'He reminds me of someone,' I said, pushing the door open, searching my memory. 'That long blond hair and the surfboard on the top.'

'Me too,' said Brian. 'Martin Bryant.'

EIGHTEEN

The best thing to do when an emotional issue was pressing hard, I'd always found, was to swamp the brain with work and push the issue right out of the picture. Genevieve used to call me cold and heartless but my technique of pushing suffering away became a survival habit when I was growing up and a great asset in our marriage. So, although my heart was heavy with the way things were between Iona and me, and my memory filled with the primal vision of last night, I continued on to work, planning my speech to Sofia Verstoek in case we should bump into each other along any of the alleyways of Forensic Services.

When I got to the office, I looked through the manila folders containing the enhanced and enlarged photographs of the soles of the boots Damien Henshaw admitted to leaving at Tianna Richardson's house. Next to these, in a separate sleeve, were the enlargements of the partial bootprint left in the soft dust near the murdered body of Tianna Richardson. I compared the images with the naked eye. It looked very promising, with similarities between the actual boot sole and its negative imprint. To take my mind off both Iona and the Brazilian, I unlocked the boots from the exhibit locker and readied myself for work in one of the examination rooms.

An hour later, after a thorough examination of the boots, I had no doubts. The bootprint we'd found at the crime scene was a faithful reproduction of the left boot of the pair we'd found at Tianna's place. Again I went over the details, the fine cracks and scrape marks on the rubberised sole and their counterparts pressed into the soil in the photographic enlargements. In court I could say on oath that *this* print came from the sole of *that* boot, and I'd demonstrate my certainty with dozens of matching points.

But what really clinched it for me, and was highly likely to do the same for a jury, was what I found in the grooves of the soles of both boots. I dug this out carefully and bagged it. I'd give them to one of the other analysts for comparison with the other samples, and that way we'd have independent findings to present to a court. But I had no doubt at all what the results would be.

Then I cleaned up again, wrote up my findings so far, made a few phone calls—including one to Kevin Waites, confirming today would be suitable to meet at the Ag Station—then called Brian.

I picked up Brian from the station and we dropped round to the address where Damien Henshaw had said he was working. No one was there so we drove to his place and walked through long grass to knock on the door. In my right hand I held a large carry bag. A young woman in jeans and tank-top opened the door and let us in like a lamb, introducing herself as Kylie. I found myself wondering if Damien's fiancée had a Brazilian.

'Hey, Damo!' she yelled as I took in the room. 'Someone to see you.'

Immediately, I recognised her for a cleanskin; she hadn't picked up on who we might be, nor Brian's profession.

A collection of beer cans and liquor bottles were displayed around the old-fashioned picture rail, posters of polished popular singers hung on the wall and cushions were piled around the floor in front of a still warm open fireplace. Several ashtrays, whose contents I felt sure could prove interesting, completed the decor. A small kitchenette was attached, piled with unwashed dishes and pots. A cold breeze came through the louvres that formed its window.

Moments later, Damien walked in, hair sticking up all over his head, tousled from sleep. As soon as he saw us, he was immediately alert and hostile, shooting a look at Kylie, who hovered in the doorway of the hall leading towards the bedrooms before disappearing.

She reappeared a few minutes later with her mobile phone and her gleaming brown hair tied back in black velvet ribbon. 'Got some shopping to do,' she said cheerfully and, waving to us all, she left the house.

Damien Henshaw's wary eyes panned between me and Brian.

'Dr McCain wants a word with you, Damien,' said Brian, eyebrows high, manner mild. 'He's found something that he thinks you might be able to help him with.'

Although what I was about to do wasn't strictly by the book, I'd always believed that good drama shouldn't only happen in the courtroom. On several occasions back in the state police, I'd seen confessions happen after some particularly interesting theatre.

I lifted up the carry bag and put it on a low coffee table, pushing aside several unwashed glasses. Then, drawing out his bagged boots, I said, 'Damien, these are the work boots we found at Mrs Richardson's place—your boots, the ones you wanted to pick up when Detective Kruger and I were at Kincaid Street.'

'Can I have them now?' His question seemed guileless enough.

'Unfortunately, no,' said Brian. 'Dr McCain will need them for some time yet.'

'How long?'

I pulled out the photographic impressions of the left sole, which I'd printed off slightly enlarged for better visibility.

'Damien,' I said, 'that's what the bottom of the left sole of your work boot looks like.'

He knew something bad was in the offing but didn't know yet how bad. He seemed to diminish, to pull himself back as if waiting behind his defences to see what might happen next.

'So?' But his manner was no longer the careless, take-it-or-leave-it of our last encounter.

'If you look closely, you'll see where I've drawn little white arrows—lots of them—to demonstrate all the areas of abrasion and individual scrape marks.' I paused, watching his face carefully as I drew out my second photographic impression. 'And this is the photograph of a footprint—a bootprint rather—that Detective Kruger and I found a couple of metres from the body of Tianna Richardson. In the car park of the Blackspot Nightclub.'

I held them up together.

'Snap!' Brian called.

Damien Henshaw's eyes darted from one photo to the other. 'But there are thousands of boots like that!' he said. 'All my mates wear these work boots. It could be anybody's bloody boot!'

I shook my head, as if in disappointment. 'Damien,' I said, deciding to help him a bit, 'you don't get it. There are tens of thousands of this sort of work boot in circulation. But only *you* have worn these particular boots in a certain way. With this sort of evidence, it's not the soleprint—as you say, they're *almost* identical with thousands of others. I say "almost" because there are always tiny irregularities that show up at high magnification. But as well as those microscopic differences, only *you* have scraped them on this or that sharp object and left a little mark in just that place.' I pointed to the first photograph and its enlargement of one small jagged tear on the sole of the boot. 'Which in turn,' here I pointed to the second photograph, 'leaves a perfect negative imprint of itself, just like the stamps your teacher used to give you in kindergarten.'

I paused to let it sink in, then said, 'Your boot,' and, pointing from the first photo to the second, 'your bootprint.'

I watched his face closely, reading puzzlement, then frowning disbelief.

'Every sole is an individual,' Brian was saying. 'It's like a fingerprint.'

'You're lying! You're just making it up to frighten me!'

'We don't have to make anything up, Damien. And neither Detective Kruger nor myself have to lie.' I tapped on the two photographs. 'This bootprint is a silent witness. Evidence that cannot lie. That cannot perjure itself.' Locard had added a caveat after these words, but I didn't quote it just then. Instead I placed the two photographs down beside the bag on the coffee table.

'Well?' Brian asked. 'You've heard what Dr McCain's just told you. Have you anything to say to us?'

'What we need to know, Damien, is how come your bootprint got to be there? Just a little distance from the murdered body of a woman you've been screwing?' I added, in a very matter-of-fact tone.

Damien Henshaw had been rendered speechless. I'd seen this a couple of times before and a couple of times it has happened to me. I knew from my own experience in moments of shock how the brain scrambled to make sense of incomprehensible data. But I couldn't speak for him. This could be the shock of the innocent person when confronted with some appalling accusation. But, equally, he could have been rendered speechless at how we'd tracked him back to his crime. I knew I needed to keep an open mind. Many years ago, when a young detective, I'd confronted a suspect with footprint evidence, telling him we'd found his bootprint outside the victim's bedroom window. The man had hanged himself in prison that night. A clear admission of guilt, everyone said. I wasn't so sure. Because I hadn't yet scrutinised his boots. That case still haunted me and now it was being brought to life again by the similarities with some of the evidence we were building up against Damien Henshaw. Later, when I *had* examined the hanged man's boots…

I stopped myself in my tracks with that one and swung my attention back to the moment. I looked hard at Damien Henshaw. Right now, was he running through a series of plausible lies? Lies that might get him out of this? Or was he completely devastated by evidence he had no way of disputing? I didn't know, but I was determined to keep up the pressure.

'How did you do it, Damien?' Brian said. 'And why did you kill her?'

I saw the colour rush back into his face. 'You can't do this! Just rock round to my place like this and start accusing me of murdering people!'

'You haven't heard the worst of it yet,' Brian said.

Damien Henshaw's panic-stricken eyes darted from me to Brian, from the photographs back to us.

'How is it that in the grooves of those boots,' I said, tapping the first photograph, 'I found coarse grey sand particles? How do you explain that the only other place I've found that coarse grey sand is deep in the wounds of two murdered people?'

'Two people?' he shouted. 'What are you talking about? You can't accuse me like this!'

'We're not accusing you of murder—*yet*,' Brian said. 'We want to know if you have some sort of explanation. We want to hear your side of things. This is your *chance*.' Brian made it sound as if Damien was in the running for some sort of prize.

But Damien, hunched forward, head in his hands, kept slowly shaking his head. 'I can't believe this,' he said, over and over.

'How come?' Brian said, keeping the pressure up. 'How come your bootprint turns up in dust at the Blackspot? And how come Dr McCain finds the same grey sand in your boots that the pathologist found on the bodies of *two* murder victims?'

'Two murder victims! What are you talking about? It's not possible! I wasn't there! I was at the pub. I told you. You can ask Kylie and the others.'

'Maybe you were,' said Brian. 'But you weren't there all night. That pub shuts at midnight.'

I was aware of the front door opening and Kylie suddenly arrived back in the room, carrying some groceries. Her smile faded. She didn't know exactly what was going on, but she knew it wasn't good.

'What's happening?'

'Tell them, Kylie,' said Damien. 'Tell them that I was at the pub the night that woman was killed. And then I went to your place.'

Kylie stood frozen. After a few moments she lowered the shopping to the floor and straightened up again, finally taking in the situation.

'Are you the police?'

Brian flashed his badge. She barely glanced at it.

'Tell them, Kylie,' Damien repeated. 'Tell them how I was with you that night.'

'Yes!' she shouted, matching his emotion. 'He was! He was at the pub with us all and then later he came back to my place—' Her speech faltered, the aspect of her face subtly altered as she raised her hand then dropped it.

'Tell them!' Damien's voice was desperate.

Brian and I watched as a silent subterranean drama played out between the two young people. 'He was with me that night,' she said, repeating Damien's words in a flat voice. Then she turned and, almost tripping over the bags of groceries, went to the front door. She wrenched it open.

'Kylie?' Brian's voice halted her mid-step. 'Has Damien told you about Karen Fleiss?'

In the small living room, the atmosphere almost crackled. I shot a look at my colleague. Who the hell was Karen Fleiss and why hadn't he told *me* about her?

'Who?' asked Kylie, giving words to my own question, looking from her boyfriend to us, then back again. All the while Damien stayed slumped in his seat, slowly shaking his head.

'Why don't you tell her, Damien?' Brian persisted. 'She's your girlfriend, sorry, *fiancée*. She has a right to know what you did. Karen was your girlfriend too, once, wasn't she?'

'What are they talking about, Damien?' Kylie's voice was a whisper as she went over to her boyfriend. '*Tell me*. Who are they talking about?' she said, voice rising.

'I think you should tell her,' Brian continued, glancing my way.

'It's none of your fucking business!' Damien shouted, agitated. 'It's none of anyone's bloody business. I was acquitted!'

'Acquitted?' Kylie was standing in front of him, hands on her hips. 'What did you *do*?'

'I didn't do anything! This stupid bitch reckoned I'd raped her. The police charged me. I had to go to court. And it was thrown out. That's all there is.'

'Seems like Damien's not going to tell you the whole story. So I will,' said Brian, looking from Kylie to me and then back to Damien. 'Some time back, a girl called Karen Fleiss was found wandering naked and hysterical on the roadway near where she lived. She said Damien Henshaw, who was then sixteen, had offered her a drink and smoked some dope with her in a disused house on the building estate where they lived. When he put the hard word on her, she said no. She was *fifteen*. He raped her.'

'She *said*!' Damien yelled. 'It wasn't rape. She was too scared to go home when it got late. She said her father would belt her. So she made up this fucking lie about some rape or something.'

'Did you do it, Damien?' Kylie said. 'Did you rape that girl?'

'I swear, Kyles, I didn't. She came with me. She wanted it.'

'He used her bra to tie her hands up,' said Brian. 'She tried to get away and he tackled her down. She was bruised all over.'

'She liked it rough! She said so! I was only giving her what she wanted!'

Kylie's face was stricken. But we had a job to do.

'Like Tianna Richardson wanted?' I said, remembering the rumour. 'Except you got too rough?'

'Jesus, Damien,' said Kylie. 'Is that why they're here? Because they think you've got something to do with that woman's murder?' She swung on me. 'What's Damien got to do with that woman's murder? He doesn't even know her!'

No one said a word.

'Do you, Damien? You don't even know her! Why don't you tell them?'

The silence lengthened.

'Why don't you say something? You didn't know that woman. Tell them you didn't know her!'

'I knew her,' Damien said, his voice almost a whisper.

For what seemed one long moment, Kylie stood, planted in front of him. I saw the struggle she had to keep her emotions from bursting out. Then, ignoring the pile of groceries on the floor, she went to the front door again.

'Get a lawyer, Damo,' she said from the open doorway, then slammed the door behind her.

Brian placed a restraining hand on Damien's arm as the young man struggled to get to his feet. 'I think we'd better do this properly at the police station, Damien.'

'I've already told you—I don't know anything about her murder,' said Damien, but the fight had gone out of him.

Brian snapped his notebook together and gathered up his things, readying to leave. I was heading for the door when a strange sound made me look back. Damien was crying.

'It's not what you think,' he said. 'There's something I haven't told you.'

NINETEEN

I jumped into my wagon, watching Brian and Damien disappear in the squad car Brian had called for. I sat there a while, unable to get Kylie's stricken face out of my mind. I knew it could take the ground from under your feet when you learned something huge and shattering about the person you thought you knew better than anyone in the world. I remembered how I'd felt when I'd first found out about Genevieve's lover.

It was looking bad for Damien Henshaw. And I was extremely curious about how the death of Albert Vaughan fitted into this. Why had Damien killed him too? Maybe he hadn't, and the appearance of the coarse sandy particles in Albert Vaughan's injuries were some sort of freakish synchronicity.

I was about to follow Brian down to the station to see if I could listen in on the interview when my mobile rang. It was Dallas Baxter, huffing and puffing.

'Kevin Waites is here, saying that you organised to see him today. I wish you'd thought to include me in your generous invitation.'

'That goes without saying,' I said, realising I'd forgotten to clear it with the boss of the Ag Station when I'd organised my meeting with Kevin earlier that morning. 'I'm on my way.'

I sneezed and cursed. My cold was freshening again. As I opened the glove box to fish out a tissue, I noticed the keys from Peter Yu's carton on their red and white plait. I slipped them in my pocket and blew my nose. My head felt heavy and a dull ache behind my eyes reminded me of how unpleasant head colds are.

I walked through the main entrance doors of the Ag Station just in time to see Kevin Waites disappearing into Dallas Baxter's office. I hoped Dallas would do the right thing and give the man his job back. Too many jobs in modern Australia offered little or nothing in the way of security, despite the fall in unemployment levels, and a cleaning job in a government department was better than a lot of other jobs. Pauline was just visible through the open door in the office beyond the reception counter, wearing a tight skirt and a blouse with frills. I filled in the visitors book and took my appointed number as Pauline clicked over in her high heels to usher me in.

'The lab book from Dr Dimitriou's lab,' I asked. 'Can you think of anywhere it might be?'

'By rights, it shouldn't really leave the laboratory, but it might be at her place,' Pauline said. 'I can't believe all the dreadful things that have been happening. This used to be such a nice place to work.'

'Tell me, Pauline, do you have any ideas of your own as to what might have happened in the Terminator Rabbit laboratory on Monday?'

Pauline cocked her head to one side, considering. 'I think someone came in from outside and killed Claire and somehow took Peter away. I just can't believe that he'd do anything to harm her. He thought so much of her. He told me once how much he admired her.'

'Did you like Peter?' I asked.

She hesitated. 'I like all the people who work here,' she answered.

I smiled quickly. 'That's nice,' I said, matching her bland response. 'Have you had any luck finding any details on Cheryl Tobin's records?'

'I can give you her last known address.'

Two years ago, Cheryl lived at an address in Turner. I took the details and thanked Pauline, then turned as I heard the door to Dallas Baxter's office opening. Kevin Waites emerged smiling and I felt I'd done something good. Maybe it evened up the balance a bit for the undoubted damage I'd already done to my relationship with Iona. I wanted to send a text message to her, something romantic, but I feared hitting the wrong note. I sometimes wondered if women knew how much we worried about—feared, even—their reactions to our well-intentioned mistakes, perhaps they'd be kinder.

'He offered me my old job back,' said Kevin. 'Said he'd been misinformed about me.'

I congratulated him and said, 'Before we go to the laboratory, I'd like you to show me where you were when you overheard the disagreement between Dr Dimitriou and Dr Yu.'

By this time Dallas had joined us and the three of us walked along the corridor down to Claire Dimitriou's former office, her name still on the door.

Kevin stepped back a few paces.

'Just here,' he said turning and looking upwards. 'I was just here on the stepladder.'

Standing a couple of metres from the doorway, he went through his story again, pointing to the light fitting he'd replaced.

'Okay,' I said when he'd finished. 'Let's go and have another look at the lab.'

'What on earth for, Jack?' Dallas's pink cheeks flushed. 'Surely a *cleaner* isn't going to be able to assist you!'

'Kevin might notice something you or I might have missed,' I said.

'Like what?' Dallas's voice was icy.

I gave him a look. 'Like the subtle changes that can be easily overlooked,' I said. 'The sort of thing someone who's in and out of an area all the time and is familiar with it is far more likely to notice.'

I could see that Dallas wasn't at all happy about this and it made me wonder why.

The three of us walked through the building towards the old Level 4 lab. As we went outside to cross to the Faithful Bunnies building, I turned to Kevin. 'She must have come back over here to the lab not long after you'd overheard them. Or maybe they went over together.'

'I can't say,' he said. 'Like I told you, Dr Yu closed the door, I finished fitting the light, then climbed down the stepladder and carried it back to the storeroom. It was time for me to start cleaning the labs at the other end of the station.'

They must have gone over to the lab, I thought, where they were isolated from everyone else. That's when he could have shot her. Or maybe he drove away, still brooding over the argument, and came back later. With a weapon. Or he drove away and never came back, because *someone else* came into the lab. Annette Sommers? Cheryl Tobin? And was the murder witnessed by Peter Yu who then bolted? Maybe the killer followed Peter Yu and dealt with him later. Doubtless, Claire Dimitriou would have opened the security doors for either of the women.

'If she worked back,' said Dallas, echoing part of my thoughts, 'Claire would have had to let him in. She wouldn't have let in a stranger.'

Maybe she didn't have to let anyone in, I thought. Maybe the killer was someone else already working in the building who didn't bother filling out the Working Alone Register. I glanced at the array of cleaning and antibacterial agents stored in the annexe before the negative pressure chamber. We stepped through. No negative airflow was necessary, nor the need for any precautions.

Dallas and I walked straight through into the laboratory, past the door with the silly little cartoon on it, leaving Kevin behind. As I stood there, looking around the sterile lab, something occurred to me that I should have thought of a hell of a lot earlier.

'What if Peter Yu *didn't* leave the premises?' I asked.

Dallas swung round at me from his slow pacing alongside the central workbench. 'Of course he's left the premises. Surely he would've turned up by now if he were still here! There were police crawling all over the place.'

'Hey,' said Kevin standing stock-still and staring at the corner. 'What's going on here? They've all gone!'

I turned to see him pointing.

'What's all gone?' Dallas snapped.

'The rabbits. They've all gone! They were all in their cages through there, in the dirty room.' Kevin stared with disbelief. 'Dr Dimitriou's rabbits.'

I followed his gaze into the corner where the stacked cages gleamed, as clean and empty as they'd been on my first visit. I turned to Dallas. 'You didn't tell me anything about any rabbits.'

Dallas blinked. 'I didn't *know* about any rabbits! I'd have to check the records.'

'But you *must* have known they had animals here,' I said, finding his denial unconvincing. 'You're the boss! You'd have to sign off things like that.'

Dallas Baxter's ruddy cheeks suddenly paled.

'I can't believe you didn't know,' I continued. Either the man was a liar or a total incompetent.

'Of course I know that Claire *had* animals,' he said, flustered. 'She'd applied for some and been allocated them. But that was ages ago. Now you mention it, I do remember the ethics committee meeting. But I'd forgotten about that. How was I supposed to know how many damn rabbits she had? I've got enough to do keeping up with staffing levels and administration without knowing where every damn mouse, sheep and rabbit is in the complex!'

'I know the staff who have animals,' said Kevin, obviously relishing this discussion—the cleaner knowing more than the boss. 'Dr Claire had six rabbits. Nice little fellows. They had numbers instead of names—1 to 6 with the initials RP.'

Rabbit pox, I thought. Six different strains. 'When did you last see them?' I asked.

'They were all here last Friday when I cleaned out the cages. Any day I come in to clean, I always give them a pat.' He threw a deadly glance at his boss. 'Well, I always *used* to.'

'Six rabbits in separate cages?' I checked.

Kevin grinned. 'They've got to have separate cages. You know what rabbits are like.'

'They're not here now,' I said. 'So where are they?'

Dallas glared at me, his polished pink brow darkening. 'I don't know. Under the circumstances, Jack, the *murder* of one of my scientists, rabbits were the last damn thing on my mind!'

'Where might they be?' I persisted. 'In another lab? Maybe the tests were discontinued and they've gone somewhere else? You know as well as I do that every experimental animal must be accounted for. They must have gone somewhere else. They can't have just vanished.'

'If they're not in their cages,' said Kevin, his voice sad, 'there's only one other place they'd be.'

Of course. I couldn't believe it hadn't occurred to me earlier. I *did* need a break, missing obvious things like this.

I looked at Dallas and, although his glare was still in place, I had no doubt he was thinking the same thing.

'We'll have to have a look,' I said. 'You'll have to check it out.'

'But I don't quite see—'

'The animal pit,' I interrupted him, impatient. 'We have to examine the animal pit.'

A long silence in which Dallas seemed stricken. 'You don't think that Peter Yu is in the *animal pit*?'

'I'll get Brian and the crime scene people back here straightaway,' I said. 'This should have been checked out earlier. Where is the animal pit?'

Dallas shook his head. 'I can't take you there.'

This was getting ridiculous. 'You don't have any choice,' I said, my voice hard. 'This is a murder investigation. The police must be informed.'

'You don't understand. I'm not refusing to take you.' His voice faded away. 'I *can't* take you. I've never actually known where the animal pit is.'

He must have seen the look on my face because he said, 'I know, I know. It seems unbelievable. But I've made it my business not to know. I'm very squeamish about things like that.' He waved an arm vaguely. 'I know it's somewhere out there.'

'I'll show you where it is,' said Kevin.

I called Brian and left a message for him to call me urgently, while Dallas and Kevin went to get the keys from the key cupboard. While I waited for them, I castigated myself. The animal pit was one place that should have been checked out thoroughly and as soon as possible after the murder of a scientist—of anyone—on these premises. I'd be having a serious chat to Brian about the search he and his crime scene team had made of this place.

But then, thinking more about it, I realised he wouldn't have known about the pit. And if no one mentioned it, Brian wouldn't know what questions to ask. Even so, this was not my job, not my case. But the second I thought about leaving the Ag Station and driving back to Forensic Services and the pile of administrative jobs that awaited me, the Brazilian filled my mind again, distracting and deterring me from anything sensible. This case was my only hope of distraction from the primal scene of last night and the mess I was making of my relationship with Iona.

Kevin and Dallas returned with the keys and I followed Kevin outside, Dallas bringing up the rear. Crickets fell silent at our passage through the sunburnt grass. After following the path for a minute or two, we arrived at a three-metre cyclone fence topped with barbed wire. Set in it was a padlocked gate and, through the wire, I could see a large, circular clearing. In the centre of the clearing the ground level had sunk to a smaller circle, about the size of a small dam, which was now surfaced with sticky mud after the rain. It looked as if the pit had been dug by a backhoe, the dug-up soil then pushed into a circular rim, like that on a shallow dish, so that animal corpses could be dropped into the pit and then soil either bulldozed or backhoed in on top of them. A shovel stood by the fence; a few scoops with it would have covered lab mice and rats. The larger beasts might need a tractor.

Brian rang as I was contemplating the pit and I told him where we were. I could hear from his voice how tired he was. He'd told me earlier how he'd spent most of the night at a suicide call-out.

'I didn't know about any damn animal pit!' he said.

'You're not the only one,' I said. 'Even the boss here didn't know where it was.'

'Damien Henshaw's still denying everything. We've let him go for the time being but I'm determined to nail that little prick.'

I listened to Brian ventilate for a moment and then explained a little more about the animal pit and how I hoped that digging it out might throw more light on the death of Claire Dimitriou.

By rights Brian should have come straight over, but I knew he probably hadn't slept for twenty hours. 'I'll send Debbie over with the camera,' he said.

'I've got my video camera with me,' I replied.

'We still haven't been able to interview Anthony Dimitriou,' said Brian, as if reading my thoughts. 'They found a whole lot of antidepressants in his gut. I'll get to him as soon as I can.'

'If you were going to murder your wife,' I said, 'would you get a third party to do it while she was at work?'

'That's what I've been thinking,' said Brian. 'It hasn't got the smell of a third-party killing.'

'Would you be happy if your wife was sleeping around with your workmates?' I asked.

'I wouldn't hire someone to kill her,' said Brian. 'Too messy.'

'And remember, it was a consensual thing,' I said. 'They were all in agreement about it.'

'Things can start out consensual and then they change. Ask a few rape victims.'

'My gut feeling is that he had nothing to do with it and is the sort of guy who can't live without his wife.'

Unaccountably, a memory surfaced from my crime scene days of a farmer whose wife had left him—the guy had tied a rope around a large tree trunk in a paddock, attached the other end around his neck, pointed the car away from the tree, then accelerated like crazy. He'd calculated it would break his neck and he was right. The rope had sheared his head right off. I'd come to the scene and stood staring for some minutes, trying to make sense of his torso still sitting up in the driver's seat. I'd found his head on the back seat.

'I'll talk to you later,' Brian was saying.

Kevin sorted the key to the gate from a crowded key ring but I told him and Dallas we had to wait. Debbie and a young bloke arrived about an hour later. Before unlocking the gate, I went back to the scullery and washed up, getting my spacesuit on and borrowing a pair of gumboots from the Ag Station stores.

Inside the wire, I filmed the surface of the animal pit. Debbie, her suit and shoes already muddied, squatted down, taking stills. The glittering bodies of flies coated the surface of the pit with a moving burnish. Despite the layers of earth moved by a front-end loader, the stink of rotting animals permeated the surrounds. Finally, I grabbed the shovel and slowly started turning the earth over, in methodical sections.

'Can't we wait till the earthmover comes?' Debbie's companion said.

'No earth-digger,' I said. 'That could destroy valuable evidence.'

'Evidence of what?' he challenged.

'That's just it, Mark,' Debbie called back from where she was discarding her filthy shoes and pulling on a spare pair of gumboots. 'Dr McCain is right. We have to do it by hand. Layer by layer.'

After Mark got his gear on, the three of us stepped into the surface muck and started to work slowly and steadily, sectioning off the area into manageable slices. Even though I'd been in this game for too many years, I still found the stink revolting. Digging around in putrefying, maggot-seething material was not how I'd intended to spend my time.

Over the next few hours, apart from grunts and curses, we generally worked in grumpy silence. Despite the autumnal weather, sweat streamed down my body as I shovelled heavy, maggoty, muddy soil aside, while Debbie carefully picked over the piles. We took turns with the hose to wash down anything interesting.

Finally, we'd dug over the whole area and all we'd discovered were dead sheep in various stages of putrefaction. The more recent burials were the worst, with stomach bags bursting their contents under the pressure of our booted feet.

'How am I going to get this filthy stink off me?' Debbie wailed, jumping back to avoid one of the last shovelfuls thrown by Mark. 'I'm supposed to be going out tonight. My boyfriend's coming down from Sydney this afternoon for a dirty weekend.'

'Give him a shovel and he can help out here,' I said, unearthing a particularly nasty conglomerate of flesh, maggots and filth. 'It doesn't get much dirtier than this.'

'Know what I hate most about maggots?' said Mark.

'I'll be the mug. Tell me,' I said, leaning on my shovel.

'When you touch the infested area, it's *warm*,' he said.

When emptied of its loosened soil and animal remains, the sides and bottom of the pit showed the unyielding subsoil, a dull grey colour, hard as stone, untouched by rain for aeons.

'We've dug over the whole area,' I said, 'and it's clear that there's nothing human here.'

'No missing scientist, that's for sure,' said Debbie, trying to wipe sweat from her face with the back of her filthy gloves.

I made one last foray through a pile of rotten intestines and my shovel knocked onto something hard. Maybe a large animal's skull or pelvis, I thought. But just in case, I squatted and used my double-gloved hands and a small garden trowel. Gradually, I uncovered something wrapped in stinking mud-covered plastic.

It was a large once-white plastic bag, the size of a green garbage bag, and, although filled with bulky objects, too light to contain a human body. Carefully, Debbie and I started freeing it from the surrounding mud while Mark videotaped the process. Finally we had it up on the edge of the pit, where Mark hosed it down.

'I don't know what's in there,' I said, looking at the strange shapes whose angles had torn holes in the plastic in some places.

'Something stinks,' said Debbie, moving back at a whiff.

'Let's bag the whole thing up and take it away for a good look,' I said.

I lifted it into the waiting bag and we carried it back inside to the scullery, put it in one of the deep stainless-steel tubs and washed it down thoroughly. Now that it was cleaner, I could see that it was tightly tied off at the top with black and white striped tape. Mark filmed while I lifted it out of the sink and placed it on a nearby bench top.

'I'm going to take it away to an examination room and do it properly,' I said.

'I can't stand the suspense,' said Debbie tearing off her filthy suit.

'You'll be the first to know,' I replied.

Debbie gave me a look. 'That was a joke,' she said.

I cleaned up and finally took the bag to the back of my wagon.

'Mark, you mind the exhibit book and finish up here,' said Debbie. 'I'm going home for a long hot soak in my tub.'

Mark and I used the facilities at the Ag Station to hose ourselves down and took showers in their wash-up area. On my way out, I called Pauline from her office and showed her the keys we'd found among Peter Yu's possessions. She looked at them and at me.

'I heard you dug up the animal pit,' she said, anxious concern in her eyes.

'And found dead animals only,' I said. 'But it's these I want to know about. Have you seen them before?'

'Yes,' she said, picking them up and frowning. 'They're Peter's keys. I remember that red and white plastic.'

'Do you know what they're for?' I asked.

'No,' Pauline said, putting them down. 'I just remember seeing him fiddling with them once or twice.'

'Recently?' I asked, thinking of my discarded girlfriend theory.

'Oh yes,' she said. 'Just last week. That's why I remember.'

I gathered up the mystery keys, said goodbye and stepped outside, pleased to be out of there.

TWENTY

Once at Forensic Services, with the bag from the animal pit duly logged, and Peter Yu's keys on my desk, I realised I was very keen to get to work on examining the contents of the bag. Close attention to this new development in the Claire Dimitriou/Peter Yu puzzle was just what I needed to keep my mind focused. I placed the bag on the clean white paper under the bright lights and could see vague outlines of what looked like lab glassware and plastic containers. I rolled the bag over and looked closer at what the other side revealed. Pressed close to the misty plastic inside was matted fur. There was no way I was going to open this bag without full protection; I needed to head out and get the appropriate gear before I could continue further.

Turning to leave the examination room, I saw Florence looking at me through the glass window in the door and I beckoned her in.

'I was hoping you'd be in today,' she said, as she bustled over, pushing thick hair back from where it had slipped from its tortoiseshell comb. 'There're a few things I need to discuss with you.' She paused, her mouth assuming an expression of distaste. 'I'll get my least favourite person out of the way first,' she said.

I again fought the memory of the Brazilian, unsuccessfully.

'Sofia Verstoek,' she said, then, looking up at me, added, 'What's that strange look on your face all about?'

I rearranged my features to business-like.

'No, I'm not going to complain. I know that's useless.' She gave me another look. 'Actually, it's because I'm *concerned* about her. It's true that I don't like her, but there's something going on. Either she's giving money to the poor, which I very much doubt,' said Florence with a dismissive snort, 'or she's paying someone off. Something's going on with her that's not right. I thought I'd better tell you.'

I signalled for her to go on, genuinely curious now, not to mention concerned.

'Yesterday, when I looked out and saw her, she was arguing with a man in a car and then she got in with him.' She lowered her voice. 'I actually thought she was going to have sex with him but she didn't. I was working back later than usual and it must have been about dusk. I could see them quite well and they seemed to be talking and then the body language got a bit brisk. Then I saw her get out of the car, go back inside and come out again a few minutes later, and then I saw her giving money to *him*!'

'And?' I asked, very curious.

'Nothing. He drove away. But I bumped into her in the tea room later and I could tell she was very upset about something.'

'There's no law against giving money to people,' I said. 'He might have been a relative. A friend with a problem.'

Knowing, as I did, that Sofia was Blue, I was hoping this incident was connected to the sharemate group. Otherwise, there could be a very ominous reason.

'It wasn't the first time I'd seen that fellow around the place either. He'd been parked outside the wire, on the road before. Wouldn't a friend visit you properly, at home? Not park on the roadside like some sort of mendicant?'

It was a good point. It was essential that I discover why one of my junior analysts was giving money to a stranger and I resolved to clear it up swiftly. But right now, I could use Florence's shrewdness in the matter of the case to hand.

'Florence, you were a friend of Claire Dimitriou's. What were your observations about her marriage?'

Florence looked away then back at me, uneasy. 'I feel bad talking like this, with him lying in Woden Hospital with possible brain damage. But I have to admit I've never liked Anthony. There's something sleazy about him. I've never felt comfortable around him. Claire adored him. But once or twice she hinted to me that he wanted—you know—kinky things,' said Florence, looking extremely uncomfortable.

'Like what?'

Florence's voice dropped to a whisper. 'She was terrified of losing him. But he wanted to experiment—sexually.'

It still didn't sound to me like reason enough for murder—most men who had affairs didn't kill their wives. Unless there was another woman involved and I made another mental note to check on this. The desire to be free of the spouse could become a *folie à deux*, and God knows there'd been plenty of such murders over the years—an illicit couple removing the unwanted spouse. Anthony Dimitriou had been at a conference, which could be cover for a clandestine affair. But if he'd bullied Claire into taking part as an unwilling member of the share-mates, this might go some way to explain her out-of-character blow-up with Jerri Quill. I sighed. In the murders of Claire Dimitriou and Tianna Richardson, there were just too many possibilities.

'What you got there?' Florence asked, interrupting my thoughts and indicating the plastic bag lying on the examination table.

'Don't know,' I replied. 'It's something from the Ag Station that needs examining. And I'm not going any further till I'm suitably attired.'

She picked up the mystery keys on the red and white thong. 'I haven't seen an old key like that for a while,' she said. 'What does it open?'

'That's just it,' I said. 'It belongs to a missing man and I don't know what the keys are for.'

'That red and white plaited thing,' she said, putting the keys down again, 'I'm pretty sure that's from one of the real estate firms in town. All their keys have those tags.'

I slipped the keys back into my pocket, grateful to Florence for this tip. It shouldn't take me too long to find out which firm the keys belonged to and then I'd be on the way to finding the property that went with them. 'Thanks, Florence,' I said.

'What for?' she said.

'Are you managing to get through your casework?' I asked as we headed towards the area where the protective gear was stored.

'Just. I've got a positive for semen from Tianna Richardson's panties and also from the vaginal swabs,' said Florence. 'I've got them up on my screens. It's easier if you come and see for yourself. Got a minute?'

I nodded and followed her down to her laboratory and over to her workbench.

'I'm not having a great deal of luck with this,' she said. 'I've been able to pull out one male. Whoever picked up Tianna Richardson at the nightclub had sex with her. But so did at least one other man in the last twenty-four hours before she died.'

Tianna, you are a complicated woman, I thought. Now we had multiple contributors.

'I can see spermatozoan all over the place,' said Florence, 'but so far, I've only been able to profile one individual.'

I felt for her. It was the sort of complication that made life difficult for us. *CSI* never had multiple contributors to sort out. Just a nice clean, clear profile. Wham! And there was the offender.

'I ran what I could isolate through Profiler Plus,' she continued. 'Take a look at this.'

She touched her keyboard and a coloured DNA graph flashed onto her screen, the printer started humming and a copy of the shimmering graph spat out from the high-speed printer. I took it from her.

'And this is from the sample sent up from the Sydney Forensic Unit,' she said, clicking her mouse and changing screens. The case number on the top of the paper—the sample from Earl Richardson, whose identity I wasn't supposed to know—now shimmered on the screen. I peered closer at the profiled peaks and valleys of the embattled widower and convert.

'And?' I asked, picking up the print-out of the DNA taken from Tianna Richardson's murdered body. Immediately I could see the difference.

'No match,' Florence was saying as she printed out the second profile. Except for the twin peaks at the first locus, the sex marker, there were no similarities. I wasn't surprised. I'd hardly imagined that Tianna had set out all dressed up to make love with her estranged husband. Earl Richardson was out of the picture as far as sex with his wife was concerned. Maybe this was the genetic ID of the mystery man who used to visit Tianna and whose discreet parking hadn't fooled the watchful Mrs Vera Hastings.

'Vic's been helping me with the tape lifts and vacuumed material from the inside of Tianna

Richardson's car. He found a quantity of fabric fibres,' said Florence, handing me a manila folder with some photographic print-outs while she scanned the report. 'Under magnification, these fibres have the lobed cross-section that is typical of carpet or furnishing fibres. Except they don't match anything at Tianna's place. Nor her car.'

Even if the killer had used her car, I thought, it would only be *after* we had found him that we could check out his environment and find the incriminating object from whence the fibres had originated.

'They didn't match any of the clothing she'd been wearing either,' Florence said, skimming Vic's results.

I recalled Tianna's black and silver outfit, the old-fashioned earrings that matched the necklace we'd found in her stepson's car and the heavy, unglamorous woollen skirt that didn't match anything else.

Florence hurriedly read on, turning a page over. 'Vic goes on to say that there are indications that the fibres could have come from a tartan or chequered fabric—red and green.' She folded the pages back down. It was a thorough report, although of little use to us just now.

'Foreign fibres could have been brought in by anyone. Including her Aunt Mary,' I said.

'Or the killer,' countered Florence.

'If there's any way of tracking him down, I'm confident you can do it, Florence. You and Vic. If the killer used her car, he'll have left something behind.'

'That's another "if",' said Florence. 'In a case full of ifs.'

'I'm still hoping we get a trace of him and that he's on record somewhere,' I said, though I wasn't feeling too hopeful. CrimTrak hadn't been able to find a match on its database. The killer did not have a record. Yet.

'*If* he's a shedder and *if* he used the car, and *if* it's not hopelessly swamped by everything else I'm going to find from that sample,' said Florence, jabbing a finger at the container. 'Tianna's DNA is all over everything. You know how it is. If I can't get anything clear this run, I'm going to have to send it over to New Zealand and get them to do Y-STRS. Pull out the male fraction that way.'

Y-STRs, male short tandem repeats similar to those we already used when extracting nuclear DNA, only occurred on the male chromosome. An automated system with this capacity could greatly help sorting male from female genetic material. Unfortunately, ours was still at the ordering stage.

'If he's left his mark I know you'll find it,' I said, moving to leave.

Florence made a dismissive gesture with her hand but I could see she was pleased. And it wasn't flattery. Florence was probably the best in the country.

'I'll do what I can,' she said, reaching over and trying to tidy up a pile of physical evidence packages. On the top, I noticed an empty package, with the serrated security seals cut through, about to fall and I scooped it back up. I read the case details upside down and the name and wished I'd been more delicate with my earlier questions.

'I am sorry about Claire,' I said, patting her shoulder.

'Stop patting me!' she said. 'Why do men always pat people? As if they're dogs, or horses?'

'Sorry,' I said, whipping my hand away.

'I'm processing Claire's samples this minute,' she said, as the automated system hummed through its cycles, extracting genetic material from the late Dr Claire Dimitriou's person and clothing. I wasn't that confident we'd be able to find anything helpful. Claire's killer had been very thorough.

I went to leave the laboratory again but turned at the door.

'Florence,' I said. 'Thanks—and I really am sorry about Claire.'

She twisted around on her wheelie chair to face me. 'So am I. She was a great researcher. That project she was developing will stall now. It could have saved billions of dollars in lost primary produce. God knows, the poor farmers round here have had it tough the last few years.' She pulled out a man's handkerchief and blew her nose. 'Three weeks ago we were all dancing at the golf club celebrating Claire's fortieth,' Florence continued. 'Now she's dead and her husband is fighting for his life.'

I couldn't think of anything to say.

Florence sighed. 'And the rabbit populations are building up again all over Australia after the *calicivirus*.'

The eternal fight between virus and host, I thought, and science's endless work to stay one jump ahead of nature herself. 'Someone else will pick it up. Her work will go on,' I said.

'Maybe, Jack. But Claire won't.'

'If you find any semen from her case, let me know,' I said.

'Semen? But Anthony was away on the ANZFSS conference,' she said, frowning, her face a study in concerned bewilderment.

'That's right,' I said.

I watched her face as she got it and glanced over at her humming hardware. When she spoke, her voice was small and sad. 'I'll let you know what I find.'

Back in number three examination room, fully suited up, I got focused on gently removing the sealing tape on the plastic bag with its murky contents. I wanted to do a good visual examination before applying anything more detailed, so I carefully opened the neck of the bag and started removing the first of the white squares I'd been able to discern through the misted plastic. Even before getting the contents all the way out, I could see straightaway that these were the first of several 96-welled plates, the sort that Dr Dimitriou's ELISA machine used in her laboratory. In some of the wells, I could see remnants of whatever material she'd been testing. But already we had a serious problem. The plastic was buckled and distorted, as if it had come into contact with high temperatures. Even so, I hoped to be able to discover what tests Claire Dimitriou had been running through ELISA. I recalled her kind words to Kevin Waites, 'My work is to stop them breeding, not breathing,' as I pulled out another of the distorted ELISA plates. By rights, there shouldn't be any pathogens involved, apart from harmless rabbit pox virus to carry the sterilising payload into the rabbits' systems.

I was interrupted by a loud knock on the examination room door; it proved to be Vic Agnew beckoning furiously through the window. Because he couldn't come into the lab and I didn't want to have to change everything to go outside and talk to him, I held up my mobile and, seconds later, it rang.

'We're hopeful of a match,' he said, turning away from the glass window, although I could still see him talking to me. This conversation was reminding me of Jacinta and Greg when they'd first bought their own mobiles, and how they used to ring each other up from inside and outside the house. Until their first phone bills arrived.

'Match with what?' I asked.

'Jane found epithelial cells. In the saliva on that half-smoked joint you picked up under Tianna Richardson's body. It's been amped and it's running through Mulder and Scully,' he added, referring to the nickname given to the CE machine.

If the DNA on the profile matched Damien Henshaw, I doubted if he could extricate himself. We had his bootprint at the scene and, if his DNA turned up on the half-smoked joint and his semen in the scrambled sample Florence was trying to unpick, he might even decide to plead guilty and save everyone a hell of a lot of trouble. Brian would have what he wanted. Damien might even be able to tell us something about the death of Albert Vaughan, I thought.

I was impatient to get on with my examination. Surely Vic could have told me this later.

'Gotta go now, Vic, I'm keen to get on with this,' I said, pointing to the bag. 'We dug it up from the animal pit out at the Ag Station.'

The door to the examination room opened and Vic walked in.

'What the hell are you doing?' I said, angry about the intrusion. 'What about my sterile zone?'

'You don't have to worry about that,' he said, pointing to the black and white striped tape that had been sealing the neck of the heavy-duty plastic bag. 'That's the tie from this bag, right? Jack, you're never going to get evidence from anything in that bag. Not when it's tied like that.'

'What are you talking about?' I said, feeling things were becoming surreal.

'That tape. That black stripe on it means the bag's been autoclaved. The tape changes colour and turns black during the process.'

Shit! I wouldn't be getting any information from residues in the ELISA plate wells. I'd been wasting my time.

'Sorry about that,' said Vic, departing.

Nevertheless, I rolled the bag right over, tipped it gently and there they were, Claire Dimitriou's faithful bunnies, very dead and very flattened by the pressure of their burial. For a moment all I could do was stare at the rabbits. If someone had killed them, thrown their bodies into the bag along with the laboratory glassware and ELISA plates, and then placed the whole lot in a bag to be autoclaved, the steaming heat and pressure would have sterilised everything.

I went to lift the first one up, but found I couldn't separate it from the others. They were welded in a large clump. When I lifted the clump out, I saw they looked as if they'd been cooked whole, their large eyes opaque white like those of a baked snapper. I could see splits in the pelts in several places and the bodies felt stiff and lumpy, not floppy as I'd imagined they would. I gently prised the small bodies apart—all of them lay in the same stiff position. I straightened up and stared at the wall opposite, trying to make sense of this. I arranged the dead rabbits in a row along the fresh white paper lining the surface of the examination table and stood back, studying the small corpses. The obvious reason for why the animals had been cooked was that protein denatures at 80 degrees Celsius—it would be almost impossible to discover anything helpful from the tissue of these animals. Even so, I decided they must be examined. I wondered who in Veterinary Science at the university might be an expert in rabbit post-mortems.

With a sinking heart I pulled more layers of plastic away to reveal Claire Dimitriou's autoclaved laptop. I lay it on the white paper and found I couldn't open it because the lid and the latch had melted together, reminding me of Salvador Dali's surreal, melting clock faces. I put my two hands on the edge of the table and bent my aching head, too pissed off even to swear. Nothing was going right. I dropped the distorted laptop into a sterile bag. Maybe, just maybe, *something* could be salvaged from the hard disk.

Right at the bottom of the bag, I found a flat parcel packaged up in layers of plastic film. I drew it out and lay it on the bench. From the weight and shape of the item, I'd guessed already what it might be and my excitement increased. All was not lost.

Carefully I opened the plastic to reveal the lab book, a substantial bound journal. The lettering on the front of the imitation leather cover had almost disappeared but I could just make out the names of the two scientists involved and the date the project had commenced two years earlier. 'Do not remove from lab' was also still recognisable, punched out in plastic embossed letters. I went to carefully open it and, again, my heart sank for heat and steam and fluids from the rabbits' bodies had stained it and the whole damn thing had fused together, baked and steamed into a papier-mâché block. I tried to unpeel one page and it almost dissolved in my fingers so I stopped immediately. This killer was expert in covering his tracks.

I needed a break, I thought, as I left the examination room with the laptop, plate and the lab book, hoping that Sarah, with her drying cupboard, might be able to get something from this mess.

On the way out, I ran into Vic again.

'You look terrible, boss,' he said. 'Go home.'

'Good idea,' I said, glancing at my watch. It *was* time to go home.

He walked with me to the door of his office. 'You'll be dead way too early if you don't lighten up,' he announced before disappearing inside.

I continued on to my office and hastily wrote up the latest events, then sat at my desk and mentally listed what I needed to do, starting with the Ag Station and continuing with what seemed like countless tasks. Underneath my workload, like the undermining of a low-grade virus, the problems I was having in relating to Iona troubled me constantly.

After making an appointment to visit the Ag Station, I rang the university and was given the runaround of just about every animal scientist on campus before finally being put through to Patrick Eadie, the expert on leporid mammals. He wasn't at all happy to be asked to post-mortem six autoclaved rabbits, but considering this was a murder investigation he'd somehow find the time. I rang off, knowing how hard-pressed for time lecturers and academics were these days. The old idea of a community of scholars had been replaced with something more like a production line turning out corporate units.

I packed up the melted laptop ready to go to our technical people and the fused lab book for Sarah. I looked at the plates, irritated. Why was I kidding myself? The great heat and pressure of autoclaving would have wiped everything. I'd find nothing on those plates.

My cold seemed to have stepped up another notch. I fished around in my pocket for a tissue, blew my nose and tried to call Brian, but went straight to voicemail and left a message telling him that everything we'd so painfully retrieved from the animal pit was probably useless. And that I intended to go out to the Ag Station and check out the autoclave. Maybe there was a logging system that might yield something. Then, hungry for information, I called the detectives at Heronvale and the young bloke, Mark, answered.

'Brian's in an interview right now,' he said. 'Can't say how long he'll be.'

'Tell him to ring me the minute he's free,' I instructed. 'Is Debbie there?'

'No. She's out. The general store at Braddon Vale was held up,' he said. 'Debbie's cruising around looking for a giant chicken with ninety dollars in cash.'

So much for her boyfriend arriving from Sydney. I was silent, the sense of unreality I'd experienced in the lab when talking to Vic washing over me again in an unbalancing wave. I hoped I wasn't going the same way as Peter Yu.

'Some dickhead dressed up in a chicken suit,' the detective explained. 'He got away on foot, according to our eyewitnesses. Great big orange feet.'

In a state where three murders had occurred in the same twenty-four-hour period, Debbie, the only other trained crime scene person apart from

Brian, had been sent out after someone in a chicken suit and ninety dollars. I rang off. No wonder they say the job's fucked.

I was just turning the corner on my way to Sarah's office with the fused lab book when Sarah herself appeared and almost collided with me.

'I'm sorry. I trod on your foot. Are you okay?' I asked.

'What've you got there?' she said, eyeing the bagged lab book.

I explained.

Sarah took it from me and held it up in its bag. 'It's a real mess but I might be able to dry it for you. Depends on what sort of paper it is. Looks like a good production.' She turned it over in its bag. 'Many lab books use archival quality paper. Just might be possible to separate those pages again. Other times...' Her voice trailed off.

'Whatever you can find,' I said, heading back to my office where I collected the soil samples taken from the Kincaid Street property. I needed to talk to Sofia Verstoek about some comparison work.

As I continued along the corridor, it became more difficult for me to keep my mind on the investigations. Sofia Verstoek worked just around the next corner and the closer I came to her domain, the more frequent and more powerful became the images from the night before.

TWENTY-ONE

As I approached the fresh, new dedicated palynology lab, images of the fair young woman clumping around in her shapeless spacesuit suddenly morphed into the vision I'd had last night of Blue and her fantastic arse and thighs and the Brazilian they'd contained between them. I had to turn back to the staff lounge just to clear my head and get my thoughts together for the questions I was silently rehearsing. I made myself a coffee at the automatic station, and, distracted, took a mouthful far too early, burning my tongue painfully. Slow down, Jack, I told myself.

I started rehearsing yet another approach as I added milk to the coffee. Then I threw the whole lot down the sink, took a deep breath and stormed towards her office door, bracing myself again as I paused just outside, sensing rather than seeing her presence.

Peering through the half-open door I could see Sofia sitting sideways at her desk, tailored slacks and pale-pink jumper visible under her white coat. She seemed completely absorbed in the notes she was making. I reminded myself I was a professional man of science, took a deep breath and knocked firmly. She jumped and turned around, her mouth pale with a pearly lipstick.

The impact when our gazes connected made me feel as if I'd been bounced off a hard surface. Perhaps I'd touched her unguarded self, hard as obsidian. She composed her face in its impassive mask again and stood up, walked over to the door and opened it further.

I hesitated until she gestured me inside.

'You didn't stay very long last night,' she said, and closed the door behind me. 'Didn't you like what you saw?' She leaned with her back against the door in a pose I'd only ever seen in Hollywood movies.

'I'm not here to talk about last night, Miss Verstoek.'

'*Miss* Verstoek today, is it?' she said, raising a downy eyebrow. 'I'm not surprised you don't want to talk about last night. After all, you completely failed to keep up your end of the deal,' she added, deadpan. With her hair pulled straight back from her face and the slight grey circles around her eyes, she looked older than I'd noticed before. Maybe centrifuging pollen assemblages by day and being Blue by night was taking it out of her.

'As far as I'm concerned, discussion of last night's incident is closed. I was acting on information received. I knocked on a door. It was the wrong door. End of story.'

She moved back to her desk and kneeled one leg on her chair, the other stretched out to the floor. It was the second pose she'd adopted in the last minute and I was sure that the half smile on her pearly pink lips was also part of the theatre.

I opened the large manila envelope I was carrying and pulled out the two containers with the reference samples I'd cut from the material taken from Kincaid Street. 'I'd like you to retest these, please,' I said, 'against any samples or lifts you might have from Ginninderra Road—and not just for palynomorphs. I want every particle of sand, clay and mineral accounted for. I want to know every trace of every component of the soils around those two houses. If those coarse sandy grains can't be accounted for from either crime scene, they could be vital in identifying the offender. I know soil profiles are not exactly your field,' I said, putting the containers down on a table near the door, 'but Florence and Vic are snowed under at the moment, Nigel's away in Indonesia and I'm taken up with administration as you know. With the way we're all stretched at the moment, everyone is having to do things that are a little outside their usual boundaries—if they have the capability.'

She jumped up almost to attention, her face hardening in anger.

'Capability? I hope these are better than the first batch! Do you know what's happened? The samples I took from Kincaid Street are absolutely useless!'

'What are you talking about?' I said.

'Contamination! And it's not the first time! That first time we met,' she continued, 'when you *strolled* over at the Blackspot—what the hell did you think I was doing? Smelling the roses?'

I went to say something but couldn't as Sofia Verstoek raced on angrily.

'The hell I was! I was getting my *own* samples first, before it was too late. Like this time. Whoever's been on the door at the Richardson house has allowed grieving relatives to put floral tributes all around the place! The pollen assemblage is completely useless! I thought I'd found a rare indicator species—the native orchid—that pointed to a crime scene. Now a defence team could argue that it probably came from some florist's shop!'

No point now in asking her about possible places to search for the native orchid, I thought angrily. On top of all the frustration of the animal pit search proving fruitless, the stress of being acting chief, plus the way I was stuffing up my relationship with Iona, came this provocation. I was furious. Marshalling every scrap of self-control I owned, I seized the extra chair and pulled it to me. Then I pointed to her chair. 'Please sit down, Miss Verstoek.'

She didn't move.

'Sit down! *Now!*' I boomed, my voice sharper and louder than I'd intended.

She threw me a filthy look, then plonked down on her chair, pushing it as far away from me as the walls of her office permitted and twisting her body to the side as if signalling she was only here because I was forcing her but it didn't mean she'd listen.

'You may not realise or care about this,' I began, 'but I have to write a report at the end of the month on all new staff members. Your job here could depend on what I say in that report.'

She jumped up again and stared at me, fury in her eyes. 'Are you trying to blackmail me?'

'Sit down!'

'You are! You're using your position to threaten me! I'm going to make a complaint about you.'

'Join the fucking queue, Sofia,' I said. 'Now sit down, shut up *and listen*!'

Whether it was the swearing or the anger in my voice, I couldn't tell, but slowly, still holding my gaze, lips compressed in a tight line, Sofia reseated herself.

'Thank you,' I said curtly.

'Don't thank *me*,' she said.

'Now let's talk like two human beings.'

She remained silent, angrily pushing back a tendril of fair hair that had caught at the corner of her mouth.

'I'm sorry to hear the Richardson house at Kincaid Street has been contaminated. But the samples I've got were taken before any other traffic and they should give you a clean reading. These sorts of mistakes happen and we have to deal with them. Okay?'

She sneered.

'I've already had complaints about your manner from a senior staff member,' I said.

'Who complained about me?' she demanded.

'And I've seen enough of your behaviour to know that the complaint is well-grounded. I've seen better behaviour in maximum security line-ups.'

'What's the matter with my work? Who's complained?'

Fortunately, I'd had years of practice dealing with paranoid, aggressive attitudes of injured innocence from Genevieve.

'A large part of the job here is teamwork. We have to cooperate with each other. We're *all* overworked. We *all* have too many urgent jobs demanding immediate attention. Extra stress is something we don't need. And the way you talk to people—your attitude—creates unnecessary pressures on people who are already carrying an unfair workload.'

'How do you expect me to behave?' she snapped, her question like a blow across the face with a glove, inviting further hostilities.

'I expect you to do your job. And while I'm the last person to tell anyone they should be available for socialising, at least please be civil to your colleagues. You don't have to like them.'

Her face remained expressionless, reminding me of the blank, impassive glare I'd perfected myself in childhood to keep the enemy adults out.

'There's something else I need to talk to you about. It concerns an incident in which you were seen having a meeting with a man parked outside our security fence.'

The blood drained from her face and she slid off the chair, walked over to her desk and started to busy herself with shuffling papers. The defiance had dropped away and I'd made a palpable hit.

'That's my business,' she said. 'Bloody spies round here!'

'You were also observed giving this man money.'

She whirled around, fear in her eyes. 'So it's a crime now? Lending money to a friend?'

'Lending money isn't a crime,' I said, keeping cool. 'Being compromised might be. At the end of the day, you work for the prosecution.'

'What is this? A lecture on my scientific responsibilities?' she said, hand on hip, the defiance back in place, before sitting back down at her desk. 'Whatever incident your nosey-parker saw has nothing to do with my work here!'

I searched my mind for a softer way to express my next thought, but couldn't find it. 'The sort of behaviour I've witnessed in you, not just now, but on other occasions, Sofia, raised questions in my mind whether you might need help—that you may have some sort of...' I groped for a phrase that wouldn't be too offensive '...emotional or psychological disorder.'

'How *dare* you!' she shrieked, jumping up from the chair.

I rose too, unsure of what her next act might be, keeping an eye on her hands, remembering a couple of times how I'd nearly come to grief during interviews back in the old days. 'I'm not saying all this to hurt your feelings,' I said, keeping my voice calm and quiet.

Sofia was heading towards the door.

'Stay and talk about this!' I roared.

She came to a sudden standstill, then swung around on me. 'It is *critically* important that I take my own samples!' she cried. 'I tried to do the same at Kincaid Street. I can't rely on the lifts and sweepings that people like Brian Kruger might eventually get round to giving me. And now I find it's too late. There are exotics all through the grounds now. It's a bloody circus! You think I was rude to you at the Blackspot? How do you think I felt when I saw this guy in black jeans and Hells Angels belt buckle walking all over my critical ground? Destroying the integrity of my crime scene?'

Even with the Brazilian still hovering in my memory, several thoughts were emerging. The first being that, despite her unfortunate nature, there was no doubting Sofia Verstoek's professionalism where her work was concerned. And the second was that when seductive overtures hadn't elicited the right response from me, she'd reverted to aggression. The third thought? Well, I didn't much like admitting it.

'You're right,' I said. 'I apologise. I had no business doing that. I've had this head cold and I wasn't thinking straight.'

'So, Dr McCain, if you haven't got anything else to say to me, I'd like to get back to my work. I'm already in the process of doing a full assay of all the pollen *and* soil components.' She picked up a folder and thrust it at me. 'Take this. There's the first analysis from the area around the house in Kincaid Street, complete with exotic contaminations.' She paused, jabbing a finger at another folder. 'And you can expect a full environmental profile of that case from out along the Ginninderra Road the moment I'm finished compiling the statistics from that area. I also went round to Damien Henshaw's place as well as the address of the painting job he's currently doing, just as you asked me to. So you'll have all that very soon, if there are no more interruptions.'

I took the completed folder from her and again she threw her hand to her hip, her stance now insulting. You've wasted enough of my time already, it conveyed. I'm working way past capacity. Just get out of here.

'Sofia,' I began, 'there's something else I need to know.'

The wary eyes flickered.

'Dallas Baxter informed me about the colour coding of the partner-swapping group.'

She gave me an ambiguous glance, sideways. 'I thought you said you didn't want to discuss last night.'

'This is not about last night. This is about the investigation into Dr Claire Dimitriou's murder.'

The wariness relaxed a little.

'And Dr Dimitriou was overheard saying something about Blue.'

The wariness returned in full force.

'In the partner-swapping group—' I continued.

'That you're not talking about,' she interrupted. 'I believe you're coded as Blue?'

'You know I am. What's that got to do with anything?'

'It means you could be connected to that case.'

'Give me a break! Now I'm part of a murder case?'

'I need to know about number sixteen,' I continued, ignoring her outburst. 'What venue is that?'

The large brown eyes glared at me.

'This is not a trick question,' I added. 'It could be very important.'

'It mightn't be a trick question,' she said, 'but it's a meaningless one. What do you mean? There *is* no number sixteen.'

'You're sure of that?'

She raised an I-should-know eyebrow. 'We only use a dozen places. Nothing like sixteen. What was said to make you think that?'

'Why? Is something worrying you?'

She shook her head. 'Why should anything be worrying me about that case? I don't even *know*—didn't know—Claire Dimitriou. It's just a job to me. I did the pollen assemblage on her clothes. In the unlikely event that Brian Kruger and his lot ever find a suspect.'

'No number sixteen at all?' I insisted.

'Absolutely not. I *can* count. You can check what I'm saying with some of the others.'

'You can be sure I will.'

It was time for me to go. The vision of the night before was starting to loom again. I needed to attempt the restoration of usual relations—not that they were cordial. But now that we'd both let off steam, it was worth the attempt. 'You're a good worker, Sofia.'

That comment brought about a seismic shift in the atmosphere between us, but not the one I'd been hoping for. Now the room was charged with dangerous energy, like that of a predator about to pounce, and my skin prickled.

'What do you mean?' she asked, wary again and unsure.

'You work quickly and off your own initiative,' I said, listing her positive traits. 'I like that. You could be a valued member of a hard-working team.'

She was unused to compliments, I thought. Whatever it was in the atmosphere dissipated and I stood up, ready to go.

'Sofia,' I said, pausing at the door, 'I've been in this game a long time. Don't make enemies of your colleagues. God knows you'll encounter enough of those in your professional life without going out of your way to *create* them.'

I picked up the folder she'd thrust at me and walked out of her office, still doing battle with the image of her naked. It didn't work and I barely noticed Vic heading towards Sofia's office.

'Is she in?' he asked.

I nodded.

He grimaced with theatrical fear, waving a letter addressed to Sofia at me. 'The secretary must have dropped this in the hall.' He gestured towards her office, 'Wish me luck', and kept going, then called back over his shoulder, 'Jack, I've left some more *Public Service* amendments on your desk. I wasn't sure where to file them.'

Great, I thought. The joy of filing government publications.

Almost at the door of my own office, I remembered that in the tension and drama of our conversation, I'd left my own manila folder with notes about Tianna Richardson's murder in Sofia Verstoek's office. I made my way back, thinking of Iona. How come I can deal with a problematic junior scientist, I asked myself, yet be so inept when it comes to my significant other?

I was distracted from these thoughts by a strange sound coming from the half-closed door to Sofia's office. For a moment, I thought she was laughing to herself. But I quickly realised my mistake.

Discreetly, I peered through the door window. With a letter crushed in her hand like a used tissue, Sofia Verstoek was sobbing violently. I knocked softly and she swung around. Instead of the impassive mask, the obsidian surface I'd previously encountered, her overlarge eyes were now despairing. For an instant, I saw the heartbreak of a betrayed child as she backed awkwardly against her desk, hands and letter behind her.

'I'm sorry,' I said. 'I'll come back another time.'

She rallied, dashing tears from her face with one hand. 'It's nothing,' she said. 'I jammed my thumb.'

'That folder?' I started awkwardly at the same time Sofia started to say something. I looked around for where I'd left it. The pile of books on the desk behind her wobbled and I realised then she'd slid the letter she'd been holding underneath them, undermining their balance. The furtiveness of the movement alerted me.

'I put it over there,' she said, indicating a table against the wall.

In the awkwardness of her lie and my curiosity about the letter, we both dived for the folder at the same time, colliding and banging our foreheads together painfully. I swore. So did she. Worse, I lost my balance and grabbing the closest thing, which happened to be the unstable wheelie chair, I went crashing to the floor, taking Sofia down too. Putting my hand out to break my fall, I grabbed her left breast instead and she clutched me in a useless attempt to regain her balance. We rolled together, ending up banging into the footing of her desk. Then we lay still, our arms still around each other.

In that split second I became painfully aware of the length of her body against mine, the swell of her belly and hips against my groin. Her tear-stained eyes looked straight into mine and I knew the Brazilian was close to my thigh and only covered by fabric. Tears magnified her large brown eyes and I had to fight a sudden urge to kiss them. Then the teetering pile of books on the desk, unbalanced by our collision, crashed all over us, the corner of one hitting me painfully on the mouth. The hidden letter fell out near my face and, as I clambered to my feet, I saw some of the words.

'Are you okay?' I asked, passing her the letter and putting out a hand to help her up. She ignored it, snatched at the letter and climbed to her feet, blood rushing to her cheeks. She shoved the letter in the wastepaper bin. The book avalanche had changed everything.

I picked up the folder and made to leave.

'You know last night,' she started as I opened the door.

I stood there and left it too long before replying. 'I said that subject is closed, Sofia.'

I didn't think my voice would have conveyed much authority in that moment.

She turned her back on me, pretending to be rearranging the books that had fallen.

'You said you knocked on the wrong door,' she said, her back to me.

'I've got to go,' I said, leaving her office about fifteen seconds too late.

I didn't even turn back when she called my name and her voice followed me down the corridor.

'Jack,' she said. 'It wasn't the wrong door.'

TWENTY-TWO

Sofia's words stayed with me, re-echoing through my mind on the drive back out to the Ag Station via the city. The memory of the way her body had pressed into mine as we crashed to the floor together, the moment when I'd looked straight into her eyes—these unforeseen intimacies were creating all sorts of interference to my normal state of mind. Not to mention the words I'd seen of the letter she hadn't wanted me to see. The letter that had made her weep. It wasn't the wrong door, she'd said. Even a man as thick as I was to these sorts of signals had to admit the woman was making a serious pass. It was a flattering thought but my heart was well and truly connected to another woman.

Once I'd signed in at the Ag Station, Pauline took me under her wing and issued me with a visitor's badge. I told her what I wanted to see and we wound through the vinyl corridors until we came to a closed door some distance from the clean-up area I'd showered in after the animal pit.

Pauline opened the door, her hand feeling inside for the light.

'This is the wash-up room,' she said, pushing the door fully open. 'We call it the scullery.'

Ahead of me was a long, narrow room, with incubators on the left and a big industrial washer for laboratory glassware. At the end stood the autoclave, like some huge clothes dryer, its door ajar. I went up to it and peered at its stainless-steel interior. This was the pressure cooker that sterilised glassware and treated hazardous waste materials from the research station. Behind it, several large bags were stacked and I noticed the black stripes on the tape that bound their necks.

'They've been done,' said Pauline, giving me my second lesson in how the black stripes indicated autoclaving. 'They're waiting for waste disposal to collect them.'

I picked up the end of a long paper tape extruded by the autoclave. Like the rolls of paper in cash registers, this one was printed with a series of dates, times, temperatures and pressures. 'What happens to this?' I asked her, the tape looped through my hands.

She shrugged. 'I'm not sure anything much happens to it. We certainly don't keep records of use. Only the fellow who comes out every so often to service it takes any notice of that.'

I pulled the tape through my fingers, noticing the pattern of use went back to last week. Monday before last, the autoclave had been used at the end of the day, starting run number 3948 at 15:34, ending its steam, sterilise, dry and complete cycle at 16:56. Tuesday and Wednesday of that week both showed similar figures, give or take half an hour. And so on to Friday. But when I came to the beginning of this week, Monday's figures were quite different. On the last Monday of Claire Dimitriou's life, run number 3953 had started much like the other days at 15:04, finishing at 16:56. But unlike any other day, the autoclave had been used a second time. Run number 3954 had commenced at 22:09 and had not ended its cycle until 01:34 the following morning. Someone had made very sure that no evidence could survive the heat, steam and pressure of intense autoclaving. Someone had killed Claire Dimitriou and, while the autoclave was doing its run, had calmly cleaned up the Faithful Bunnies lab. They'd then come back, unloaded it and taken its contents down to the animal pit. If we hadn't dug through the pit, we'd never even have known about this anomalous run.

'I'm taking this section,' I said to Pauline, snipping off the length of tape and furling it into a protective envelope. More than anything else, I wanted to know what had happened in that laboratory.

'One more thing, Pauline. The digital print-out of Claire Dimitriou's key number.'

'I have it back in my office,' said Pauline, returning soon after with some pages in a protective sleeve.

'Is this Claire's code?' I asked. 'Four, seven, zero, eight?'

'Yes,' said Pauline. 'She could never remember it so she had a post-it note stuck on her computer with the code on it. You can see where she's checked in every fifty-five minutes on Monday evening and even in the early hours of Tuesday.'

I studied the log: fifty-five-minute intervals of the twenty-four-hour clock with 4708 printed beside them, the last one appearing at 02:15. I glanced back at the autoclave records. The last cycle of Tuesday morning had ended at 01:34, a little under three-quarters of an hour before Claire's last keyed-in number. That would give the killer nearly three-quarters of an hour to unload the autoclave and take the contents to the animal pit, then come back and clean up in the showers, make one last entry of Claire's code and leave the premises.

'Once the building is empty, the automatic alarm resets itself,' Pauline was saying. 'Security would only be alerted if the sensors detected someone moving around on the premises and alerted the remote monitoring service. But the alarm didn't go off and I was the first to arrive at the building that morning. There was nothing out of the ordinary.'

Anyone knowing Claire's security code could have keyed in her number, I thought, on the drive back to the city. According to Harry, time of death was sometime between 9 p.m. Monday and the early hours of Tuesday, give or take a few hours. In the dead of night, the killer had had all the time he or she needed to cover their tracks—do the clean-up, kill the rabbits, run the autoclave, then dump the bag in the animal pit.

Whoever had put the bodies of the rabbits, the ELISA plates, Claire's laptop and the lab book into the autoclave, and then dug them into the animal pit, had to have hung around till 1.34 a.m. before he or she could open its door. That someone would have been dirty. Even if the steam-cleaning had been done at speed, such an action would have to take half an hour or so. The killer could not have left the premises until some time after 2 a.m. This was the sort of killer who would take every precaution. The clean-room annexe to the Faithful Bunnies lab was full of protective Tyvek suits and polypropylene shoe covers. The killer could ditch them and get into his or her car and drive home, neat and clean. And out here, with only paddocks fronting the road and the homesteads half a mile away at the end of a long driveway, the chances of anyone having seen a person leaving at that hour weren't good. North, south, east or west, whichever way he took, the killer had a good five or six hours, maybe longer, to get away, before Pauline had noticed that Dr Dimitriou was not answering the calls switched through to her lab and then investigated further and noticed that her car had been there all night and she'd failed to log off.

It had been a long day and I knew I should have headed home, but instead I found my car pointed back to work. When I got there, I found a folder from Sofia Verstoek pushed under my door—the results of her soil profiles from the Kincaid Street house and the house out along the Ginninderra Road. I slipped them in my briefcase, checked for any messages and then locked my office. But I couldn't switch off from Claire's murder. I replayed the overheard conversation between the two scientists, trying to make some sense out of the scant information, again trying to work out what they might have been disagreeing about. She wanted to do something and he was dead against it. I had to find another way of looking at this. There were six other deaths to consider. Why did the rabbits—RP1, 2, 3, 4, 5 and 6—have to die? What if the argument had not been about sex but about science?

I rejigged their words, trying to imagine what sort of scientific dispute might have led to such passion. But after examining the dialogue from this angle, I still ended up nowhere. Finally, I had to admit that the argument between the two scientists could have been about any damn thing, from whether to approach the Meyer Foundation for funding or whether they should put all the tea money on a sure thing in the fifth at Randwick. There were a million possibilities.

Nevertheless, a new series of questions and ideas about why Claire Dimitriou had died was starting to emerge in my mind.

I looked at my watch and realised I was probably going to miss dinner at home. I didn't want to think about Iona, so I decided to follow up one more lead.

●

I parked on the street outside the address Pauline had given me for Cheryl Tobin—a bungalow with a well-established garden. My mind was still preoccupied with the reason for the heated argument between Claire and Peter Yu, right up to the moment someone answered my knocking.

'Who is it?' said a frightened female voice.

'Cheryl Tobin?' I asked. 'I'm a scientist who works with the Federal Police. May I have a moment of your time?' I held up my ID near the door that had opened a crack.

'Have you seen Cheryl?' the woman asked, opening the door wider. 'She hasn't been home for a week. I'm worried sick about her.'

The lined and harassed face belonged to a woman in her sixties; her anxious eyes scanned mine. I realised she hadn't taken in anything I'd said.

'Are you her mother?' I asked, after repeating my greeting. She nodded. 'I want to talk about Cheryl,' I said, quickly adjusting to the situation. 'May I come in?'

She stepped back and I followed her through into a living room where she indicated a chair for me and sat opposite, right on the edge of her seat, hands clenched.

'Have you heard something?'

'I'm sorry, I haven't any news of Cheryl,' I said. 'Maybe you could help me find her, Mrs Tobin. I believe she used to work at the Ag Station a couple of years back?'

'She hasn't worked since,' said her mother. 'That's when she just went to pieces. I didn't know what to do about her. She started drinking heavily and then, God knows what else... I'm at my wit's end.'

I'd heard this sad story so many times in so many different guises. A big disappointment happening to a stunted spirit resulting in growing drug dependency. I'd lived it myself. Eventually, the corrosion of addiction destroyed whatever remained of personal relationships. As I listened to Mrs Tobin's anguish, I thought she could have been talking about Jacinta, or about me twenty years ago.

'I'm sorry to hear that, Mrs Tobin,' I said. 'I've got a few friends around. I'll ask them to keep their eyes open for her. Ask her to contact you.'

'Sometimes I can find her hanging round near the Civic mall,' she said.

'Have you a photograph of her that I can copy?' I asked.

'I have, but it wouldn't be helpful,' she said, and I followed her gaze as it lit on a framed portrait of a beautiful, beaming girl with classic features in mortarboard and robes, holding her furled degree. 'She doesn't look like that any more.' Mrs Tobin's eyes filled with tears.

I stood up and so did she, accompanying me down the hall back to the front door.

'I'm very sorry to hear what's happened to Cheryl,' I said. 'If it's any help to you to know, I have a daughter a little younger than yours and she was living the life of a street addict. She's now clean and straight, studies hard at university and cares about herself and others. People *can* get well.

They can learn to grow their spirit—learn to deal with the problems that drove them to drugs in the first place.'

I wasn't sure if she could hear me, but it was the best I could do as I took my leave. I turned back to her and saw the grief and anger in her eyes.

'You must look after yourself, too,' I said. 'Be gentle with yourself. You look worn out.'

I left her with the tears running down her face. I knew how she felt.

On the drive through town back to the cottage, my own words kept ringing in my ears. Had I learned to deal with *all* the problems that had driven me into alcoholism? I thought long and hard and came to some conclusions. I may have learned how to be a responsible father and workmate and possibly even brother and friend. But when it came to romance, I had to admit I had a big problem.

Women had always confused me. Beginning with my mother. I didn't understand what was going on with her when I was a kid and, forty years later, I still seemed powerless to decipher what a woman wanted. I knew how to comfort women, but that wasn't enough. Healthy people didn't need comforting. They needed an equal relationship. I thought of my various misdemeanours with women over the years—not a huge number, but all had ended in tears. I recalled the words of Annette Sommers as she described Peter Yu and the thought that my relationship with Iona was doomed to the same sad ending evoked in me a dark and desolate mood.

Unlike earlier occasions when my heart would lift at the sight of Iona's car and the lights on in the cottage, I felt tired and defeated as I walked inside. Noting the closed door of our bedroom and the absence of the letter I'd written her that morning, I hoped Iona was having a nap and had forgiven me. Again. I decided to leave her be and followed my nose to the kitchen where Charlie was making pizzas.

'Have Jacinta and Greg gone?' I asked. 'Her car's gone.'

'Yes,' said Charlie. 'Back to Sydney. Jacinta was really worried about Shaz and said to say goodbye and that she'd ring later. Want a drink?'

Charlie passed me the wooden spoon and pushed me towards the tomato sauce simmering on the stove.

I started stirring the sauce when my mobile rang and I cursed it.

'Yes?'

'Damien Henshaw didn't get to Kylie's place till well after 2 a.m. the night Tianna was murdered,' said Brian. 'She's just made a statement.'

'Is he trying to tell you that he was with another woman but he won't give you her name to protect her honour?' I suggested.

'Not quite,' said Brian.

'He reckons he doesn't know her name?'

'Got it in one,' said Brian.

'Years of experience.'

'I'm not letting him go now. I'm counting on you, Jack. Give me more physical evidence.'

'More than those boots?'

'The boots are okay. But someone else could have worn them. I want something that can't be explained away by counsel. I want something that puts *him* right there at the killing. I've got a feeling about this guy. He's a smug little shit and, if he did it, I'd hate to see him getting away with it.'

I recalled the epithelial cells Vic had told me about from the half-smoked joint. 'I'll check up how we're doing with our analyses. We might have a DNA result for you soon.'

'I thought you said the palynologist found some rare native orchid pollen? That could help us pinpoint the primary crime scene.'

'Sadly,' I said, 'that evidence was compromised. Contamination by floral tributes at Tianna's place. Our palynologist could probably make a reasonable case around prior deposition—'

'Sorry?' Brian said.

'She could probably show that one type of pollen was laid down at an earlier time than the pollen introduced to the scene, but it's still not the sort of clear-cut evidence that a jury likes.'

Brian grunted.

'And before you go,' I added, 'there is no venue sixteen used by the partner-swapping group. I spoke to the person coded Blue and she denies knowing Claire Dimitriou.' I gave Brian the details, rang off and returned to stirring the sauce and filling Charlie in about the arrest in the Tianna Richardson case.

'What about the son?' Charlie said when I'd finished.

'Stepson?' I said. 'He's definitely a possibility.'

'Why not have a look at their family of origin?' said Charlie. 'That could help you close in on one rather than the other. If there's a violent family background in one case and not in the other, I know which possibility I'd put the money on.'

'Maybe one day we'll get to that sort of sophistication,' I said, 'where we can run the factors through a program and come up with a statistical result. It might point us in the right direction quicker.'

When dinner was almost ready, I went to the bedroom door, intending to let Iona know. I knocked gently before going in. Iona wasn't having a nap.

'What are you doing?' I asked, not prepared to believe my eyes.

Two suitcases lay on the bed, one of them filled to capacity, the other with an assortment of her clothing.

'As you can see,' she said. 'I'm packing up.'

'But you can't!' I said, 'This is crazy.'

She paused in her folding of a large creamy jumper that I loved to see her wearing. 'No, this isn't crazy. What's crazy is what I've been doing the last six months, Jack,' she said gently. 'Having the same conversation with you over and over. Waiting for you to give me some scraps of your time.'

'Scraps?'

She nodded. 'One picnic, duration two and a half hours nearly six months ago. Do you have any idea how many times you rang me to say you'd be home late? That I should eat alone? Most weekends you're not here.'

'But why suddenly now?' I asked. 'Sorry. That was a stupid thing to say. It's not as if you haven't expressed these concerns before.'

'After the other night's conversation...' She paused, then said, 'I realised I was turning into one of those women.'

'What do you mean? That conversation had nothing to do with you. With us. I was talking about a case I'm working on,' I said.

'That's right. And I had to ask myself the same question: why am I staying with a man who keeps hurting me?'

Her words hit me like a stunning blow. I felt winded. I hadn't realised that I was *hurting* her.

'I'm so sorry,' I said. 'I didn't realise.'

'Jack, I've been asking you for months. I'm starting to feel like some pathetic supplicant, begging for favours. I'm not doing this any more and I've made my decision to go.'

'But where will you go?' I said when I could speak. 'Where will you stay?'

'I'll look around for a short-term lease in town. Finish the term up at the college. Then I intend to go back to Sydney. I'll stay with a friend for the rest of the year and then move back into my house when the lease runs out.'

I went over to her and held her. Tears were running down her face.

'Please, Iona. Please,' I said. 'Give me another chance.'

She gently disengaged from me, searching her pockets for something to wipe her eyes.

'Here,' I said, passing her my handkerchief. 'Use this.'

She took it and wiped her eyes and blew her nose, tucking the balled-up hankie into her sleeve. 'I'll take these things with me in the morning and come back for my other stuff later,' she said, indicating the scattered possessions. Then she gathered up her towel and dressing-gown and headed for the bathroom, leaving me sitting on the bed, my head in my hands, exhausted and with no words left. I wasn't used to this sort of ending. The end of all my other affairs had exploded with screaming accusations, recriminations, pent-up fury finally unleashed. Not this sad and resigned dignity.

When I could, I stood up and walked out through the front door onto the verandah overlooking the garden. The night air was sharp with frost and an eroded moon hung over the hills, etching the edges of trees along the skyline. Small night creatures rustled in the old hedges. I couldn't remember when I'd last felt so bad. This was so different from all previous separations and I didn't know how to deal with this sad, steely resolve of hers.

Aware of a presence, and for a moment absurdly hopeful, I swung round but it was only Charlie.

'I'm leaving tomorrow, bro.'

'So's Iona, Charlie.'

A long pause.

'What are you going to do?'

'What can I do, Charlie? She's made up her mind.'

Charlie put a hand on my shoulder and I was grateful for its warmth. 'You know what to do, Jack. The problem is, you won't do it.'

'Jesus, Charlie, I *can't*! I'm in the middle of three really tough cases. I can't just walk away from them at this stage.'

'I guess you can't,' said Charlie. 'And that's the whole problem in a nutshell.'

I looked up at the sky to see a shooting star sliding through the immense and silent blackness. In ancient days, such things were seen as bad omens and that seemed very apt just now. Charlie left me and I stood a little while longer in the cold night air then I went back into our bedroom.

It looked sad and stark because Iona had taken down her paintings and stacked them, faces against the wall, and her other personal items, like the old-fashioned silver-backed hairbrush and mirror set that I'd first seen on the Victorian cedar dressing-table in her house at Annandale, were missing. Iona was kneeling back on her heels, wrapping tissue paper around something fragile.

'This can't be the end, Iona. I'll meet you tomorrow. We can find a way through this.'

'Don't, Jack,' she warned. 'The time for talking has come and gone. Several times. I'm starting to lose my self-respect.'

'But you can't just go like this,' I said, watching her helplessly as she battled with the lid on the bulging second suitcase. Instinctively, I went to help her.

'Why am I doing this?' I said, pulling back. 'I'm not going to help you leave!'

But I ended up zipping the suitcase all the way round while Iona sat on it.

'This is crazy,' I repeated. 'Don't go.'

'I'm weary, Jack. I can't keep arguing like this.' She walked to the door. 'I'll sleep in Jacinta's room tonight.'

'You've got to tell me where you're going,' I said.

'I'll be staying with a friend in town.'

'What friend?'

She told me. It was one of the women she taught with who had an apartment in Ainslie. I scribbled down the address, vaguely remembering the place from the time we gave Anne-Marie a lift after school.

And that was it.

I looked at the two bulging cases and rebelled against carrying them out to be near the front door. Charlie could do that, not me.

I tossed and turned and once even got up and went down the hallway, wanting to knock on the spare bedroom door and talk her out of it. But I knew when I was beaten. There was a steel in Iona that had helped her survive the events of her life and now she was using it against me.

At about 3 a.m. I got up and went out to the lounge room and rebuilt the fire. Even when it was crackling along, I felt cold to the bone and I couldn't tell if my head cold had turned into a fever or if I was just sick and cold with grief.

I ended up dozing off on the lounge and woke just as dawn was streaking the skies above the eastern hills. I wrapped one of Iona's mohair throws around me, went out to the kitchen and put the kettle on. I didn't think I could bear being here when Iona moved out so, while it was still dark, I wrote a note, rolled the car down to the gate and left for work. I made a plan that I'd go round to Anne-Marie's later in the day. Maybe by then I might have found the words that would make Iona change her mind.

TWENTY-THREE

At Forensic Services, there was no one else around at this hour on a Saturday, just the soft hum of automated processes moving through their cycles behind closed doors. I was relieved because talking to anyone just now would have been a strain.

I sat at my desk, staring at the Venetian glass paperweight, a gift from Iona in happier days. Restlessly, I got up and paced around. Finally, I rang the cottage then killed the call. There was no point and I didn't want to become a nuisance. Work, I told myself. The old standby.

I pulled out the results I'd got back from Vic, laying them out on the low coffee table together with my own findings and those of Sofia Verstoek: the tables of soil analysis from around the grounds and gardens of three houses—one in Kincaid Street, another from a tiny hamlet on the Ginninderra Road and the last from Damien Henshaw's place. Apart from botanical variances, the statistical measurements for the soils at all three places shared certain characteristics of the locality: various degraded metamorphic rock mixed with mineral inclusions, as well as diatoms, pollen both fresh and fossilised with clay fractions. But there was no explanation for the coarse grains we'd found embedded in the head wounds of both Tianna Richardson and Albert Vaughan. Someone had brought those particles in. From somewhere else. And that someone was their killer.

I glanced over the soil analysis from Damien Henshaw's place; stapled to it was a fourth profile, from the house he was currently painting. Finally, I read and reread through the complicated graphs and charts. Nothing Sofia had found matched the coarse sandy particles. The rare native orchid pollen could not be accounted for either, in any of these locations. I threw the report down. The soil profiles would not help us locate even the general area of the primary crime scene.

My mobile rang. It was Brian, wanting my company on a visit to the remand centre. 'Damien Henshaw tried to off himself last night. I told you he's guilty as hell.'

'Is the remand centre open for business already?' I asked, looking at my watch.

'Crime never sleeps,' said Brian, 'and neither does the remand centre.'

'Could be hopelessness,' I said, thinking of Anthony Dimitriou as well as the hanged man whose death still haunted me. 'I had a case once where a suspect suicided when we confronted him with bootprint evidence.'

'Case closed,' said Brian. 'Good as a guilty plea and saves the state a motza.'

'Except the evidence didn't exist,' I said. 'I was just a youngster then. And when I did examine his boots, they were completely different.'

That took Brian aback a little. 'Then why did he off himself?'

I paused, though I'd had years to consider this one. 'Because,' I said finally, 'he knew he couldn't win against the cops. He was a nobody, a petty crim. It was despair, not guilt.'

'Don't let that get in the way of your dealings with this little shit,' said Brian. 'This isn't just any old bootprint, remember. We've got other ways to hang him out to dry. The bootprint, the admitted argument, the dodgy alibi. Shit, Jack, I reckon it was him. When you get the DNA results we'll be able to nail him.'

I couldn't argue, but something was still worrying me.

I recalled part of my earlier conversation with Charlie. 'Did Damien Henshaw grow up in a violent household?' I asked.

'His parents are Quakers,' said Brian. 'Complete pacifists. So the little creep's got no excuses. But I'm determined to find out why he killed Albert Vaughan, and I want him to tell me. I don't like mysteries.'

'Albert Vaughan was out late Monday night, remember,' I said. 'He told the pharmacist he'd just seen someone he knew.'

'Yes, but who?'

'He saw something that he shouldn't have,' I went on. 'And that's why he had to die.'

'If *you'd* just seen someone murdered, you'd say to the pharmacist "ring the police" or "I've just seen a woman murdered" or something like that, asthma attack notwithstanding,' said Brian. 'All Vaughan said was he'd just seen someone he *knew*. It could've been anyone.'

I climbed back into my car and drove to the remand centre where I met Brian and sat with him and Damien Henshaw in one of the sterile visiting rooms, a staff member of Corrective Services standing discreetly nearby. Opposite me, Damien Henshaw, no longer the cocky little rooster I'd seen last time, sat hunched in his too-big jacket. His hair was cut short back and sides and he looked like he'd already lost weight.

'Damien, you'd feel a lot better if you just got this whole business off your chest,' said Brian. 'You don't look well. I hear the medical staff are concerned about your mental health. You tried to kill yourself last night? Tell me why you killed Tianna and Albert.'

Damien looked up from under his eyebrows. 'You don't know what it's like in this place. I'd rather be dead than in here.'

'Answer the question.'

'I didn't fucking kill anyone,' he said. 'I shouldn't *be* in this place.'

'I believe you're in the right place, Damien,' Brian said. 'I just want to know why. What happened the night you killed Tianna and poor old Albert Vaughan?'

'I didn't kill anyone,' Damien repeated.

'I'm still not quite clear on a couple of things,' I started.

'But we've got the big moves sorted out,' interrupted Brian.

'There weren't no big moves,' Damien muttered. 'Not by me, anyway.'

'You took Tianna to the Blackspot that night, but you'd had enough of her,' said Brian. 'She was threatening to tell Kylie about your casual infidelity and you couldn't risk that. You really love Kylie, don't you?'

I saw Damien tear up but pressed on. 'So, to protect Kylie from knowing the truth about what you're really like, you had to shut this woman up.'

I tried a line that had worked for me with suspects over the years when I was a detective. 'You didn't mean to kill her. You're not really a murderer,' I said. 'But Tianna wouldn't shut up. She wanted to go to the Blackspot with you. She was sick of being hidden away. She was going on and on about it. So, finally, you took her to the nightclub. You even had a joint with her outside. Maybe you tried to sweet-talk her, change her mind. You hoped that with a bit of dope in her, she might forget her threats and the whole thing would blow over. You could keep dropping in and up-ending her once or twice a week, just to keep her on side, and Kylie need never know.'

I paused. Damien's head had sunk lower on his chest. I wasn't even sure if he was listening.

'This part I'm not too clear on and I'll need your help,' I continued. 'But you took Tianna somewhere else—somewhere where there are rocks or stones comprised of coarse grey sandy particles—and you caused her to fall back against something hard, at speed, or you pushed her in such a way that she bashed the back of her head in. You panicked. Look, if you just admit it we can try and get the charge reduced to manslaughter. We know you didn't mean it.'

Still no response.

'You decided to dump her back at the Blackspot, but somewhere between picking Tianna up and dumping her back at the club, you realised something. Somewhere, Albert Vaughan had seen you!'

As I said this, Claire Dimitriou's words flooded my mind. 'She saw! She saw!' I had to deliberately refocus my mind. I wanted this man to confess, too. Maybe that way I could get the death of that old lag all those years ago out of my mind for good.

'I don't know what you're talking about,' Damien muttered. 'Who's this Vaughan?'

'You knew that Albert Vaughan would dob you in, one way or another. Even if what he saw didn't seem ominous at the time, once the murder became public he'd remember what he'd seen and mention it to someone. It would get back to the police. This all raced through your mind. Your adrenaline was pumping, you'd already murdered one person. Once you've stepped over the homicide line, it's easier—all the old crims say so. So you knew you *had* to shut him up before he could do this. And it had to be done immediately. So after you'd dumped Tianna's body at the Blackspot, you went back to deal with Albert Vaughan and found that you were in luck. It was a golden opportunity—you didn't even have to break into the house. Harry Marshall thinks the weapon used was probably a tyre brace. One of your work tools? Then off you went and you believed that no one would ever know what happened.'

'I never killed anyone.' The monotonous, hopeless voice. 'Never touched her or the old man.'

'It was such rotten bad luck, wasn't it?' said Brian. 'Old Mr Vaughan spotting you like that. Old invalid like him. Just happened to be out and about at the wrong time. Maybe he saw you with her in the car? Maybe he saw something more damning? But he saw something and he had to die.'

Again, the strange dialogue from Claire Dimitriou intruded in my brain: 'She saw! She saw!' And so had Albert Vaughan.

I'd been at similar interviews and watched a perpetrator's eyes get rounder and rounder as someone recounted a reconstruction of the sequence of events leading up to a crime. But that hadn't happened here.

I looked at Brian then looked away. From somewhere came the liquid notes of noisy miners. We waited. Nothing happened.

Later, outside the remand centre, we walked towards our cars.

'It was worth a try,' said Brian. 'Save the people a lot of money if the little shit would just sign a confession.'

'Brian, maybe we've got the wrong man,' I said.

Brian gave me a look. 'You put him there, mate, with your physical evidence. There's no way round that. This isn't like the incident you feel guilty about,' he said. '"This is physical evidence that cannot lie,"' he quoted.

'"That cannot perjure itself,"' I said, and continued with the Edmund Locard quotation: '"Physical evidence cannot be wrong; it cannot perjure itself; it cannot be wholly absent. Only its interpretation can err. Only human failure to find it, study it and understand it can diminish its value."'

'But why then hasn't your team found any trace of the large grey particles at Damien's place or in his vehicle? And I still haven't heard anything back from Bob about the photograph I sent him of Tianna's mystery man.'

'We've got enough,' said Brian.

I brought him up to date about how I planned to find a home for the mystery keys we'd found in Peter Yu's cartons and we parted.

The mystery man and Locard's words continued to trouble me as I stopped the car at a phone box and, miraculously, found an intact phone book. I went back to the car and made a list of the local real estate offices. This was one of the times I wished I had a fifteen-year-old junior back at the office to send out on an errand to track down which office used the red and white plaited tags. I looked at my watch and saw it was past nine so started ringing around. By the fourth call, I'd discovered that Fletcher Daley Real Estate used red and white thongs for their keys. I double-checked the address and headed straight over. As I drove I realised Locard's words kept running through my head like a mantra to keep my mind from turning to Iona.

At Fletcher Daley I spoke to a pretty young woman who confirmed the keys did belong to one of their rental properties but because the identifying tag was no longer attached, she couldn't really say which property. She thought one of the managers might know.

'Could you ask him?' I suggested. But Mr Vernon was on holidays.

'I'll leave them here and if anyone remembers or has any information on them, please ring me immediately,' I said, leaving my card with all my phone numbers circled. She promised she'd see to it.

I arrived back at my office and, as I passed Sofia Verstoek's closed office, was reminded of the palynologist's final words before I'd hurried away yesterday. They kept replaying themselves in my mind and my body couldn't help but respond to what had been a clear invitation. For a moment, I tried to tell myself that having a lust-driven affair with her might take my mind off Iona, and tried to suppress this idea by remembering that her invitation to sexual favour was somewhat indiscriminate. I also recalled how my last lust-fuelled affair had ended and rejected the idea completely.

However, even rejecting the idea unfortunately took me straight back to the vision in Suite 12 at Olims.

I picked up the desk phone and dialled Bob on his mobile. 'Any luck on that photograph I faxed you?' I asked, dispensing with pleasantries.

'Yes,' said Bob. 'I tracked him down and he was going to ring you. Has he?'

'Not so far,' I said. 'What's his name?'

'Adam Shiner,' said Bob and I noted it down.

'He said he was going to call,' said Bob, 'but here's his number in case.'

'I owe you one, Bob.'

'You'll keep,' Bob replied.

'Before you go,' I said, 'do you remember a conversation at the Glebe morgue about pollen? Bradley Strachan, you and me. I'd just dropped in because you'd been working on a case of unidentified remains and there'd been some rare pollen found on what was left of his clothes.'

'Do I remember?' said Bob. 'Mate, I helped dig him *out*—what was left of him. Remains of a young male found near Queanbeyan wedged under a rock shelf and covered over. A dog brought his jaw bone home and that's when the local cops called the forensic pathologist. You know what bones are like when they first turn up—filthy, lots of dirt and other accretions. Bradley was on leave at the time he was found and we brought him up to speed when he came back. You arrived while we were talking about it.'

'That's right,' I said, relieved now that I'd remembered.

'Unknown Male 17/2000. He's on my UHU list,' Bob said.

'Because of the pollen?'

'That, and a few other bits and pieces that are in the box with him that might yield something,' said Bob. 'Why?'

'I want him. Tianna Richardson's head wounds also carried traces of a rare species, although there's been some contamination apparently. I'd like to check out the pollen in both cases. Might help us with a primary crime scene in her case. Just maybe your unknown male was killed in the same area and the physical evidence accompanying him might give us some more ideas.'

'It's a bloody long shot,' said Bob.

'I'll pick him up. I have to come to Sydney to talk to someone,' I said, thinking of Jerri Quill. While I was telling Bob about her I was interrupted by Sarah knocking on the door of my office. I rang off as Sarah came in.

'You're here too?' she said. 'I thought you were supposed to be taking some time off?'

Her words made my heart ache but I shrugged. 'You know how it is,' I said.

'I've finally had a chance to dry out that lab book and, seeing as you're here, you might as well come and have a look. Got a minute?'

'Sure,' I replied and accompanied her back to her examination room, donned a pair of gloves and took a look at what she'd done.

'The pages dried easily enough,' she said, carefully lifting the lab book out on its supporting plate. 'We're in luck. It's very good quality, acid-free, with a calcium-carbonate buffer. It's been produced to resist deteriorating. And the whole book has been well bound in sections. Last for a hundred years, this stuff would.'

'Did you use a drying cupboard?' I asked, impressed.

Sarah shook her gleaming head. 'I used my special forensic tool,' she said, nodding to a hairdryer residing in its box on the bench. 'That plus a lot of patience did the trick.' She drew the lab book closer and carefully, using gloved fingers and the tip of a small probe, teased open one page then another.

'Well done, Sarah,' I said.

She looked up at me. 'Give me a pay rise then.'

'If it were in my gift, I would,' I replied. 'You deserve it.'

'Here. This is the bit I want you to see.'

Sarah had opened the lab book to the most recent entry. I picked it up and studied what seemed to be the results of standard assay runs on the ELISA system. 'This looks okay as far as I can tell,' I said, deciding that, just in case, I'd visit Dr Leonie Pringle and make sure I wasn't missing anything.

Sarah said, 'Look at the date.'

I looked closer. 'These results are from the week *before* Claire Dimitriou was killed,' I said. 'Where's that Monday? The day of the upset with Jerri Quill?'

Sarah nodded. 'At first, I just thought they'd been a bit lax and hadn't got round to writing up the day's work. But then I noticed this.'

She took another probe from a glass flagon and, using the two probes like chopsticks, pulled the centre of the page open. 'Look closely there and tell me what you see.'

She passed me her magnifying glass, a dramatic lorgnette edged with diamantes.

I looked closely at the centre binding of the page. I could see tiny irregularities, little worms of paper just discernible near the cotton binding thread. 'A page is missing,' I said.

'That's right. That's why he or she would have to dump the book. I'm relieved—and amazed— they didn't shred the damn thing. Have you ever worked on restoring shredded documents?'

I hadn't, but I'd seen colleagues sitting in piles of the stuff, week after week, trying to find the matching pieces.

'Probably couldn't afford the time,' I said. 'It's Monday's page that's been ripped out.'

'And it's just too bad,' said Sarah. 'I can work miracles routinely, but even I can't materialise missing pages.'

Before I could ask her the next question she'd already answered it. 'I tried ESDA on the preceding pages but it wasn't possible to get any clean impressions of the missing page. The last few pages have been done with a felt tip, not a ballpoint. Not enough pressure exerted.'

I straightened up, frustrated and pissed off. We'd come so close. Now we'd never know what had happened in that laboratory on Monday.

'So,' Sarah asked, 'what does it all mean?'

I considered.

'Why would someone rip out a page?' I asked before answering my own question. 'Because there's something on it that they don't want anyone to see.'

'What other reason could there be?' asked Sarah, poking the corner of the page with her probe. 'But the supervisor would have noticed anyway, because the pages are numbered. A missing page would stick out.'

'I'm sure an excuse could be found,' I said. 'Like spillage ruining the page.'

'Whatever it was, we'll never know now,' she said.

I went back to my office, feeling defeated. I needed to track down Jerri Quill and find out what that fight had been about.

I looked through my diary, checking the best time to get away for a day or so and talk to her. I was ambushed by a pencilled note in my diary concerning Iona's upcoming birthday. I'd planned to take her out for a surprise dinner and present her with the little leatherbound daybook she'd admired. Now, there'd be no dinner. No gift.

Grief was a dangerous emotion for alcoholics because it could undo the sort of sobriety that merely capped the deeper wells of sorrow and kept them pressed down. I knew I had to allow my grief to flow if I wanted to heal fully. These grave thoughts were interrupted by a call on my mobile, this time from one of the most revered forensic scientists of the generation before me. Ellis Smith said he'd just typed up his official report on the grey particles we'd found embedded in the wounds both of Tianna Richardson and Albert Vaughan, but he'd decided to ring through his basic findings and say hello at the same time.

I thanked him for his generosity in working on a Friday night and Saturday and picked up my pen, ready to take notes.

'Those large particles come from an aggregate that was around fifteen or twenty years ago,' Ellis Smith said. 'I remembered it as soon as I saw the samples and when I went to compare it with my old records, there it was. It was manufactured by a company in Victoria called Universal Cement. They used to make a block that was basically a mix of granite chips and cement. It was mainly used for gardens and outdoor constructions—ponds, steps, retaining walls, that sort of thing. The blocks came in two shades, a golden one called Colonial Classic and this one, which I'm convinced the particles came from, a grey-white called Roman White. It was discontinued some time back. They went into liquidation. But you could check local outlets. See who used to stock it. If they remember.'

'Thanks, Ellis,' I said, immensely grateful.

'How's it all going? Have you locked up the case?' he asked cheerfully.

'Not quite. Someone's been charged but there's a whole trial to go yet,' I said. 'How's retirement treating you?'

'Marvellous. Should have done it years ago. Although it was interesting looking at your samples. Haven't had any business put my way in ages.'

'That's why you were so prompt,' I said.

When I rang off, I leaned my head in my hands. Normally, I'd have felt elated at such an easy breakthrough and would have started ringing around to see if local stockists remembered these two composite blocks from Victoria. But I had no enthusiasm. Instead, I rang Brian and passed on what Ellis Smith had told me. Keep busy, Jack, I told myself. And go to an AA meeting. I looked at my watch. There was a midday one at St Kelvin's church hall. I had to make myself go.

Even the meeting, with its mix of suffering newcomers, old dinosaurs and smart youngsters with a good grasp on sobriety, couldn't take my mind off the images in my mind of Iona collecting her things and packing her bags. But at least I was reminded by listening to them all that I wasn't alone. That loss and separation was part of our lives. Still, I didn't know how I was going to face the cottage now that Charlie had gone, when every room now held memories of Iona.

After the more formal proceedings, I hung around with a couple of people I hadn't seen for a while and had an Iced VoVo and a cup of teabag

Ceylon while I listened to a newcomer telling me he didn't really have a drinking problem.

'See, I can stop whenever I want to,' he said.

I passed the plate of Iced VoVos to him. 'We can all do that,' I said. 'But obviously you haven't tried *staying* stopped yet.'

He stared at me.

'That's the hard part.'

I picked up a souvlaki roll from the Cretan and drove back to Weston where I ate it in my office as a late lunch. I made myself another tea and rang Jerri Quill's parents.

She was there and she was willing to talk to me. She'd only just heard of Claire Dimitriou's death so she was pretty shaken up. Being a log-keeping scientist, she'd already written an account of the events of that Monday and she'd read over it to refresh her memory. I told her it would take me several hours to get to her parents' place but I'd be there as soon as possible.

Then I dialled the number Bob had given me.

'Shiner,' came the laconic greeting.

'Adam Shiner? I'm ringing you in connection with a murder case,' I said, giving my name and details.

Shiner didn't miss a beat. 'Bob Edwards said you've been looking for me. Tianna Richardson? I used to see her from time to time,' he said. 'But I hear you've charged someone.'

'That's so, but we need to eliminate you officially. I'll be in town this evening,' I said. 'I'd like to catch up with you.'

'I'm a married man, Dr McCain. But I can meet you somewhere.'

He lived at Ryde and we agreed that I'd ring him as I approached Sydney and make a time and place to meet that evening.

I went over Brian's words again and listed the facts. It seemed clear enough that there was sufficient evidence against Damien Henshaw to get to committal. If only, I thought, leaning back in my seat and stretching my aching neck and shoulders, we'd been able to gather such undeniable links to a suspect in the case of Dr Claire Dimitriou's murder. I stood up and pushed my chair back under the desk. That investigation had hit a brick wall.

I packed my notes together, jamming everything into my briefcase. I wanted to fill every minute with work so that there was no space left.

TWENTY-FOUR

Half an hour out of Sydney I rang Adam Shiner. I told him I had an appointment in Lane Cove and he suggested we meet later at the Country Comfort on the Pacific Highway. I agreed, grateful to be busy at this hour and not sitting alone beside the fire, knowing that Iona's car would not be pulling up outside the cottage any more.

About an hour later, I was at the door of Jerri Quill's parents' house. I knew it was her the moment she opened the front door to my knock—piles of tightly curled hair surrounding a wide, intelligent face. She wore a long striped jumper over tights, her face was scrubbed and she resembled a dancer more than someone involved in postgraduate science studies.

After our initial introductions, Jerri took me through the large old house to her untidy room at the rear. Her desk was piled high with papers and folders and the bench tops were littered with specimen jars and other glassware. There was a decent microscope in the corner and a wash-up sink and drainage board.

'Brian Kruger sent someone to take my official statement,' she said, 'not long after we spoke on the phone. I can't believe Claire is dead.'

'Jerri, this is not official,' I said. 'I've heard about the scene with Dr Dimitriou from your flatmate in Canberra. Now I'd like to hear it from you.'

Jerri reached for a bottle of water and drank some, apparently nervous.

'I've already explained all that in my statement. That scene, as you call it, couldn't have had anything to do with Claire getting *murdered*! It was just one of those things. People working close together. Getting in each other's hair. Working long hours. Tempers get short.'

'From what I've heard, it sounded far more serious than just the stress and strain of a long day in the lab. You left town over this dispute. Wendy told me you're considering throwing in your scientific career.'

She turned away from me and went to stare out the window, fiddling with one of her tight curls. She wasn't all that much older than Jacinta and I felt for her.

'Please, Jerri, I wouldn't be here except we're just not getting anywhere with this case. I need your help. Please tell me what happened.'

I saw her shoulders lift in a huge sigh before she slumped down on a large cushion in the corner.

'Sit down,' she said. 'I'm forgetting my manners with all this stress.'

'You're doing fine,' I said. 'You shouldn't let someone's unfortunate overreaction ruin your whole career.' I would have said the same to Jacinta if she'd been in this position.

'It was awful,' she said after a silence. 'I still get upset when I think about it.'

'Tell me.'

'I made a mistake. With an assay,' she said.

'We all do,' I said. 'It's part of being human.'

She gave me a wan smile. 'Dr Dimitriou didn't seem to think so. The way she went on, it was like I'd committed an unforgivable sin.'

'What did you do?'

She was silent a moment. 'That's just it. I wish I knew. I don't know what I did. When Claire went off at me I felt like a little kid again, when some stupid adult won't tell you *why* you're in trouble. Just that you're in it big time.'

I remembered that feeling only too well. *You're so wicked, so lost to goodness, that you don't even recognise a terrible sin when you commit it.*

'I thought I'd done everything according to the instructions,' Jerri continued. 'I'd even opened a new kit. We'd recently switched to a new supplier of reagents and ELISA plates. They were brand new and uncontaminated.' She reached over to get her bottle of water.

Any sense of achievement I might have felt at finally talking to Jerri Quill evaporated. Even *she* didn't know what she'd done. 'So when did it happen?' I asked.

'The Friday before Claire was killed was the beginning of it.' She looked down at her hands, shaken by her own words. I wrote down 'Friday' in my pocket diary.

'Things had been tense in the lab for some weeks before that though,' Jerri was saying. 'Peter had been getting weirder.'

'Tell me,' I said, feigning ignorance.

'He'd got all religious suddenly. Or something. I think he was involved with a cult. He'd brought his Bible into the lab and kept reading out all this death and destruction stuff. It got so bad that I used to dread going there.'

'Okay,' I said. 'So Dr Dimitriou yelled at you on Friday?'

'No, no,' Jerri interrupted me. 'I prepared the assay for the automated process on Friday, but the result wasn't apparent until after the weekend. She didn't yell at me till Monday, when she saw the results of the assay. At the time I was writing up the results.'

'You'd better tell me the whole story,' I said.

'I'd been rushing to leave the lab on the Friday,' she said, 'because my flatmate and I were hoping to get to a six o'clock screening of a movie we wanted to see. Dr Dimitriou asked me to set up the ELISA machine so that we could run an assay on the rabbits' antibody levels over the weekend. Do you know how those tests work?'

'Not really,' I said, hoping she'd give me more details.

'With the Terminator Rabbit project, we've been working with six different strains of the rabbit pox virus—all of them carrying the sterile gene. But naturally one strain is always going to be more effective than another.'

'Dallas Baxter told me a bit about this,' I said. 'But I'd like to hear it from you.'

'Okay,' said Jerri, leaning back. 'We've been working with six rabbits who are variously immune to the six different strains of our specially treated rabbit pox virus. We're trying to find—I mean, we *were* trying to find—the best strain to develop out of the six. Whichever strain we select has to satisfy two criteria. It must be lethal, at least among the feral rabbit population, and it must be efficient in delivering the sterile factor—the Terminator Rabbit gene. Once we've got evidence of infection, we'd be testing to see if the sterile factor has combined with the test rabbits' own DNA. Then the next step will be to see if that in fact does make them sterile. Or if they can still reproduce but pass sterility on to the next generation.'

'So you use rabbits who've been immunised against rabbit pox,' I said.

'That's right,' she said, nodding. 'We don't want to kill them. But we want them to have a non-lethal dose of the disease so that the virus combines with their genetic material. Then we can test further to see if sterility has been factored into their DNA. That part of it is some way down the track. At the moment, we're still refining the different strains of the virus.'

'I don't know anything about rabbit pox.'

'It's a disease of laboratory animals and not yet described in the wild,' Jerri said. 'It's quite harmless to any living creature except rabbits We're hoping to use it eventually against the wild populations and the theory we'll be testing is that after we've introduced some future rabbit pox epidemic, the 5 to 10 per cent of rabbits that tend to survive the virus without immunisation, and which under normal conditions would start breeding up new generations of resistant animals, will now be carrying the sterile gene in their DNA. The way things stand now, that 5 to 10 per cent that do survive pass immunity on to their offspring and so the populations start building up again. That's what happened with myxomatosis. And it's happening now, after the *calicivirus*. This way, we aim to breed out any of the survivors by having the resistant animals carry this fatal flaw in their chromosomes.'

'Because of the sterile gene that's now part of their DNA after they've beaten the infection,' I said. 'It's a very smart hypothesis.'

'Science is full of smart hypotheses,' said Jerri with a faint smile. 'It's seeing if they work in practice that's important.'

'So the immunoassay that you'd set up before the weekend was to test the rabbits' antibody responses?' I asked. 'To make sure they'd contracted the disease?'

'That's right,' said Jerri. 'Just to make sure they'd had a dose sufficient to deliver the sterile gene.'

'So what happened?'

'I did exactly what I was supposed to do. Standard procedure. I set up an ELISA immunoassay to determine whether or not the rabbits had been infected by a dose of rabbit pox. I've done this dozens, hundreds, of times. I set up the plates and the various dilutions of rabbit serum, started the ELISA run and off I went to the movies.'

'Where were Dr Dimitriou and Peter Yu?'

'Not sure. They often worked over in the office area, either alone or together.'

'Help me get a picture of what the assay involved,' I said and gave what I hoped was a reassuring smile. 'It's been a long time since I've done anything like that.'

'The plates come already coated with serum,' she said. 'I added our six test animals' serum to the wells—two rows per rabbit—to test the six strains. They're coded RP1—that's Rabbit Pox 1—and so on to RP6.'

'You allow two rows per rabbit?' I repeated to make sure, jotting down some notes.

'Yes. Each rabbit has a replicate row, just to make doubly sure.'

'That's two by eight lots of wells per rabbit,' I said, half-thinking aloud. 'And then after the immunoassay has done its run, the tests show either positive or negative results.'

'Yes,' said Jerri. 'If there's been no exposure to the disease, there's only a negative reaction and no colour development. But if it's positive, the colour development intensifies and the material in the wells turns blue.'

'Blue,' I repeated trying to integrate this new information and thinking that two by eight equalled sixteen.

'So tell me what happened on Monday.'

'I arrived early and I was the only one there. The green lights on the machine told me the assay was finished. I was writing up the results when Claire arrived.'

'What were the results?'

'That's where the problem started,' Jerri sighed. 'As soon as I took the plate out, I could see that it hadn't been a successful run. The colour hadn't developed in most of the wells. Usually—depending on the degrees of immunity in the individual rabbits and which RP strain they've been given—all the wells are *some* sort of blue. Paler or darker. But except for RP4's two rows, none of the other wells had developed any colour at all. Either the other five rabbits had become so resistant that their systems were no longer even recognising the antigen as a threat and no longer making antibodies, or I must have put the wrong dilutions in or something. But I swear I did exactly the same procedures as I've done many times before. Why would I alter things? I knew the routine by heart. I wondered then if the plate had lost its integrity, been exposed to sunlight or got wet or something. But I knew it had been a brand new sterile pack I'd opened from a brand new carton of supplies. And after all, RP4's wells were showing the deep blue colour development of a positive reaction. So the plate *must* have been viable. All I could do was start writing up the results. And that's what I was doing when Claire came in. I told her about the results and she looked at the plate. She kept staring at me and then at the plate. I asked her, "What is it? What's wrong?" But she seemed speechless. She stood there, pointing to the plate and staring at it. Then she started screaming at me. "Can't you see what's happened here? What have you *done*?"

'I tried to tell her I'd done exactly what I always did. I tried to calm her down. But she was crazy. She kept saying: "Can't you see what you've done? Can't you see what's happened here?" What did I think I was doing using that plate, she asked. I kept telling her it was brand new, from the new supplies. But she couldn't seem to hear me. She kept saying, "What the hell have we done here?" Then she snatched the lab book out of my hand.'

'Did you see what she did with it?'

'No,' said Jerri. 'She just grabbed it, going on about this terrible thing I'd done. Then Peter came in and went over and had a look. They started arguing but I couldn't take any more so I ran out.. I didn't want him to start on at me too.'

'Don't make any hasty decisions about your career yet,' I said after a silence. 'I'm sure the board of examiners would understand your distress—under the circumstances—and you could switch to another research lab without penalties to your doctorate.'

Jerri stood up and went to the window. 'I just don't know. I'm not used to that sort of behaviour. I didn't think science was like that. I don't want to work in a world where people behave hysterically. And Peter had been freaking me out with his religious stuff and, before that he'd been stressed out of his head. And now, with Claire murdered... Everything's gone crazy and irrational.'

I had to keep a straight face. What did Jerri Quill think the world was *like*? Irrational was a defining characteristic.

'I hope I've been of some help. I can't cope thinking that Claire's killer is out there somewhere,' she said, taking her glasses off and slipping them in a pocket.

'Wendy asked me to send you her love,' I said, remembering after a pause.

'Before I go,' I added, paying great attention to her face, 'did you ever see anything between Claire and Peter of a romantic nature? Anything to indicate that they might be more to each other than workmates?'

Jerri shook her head. 'Absolutely not. Claire was a very proper woman.'

I smiled to myself. If only she knew.

'She didn't approve of Peter Yu at all.'

'She knew about his girlfriends?' I asked.

'Everyone knew about his girlfriends! He had a new one every month! He was notorious. Even a humble little doctoral student like me knew about it.' She looked down at her fingernails. 'He was pressuring me at one stage—wouldn't let up until I practically had to insult him.'

As I was leaving, I turned to her. 'Wendy misses you. Don't lose sight of your ambition, just because of this. Your life's too important.'

'Maybe.'

'No maybe about it. Because one day, if you finish your doctorate, I might need to call on you. Jerri, we all need each other in this game.'

I sat in the car, thinking about what I'd just heard from Jerri, keeping my mind away from Iona by working hard at putting things together, trying to fit the pieces in the right way. Something had happened in the Terminator Rabbit lab, something to do with a rabbit pox assay and whatever it was, it had created the necessary conditions for the murder of a scientist. 'She saw sixteen blue... *something*' Claire had repeated to her partner in the heated argument overheard by Kevin Waites. Sixteen blue *wells*. Claire must have been referring to Jerri and the assay results. But why? Why did sixteen positive wells create such a disturbance? Wouldn't Dr Dimitriou have been more disappointed with the *negative* results from the other five test rabbits? At least RP4 had responded to the infection successfully.

Taking a break from trying to make sense of all this, I rang my daughter and left a message to tell her that I had some jobs to chase up in Sydney and that I'd be spending the night at Malabar, arriving later.

I stayed sitting in the car. I kept rerunning a scene in my head, like a video replay, of the grief counsellor brushing dandruff from a man's suit. The intimacy of that gesture had been troubling me, stirring under the surface of my everyday mind. While in Sydney I was going to drop in on Earl

Richardson. As far as I was concerned, he wasn't out of the frame for his wife's death. Then I turned the car in the direction of the Pacific Highway and aimed for the Country Comfort.

I didn't recognise Adam Shiner immediately but I could hardly be blamed—this was the first time I'd seen him clothed. I looked around the restaurant and, seeing a fair man sitting alone at a corner table, took a punt and won.

Shiner had unruly fair eyebrows, cagey eyes and a thin mouth. He watched me warily as I approached to introduce myself. He didn't offer me a chair but I sat down opposite him anyway.

'You having a drink?' he asked and I shook my head.

'Why didn't you come forward earlier? You must have known we'd turned up your photograph,' I said.

'I thought the reason would be pretty obvious,' he said after a pause. 'Like I said on the phone, I'm a married man. You know how these things are. Besides,' he added, 'I was with Tianna the afternoon she died. It wouldn't have looked good.'

'It looks worse that you didn't come forward,' I said. He shrugged and I knew only too well what that meant. Don't get involved. Never admit anything. Deny everything. Don't get involved was the name of the game, and most men would stay quiet if they thought they could get away with it, especially cops. He was only here now because of the teamwork of two old partners, Bob Edwards and me.

'What time did you leave?' I asked, thinking of the fight with young Damien in the evening.

'Must have been about three thirty, four o'clock when I left. We had lunch, then went back to her place and had sex. And she was alive and well, I can tell you,' he leered.

'We'll need a DNA sample from you,' I said.

'For elimination purposes,' he said dryly before I could say it myself.

I took down his details and got him talking about his background with the NSW police. He'd spent some years with stolen vehicles, circulated around various squads, including some time with South Sydney crime scene. Currently he was working as a detective in South West Sydney region.

'Tell me,' I said, 'how and when did you meet Mrs Richardson?'

'I was on a secondment down there, with the Feds, a couple of years ago. I went to the Blackspot Nightclub. I'd heard a bloke could do all right for himself there.'

'I wouldn't know,' I said.

'Tianna and I hit it off. I used to drive down when I could. Do a bit of fishing. Maybe once every month—six weeks or so.'

'You must have realised we'd want to talk to you,' I said. 'That we'd find those photographs.'

'Which photographs are you talking about?'

I told him about the one taken at the Cat and Castle and he remembered it. Then I mentioned the others, the athletic series.

'Christ,' he said. 'She must have set that up without me knowing. I was very uneasy when I found out she was separated from someone who used to be in the job. I didn't want a jealous husband on my back.'

'Do you know Earl Richardson?'

'A bit. He graduated from the academy same year as me. But I never had anything to do with him. We moved in different groups. I'd spoken with him a couple of times over the years before he left the job. Funny that your mate Bob Edwards was in the same intake as me, too. We marched together on graduation day.'

'We'll need an alibi from you,' I said, uninterested in his graduation day reminiscences.

'No probs. I had to hurry back to Sydney that night for a get-together at a mate's place. I was there most of the night.'

I knew how a mob of cops could scrum down and rehearse a story, particularly if it meant protecting one of their own. But if he was telling the truth, I thought, taking the mate's name and number and making a quick calculation, Adam Shiner was off the hook. According to Harry, Tianna had died later in the evening—somewhere around ten—give or take a few hours.

'I'll get my mate to do a formal statement,' Shiner was saying 'and bring it with me when I drive down for the forensic conference.'

That was almost upon me. With everything that had happened recently, it had dropped out of my mind.

'That won't be necessary,' I said. 'It'll be followed up in the usual way.'

Shiner signalled a waiter and called him over.

'Sure you won't change your mind?' he asked, ordering a beer.

'Very sure,' I said.

'There's quite a big group of us coming down for the conference,' he continued. 'We're going to get together one night and have a dinner—an informal reunion celebration somewhere in town. The accommodation at the AFP academy is booked solid.'

'I heard a rumour that Tianna liked it rough. Was that your experience?'

Shiner, head on one side, considered. 'No,' he said. 'But I heard that too. And quite recently.'

'Where?' I asked.

'You know how these things get bandied around.'

I murmured something. It was time for me to leave; I could feel the grief and weariness combine and I wanted to be alone to lick my wounds.

I took my leave of Shiner and, back at the car, left a message on Brian's voicemail giving him the name and number of Shiner's mate. Then I rang Bob to see if he was coming down for the conference, saying he was welcome to stay at the cottage. Like me, Bob had never been one of the boys and I knew he'd rather bed down with a king brown than with a whole mob of police.

TWENTY-FIVE

I drove up the rise to my Malabar house, smelling the salt on the night air and listening to the pounding of the waves against Boora Point, always louder at night when other sounds fell still. An inside light was on, but Jacinta's car wasn't there.

Inside, I made myself a toasted cheese sandwich for dinner and sat down at the kitchen table, bringing my notes from the discussions with Jerri Quill and Adam Shiner up to date. I was almost finished when I heard the sound of Jacinta's car arriving and I put the kettle on and went to the front door to welcome her.

'What is it, Jass?' I asked, alarmed by the expression on her face, the way she barely kissed me, but hurried inside with me following.

'It's Shaz,' she said. 'She didn't come to lectures yesterday and she's not answering her phone. I want to go round there. I've just been discussing it with Andy.'

'Don't,' I said. 'Tell her family.'

'As if they'd care. Her mother thinks I'm jealous. She's hoping Shaz will *marry* this pig! He's a perfect gentleman, she told me.' She paused. 'I want to go round tomorrow and make sure she's okay. Andy reckons I should stay out of it—that it's Shaz's business.'

'She's the only one who can make the decision to break it off,' I said, 'but if he's bashing her, that's everyone's business.'

Automatically, I put some more toast and cheese on for her. 'I've got some time tomorrow,' I said. 'I'll come with you when you go.'

'There's no need, Dad. Don't make it into a big drama. Shaz lives in a share house anyway. There'll be other people around. I don't want you to come. You upset her dreadfully last time you were with her.'

'I think it's more upsetting to be used as a punching bag,' I said. 'If having the truth pointed out is worse—'

'Dad! Give it a rest!'

'And what if he's there or comes round while you're trying to talk her out of leaving him? Have you thought what his reaction might be?'

'Dad! Stop worrying! I'm going tomorrow and that's it. Okay?'

'Make sure you don't go alone,' I said, knowing it was useless to argue with my wilful daughter. 'I don't want you going to a place where you might have to confront a violent man. Okay? Now wash your hands and come and eat something.'

She didn't say anything as she went to the sink and scrubbed up, returning to the table and sitting down to the plate of toasted cheese sandwiches.

'Has Iona moved out?' she finally asked.

'As far as I know,' I said. 'I couldn't stick around and watch. She moved out today.'

'Dad, I'm really sorry.' She got up and came around to stand behind me, kiss the top of my head and drape her arms around me. 'I think you'll get back together,' she said. 'I feel sure.'

'Jass, it's me. I can't seem to take the time off. I mean to, but I can't turn my back on my responsibilities.'

'You're hopeless,' she said. 'Mum used to say you were never there.'

I sighed. I didn't want to discuss this with my daughter right now.

'Promise me,' I repeated. 'You'll take Andy. Or better still take Bob when you go round to Shaz's place.'

Finally, I extracted the promise that she'd call Bob and, if Karl Docker arrived, she'd leave immediately. 'That's the deal,' I said. 'You don't know how these things can escalate when you're dealing with a man with no impulse control.'

'Dad! You're sounding like Uncle Chas! Stop worrying so much. Mum was right. You only look for the worst in every situation.'

I didn't say, I don't have to *look* for it, the worst has always been there. Instead, I made her promise one more time that she would not go round to Shaz's place without Bob.

She went into her room and closed the door, leaving me sitting at the kitchen table feeling as lonely as I used to when I was a little kid.

I needed an early night but I lay awake a long time, listening to the thud of the waves.

Next morning, Jacinta and I breakfasted together and before she left for the library I made her renew her promise about visiting Shaz.

'You have a good day,' I said. 'I'll ring tonight when I get back.'

'What are you going to do about Iona?' Jacinta asked.

'What do you recommend?' I replied. 'Any suggestions gratefully received.'

'Me and Greg got used to you not being around,' she said, shrugging. 'Kids have to stay. We didn't have an alternative.'

'You're saying Iona is exercising her option. That's not a suggestion.'

'You really want a suggestion? There's something you should've done a long time ago.'

'What's that? Leave the job?'

'No. Reorder your priorities.'

I waved her off, considering her words, then rang Bradley Strachan at the Glebe morgue. I was in luck as he was on duty on a Sunday and I arranged to borrow the box containing 17/2000 from the bone room.

Bradley wasn't there when I arrived, having been called out in the interim, but one of the technicians helped me locate the remains I was looking for and I filled out and signed the necessary receipts. I had a quick look at the contents—a badly damaged skull sat on top of the rest of the bones and under all this were plastic bags and containers holding the pitiful bits and pieces found with the remains.

With the box safely in a carry bag, I headed for the address I had for Earl Richardson. A semi in Glebe, it was easy to find and I pulled up across the road from it. Like most of those places, it fronted the main street with a lane at the back and I found its backside and looked over the sagging old timber fence. I stared at the clothes line running the length of the back of the house. Maybe Earl had a sister or other female relative staying with him and the sexy bras and panties swaying in the morning sunlight belonged to her. But I thought not. I walked back to my car and sat there thinking a moment. Then I rang Bob.

'I've just taken delivery of one of your old friends, 17/2000, and I'm going to have another look at the physical evidence in the box with him. We'll cop any expense.'

Bob was happy to hear it. It meant one less job for his Unsolved Homicide Unit and a little more in the budget kitty.

'But there's a catch,' I said, giving him Earl Richardson's address in Glebe. 'There's a place I want you to keep an eye on. See who comes and goes.'

I continued my drive south, linking back up with the freeway, travelling on automatic pilot, the speedo needle sitting on 110. I tried to make sense of Claire Dimitriou's extreme reactions to a routine immunoassay result. After questioning Jerri

Quill, I was still trying to work out what might have happened in that laboratory. Something had changed when Claire saw the assay plate results. Maybe with her husband away on a conference in New Zealand and finding her work partner seriously unbalanced and becoming irrationally religious, Claire Dimitriou overreacted to an otherwise minor error on the part of her student. Perhaps I'd never discover what happened in that laboratory nor why Claire Dimitriou had died. We seemed to be no closer to finding the truth about who had killed her or why.

By the time I took the left hand of the Y-junction at the turn-off to the Canberra road, I was still wondering about the motive for her murder. Thinking about the enormous sums of money to be made from scientific improvements in pest control, I was starting to consider that Claire Dimitriou's murder had been less about sex and more about science.

Once back at Forensic Services, I kept busy, trying not to think of the drive out to the cottage I had to make this evening. I logged the box containing the skeletal remains and, gloving up, sorted through the packets that lay at the bottom of the box. I found the labelled packet that I hoped would contain traces of the rare native orchid. God knows it was a long shot, but until we found a primary crime scene for Tianna Richardson's murder, the investigation was handicapped. At the same time I could test for DNA, because every year the extraction and amplification of nuclear DNA was being refined and improved. Even though bone itself didn't provide nuclear material it was just possible that there might be traces of protected genetic material in the cracks and fissures of the leather sandals that Bob's unknown male from Queanbeyan had been wearing when he died. With our ability to amplify even the barest traces, it might be possible to make a nuclear DNA profile. At least give a family the chance to bury their son. A gravesite was better than never having anything at all.

Even though it was Sunday, I rang Gavin Samways home number and he agreed to do a plaster cast of the skull after Sofia Verstoek had taken anything helpful for her pollen assemblage. As I rang off, I realised I'd hardly thought of the Brazilian—Iona's decision to leave me had swamped all my other recent concerns.

To prevent further brooding on this issue, I set to work worrying at one of the things Charlie and I had discussed previously. I had to admit to myself that it was almost impossible for me to do the very thing that Iona wanted from me—to simply be. I had to be *doing* or I started to feel like I was feeling now.

One day, I thought, I should find out what happens if I don't allow the restlessness to push me into further action. What would happen if—as I'd suggested to the reality-denying AA newcomer about drinking—I stopped and stayed stopped?

One day, I vowed to myself, I'd find out. But not right now, with every spare moment needing to be filled. No way I wanted to sit in the cottage alone. A drive would get me moving so I looked up the address Brian had given me and headed out to the foothill country. I wanted to find out more about Jason Richardson's childhood.

It was a pleasant drive and in less than forty minutes, I'd found the small foothill village and taken the turn-off to Sparrows Ridge Road. As I pulled up at the address, I saw Jason's panel van and a small two-door hatchback parked in the driveway outside the cottage, which lay partly hidden in a garden of native vegetation.

I rang the doorbell and soon after a pleasant woman in her sixties answered and ushered me inside while shooing her over-friendly golden Labrador out of my way.

'Jason's told me about the necklace,' said Alana Richardson, after I'd explained why I was there. 'It was very wrong of him to take it. But it's good to know where it is.'

'Where is Jason?' I asked, smiling reassuringly. Behind Mrs Richardson, wide picture windows looked across a valley.

'He's out the back. Fixing the back fence. Earl's father was going to do it, then Earl.' She opened her hands in a gesture of helplessness as if to say 'Men!' 'I've told Jason he'll have to pull his weight if he wants to stay here. I love him but I've made it clear I don't think it's right for a young man to be idling away his life like he is. I keep telling him he's got to settle down and *do* something.'

I nodded in assent, sympathetic but wondering for a fleeting moment if Jason could give me a few tips.

'We've all been in shock, I think, with Tianna's death. The way it happened. It's time to move on and make the best of our lives.' She turned away quickly and went to put the kettle on.

'How did Jason and Earl get on?' I asked.

Alana shrugged. 'Okay. There were fights. But then that happens in any family.'

'What were the fights about?'

'Earl is a pretty tough father. He's always expected a lot from Jason.'

'What about when he was a little fellow?' I asked, remembering Charlie's hypothesis about violent backgrounds. 'Was Earl tough then?'

'Earl's always been tough,' she said. 'His father was too. In the last few years, the fights were usually about Jason's lifestyle. The way he just travels round Australia surfing. He'll be twenty-one soon. And he doesn't seem to understand that he's going to have make a living for himself. A *life* for himself.'

I thought about what 'tough' might mean to a two- or three-year-old. And then I thought about the kids for whom there were no decent jobs. Even after Jacinta and Greg had finished their studies, there were no guarantees of employment at the other end.

'The sad thing is that Jason absolutely adores his father. He'd do anything for him. If only Earl would just soften a bit, not come down so hard on the kid, he could have Jason eating out of his hand. He responds so well to me when I'm encouraging. But he really needs his father.'

'We all do,' I told her, feeling an ache in my own heart.

Alana Richardson suddenly looked embarrassed, as if she'd exposed too much family business.

'That necklace,' I said, 'is worth a couple of thousand dollars. The jeweller gave me an estimate.'

'I hadn't realised,' she said. 'And I doubt if Lily realises it either.'

She saw my puzzlement and explained. 'It's not mine. It belongs to Earl's first wife, Lily. Lily Meadowes she was. Such a pretty name and so is she—or was, when I knew her. There are still a few of her things around my place.'

'What was Jason's mother like?' I asked.

'Lily?' Alana Richardson thought a moment then reached behind her for a small framed coloured photograph. 'Here she is.'

The image quality wasn't good, with its fading eighties Polaroid colours showing a young girl looking down at a baby in her arms. It was hard to see her features because her thick, dark hair all but hid her face. I turned it over and read the date and inscription: *Jason's first birthday 23.3.84.*

Twenty-third of March, same month as Greg's birthday, I noted, as Alana continued.

'She and Jason had the same birthday nineteen years apart. She was just a kid and I think it was all too hard for her, leaving the UK, new country, new family.' Mrs Richardson took the old photo from me and replaced it on the shelf. 'Then later, after she left Australia, I think she just wiped her hands of us. I know she found it hard being a mum. I did all I could to help, but she resented me a bit. The intrusive mother-in-law. Jason was a difficult little kid. Spitting image of her. And had her temper too. You know what little boys are like.'

I felt a pang of guilt. I hadn't been around much when Greg was a little fellow. I'd left most of that to Genevieve.

'Lily never had a mother herself,' Alana was saying. 'She was raised by her grandmother too, like Jason. So I used to make allowances for her.'

Family patterns, I thought. Charlie could tell Alana Richardson a thing or two about these mysterious repetitions.

'I keep Mum's and Lily's little pieces—not that there are many—in here.' She stood back from the living room door to let me through.

I couldn't help showing off. 'I think I know where they are,' I said.

She turned, surprised.

'They'll be in a drawer. At waist height. I'd look for them in your bedroom. Probably your dressing-table.'

'How did you know that?' she said, shocked.

'I'm an old hand,' I said.

'In women's bedrooms?'

We both laughed as we walked into one of the smaller rooms off the hall and, sure enough, she went straight to her dressing-table, opened the waist-high drawer and drew out a long black leather box. I could see she was still deep in thought and memory.

'It must have been hard, being married to my son. Earl has some of his father's old-fashioned attitudes about women, I'm afraid. And I think they've got worse since he got religion. He and Lily were staying here before they separated.' She sighed. 'It was a sad time. I'd been away at a girlfriend's place and so I didn't even get the chance to say goodbye. I got a couple of postcards from Lily and then one saying she'd decided to go back home to the UK. After that, she just stopped writing.' She opened the box without looking into it, still reminiscing. 'And I have to say, I was angry with her for a long time. What sort of woman leaves her baby like that?' She tried to lighten up. '*And* her jewellery? Anyway, her earrings are—'

She stopped as she looked into the narrow container. It was quite empty.

'Were they supposed to be in the box?' I asked.

'Always! With the necklace.' She turned round and called out the window. 'Jason? Come in here this minute!'

She turned back to me. 'Why? Where are they?'

I told her where they'd been found and she was suddenly very quiet.

'I don't understand. How did Tianna get hold of them?' She started looking around in the opened drawer, pushing underwear aside. 'And Granny's things aren't here either.'

'What else is missing?' I asked.

'I had a small bag of my late mother's personal items. Nothing valuable. Her rosary beads, her glasses, good Christian Dior ones that I keep meaning to give to St Vinnie de Paul with her old dentures. And *her* mother's Victorian mourning brooch with a lock of her mother's hair in it.' She gave a little smile. 'Bit grisly, really. I suppose it might have some value as an antique. It was nicely set in gold, glass on both sides, a few pearls, I think.'

We left the bedroom, and she marched over to the window and yelled Jason's name again. Finally, he came in, dusting himself down, work boots and old hat in place.

'What's up?' he asked and then he saw me and his face registered shock. Slowly, he took off his hat, his hands clenching it in front of him. Although his grandmother was brandishing the empty jewellery box at him, it was a moment before he could focus on what she was saying.

'You didn't say anything about pinching Granny's things. And the earrings!'

'What things? What earrings?'

I watched carefully. He looked genuinely bewildered.

'I didn't take anything else. I told you about the necklace!'

'I find that hard to believe, Jason,' I said. It was possible Mrs Richardson had mislaid her late mother's personal odds and ends but she'd said the missing earrings had been together with the necklace in the black box. 'Why would you take the necklace and leave the earrings behind?'

'Because there *were* no frigging earrings to leave behind!'

'Don't speak like that, Jason!' said Alana.

'Like what? The only thing inside that case was the necklace! I don't know anything about Granny's other things or any earrings! Maybe Tianna came over and took them herself.'

Alana Richardson turned to me. 'She did ask to borrow them once, when I showed her Granny's things. But I said they weren't mine to lend. Now what am I going to tell Lily when she wants them back?'

'Stop dreaming. She's never going to want them back,' said Jason. 'She's forgotten all about them by now.'

There was a sadness in his voice. Peridots and pearls weren't the only thing Jason's mother had left behind. I felt both anger and sympathy rising in the heat at the back of my neck. Like my mother, Lily Richardson had left the upbringing of her son largely to chance.

'Why did you take the necklace, son?' I asked.

The youth seemed embarrassed, sheepish even. 'It wasn't like I was thieving,' he said finally. 'I was going to put it back after a mate took a photo of it so I could put it on the web.'

'For eBay?' I asked.

Jason's eyes looked like those of an injured dog as he slowly turned his long, narrow face away from me. 'He was going to take a photo of it to attach to my ICQ program. So I could email it. I thought if she wouldn't come home for me, she might come home for her bloody jewels.'

Lily, I thought, you've stayed away too long. You really should come home and see your son. Attend to unfinished business.

'I wanted to find her,' Jason continued. 'Show Dad that I'm not the useless bastard he thinks I am.'

'When did you take it?'

'Couple of hours before you found it in my glove box. Lucky, aren't I?'

After we'd talked a bit longer, Jason returned to his labouring. I watched him out the window, back at work, lifting blocks onto a retaining wall. Then I thanked Alana Richardson and turned to leave.

Suddenly I noticed that the Polaroid of the young woman and the baby had gone. Jason must have pocketed it.

'Speak frankly,' I said, turning near the front door. 'This is just between you and me. Tell me about Tianna. What sort of woman was your late daughter-in-law?'

Alana hesitated a moment. 'I did my best for Earl and her. I used to invite them here for dinner at least once a month,' she said and paused. 'But Tianna and I, we just never saw eye to eye. Maybe it was the generation gap. Maybe it was because I wanted more grandchildren. I never actually said that, but I was disappointed and I think she picked that up.' Her face softened with sadness. 'But Tianna didn't want babies. Tianna just wanted to party.'

'Thanks for being so frank,' I said. 'I appreciate it.'

'Don't be too hard on my grandson,' she said as she opened the door. 'Apart from that photograph, the jewellery is pretty well all he's got of his mother.'

He'd got a better deal than I had, I thought, getting back into my car, thinking of the sad kid and the necklace. The only thing I'd got from my mother was alcoholism.

TWENTY-SIX

As I pulled the seatbelt on, I sniffed, thinking for a moment I might have brought a memento of the Labrador with me on my shoes. But then the smell vanished.

On the drive back to Forensic Services, I mulled over some possibilities. If Damien Henshaw hadn't killed Tianna, it was possible Jason Richardson had. I knew more than most what it felt like to be angry with a mother—a stepmother might be even more problematic. By killing Tianna, Jason could have avenged himself twice: once for the way he was abandoned by his birth mother, and once to punish the woman who'd replaced her.

The earrings, although they weren't any sort of proof—Tianna could have taken them herself any time, sneaked into the house when her mother-in-law was absent—still teased me, as did the woollen skirt Tianna had chosen to wear that night. I'd held in my own hands the perfectly fitting, matching skirt that went with her ensemble, the black and silver earrings bought that day to go with the black and silver two-piece outfit. Why hadn't she worn them? What had turned her off them? Again, I had the strong feeling that if I knew why she'd worn Lily's earrings that night, I'd be halfway to knowing the whole story.

Back in my office, I revisited in my mind's eye the crime scene in the car park of the Blackspot and reviewed all I'd found there. I did the same with Tianna's pretty bedroom. Somewhere, these questions had answers, but I just couldn't see them. Jason, Tianna's angry stepson, was a very credible suspect and Adam Shiner, the smooth and plausible Sydney detective who used to drive down from Sydney from time to time to visit Tianna, was also not to be dismissed too quickly. On the surface, he had no motive to kill a woman who, from all accounts, was quite happy to oblige him. But what if Tianna had threatened to tell Shiner's wife about their liaison, as she'd done with Damien Henshaw and his fiancée? Too many people might have wanted Tianna Richardson dead and, despite the mounting evidence against Damien Henshaw, I was still uneasy. I stood up and walked to the window. The weather had turned bleak and cold and the thought of the empty cottage chilled my soul as well.

I rang Charlie. 'I thought about what you said and I've got a problem,' I admitted, once we were through the greetings.

'You sure have,' said Charlie. 'But what are you going to do about her?'

'That's not what I meant,' I replied. 'Brian's arrested a fellow for the murder at the Blackspot Nightclub, but there are two issues that concern me. The first is, the suspect doesn't have a violent background—'

'How do you know?' Charlie interrupted.

'His parents are Quakers,' I said.

Charlie considered. 'That might be so, but it's impossible to say that someone didn't have a violent childhood. These things are often kept very secret.'

'And the second point,' I said, pressing on, 'is the case keeps reminding me of something I was involved with years ago that I've always felt bad about. A long time ago, when I was in my old job, I did something dishonest—'

'No!' said Charlie, feigning dismay. 'You *didn't*! And you a New South Wales police officer!'

'And the suspect suicided,' I went on, ignoring him again. 'So now I'm plagued with the thought that the kid Brian's charged with the Blackspot murder isn't the right man.'

'So you want to make a full and frank confession concerning one of the sins of your youth,' said Charlie and paused. 'Did you say "murders"?'

'Yes. Both victims were murdered the same night and physical evidence links them to each other.'

I told him about the grey granite particles and I could tell from his tone that he was hearing me, taking me seriously now. I told him more of what I'd discovered regarding Jason Richardson and his unfortunate family situation.

'You sure you're not projecting *our* mother onto his?' asked Charlie. 'Just because you'd like to have murdered your mother doesn't mean that young man does.'

I wasn't sure what to make of this. Charlie's remarks sometimes took me by surprise.

'Oh, by the way,' he said, 'I ran into Genevieve shopping.'

I was surprised. Genevieve and my brother had never liked each other.

'She asked me to dinner,' said Charlie. 'I couldn't believe my ears.'

'She's got a new man. Maybe she's feeling happier,' I said, remembering something Jacinta had told me a few weeks ago.

'Maybe she wants to talk about him, run him past me. She's hitting midlife. It's often the time when women start looking at their pattern in choosing men. She might be seeing at last that she chooses dreadful men.'

'Thanks a lot.'

'I should have said "unsuitable". You've improved a lot, Jack,' said Charlie. 'You're a new man since you gave up the booze and certainly not the man Genevieve married. But you really need to look at why you're stuffing up with Iona. It's not too late, Jack. You could still retrieve the situation.'

I remained silent, defeated by my own deficiencies.

'Look,' said Charlie, 'as to your earlier confession. I'm not unsympathetic to it. In fact, it's something I'm working with right now. I have a client at the moment who was in the job in New South Wales for over thirty years. He's seeing me because of something a bit like what you mentioned.'

'So how do you think you'll help him?' I asked. 'You can't undo what has been done.'

'No, you can't,' said my brother. 'But you can talk about it. Let it out of the secrets bag. He's done that and he's come up with an idea. Atonement.'

'What?' I couldn't believe the word my brother was using.

'That's what I said. Or rather, what *he* said. Think about it. Haven't you got a similar tradition in AA? Making amends.'

He was right. I hadn't made amends to anyone for a while. And it wasn't because I hadn't offended anyone. It was because I didn't know what to do—how to make amends to the woman I loved. Until I discovered how to be the man she wanted, there was little point in trying to make amends.

If that ever happened at all, I thought, it would have to come from a very different man to the one I was right now.

I glanced at my watch, then headed with the box of bones to the palynology building with its centrifuge and the special facilities for storing the very dangerous hydrofluoric acid used in obtaining the pollen assemblage. Hydrofluoric acid was something like the acid made by Sigourney Weaver's aliens—capable of eating through everything.

Carefully, I lifted out the bones and placed them on the clean white paper on the table. For this case, there were no accompanying pile of papers in a folder, no brief, no casenotes. No witnesses to interview, no suspects to follow up. Nothing except these bones, a case number and the pitifully few details scrawled and photocopied then stuck on one side: *#17: unknown male, Queanbeyan, 2000.*

It was apparent that large sections of the skeleton were missing, but the skull and separated mandible were both present, as were some of the ribs, sternum, arm and leg bones, part of a pelvis, and numerous vertebrae, plus bits and pieces of the delicate hand and foot bones. These smaller bones tended to be the first ones lost to scavengers and weathering. I was no expert with bones but I could see these no longer had the waxy quality found in fresher bones and the colours ranged from fawns to browns. They were clean and old.

In a bag at the bottom of the box was a small plastic bag containing fragments of clothing, some rotted denim, bits of a discoloured fabric and, in a separate packet, some pieces of light brown hair, fairer at the ends. I pounced on those and looked at them more closely, observing there was no follicle attached to any of them. All tissue had perished long ago.

From one of the plastic packages I pulled out a stiff leather sandal, turning it to see the worn sole and then back again, revealing the embossed straps of the upper, still in fair condition. I put the rotting sandal down and picked up the mandible. I saw that the teeth looked healthy and the gracile nature of the jaw indicated a slight-framed youth, like Greg had been until the last year or two when he'd started to fill out.

After replacing the jaw bone, I turned my attention to the plastic bag again, carefully drawing out what was left of the fabric, dull blue and yellowish brown with what looked like the remnants of a floral pattern, possibly from a Hawaiian shirt. As I did, bits of soil and other traces fell to the paper. Sofia Verstoek would take samples from this as well as the bones; it would give her something to sink those fangs of hers into, besides her colleagues. An environmental profile would reveal traces from the environment where the remains had turned up. In all likelihood, that was a secondary crime scene, such as that at the Blackspot car park, but I was hoping we just might get lucky with a trace profile of the primary scene and match this against the profile from Tianna Richardson's scene. It was time I had a bit of luck, I thought. Things couldn't get much worse for me in the personal area.

I returned my focus to the bones, doing my best to stack a section of vertebrae in order so that they nestled together. The spine was a beautiful piece of engineering and I sat the skull atop the atlas, where it balanced a moment, before rolling off to reveal the large anterior hole with fine radiating fractures around it. It was quite clear what had killed the youth. Someone had bashed his head in.

Holding it in my gloved hands, I studied the back of the skull more closely, just in case there was evidence of scattered shot injuries. None showed. Until we'd discovered his identity, we didn't have a hope in hell of finding out who might have killed him, nor the weapon used.

Unidentified bones asked a question as poignant as the ruins of an old homestead, I thought, as I peered into the orbital sockets right through to the ruined cranium plates. Once a young man's consciousness had lived in here and this present emptiness behind the sockets never quite ceased to amaze me. Carefully, I put the skull down and picked up one of the kneecaps, the small patella. There was no point in taking samples for mitochondrial DNA unless we had a maternal sample against which to match it. Our lab dealt only in nuclear DNA from the tissue samples sent to us by various physical evidence personnel—traces of blood, saliva, semen or shed skin cells. No one in Australia worked with mtDNA and now that the FBI didn't do it for us any more, we had to send samples to England, to a facility where a whole lab had to be dedicated to just one sample because of the extreme sensitivity involved and the dangers of contamination.

I carefully put the skull down again, placing it together with the rest of the bones and sweepings from the paper, making sure nothing was lost.

If only we could get a useful environmental profile, I thought, recalling a couple of recent interstate cases where forensic palynology had swung a conviction. Living things were not distributed randomly but had very specific needs, which restricted them to areas that matched those needs. With a little luck there was an outside chance that Sofia might come up with a possible location that matched the botanical, sedimentary and mineral distributions found on Tianna Richardson's clothes and, by refining this further, we might gather a little more information about the rare native. It could help narrow down a potential primary crime scene. And this in turn, if it was the same orchid, could help with the unidentified youth's case. Of course, it might turn out to be a completely different species and then my efforts with 17/2000 would have been in vain. But, right now, I needed to keep busy like never before.

For a split second it occurred to me that Iona had left me because I was always busy and that my defence against her leaving had been to increase my level of busyness. But I brushed that insight aside and focused on the bones in front of me. I had another hope about examining these remains: that there would be sufficient nuclear material left for me to produce a DNA profile. This could then be matched against any families who'd lost an adolescent son about twenty years ago.

I took the packages that had come with the bones and carefully cut samples from the anonymous floral shirt as well as probing and scraping the inner sole of the cracking sandals. These were very lightly made, but I hoped that perhaps there'd still be some trace genetic material in the grooves of the discoloured stitching that ran around the edges.

Finally, I was satisfied that I had enough material to reveal whether or not any nuclear DNA had survived the elements. DNA breaks down rapidly with radiation, but this body had been stashed under a rock ledge and then partially covered. There was just a chance.

I took the samples from the examination room and soon had the system up and running. I could get on with all the rest of my life while Profiler Plus worked its automated magic.

I was degowning in the disposal area when I saw Sofia Verstoek approaching. I wasn't expecting to see anybody—least of all her. I cleared my throat.

'I have a job that I need you to do. From unknown bones,' I said. 'I'm wondering if you have time to look at it.'

She came right up to me and this time her face and voice were soft. 'That's not a problem.'

I was relieved at this turn of events. Maybe our physical collision had done something to the energy between us. 'I've got them right here,' I said.

She put on her protective gear and took what she needed away.

I went back to my office to catch up on paperwork until her results came through. Finally, there was knock on the door.

'I'm running it all again,' Sofia said. 'This is the third time. I wasn't satisfied with the first soil profile.'

'Why?' I asked.

'Ever since the Kincaid Street property was contaminated by foreign pollen from those wretched floral tributes I've been doing everything at least three times so as to cut out the exotic contaminants. But, in spite of that, I keep getting an anomalous result. I'm going to keep redoing the assemblage until I get a result that makes sense.'

My mobile rang and I snatched it up, nodding to Sofia as she left. It was Mr Vernon from Fletcher Daley Real Estate. I was surprised to hear from him on a Sunday but was pleased when he told me he could help me with the provenance of Peter Yu's set of keys.

TWENTY-SEVEN

An hour later, I was in Brian Kruger's car driving through the late afternoon, the address Mr Vernon had given me written on a piece of paper in my pocket, together with the keys.

'Anthony Dimitriou went home from hospital,' said Brian. 'We've crossed him off the list of suspects.'

I was silent a moment, thinking how quickly life could change from the routine and predictable. Then I brought Brian up to speed.

'Mr Vernon told me it's not really one of their lettings but they act as a drop-off point for keys. It belongs to a cocky and it's a peppercorn rental.'

Brian turned off the road, through an open wire gate and roared up a short dirt track. He pulled up outside a small weatherboard house, the sort built around the turn of last century for a married stationhand.

'This place has no power and only tank water,' I said, as we got out and looked around. 'Usually only hippies live here, according to the real estate agent.'

I could hear a low humming from inside the house and, because I'd been out of constant crime scene work for years, didn't immediately recognise it. Then Brian looked at me and I remembered what it was. As we turned the corner to the back of the house, the humming grew louder. It was the unmistakable sound of massed blowflies and, sure enough, there they were, coating the back wall in their teeming numbers, clustered and swarming, or buzzing in and out of the louvre windows, which were positioned too high to look through.

As I approached the back door, the stench grew and when I looked more closely at the door, I realised it wasn't completely shut. With my shoe I touched it open, then ducked as blowflies hurtled past. But I'd seen enough of what lay on the floor ahead.

'Looks like a job for you,' I said to Brian, retreating.

'Thanks, mate. Just what I need.' He grimaced as he looked through the half-opened back door. Over his shoulder, I saw a black cloud of flies rising from something on the floor in the corner, disturbed by the dim light and movement created by our presence and the opening of the door.

We climbed back into the car and Brian drove up the bumpy dirt track and around the paddocks until he came to the landowner's comfortable house. I waited in the car while he informed the landowner, who, shortly afterwards, climbed into his Range Rover and followed us down the track, locking his gates behind us.

'Are you going to go inside?' he asked.

'We can't really,' I said. 'We haven't got the equipment we need for this.' I'd noticed a generator near the back wall but its fuel gauge showed empty. 'There's no power source here. We need lights and crime scene gear.'

'I'll need to go and get my stuff,' Brian said.

'I can wait here,' I told him, realising I'd do almost anything not to go back to my empty cottage.

'I'll be back at the house if you need me,' said the property owner and walked back to his 4WD.

As the sky darkened, the sound of the blowflies eased and finally stopped. It would be more merciful for us inside later rather than in daylight.

Despite my best intentions, I rang Iona's mobile without result and the line at the cottage as well. But she hadn't changed her mind and the call rang out in an empty room. I didn't let myself think too much and busied myself making other calls. I spoke to Dallas Baxter, reminding him of the staff lists he'd been promising me for some days now and telling him that we'd probably found Peter Yu but to keep it to himself until it became official.

'I'll drive over to work,' he said, sounding shaken, 'and meet you there later.'

Finally, Brian returned with a wagonload of gear. 'I didn't bring Debbie with me because I've got you, mate,' he grinned, passing me a Tyvek suit and shoe covers and getting me to help him lift the generator out of the back.

When I told him I didn't mind, I wasn't being dishonest—I needed the distraction because my mind kept turning to Iona and her words of two nights before and my heart ached hearing them afresh in my memory.

Once the police generator started up and the powerful lights beamed into the back area of the farmworker's weatherboard, Brian and I went inside. At this stage, we didn't know what we were walking into—another murder, a freak accident, a suicide or a sudden natural death. But we took every precaution, not touching anything, leaving doors and surfaces for the fingerprints people.

'He's bloody overripe,' said Brian as I followed him in, flinching at the intense stench, wielding one of the powerful flashlights in my gloved hands and using it to penetrate into unlit corners and black shadowed areas cast by the bright lights.

The body of the man I presumed to be Peter Yu lay on the linoleum floor in the kitchen near the doorway to another room in a pool of stinking body fluids, discoloured and swollen. Harry Marshall would give a much better estimation of how long the man had lain dead, but my guess was that he'd died not long after Claire Dimitriou.

The place looked unloved, just short of derelict; dusty and neglected, with two or three pieces of old, cheap furniture that no resident had wanted standing in the kitchen. In the cramped, walk-in pantry off the main area, Dr Yu had set up an ad hoc darkroom, I realised, as I peered in at the trays and the battery on the floor from where he'd run lights.

The ancient black range looked like something my grandmother might have used, and near it stood an old kerosene fridge. Kerosene lamps hung from large butcher's hooks on the walls and low ceilings. Ancient linoleum peeled from the floors.

'Looks like he might have shot himself,' said Brian, raising his camera, standing on the other side of the corpse.

I came round to take a look and saw the hole in the right temple that had leaked matter onto the floor.

'There's that Browning you've been looking for,' I said, as Brian took photos of the body and the weapon lying loose in Peter Yu's right hand.

I looked around the kitchen and tried to open some of the dusty windows. Once, they'd slid open, but not for a long time. The timbers had distorted and swollen over the years and they were jammed shut or open, whichever way they'd been left.

On the floorboards, I could see the black stains where Peter Yu had first fallen and the blood splash on the walls.

Carefully, I stepped through the doorway of the room near the body and flashed my torch around the walls. I stood there, stunned for a few seconds. Peter Yu must have slept here, I thought, looking at the sleeping bag on the floor, the small camp stove in the corner and its bottle of liquid gas. But it was the walls that had captured my attention.

'Brian, step in here a moment.'

Brian appeared in the doorway and, like me, stood stock-still before joining me further inside the room.

'I never got my head around that giant multi-crystal business,' said Brian. 'But what the hell is this? Is that how science thinks of God?'

'I don't think it had much to do with science or God,' I said. 'I think it's in the realms of complete emotional breakdown.'

'You mean he was Captain Rats?' Brian asked.

'That's one way of putting it,' I said.

It was like walking into an art installation. Every surface, including much of the ceiling, was plastered with blown-up images of galaxies, landscapes and pathogens, enlarged scanning electron microscope images of bacteria, medical imaging of viruses, rampant in their toxic beauty. I thought I could discern what Peter Yu had been aiming at, the intelligent sense of design touted by theists, of repeating patterns, like fractals, of unfolding fern leaves next to a sagittal section through a trumpet shell revealing an identical symmetry.

When I painted, I often marvelled at the way nature used and reused a successful structure, noticing repeat patterns in the macro and micro worlds. The flaky bark of pine trees appeared almost identical with microscopic images of flaky hair shafts. Spirals repeated themselves throughout our world, from the misty twists of galaxies millions of light years away, right down to the intimacy of the way the DNA wound in our chromosomes. For a split second, I touched the edges of what Peter Yu might have been trying to compose.

'This was his chapel,' I said. 'This is what he was struggling to explain to Annette Sommers.'

'Okay. Quite apart from all the giant crystal business, where does the death of his colleague fit in?' said Brian, dispelling the light out of my insight somewhat, so that now only a jumble of miscellaneous images jostled together on a grubby wall.

Slowly, I walked around the small room.

'What do you think, Jack?'

'I'm not a psychic, Brian. I don't get it either.' It wasn't quite true, but I sure wasn't getting the reason for the crime. 'We might never know what happened in the Faithful Bunnies lab.' I paused, reading the contents of a note pinned to the wall under a huge enlargement of the horse head nebula. 'Although this might help us understand more.'

Brian came up to read it out. '*I had to do a terrible thing to stop a blasphemy. I've cleaned up everything. Forgive me.*'

Blasphemy. What a word. He certainly had cleaned up everything. 'It sounds like an admission,' I said. 'But it's still ambiguous.'

We poked around a little longer. 'If your team finds anything that resembles a torn-out page with scientific processes written up on it, let me know,' I said to Brian.

'The missing lab book page? I don't think we'll ever find that.'

I didn't hold much hope either. Whoever ripped out that page had wanted its contents hidden, never to be seen.

Brian finished his recording and photographing and called up the contractors to come and pick up the body while I rang Sofia, inviting her to take samples in the morning.

'God,' said Brian, overhearing me. 'Make sure you give me plenty of warning, so I'm not here when she is.'

After we'd secured the place as well as we could and reloaded the wagon, Brian drove me to the Ag Station so I could pick up copies of the staff lists.

'I want to know what happened,' said Dallas, as soon as he let us into the station. 'Did Peter Yu kill Claire? And then suicide?'

'We did find a note that suggests what you're saying is likely,' said Brian. 'It looks like a murder suicide.'

'It's too early to be definite,' I said. 'We'll have to wait on Harry Marshall. But I think that whatever happened in that laboratory—the reason it was so thoroughly cleaned up to the point of murdering Claire and destroying the page in the lab book—has everything to do with something in that assay that caused the uproar with Jerri Quill on Monday morning.'

'But how could an immunoassay of rabbits create such a situation?' asked Dallas and in the short silence that followed I turned this question over and over.

'The sixteen blue incident was the assay result we need to focus on,' I said. 'Peter Yu went religious I know,' I said, thinking of the extraordinary word Yu had used in his suicide note, 'but how long ago was that?'

Dallas considered. 'I don't know. Two months maybe? People were starting to talk about him by then.'

'And the rabbit immunoassays have been running all that time?' I asked.

'Of course,' said Dallas. 'These routine research tests go on for many months, years sometimes.'

'Yet one particular assay result created a terrible scene last Monday,' I said.

We walked on in silence, past several stacked plastic cartons.

'Look at all these,' said Dallas. 'All waiting for me to check them off invoices. Otherwise we end up being charged for things we don't need or didn't even order in the first place.'

Through the plastic, I could see a number of stacked ELISA plates. Like me, Dallas was expected to do more and more paperwork. Once, before economic rationalisation, we'd had full-time storemen and could get on with our real jobs.

'As if I haven't got enough to deal with,' he complained. 'Two researchers dead, my staff being upset, police everywhere, questions, the media.' His voice cracked and I thought he might start crying. 'Last month I was sent human sera plates in error and spent most of an afternoon chasing them and writing up the returns paperwork. We need animal antigens here,' he said, his voice rising. 'Rabbits, sheep and cattle. These days, it's all requisition orders or countering wrong orders—I waste so much time doing that sort of thing. I'm a scientist, not a bloody clerk.'

I felt sorry for Dallas. He was dealing with the shocking events that had overtaken his research station in his own way, projecting his distress onto less threatening problems like cartons of equipment and wrong orders. Gently, I tried to draw him back to my line of inquiry. 'So, last Monday, you didn't hear anything untoward about the assay result?' I asked.

Dallas frowned. 'I didn't hear anything. It was just another one in a routine series of hundreds—maybe thousands even—of rabbit pox tests,' he said. 'I know how these tests go. Sometimes all the wells show positive, sometimes only some of them, occasionally none of the wells show any antigen reaction. Mostly, it's a mixture because of the different levels of infection. I'm still trying to make sense of what it was about this particular result that meant two of my best people are dead.' He looked at me and his eyes were magnified with tears.

Blasphemy, I thought. Peter Yu had identified a blasphemy and he and Claire had died because of it.

'I still can't answer that,' I said. 'But the sixteen blue incident was the assay result we need to focus on.'

Dallas disappeared into his office and returned with the copied staffing details. I thanked him and put the envelope in my pocket.

'That other information doesn't have to come out now, does it?' he asked anxiously.

'I can't say that, Dallas.' Again I felt sorry for him. Poor bastard, with his fancy house and rich wife and storeman job trying to keep it together, except for the bit he wanted to keep well apart.

'Dallas, how well do you know the Bible?' I asked.

'I used to know it quite well once,' he said. 'When I was younger.'

'Is there any well-known chapter or verse 16?' I said, wondering about blasphemy.

'Like Micah 12, you mean? Not that I've heard of,' he replied.

We parted and I walked back to the car to find Brian half out of his seat, holding up his mobile. 'It's your daughter. Reckons you've been off the air.'

I swore and grabbed his mobile. 'Jass! Are you okay?'

'Of course I am. Why was your phone switched off?'

'I must have switched it off,' I said, thinking this was the sort of thing that happened when a person was in emotional upheaval. 'What's the problem?'

'You always ask that.'

'There usually is one,' I countered.

'Well, clever dick, this time you're wrong. Shaz's left that bastard and Bob's fixed her up in a nice motel while she finds another place to live. A friend of his runs it at Maroubra.'

I knew the place and the man who ran the Maroubra motel; Bob and I had used it in days gone by as a safe house for other people who needed to lie low.

'That's good news. What happened?'

'We went to her place and her flatmates told me she'd gone back to his flat. We found her there. Oh, Dad, you should have seen her. She still had the black eye and he'd split her lip too. She was in a terrible state. But the good thing is, she's finally had enough. So she came back with us and Bob drove her to the doctor's to get her lip stitched, then we helped her pack up while Bob organised the motel. The owner says she can stay there until she finds another place to live. I think Bob's paying.'

'I doubt it,' I said, knowing my old friend and his system of leverage. 'Great work.'

'I feel so much better knowing that she's finally free of him,' she said.

'Sometimes, Jass,' I said, 'I am ashamed of my sex.'

'And guess what? Sometimes I feel ashamed of mine.'

We laughed, I made some mumbling comments about her need to study and she scoffed at me with a line about dickbrains who forget to switch on their mobiles. Suddenly she was serious. 'How's Iona?' she asked.

I didn't want to talk about that right now and told her I'd ring later when things were quieter.

She farewelled me with a kiss blown down the line.

I handed Brian's mobile back to him.

TWENTY-EIGHT

It was bloody hard driving up in the darkness to the cottage, knowing that the place was cold and empty and that Iona wasn't coming home. I parked the car and overwhelming grief surged up in me. What had I done? Why hadn't I been able to give this woman I loved so much the only thing she wanted from me—my time and attention?

I turned the key in the door and walked into the chilly atmosphere; it smelled of dead fireplace. To dispel the sadness, I went round the back and, by the shed light, swung the axe, splitting a good stack of firewood to replenish the pile depleted by my guests.

I couldn't settle. I paced around after making the fire but the loneliness of the place got to me. Once, I'd been content to sit here, night after night, alone, reading, watching television, reviewing some work project, but now the prospect of an evening alone with my grief seemed intolerable.

I damped the fire down, put the wire screen in front of it and left the house. I drove out to Weston, logged myself in and walked down to the lab to check if the automated run I'd started from the samples I'd taken from the unknown male's sandals had finished. They hadn't so I got back in my car and drove to Ainslie, sitting across the road from the apartment where Iona's friend, Anne-Marie someone, lived.

The lights were on, but the drawn curtains did not permit any decent surveillance, and besides, I was feeling ashamed of myself. After about ten minutes I drove away, heading for the Cretan's café.

I ordered moussaka and sat in front of it, defeated.

'Something wrong, Jack?' the Cretan asked, coming over to my table.

'Not with your food, Yorgo,' I said. 'With me.'

'Ah,' he said. 'Woman trouble?'

I nodded.

He left, coming back with a small liqueur glass of Aphrodite brandy which he placed on the table with a flourish. 'You have this. On the house. Warm your heart up. Make that woman love you too much.'

'Thanks, Yorgo,' I said, looking at the volatile liquid. 'You'll have to drink it for me. I don't drink alcohol.'

'Just this little one. It will do you good.'

'Okay,' I said, not wishing to offend his generous spirit. When he wasn't looking, I tipped the brandy into a planter box of fake ivy beside me. 'Here's to you, Iona,' I said, as I emptied it.

Finally, I went home and, somehow, ended up going to sleep in front of the fire to awaken, stiff and cold, in the early hours when I finally went to bed.

Next morning, I woke from a dream where Iona and I were translating something from a book together down on the river bank. It took me a second or two to catch what had happened and, as I swung out of bed in the darkness before 6 a.m., I tried to remember what had been written in the dream book. I took a shower, distracting myself with making a list in my head of jobs that needed to be done today.

As I swiped myself through to the office area at Forensic Services, I decided I needed to talk to Sofia, but before that I hurried down to the laboratory where I'd started the amp run yesterday. The green light indicated that the run had finished, genetic material had been extracted and amplified and now it was a matter for Profiler Plus, the DNA program, to construct the profile of Bob's unknown male 17/2000 into a graphical diagram. If possible. I wasn't all that hopeful as I set the next step in motion. But, fingers crossed, we might have something.

I rang Sofia's office phone. Despite the early hour, she was in and yes, now was a convenient time. Her voice was clipped, artificially polite. That, at least, was something, I thought.

As soon as I'd closed the door behind me, I could see she'd been crying.

'I'm fine!' she said defiantly, when I asked her what the matter was. 'And I'm *very* busy.'

'I realise you've been under a lot of stress,' I said, grabbing the spare wheelie chair and sliding it towards me so I could sit closer to her. 'And I can see you're upset right now.'

She went to interrupt me, but I silenced her. 'What I'm trying to say is that you don't have to fight me to get what you want. Why don't you just ask? If there's something worrying you—and I have reason to believe that there is—why the hell didn't you just knock on my door and come in and sit down and have a chat?'

She looked at me in disbelief. 'You think it's that easy?'

'With me, yes. It *is* that easy. And before you say anything else, I want to tell you something about me. Maybe that'll make it clearer to you. I want to tell you something personal. And no, it's not about sex.'

At those words, she raised her head. She sure hadn't been expecting this.

'It's much more intimate than that.'

I had her full attention now.

'Sofia,' I started, 'I'm a recovered alcoholic. Until twelve or thirteen years ago, I lived life very differently. I want you to know I've done every stupid, cruel, self-centred, bloody-minded, phoney and plain wicked thing that you can think of. So I'm in no position to judge anyone else. But in leaving that life and making another one, I've learned a few things and I've noticed things—things that often people who haven't lived two lives fail to notice.'

She was silent, listening—bristles, hackles, defences, for the moment, folded down.

'So when I tell you that I've worked out what's going on with you, I hope you don't feel any sense of shame. I know what it's like to have a past that is painful, that you'd prefer to keep hidden.'

Her eyes widened. 'What do you mean?' Her voice was full of fear.

'It's very important that, as scientists, we remain uncompromised. Objectivity must be maintained at all times. All we have is our objectivity, our impartiality. Some time back, a fellow at another lab falsified his findings. Certified that he could find no evidence of heroin in an item—when, in fact, there was a lot.'

'What are you talking about? I would never do that!'

I ignored her interjection. 'He later suicided. He knew he was finished as a scientist. Because of his own addiction, he was also pretty well finished as a human being. At least in his own eyes. He'd sold himself to a crim. Because he had a secret that he believed he had to protect. I think of that poor bastard from time to time.'

She shifted uneasily in her seat, eyes wary. 'Why are you telling me all this?'

'Because I believe you are potentially being drawn into a situation that could one day—maybe quite soon—turn round and bite you. It could also cast a shadow over your objectivity—your scientific *honour,* if you like. A situation that could destroy you.'

I heard her sharp intake of breath and she jumped up and stood near the window, turned away from me. Then she leaned against the window, head down.

'Shit!' she said.

'You want to tell me about it?'

An hour later, we sat in my car, overlooking a pretty valley about fifteen kilometres away from work. Sofia had been crying a lot and I'd made no move to stop her, apart from passing the tissue box to her now and then. I'd learned to let angry people be angry and let crying women cry.

'That's how I supported myself while I was doing my postgraduate studies,' she said. 'I was a worker three nights a week. Because I was young and good-looking and was free to go away with guys for the weekend, I made quite a lot of money. Mostly overseas businessmen from repressive countries. They loved going with a blonde woman who could fuck.' Her voice was hard and contemptuous.

'That's why you reacted so strongly when I said you were a good worker,' I said. 'I meant it in the context of your work here.'

She nodded. 'I realised that. But when I heard that word—it's a loaded word for me. It's so hard maintaining privacy.'

I watched a small hawk hanging in the air beneath us, head turning from side to side as it sought movement on the valley floor, and thought about an old saying: 'We're only as sick as our secrets.'

'But someone from your past recognised you?' I asked.

'He said he'd tell my boss if I didn't have sex with him for nothing. I told him I didn't do that any more. Then I had to buy him off.'

'But he kept coming back. That's what they do,' I said. 'Who is he?'

She leaned back in the car seat, covering her face with her hands.

'The guy who manages the Blackspot. Endo Bremmer. He recognised me that morning, despite the glamorous Tyvek overall. Later, he accosted me when I was packing my gear in my car. It didn't take him long to find out my real name. He'd only known me as Demi from Bondi.'

I closed my eyes. Demi from Bondi was now an analyst in my team. This might turn very nasty. Murky, murky waters. A crime scene professional gathering evidence at a murder scene connected to a man who was blackmailing her.

'What is it?' she asked, picking up my mood.

'Think about it. You're working crime scene and being blackmailed by someone who might be involved in the crime scene you're investigating. Can you imagine what the defence could do with our evidence if that came to light? Prosecution scientist named in evidence scandal,' I intoned, as if reading headlines. I leaned back in my seat, drumming my fingers on the steering wheel.

'What am I going to do, Jack?' This time, I heard the little girl's voice instead of the angry bitch. She might have been Jacinta.

'Leave it with me. In the meantime, tell him it's finished. No more money. Never, ever. No matter what he threatens.'

She nodded.

'Okay,' I said. 'Let's grab a takeaway espresso and get back to work.'

When I drove into the car park, I saw Vic Agnew give me a look as Sofia climbed out of the passenger seat.

'It's not what you think, sonny,' I said, as I walked past him.

'How do you know what I was thinking?' he called after me.

At the top of the stairs Sofia was waiting for me to catch up. 'I meant to give you the final analysis from the pollen assemblage and soil profiles when you came to my office earlier, but I forgot what with everything,' she said. 'I feel like a huge weight has been taken from me. This is the first time since I've been here I haven't felt completely alone. And in danger.'

'We've got to deal with this Bremmer character first. He's poison,' I said.

'I had a very strange family,' she said, wanting to explain more. 'A very odd upbringing and I never learned the ordinary niceties. Plus, I don't trust anyone, especially men.'

'How come you talked to me?'

'Because you told me a big secret of yours. And I believed you weren't judging me.'

'I wasn't,' I said. 'Maybe one day you might tell me some more about yourself.'

She cocked a fair eyebrow. 'You know too much already. Demi from Bondi is enough.'

I waited near my office door while she disappeared, returning a few minutes later with two folders, one containing the third attempt to get clean results from the body and surrounds of Tianna Richardson, and the second from unknown male 17/2000 and whatever she'd been able to extract from the sandals, the few strands of hair and the rags of clothing that accompanied the bones.

I thanked her and took the complicated analyses into my office. I glanced through the pollen assemblage that gave an indication of the general vegetation of the two areas, the differences between the car park area of the Blackspot and the bushland of the shallow gravesite. Then I saw that Sofia had highlighted the pollen she'd found, the rare indicator species, and, if I was reading these diagrams correctly, she'd found this rare pollen at both places. I looked again, switching from one diagram to the other, while walking back to her office.

'Sofia,' I said, knocking on the door. 'These results. Does this mean what I think it means?'

'That's the anomalous result I was telling you about,' she said, bringing me inside. 'The mystery. I've checked that pollen out with my former doctoral supervisor. Native orchids are his specialty. This one's very rare. Only grows in two places in Australia. Well, that we *know* about, because its needs are very specific. That's why I kept redoing the samples. I used separate labs for each of them. In spite of all the care I took, I thought I must have contaminated them somehow.'

'So is there a rare orchid growing near the Blackspot?' I asked. 'Is that one of the two places?'

'No,' she said. 'Not a trace of it. As I remember, the two places it's been reported are both in Victoria.'

Yet 17/2000 must have come into contact with the orchid too. The coincidence was staggering. Then I thought of something obvious. 'But pollen can be windborne. Couldn't it have blown onto them? Our topsoil is already decorating New Zealand's high country.'

Sofia shook her head. 'Not this orchid. It only makes a tiny amount of pollen. It's one of the types that disseminates pollen via insects, or birds. Something has to actually brush against it to pick up traces. It's not designed to be windborne at all. So you're going to have to get that suspect to confess. Tell us where the primary scene is. My old orchid-crazy supervisor will love him for that.'

'He's still denying he knows anything about the murder. He's light years away from spilling the beans about the primary crime scene.'

'Maybe he's telling the truth. Maybe he really doesn't know?'

I shrugged.

Her frown deepened. 'And the reason I know it's associated with the primary crime scene is because it only appeared in conjunction with those grey particles.'

'On Tianna's injuries?'

She nodded.

'I'm surprised you found such a rare orchid pollen on 17/2000,' I said.

'I found some very small residual traces in the hair strands.' She looked up at me from her detailed charts. 'That egg-shell fracturing of the skull...' She paused. 'Did you notice? I thought it was odd that they both had similar injuries. And this pollen in common, too.'

'And you're sure there hasn't been any contamination?'

'As sure as a scientist can be,' she said, after a moment's hesitation. 'I followed the strictest protocols.'

Knowing Sofia, I was sure she would have.

'It's the sort of coincidence that makes me want to write an article for the palynological association,' she said. 'It'd be interesting to do the stats on such a thing happening twice in two such different murders and dump sites.'

'What about the Albert Vaughan samples?'

She shook her head. 'No. The granite particles turned up in his injuries, but no orchid pollen. The pollen profile in his case was what I'd expect—consistent with local vegetation.'

'You're right,' I said, considering something she'd said earlier. 'They both had similar eggshell fractures.' I'd seen the damage to Tianna's skull, the radiating fracture lines, the massive off-centred damage, the blow-down of the superior orbital plates that Harry had pointed out to me. And I'd held Bob's unknown male skull in my hands, noting the same set of extensive injuries. Now here was another coincidence, another oddity—same damage, same orchid. 'That *is* very curious,' I said. 'Somehow we've got two cases, both linked to this very rare indicator species.'

'That's what the evidence would suggest.'

I considered. 'Could you do an environmental profile?' I knew that the reconstruction of an environment was possible; traces of animals, plants, soils and sediments can yield a 'landscape' that an experienced interpreter can read.

'It's not an area I've had much experience with,' she said.

'I've seen orchids at one household,' I said, trying to make sense of this, remembering Vera Hastings and her late husband's interests. 'Near where Tianna lived—did I mention that?'

Sofia shook her head. 'It doesn't matter. When I say rare orchid, I mean rare. Native. There's *no* way you'd find this in a house. They only grow in the wild. It's truly weird.'

She'd used exactly those words when making another observation and I reminded her. 'The clothes Tianna Richardson was wearing. At the crime scene,' I said. 'You said there was something weird about them. Back at Tianna's house I found a nice black and silver pair of earrings, like little chandeliers, still in their wrapping on Tianna's dressing table. And the matching skirt that went with that suit was draped over a chair.'

'So why didn't she wear them that night?' Sofia asked.

'I can't be sure, but I'm beginning to wonder,' I began. 'The skirt was a perfect fit. We tested it down at the morgue.'

'Maybe she was interrupted while she was dressing. And didn't have a chance to get the skirt on,' said Sofia.

'But she did get *a* skirt on. The one you described as daggy.'

'You said you were beginning to wonder... what?' Sofia raised her eyebrows.

'You thought a man wouldn't notice something like that,' I said. 'And that's what I'm thinking happened. The killer put that skirt on Tianna.'

'But why?' said Sofia, bewildered.

'That's what I need to think more about,' I said.

'It's a mystery,' she said. 'Like this orchid popping up in two places.'

Her phone rang and she picked it up. She didn't speak and the colour drained from her face.

'Give it to me,' I said.

She hesitated, then passed it over.

'I know who you are,' I said. 'And I'm Sofia Verstoek's boss. You are not to contact her again in any way. Understood?'

'It's a free country,' he said. 'I can do what I want.'

'Try it, pal, and you'll find out just how free you are,' I said.

His voice was cocky and full of sneering. 'You like employing sluts?'

'If you attempt to contact Miss Verstoek or any of my staff members again,' I said, 'I'll make sure your nightclub is closed down and that you're out of this town so fast you won't know what hit you.'

'Are you threatening me, man?'

'Not yet,' I said and hung up.

Sofia had a hand covering her mouth.

I was indignant. 'A prick like that getting money out of you.'

She raised one of those fair eyebrows. 'I've had a lot of money out of pricks like that.'

'If he so much as thinks about you,' I said, 'you let me know. Okay.'

She nodded.

On the way back to my office, I thought about the scene with Sofia. Why was it, I asked myself, that I could act immediately and know what to do with a woman in trouble, to the point of maintaining an open-door policy, and yet when it came to my relations with Iona, I couldn't seem to make the time?

TWENTY-NINE

This question lingered in my mind as I took the pollen profiles and soil profiles back to my office, puzzled. A rare orchid that had to be brushed against to deliver its pollen had turned up on a woman, only dead a little over a month ago, and again on a youth, dead a long time, perhaps two decades. Both were bearing similar injuries. Whichever way I examined it, as coincidence or connection, it seemed equally unlikely.

I rang Brian and told him what Sofia had discovered, that the rare orchid pollen only appeared among the granite particles embedded in Tianna's head, with traces showing up again on 17/2000's hair. Then I asked him what he knew about the licensee and the manager of the Blackspot Nightclub and gave him the name Endo Bremmer. Without mentioning Sofia's previous work history, I briefed Brian about the situation. He said he'd look into it.

Then it was time to see if Profiler Plus had come up with anything in the way of reportable DNA concerning 17/2000. I seated myself before the monitor and opened the print program, waiting to see what the finished profile looked like as it appeared on the screen. I was no expert in reading these graphs, and I'd certainly take it down to Florence to get an expert eye examine it as well, but I could see straightaway that the program had come up with NR—Not Reportable. I was disappointed. Even though I'd known beforehand that the chances of finding any non-degraded genetic material were probably non-existent, I'd been hanging onto the hope that *something* had endured. But genetic material produced by the amplification process had been too degraded after all. The way our system was set up, the sex marker came right at the beginning of the profile, followed by nine other loci. In very degraded samples like this one, sometimes it was only the sex marker that could be read, but we already knew this was a male. I'd wasted valuable time and resources.

I was about to turn the program off, when I glanced at the first locus and blinked. I hadn't noticed it at first, being so dejected at the overall picture. It took me a second or two to take in what I was seeing.

'Holy shit,' I said to the empty laboratory.

I checked it again. Sometimes my eyes didn't focus all that well, especially when I hadn't had a good night's sleep. But I wasn't seeing things.

I grabbed my mobile and rang Harry Marshall.

Harry was doing the rounds with a young postgraduate pathologist, Rosalie Hughes, when I arrived, 17/2000 in the box under my arm, the print-out of the DNA profile in my briefcase. He seemed pleased as punch, as if the young woman was in some way his work.

'Rosalie will be helping me here, from time to time,' he said.

Rosalie Hughes was very keen to see what I was carrying, both the unidentified remains and the DNA profile.

'Peter Yu, have you done with him?' I asked.

'Yes,' said Harry. 'Self-inflicted gunshot to the head.'

The three of us gowned and gloved; Rosalie, the white gown covering her pink gingham blouse, suddenly transforming into a purposeful-looking professional. We went into a spare examination room and I put the box containing 17/2000 on the table with the DNA profile beside it.

'You'll have to show me what this is all about,' said Rosalie, moving closer, indicating the printed-out profile. 'I don't know much at all about how you extract and process DNA for identifying people.'

I lifted the skull out and put it on the table. 'I will,' I said. 'But first, tell me what you see.'

Rosalie picked the skull up, studied it for a moment, then deferred to her senior colleague and passed it to Harry.

'Who's this?' he asked, turning it round in his hands.

'It's one of Bob Edwards' cold cases. He dug it out of a Queanbeyan gravesite some years ago and

I requested it because of trace pollen evidence that showed up on some of the hair strands similar to that found on Tianna Richardson. He's been listed as an unknown male,' I said, tapping a gloved finger on the skull. 'With severe injuries at the back of the skull. I want to take another, closer look. I want another opinion.'

Rosalie carefully lifted out the fragments of fragile fabric and what was left of the stiff, cracked sandal soles, handling them with gloved reverence. I immediately liked her as she smoothed out the fragile fabric, holding up the front of the blue shirt, checking one of the two remaining blue plastic buttons, peering at the thin strands of hair in their packet then turning her attention to the old leather sandals.

Harry frowned under his heavy eyebrows, his kindly eyes magnified by his glasses as he rotated the ruined skull under the gaze of his protégée. 'Maybe the junior member of our consulting group should be allowed first examination?'

Rosalie, looking up from under her curving fringe, demurred a moment, then took the skull back from Harry, turning it over to reveal the gaping, off-centred hole, the spidery fracture lines running away from the edges. She studied the jagged gap for a few moments. 'Severe damage to the cranial vault area,' she finally said. 'Especially the superior orbital plates, with extensive radiating fracturing plus extensive base-of-skull fracturing.'

'Yes,' said Harry. 'Plus blow-down of the superior orbital plates.' He paused. 'Suggest anything to you?'

'Yes,' she said. 'Blunt instrument?'

'Mmm,' murmured Harry. 'It's difficult without seeing the front of the brain, but I'm thinking something different. A fall from a height.'

'Male or female?' I asked.

Rosalie frowned and looked hard at the front of the skull. 'Gracile, no marked post-orbital ridge.' She turned it sideways and squinted at it, then looked at it face-on again. She put it down and sorted through the box until she found the femur and part of the pelvis.

'Again, I'm not a hundred per cent sure,' she said, 'but from what I've seen, I'd say more likely to be female than male.'

'Congratulations,' said Harry. 'That would be my conclusion.'

I passed her the profile. 'And here's the genetic confirmation of your decision,' I said, pointing to the single peak at the sex locus. 'If it had been male, there'd be two peaks there, one for the X and one for the Y chromosome. Two XXs, which indicate female, stack up on top of each other, making only one peak.'

'Bob's not going to be happy about this,' said Harry, looking over Rosalie's shoulder.

'Why?' Rosalie asked.

I explained that these remains had been sitting in the bone room at the Sydney morgue for the last four years, logged as male.

'It happens from time to time,' said Harry. 'Especially if all the remains aren't available. And inexperience plays a part in wrong identifications.'

I remembered Bob saying Bradley Strachan was on leave when the remains were found, so it would have been a locum pathologist who'd accompanied him down to the gravesite. Then I opened the packet of hair and teased out a few more strands. I intended to ask Jerri Quill's flatmate, Wendy, to try and reconstruct the face. I'd have to ring her straightaway.

Rosalie was silent a moment, considering. She held the skull at eye level, gazing through the empty sockets. 'Who *are* you?' she asked.

'At the moment, she's missing female, 17/2000, aged somewhere between twenty and thirty,' said Harry.

'She could be me,' Rosalie said, tracing the sutures of the coronal fissure.

'You'll make a great pathologist one day, my dear,' said Harry, patting her arm. 'Getting the sex right, despite the writing on the box.'

'Actually, I cheated,' said Rosalie, smiling broadly as she helped repack the bones and the accompanying items.

'How's that?' I asked, puzzled.

'The scraps of the blouse. Didn't you see? It buttons on the female side.'

Before I'd got back into the car with the box of bones I was on the phone to Wendy.

'What would you say to the offer of a New South Wales cold case skull to reconstruct?'

'I'd jump at it,' she replied.

'Not quite sure how we'll pay you. But I'm sure we can come up with something,' I said.

'That's cool. At the moment, I'm more interested in building up an impressive CV.'

There was no mistaking the excitement in her voice and, as soon as I hung up, I rang Bob.

'So now I've got two *women*,' I said, 'both killed in the same way and both coming into contact with an extremely rare orchid at the site of their respective injuries. But many years apart.'

'Mate, you're onto something,' said Bob and I could imagine the grin on his face.

'Yeah. Something. But what?'

Bob's sigh came down the line. 'I'm going to have to go through all the missing females from the last twenty years. As well as keep up to speed with everything else.' He was right. I didn't envy him.

'But at least with Ms Seventeen Two Thousand,' I said, 'you'll soon have a face to work with.' I filled him in on Wendy's work.

'I heard you'd already charged someone for Tianna Richardson's murder,' Bob said. 'So maybe you should have another look at your suspect in the light of this new discovery. Same MO.'

I did a quick calculation. 'Nice try, Bob, but at the time of 17/2000's death, Damien Henshaw would have been about five.'

'So much for similar MO,' said Bob.

'It's still similar MO,' I said. 'But no loading it onto Damien Henshaw. I'm not a hundred per cent happy about him anyway. I'm not sure that he's the right man.'

'I've got a bit of hot gossip for you,' said Bob. 'Earl Richardson is getting over his grief with the bereavement counsellor in ways not prescribed in the manual.'

I recalled the lacy bras and undies fluttering on the clothes line at the back of Richardson's house.

'Well-built blonde?' I asked, recalling the woman at Tianna's funeral.

'She lives there,' said Bob. 'I had a good gossip with next door. Can't blame the man for seeking comfort with a professional.'

I thought about those words all the way to Wendy's place, and then again on the drive back to work.

In my office, I tidied up my desk. Bob was back to square one with his case, and I was now convinced that Brian had the wrong man in the dock for Tianna Richardson's death. To top it all off, the wretched forensic conference was almost upon me. People were running around organising things that the organisers should have done weeks ago. I sat at my desk, debating as to when I should next contact Iona and while I was fighting off the urge to do it right then, the desk phone rang. I prayed it would be her saying she'd made a big mistake. 'Patrick Eadie,' said the voice. For a moment I couldn't place the clipped, abrupt tones of the leporid man.

'I've got some preliminary findings for you,' he said into my silence, 'from my examination of those six rabbit carcases you sent me.'

I thanked him then picked up a pen and waited.

'These are the main points,' he said. 'I found evidence that the animals had been dead for some time prior to undergoing the pressure and heat changes due to the autoclave process—which compromised my findings considerably. But despite that, I was able to see that all of them showed some traces of disease symptoms, skin rashes, subcutaneous oedema, especially of the mouth and body openings, tissue swelling...' He paused. 'Ah, here it is.' I heard the rustling of paper. 'And that these findings are symptomatic of rabbit pox.' He paused again. 'I've cut and pasted a section from one of the reference texts concerning rabbit pox. That might be useful to you. Give me your fax number and I'll fax it over to you.'

I gave him the number and thanked him again.

'Who gets my invoice?'

Our budget was heading for the red and I'd committed to pay a fee to Wendy Chen. 'Dallas Baxter,' I said. 'At the Ag Station. Send it to him.'

On the way home, I drove by the Ainslie address of Iona's friend and was sitting there, listening to the Drive Time program, watching a couple of late joggers puffing past, when I was startled by a presence by the window. I wound it down to see Iona's friend from the college beside the car, tugging her gloves on, the disapproving frown and dark scarf over her head lending a touch of severity.

'This is not a good idea,' she said. 'This is the second time I've seen you here in as many days. The word "stalking" comes to mind.'

'Have a heart,' I said. 'I just want to talk to her.'

'From what I hear, there's been too much talk already.'

'Is Iona in?' I asked.

'Please go,' she said. 'Iona doesn't want to see you or talk to you. She says it's too painful.'

'So it should be!' I said, feeling a dark pleasure that I was important enough to Iona for her to ache about me.

'She said to give you this, and now I think you'd better go,' she added, giving me a look of pure dislike.

I wound up the window and switched on the cabin light.

> Dear Jack, please don't try and contact me. It's not helpful as we'd only end up having the same endless argument that we've been having almost since I moved in with you. I understand that you've done your best to change.

I wanted to cry, but I couldn't. Her letter gave me no hope at all and I folded it up and put it in my jacket pocket, feeling the chill darkness of the oncoming night in my heart.

THIRTY

Tuesday morning I woke and immediately started to fight the desire to call Iona, wanting to say, if it hurts talking to me or seeing me while we're separated why don't you for God's sake just come home? But sanity prevailed and I distracted myself by reading Patrick Eadie's faxed post-mortem report and making my own notes. Concerned though I was with what he had found, I was still very unsure of what the full implications were, so I put my notes aside to look over the local newspaper.

On the second page I saw a small piece about the closure of the Blackspot Nightclub. Since the murder of Tianna Richardson, the place had been virtually deserted and now the manager, Endo Bremmer, had been charged over licensing irregularities plus a whole lot of other charges—obstruction, resist arrest, attempted bribe. The last one surprised me; maybe it hadn't been big enough. Jack, you're a cynic, I thought. But, despite my heartache, I couldn't help smiling. Some people were their own worst enemies.

I turned the page to find a double-page spread: POLICE BAFFLED BY MOTIVELESS MURDER–SUICIDE OF LOCAL SCIENTISTS. I was baffled too, I thought as I read it, sitting with a dish of rolled oats and honey in the kitchen at the back of the cottage.

Pale sun shone through the glass of the windows and, because the fireplace in the lounge room didn't warm this end of the place, I had a dinky little electric heater near my feet. I should get the old range going, I thought. It would warm the whole back of the house.

Outside, a flock of galahs shrieked as they flew overhead while I reread the article and a boxed story on the same page featuring my friend the Calvinist barman, telling what he knew about the partner-swapping group who used to meet at the Cat and Castle. 'Downright disgusting,' he'd called it. I looked at his disapproving sneer in the small photograph. It was a warning, I thought. When you couldn't get something, you often ended up hating it. I didn't want to end up like that, nor turn into a bitter old man like my father. My father. It was ages since I'd contacted him. I tried to force myself to pick up the phone, but I just didn't have it in me. My mobile rang.

'Dad?'

I could read my daughter's voice like I can read A B C. Immediately, I knew something was wrong. 'What's up?' I asked.

'Shaz. She's gone.'

'What do you mean gone?'

'I drove over to the motel to bring her some gear, girlie things, and she wasn't there. Her stuff's gone. She didn't have much, just one bag with clothes and textbooks. I rang Bob straightaway and left a message.'

'Ask the owner if he saw anything.'

'I did. He hadn't seen anything. He was at the front in reception and no one came in that way.'

I didn't imagine Docker would advertise his visit.

'Dad,' said Jacinta. 'I'm really worried.'

'I'll ring Bob and he can alert the local police. Try not to worry. Let me know if you hear anything,' I said, and did exactly that, leaving a message on Bob's voicemail.

I turned my attention back to the bare facts of Dr Claire Dimitriou's murder and Peter Yu's suicide as presented by the newspaper. I knew that I was going to have to do the same as Bob with his cold case. When you were baffled, there was only way to go. Start all over again. From the beginning. From that Monday morning in the laboratory when Jerri Quill made her mistake. Science began with a hypothesis and then tested it.

I couldn't deal with hanging around the empty cottage so I grabbed up Eadie's report and anything else to do with the case and headed back to Forensic Services.

Most of the offices and labs were still empty when I arrived and so, in the quiet permeated only by the soft humming of distant automated processes, I went through the whole story again. Acute grief cleared the mind of all petty concerns, focusing it into a sharp, painful point. In the light of that clarity, I went right through the steps of what had happened in the Faithful Bunnies laboratory, beginning with the almost hysterical overreaction to the results of a routine assay, sixteen blue wells, the heated argument between the two scientists, the charge of blasphemy, moving right up to the murder of Claire Dimitriou in her steam-cleaned laboratory, the obliteration of any records from that day, and ending with the suicide of her unstable partner.

I went over conversations I'd had with Dallas Baxter, another overworked chief like me. *I had to do a terrible thing to stop a blasphemy*, Peter Yu had written. I stood up and walked around, unaware of the office, putting myself back in that lab, looking down at Jerri Quill's immunoassay plate in my mind's eye, seeing the strong reaction to the infection in the case of RP4, one of Claire's six rabbits. What could be more terrible than two deaths, I wondered.

The answer was simple. I turned away from the window through which I'd been sightlessly staring and almost flew the couple of steps back to my desk. Eureka moments could do that and that was what I was experiencing as I snatched up the phone to ring Jerri Quill.

'I need your help,' I said and outlined what I had in mind. After some hesitation, Jerri agreed, but said she'd need a day or so to organise the trip.

'I'm still not sure what to do,' she said. 'At the moment, I feel the rug's been pulled out from under me. Here I am, in the latter stages of my thesis, and I make some stupid mistake.'

'Jerri, you didn't make a stupid mistake. A mistake was made, but it wasn't yours. I've worked out what happened.'

'*Tell* me,' she said.

'You'll see for yourself on Thursday. Once I'm a hundred per cent sure.'

'Okay. I'll do what you've asked and write everything down,' Jerri said. 'And I'll drive down tomorrow evening. That way, we can do it in the morning. Just like it happened the first time.'

All that remained was to call Dallas Baxter. Although I didn't tell him what I now suspected had gone wrong in that assay, I told him enough to enlist his help in a reconstruction. He assured me Pauline would do anything in her power to assist, promising to ring her so that she'd be ready too.

Early Thursday morning, Jerri called me on her way out to the Ag Station. After shovelling down the last of my scrambled eggs and coffee, I cleaned my teeth, grabbed a clean jumper and jumped into my wagon. I was doing okay, I thought, after Iona. The night before I'd rung Bob about Shaz but he had no news of her.

It was nice and early and most of the staff hadn't yet arrived. Sheep were bleating and I saw a utility parked near their external pens and a man hauling bales of lucerne hay to accompany their usual feed-lot breakfast.

Dallas was unlocking the building that housed the Faithful Bunnies lab as I pulled in and Pauline was getting out of her car. A moment after I had parked, Jerri arrived.

As we were entering the building, I heard someone calling and looked across to see Brian hurrying across the frosty grass. He made his apologies for being late. The giant chicken had struck again at Woden, but this time the angry shopkeeper had tackled him down. Brian had been up most of the night trying to get some order into his paperwork and some sense out of the captured chicken.

The five of us were oddly silent as we gowned up and then stepped into the erstwhile Faithful Bunnies laboratory, which still smelled faintly of antiseptic and rabbits.

Jerri walked a little ahead of us, turning uncertainly halfway over to the central workbench, looking absurdly young in her lab gear. 'What should I do?' she asked.

'See if you can repeat what you did last Monday morning, when you came in,' I said.

Over the last two days, I'd used my notes to make rough scripts of what Jerri had told me had passed between Dr Claire Dimitriou and herself that morning and now I handed Pauline and Dallas a page apiece. 'You can use these when you play your parts,' I said, then turned my attention back to the young woman. 'Jerri, what did you do first when you came in?'

'First thing I did was go over and say hello to the rabbits.'

'Do that,' I said.

Jerri headed for the room at the other end of the laboratory space, where once the experimental animals had lived in their locked and airconditioned space, now neither locked nor airconditioned. Jerri paused at the unlocked door and stood at the threshold. 'Hi guys,' she said, to the six empty cages, her voice trembling. She turned round to explain. 'My favourite one was RP4, the smallest one, and I went over to him and patted him through the cage. Then I had to wash my hands and get my gloves on.' She went through the motions of this while we stood around, watching.

'This really feels strange,' she said.

'You're doing great,' I told her. 'What happened next?'

Jerri approached the ELISA machine then hesitated. 'I walked over here and checked that the run was finished. It's like an incubator and the green light tells you when the process is completed. You'll have to imagine the little green light there is on.'

'Okay,' I said. 'The green light is on, so now show us exactly what you did.'

Jerri undid a fitting at the base of the machine and pulled out a sliding tray. 'I pulled out the tray like this,' she said. 'And lifted the plate off it.'

'Let's get an ELISA plate, for realism,' I said. 'Where are they stored?'

Jerri pointed to a large white cabinet near the entry to the lab. 'The glassware and stores are kept in there. Down the bottom. You'll see the carton on the floor. Each unit is sealed in a sterile pack. You'll have to open one.'

I went over and opened the cupboard door and pulled out the large laboratory supplier's carton that was taking up almost all of the space. The handling instructions were printed down the side and the contents and quantities, in small print, were partially obscured by brown masking tape. I peered closely at what was written and felt the triumph of a suspicion vindicated, however I kept this to myself just for the moment. I ripped off some of the masking tape to make things easier and lifted out one of the tightly packed units and took it over to Jerri. She tore the pack open, lifted the sterile vacuum seal and pulled out a 96-welled plate in her gloved hand. I came up close, to watch exactly what she was doing.

'Here. The plates fit in that housing. Like that,' she said and secured it before closing the door.

'Okay,' said Brian. 'So let's imagine it's been cooking over the weekend and now it's ready for you. What happened when you took it out again?'

Jerri undid the housing once more and drew out the new plate, which was light grey in colour, reminding me of a miniature egg-carton suitable for 96 tiny pointed eggs. 'This one's unused,' she said, 'so all the wells seem empty and colourless but they're not empty. Each one comes coated with a very fine layer of refined rabbit serum which is barely visible. But it's there.' She looked around at us. 'I don't know how technical you want this to be?'

'Keep it simple,' I said. 'Brian and I are outclassed here.'

'Please,' said Pauline, 'I'm not a scientist.'

'And I'm no teacher,' said Jerri, 'but I'll do my best to explain it. I'd already made dilutions from the blood of our infected rabbits. Because our rabbits are infected with rabbit pox, their blood has disease antigens in it and once I've dropped this into the clean rabbit serum at the bottom of each of those 96 wells, a reaction starts. Just as a real rabbit's system would, the serum recognises the presence of dangerous foreign disease material and starts to make antibodies—these are proteins produced by the immune system when it recognises the threat posed by the infected blood. And when antibodies start being made, this creates a reaction and the colour in the wells starts changing.' She looked around to see if we all understood.

'That's what I'd done on Friday,' she said. 'I'd added disease dilutions from our rabbits to each of the wells—the wells that came coated with clean rabbit serum.'

'Two rows of eight wells for each rabbit,' I added, so the others would understand what was going to unfold.

'That's right. Over the weekend, because of the disease proteins that I'd added from the rabbits, the serum at the bottom of the wells started producing antibodies, demonstrating that our rabbits have come into contact with the rabbit pox virus. In other words, they're infected and making antibodies against the infection. We want to know that they're infected properly so that later, when we release this into the wild, we'll be confident that the virus will spread through the rabbit populations and start mixing it with their DNA.'

'So what did the wells look like that day?' Brian asked.

Jerri looked at me. 'Like I've already told Jack, I must have done something wrong. Instead of all the 96 wells going blue, only two lines of wells were demonstrating the colour change.'

'Sixteen blue,' I said.

'You didn't expect this?' Brian asked, his pen poised over his notebook.

'No way. I would have expected *all* the wells to be showing lighter blue or darker blue, depending on the strength of the dilution and how strong the antibody build-up in each rabbit is.'

'So what did you do next?' I asked.

'I racked my brains, trying to work out what I might have done wrong and I checked the steps in the previous records in the lab book. But there was nothing there to help me. I'd done exactly what I always do when I run this assay on ELISA. There was nothing to account for this. So I did what a good scientist does—I started noting down the results, describing the lack of reactions, noting that only RP4 had developed antibodies this time. And querying this response. I wrote that the experiment would need to be repeated so as to discover what was going wrong.'

'Then what happened?' I asked.

'Claire came in,' said Jerri.

'Okay, Pauline,' I said. 'This is your moment. You come in now. Have you got your lines? Jerri, where were you?'

'I was sitting at the bench, writing in the lab book. Like this,' said Jerri.

'Good,' I said. 'Do it just like you did that day.'

Jerri hunched over the book, head down, writing away.

Pauline walked over, glanced at her lines then fixed her attention on the ELISA plate sitting beside the machine.

'What have you done?' she cried in a theatrical voice. 'What's going on here?'

'I'm not sure!' said Jerri, paling. 'What is it?'

'Can't you see what you've done? Can't you see what's happened here?'

'I know there's been an unexpected variation in the antibody reactions,' she said.

'That's what I'm talking about! Don't you see what's happened? What that *means*?'

Jerri, about to respond as she had done that day, suddenly abandoned her script and stood up, out-of-role and shaken. 'This is awful going over it like this. It's bringing it all back to me. And now Claire's dead. My heart is racing.'

I hurried over to the cupboard near the door where the carton of new plates was stored.

'Come on, Dallas,' I said, 'this is where you come in.'

Dallas, very pink in the face, playing the role of Peter Yu, strode into the centre of the lab and stood next to Pauline. 'What's the problem?' he demanded self-consciously. Then to me, 'Is that all I'm supposed to say?'

'You're doing a great job. Just finish your walk-through,' I said.

'Look what she's done! Look at that plate!' Pauline was thundering, enjoying her role.

Dallas, acting the part of Peter Yu, grabbed the ELISA plate from Pauline. I watched as the colour drained from his face. 'Oh my God!' he cried and he wasn't acting.

I hadn't scripted that line. But it was the right one.

Dallas stared at the plate, turning it over in his hands.

'This is not the right sort of plate!' he said.

I certainly hadn't scripted that line either, but it was perfect. I took the empty plate from his hands, looking around for something to make this more realistic. A container of blue fluid—window and glassware cleaner—stood on the bench and I grabbed it up, dripping some into two rows of wells.

'Remember,' I told them, 'that the wells on the plate containing RP4's antibodies had reacted very strongly. Isn't that right, Jerri?'

'That's absolutely right. RP4's wells were the ones that had turned blue.'

Dallas looked up at me. 'Sixteen blue,' he said.

I nodded. 'That's right. Sixteen wells turned blue.'

'Stop it, Dallas!' Jerri's distressed cry brought me back to earth. 'You're frightening me! That's just how Claire was looking at me! She was staring at me just like you are now! As if she couldn't believe her eyes!' Her eyes filled with tears. 'For

God's sake, *tell me*! Tell me what happened here last week!'

I went to her and took her arm. 'It wasn't your fault,' I said.

'You used the wrong plate!' said Dallas.

'That's just what Claire said too! What wrong plate?'

Pauline put her arm around the distressed girl. This had gone on long enough.

'Do you want to explain, Dallas? Or will I?' I said.

'The new suppliers,' he said. 'There was a mix up last time and they delivered some cartons of the wrong plates. I thought I'd collected all of them but this carton must have been overlooked. Nuclear biology is not my forte.'

'What do you mean wrong plates?' Brian asked.

'My God,' said Dallas, looking at me. 'I hope I'm not held accountable for this.'

'Will someone please tell me what the hell is going on?' said Brian.

'You thought some mistake had been made, Jerri, because it looked as if only RP4 had developed antibodies this run, except that it wasn't rabbit serum on that plate.'

I glanced at Dallas, who was studiously avoiding my gaze. He knows, I thought. He's worked it out too.

Jerri picked up the plate and looked at it, frowning. 'What was it then? The plate does look a bit different—a slightly different colour—now that I look at it closely.'

'And you quite reasonably thought it was just a variation because of the new suppliers. But this plate was one of several cartons—a wrong order that came through the same new supplier—*human sera* plates, not rabbits'.' I remembered Dallas's complaining about the wrong delivery. 'What Claire Dimitriou and Peter Yu saw that morning— and what you'd failed to see, because you hadn't realised what sort of plate it was—' I stopped speaking because I was watching Jerri's face as she returned from checking the side of the carton.

'Oh God. I think I know now what happened,' she said, eyes widening with shock.

'For Christ's sake, will somebody tell me what's going on? What the hell happened here?' Brian demanded.

I waited for Jerri. After what she'd been through, it was her moment.

'One of the strains of the virus—the strain from RP4—had caused a violent reaction. In *human* serum,' she said and raised her eyes to mine.

I nodded. She'd got it all right. 'That means,' I said, 'that the rabbit pox had mutated. The virus had jumped species.'

And there was something more troubling even than that, I thought as we waited in silence while Dallas locked the lab. We degowned, still quiet, still thinking about what had happened in the Terminator Rabbit lab and I could see the puzzlement still in the faces of Brian and Pauline as the implications took longer to sink in.

Dallas invited us to his office, where he poured everyone except me a large brandy. I found some tonic water in a cupboard and, once Dallas had us all settled, he closed the door and we sat around, silent for a while longer. He was ashen. Like me, he was thinking that things were worse than a virus jumping.

It was Brian who finally spoke, pulling out his notebook, looking around like a puzzled schoolboy, eyebrows at twelve o'clock. 'I'm just a country cop,' he said. 'Spell it out.'

'Viruses are always jumping around,' I said. 'They're extraordinary life forms. A strain of bird flu has now become a big human problem and humans are dying from a disease that once only infected chicken and other birds.'

'Do you mean the rabbit pox could make people sterile?' Pauline's eyes widened with concern.

'The genetic payload was made from and for *rabbit* genes,' I said. 'Targeting rabbits, not humans. That's not the problem as I see it.'

'Then what is the problem?' asked Brian.

'What happened demonstrates that yet another virus, a close relation of the vaccinia virus—that's the one used in vaccinations against smallpox—has become capable of infecting humans. But more alarming, that virus has killed six rabbits—rabbits that had been *immunised* against it. And that is a big worry. Not only has it jumped species, it's also increased in lethality. God knows by how much. I'm guessing here, but I think that the dangerous strain was the strain developed in number four rabbit.'

'There are people in the world,' said Dallas, 'hostile to life, who would be very interested in this sort of discovery.'

'Claire and Peter realised what had happened,' said Jerri, 'but I didn't. Because I didn't know it was human serum in those wells.' She frowned. 'They must have been arguing about that. They would have both been shocked and distressed.'

'I still don't get it,' said Pauline. 'Why didn't they *do* something about it?'

'I believe they did,' I said. 'Or one of them was about to. I asked myself: if they're not arguing about sex, but rather science, then the obvious point for discussion would be: what the hell are we going to do with this knowledge? Just the same question Ron Jackson and Ian Ramshaw had to ask and answer for themselves only a few short years ago, when they saw what had happened to the mice they'd tested after genetically tweaking their immune systems. They'd found a way to increase the lethality of mouse pox.'

I paused and saw light dawning on Brian's face.

'All their test animals died too. And they were all vaccinated mice. Jackson and Ramshaw had to face the fact that their research could have huge implications. They didn't know what to do with their findings or if they should even publish them. I believe that the argument Kevin Waites overheard was a similar argument, Claire taking the line—in my opinion, the right line, in fact, the *only* line—

that they *must* publish the facts about this event and Peter Yu saying no, they mustn't. It would be too dangerous. In my reconstruction of these events, he was arguing that this information must be suppressed. No one else need know, he might have said. We rip the page out of the lab book, destroy the rabbits' bodies and stop this line of research dead in its tracks. The rabbits are disposed of, the RP4 strain is dead, the lab steam-cleaned and no one need ever know how this virus not only jumped but also increased its toxicity. They didn't even have time to worry about whether or not they'd caught it themselves.'

'God,' said Jerri. 'What if I'd caught it? And they hadn't even thought to tell me!'

I finished off the last of my drink. 'Kevin Waites overheard Dr Dimitriou saying, "Don't you see now we have to!" And to strengthen the urgency of the situation, she reminded Peter that Jerri had seen the sixteen blue wells on the ELISA plate, the intense antibody response, and might, in due course, realise that her test run had inadvertently been done with human serum. "She saw sixteen blue wells!" It was essential, Claire thought, that they make their findings public so that the scientific world could be prepared. "Forewarned is forearmed",' I quoted, 'and in these days of bio-terrorism, being forewarned is essential. Seen in this light, their argument had nothing to do with extramarital sexual liaisons, as Brian and I first suspected, and everything to do with Terminator Rabbit.'

'Why didn't they destroy the rest of the carton then?' Brian asked, looking over at the cupboard.

'Because there's absolutely nothing sinister about a carton of human sera plates. They were just part of an ordering error. They would have been eventually sent back to the manufacturers and replaced with the right ones. It would have been much stranger if they had destroyed them. That would have been something to explain. Wasting valuable resources.

'So Claire's saying "We must publish" and Peter's saying "We can't". And he felt so strongly about this, what with his newfound belief that he knew the mind of God, that when he saw he couldn't budge his colleague, he left the Ag Station, got the weapon he'd obtained previously, came back later that evening when Claire was working back—'

'—and shot her,' said Brian. 'And cleaned up very thoroughly.'

'So what do we do next?' Jerri said.

'*You* find another place to finish your doctorate,' I said. 'And keep the standards of science shining bright. Don't be discouraged by what happened in the old Faithful Bunnies lab.' I looked around the group, put my glass down and stood up. 'Me? I'm going back to work.'

On the way back to Forensic Services, I diverted via Wendy Chen's flat.

Shyly, she led me into the well-lit room to show me the work she'd begun on 17/2000. The reconstruction was well underway, with the eyes in place and muscle tissue building up around the pegs that marked the depth, but because the muscles around the eyes were not yet fleshed out, the face had a shocked look, staring wildly out of the clay. A decomposing body I'd worked on in the old days had shown just such an expression—the face also incomplete, but in that case falling away.

'I've bought some hair. There was just a little left.'

'That's a great help,' she said, taking it and studying it in its plastic protector. 'She'd had her hair tipped,' she said, showing me. 'Little blonde tips.'

We were both silent a moment with the poignancy of it.

'Would you like a drink?' Wendy offered, breaking the silence.

Today she was wearing a tight lime green leotard under the too-big, clay-spattered shirt. Reminded by this feminine presence, my heart jumped to another woman. In the excitement and drama of the reconstruction of the fatal events in the Terminator Rabbit experiment, my sorrow about Iona had receded for a little while.

'Maybe, when she's finished,' I said, 'I'll buy something to celebrate.'

'It's hard to believe,' Wendy said, 'that no one has noticed a young girl like this going missing. Where is her mother?'

I explained that not everyone had a mother, that some kids were raised in institutions, or in families where no one gave a shit. As I spoke, my body was infused with the older pain that arose about my own mother.

THIRTY-ONE

Over the next few days, the excitement generated by what our re-enactment had unearthed reached almost hysterical proportions.

Brian and Dallas were plagued by journalists, and the Ag Station itself, now the subject of an inquiry, had to pull the always-open boom gate down and put a security man on duty. Dr Leonie Pringle was said to be considering resigning from the board of examiners. There were calls for more stringent protocols on research projects and, for a while, the jumping virus was very hot news.

Then, as was always the case, another scandal, another disaster, took precedent in the press and the fuss died down. Sober articles from senior scientists drew attention to the facts that human beings posed the greatest threat to each other and that nature herself, without any genetic tweaking, was the mother of all terrorists, the Spanish flu of 1918 killing between 20 and 30 *million* human beings; the AIDS epidemic responsible for a similarly huge number of deaths over a longer period.

But it was always more menacing when human malice took to the laboratory to do harm.

With both investigations now coming to an end, I found that the grief around my loss of Iona was worsening. I tried to fill in the silent hours of the weekend back at the cottage by taking out my water colours and attempting to capture the soft grey mauve of dusk over the worn, dry hills.

At work on Monday morning, I tidied up, preparing at last to take some time off and go to Sydney for a while. I put Bob's box of bones, 17/2000, in a large sealed bag and signed off for them, calling Bob to tell him I'd act as courier myself and deliver them to Bradley Strachan at the Glebe morgue on the way in to Sydney. Then I rang Wendy Chen to see how she was progressing with the facial reconstruction.

'Come and see for yourself,' she said. 'And bring that bottle with you.'

'You've just missed Jerri,' Wendy said, letting me in. 'She'll be disappointed.' Today she was wearing a tight red jumper with jeans and her glossy black hair fell around her shoulders. She looked about fourteen years old.

'I hope she forgives me one day for what she had to do in the Terminator Rabbit lab.'

'She told me all about the re-enactment,' said Wendy, as I followed her through to her workroom.

'I'll get some glasses,' she said, taking the bottle of Australian champagne from me, 'and then you can come and have a look at the progress we've made with your unknown young woman.'

I wasn't sure if it was progress or not to have an unknown male turning into an unknown female. But when I stood in front of the head that Wendy Chen had rebuilt from a cast of the stark cranium and mandible from the bone room, I felt something like awe, not to mention a powerful sense of recognition that was just out of my reach. Somehow, I *knew* this young woman. Somewhere, I'd seen her.

I viewed the restored head from all angles, the sense of recognising her growing stronger every second. *I know this person,* I thought. But how could I? A young woman murdered at Queanbeyan probably two decades ago. I wasn't even working in Canberra at that time.

Wendy had placed the head on a table, where there was room enough for a vase of violets. Their delicate, old-fashioned fragrance reached me as I walked around again, examining the work. The unknown woman's eyes, now set finely in their fleshed-out orbits, fringed with lashes, gazed a little to my left so I moved until I was in the right place. Now she was looking straight into my eyes. Soft hair, bleached at the tips, waved around her cheeks, a mid-length style that would allow viewers to imagine it shorter or longer as they needed. Wendy returned with two glasses.

'Let me,' I said, seeing her about to tackle the champagne bottle and taking it from her.

'What do you think?' she asked.

'You're a genius,' I said. 'It's almost a breathing presence.'

'Kind of you to say so. I'll probably never know if I got it right, or even if I was close.' She poured two glasses of the home-grown champagne—nothing sham about the pain, I used to think, the morning after.

'I don't drink,' I said, 'but I wanted you to pour two glasses.'

I picked up the tall glass, with its bubbles beading in horizontal lines up the sides, and placed it carefully near the vase of violets. 'This is for you,' I said, 'whoever you are, wherever you are. This is an offering for you.' When I turned to Wendy, I saw she had tears in her eyes.

'If I can take her and get our technicians to post a photo of her on the Missing Persons link, it could have results. I promise I'll take great care of her.'

'Sure,' said Wendy. 'Just don't let her out of your sight. What can I get you to drink then?'

I said I'd settle for anything soft. Wendy poured herself a second champagne.

'That was a lovely thing to do,' she said, 'to make an offering of wine.'

I signalled with a lifted hand. 'It was the least I could do.'

'And I'm really pleased with how she turned out,' she said.

'You should be,' I said. 'She's so good, she looks familiar. I feel I've seen her somewhere.'

'Remember, it's not like a photographic likeness or anything. It's only ever going to be a passing resemblance. We don't know the habitual expressions that made her face her own. We can't derive that from statistics.'

I kept staring at the dead woman's serene gaze and I felt uneasy. The familiarity worried me.

'Maybe you met her once,' Wendy said. 'Years and years ago.'

'That could be it,' I said, not wanting to labour the point.

When it came time to leave, I placed 17/2000's reconstructed head, wrapped up in tissue paper and an old evening gown that Wendy was happy to contribute for the occasion, and put her on the passenger seat beside me, cradled in a box and seatbelted in.

On the drive back to Weston, I came to the conclusion that the sense of recognition I'd experienced when looking at the face of the unknown young woman hadn't derived from twenty years ago. Impossible though this was, I recognised the features of 17/2000.

I was *sure* I'd seen her quite recently.

Back at work, and still puzzling about the impossibility of this, I walked down to the technicians who would scan 17/2000's head onto our records for posting on Missing Persons and other police sites. After giving them the reconstruction, we discussed a press release and decided that if we didn't get any results from the first line of exposure, we'd go to the newspapers with the likeness.

In my office, a phone call reminded me that a group of Sydney detectives were arriving the next day for the forensic conference and I wondered if Wendy would be available at such short notice to give an off-the-cuff talk about her work with cranial and facial reconstruction. I rang her and asked. She liked the idea, but...

'I've never done anything like that before,' she said. 'I'll be very nervous.'

'Consider it practising for invitations in the future. There would also be a guest speaker's fee in it as well as your payment for the job,' I bribed. 'Remember, you're an impoverished postgrad student.'

That clinched it.

I reclaimed 17/2000 from the technicians, who'd finished with her, and, remembering my promise to Wendy, installed her on top of my tall filing cabinet where inactive paper files were still stored. I couldn't resist hanging the evening dress down the front of the filing cabinet and, together with a Brumbies football team scarf that someone had left lying in the meal room ages ago, I draped the exposed top area of the cabinet. I smiled to myself as I stepped back to admire my handiwork. At first glance, it looked as if a tall woman dressed for an evening out was standing in the corner of my office. She looked very good there, and the slight angle I'd given to the bust gave her eyes a come-hither look. Maybe it was a strange thing to do, possibly even pathetic, I thought. Was this the only sort of woman I could make it with? I sat at my desk with my head in my hands, staring at the Venetian glass paperweight and wishing like hell I knew how to get Iona Seymour back into my life.

After that, I spent a long time bringing my records up to date and dealing with the endless mountain of mail, from both the outside and internal world. Days like this, I'd like to track down the liar who promised us a paperless office twenty years ago.

My mobile rang while I was absorbed in this and I grabbed it up. When I heard who it was, I wished I hadn't.

'Jack, I'm in town,' said Earl Richardson. 'Drove down with some of my old mates from the academy.'

I tried to think of something to say.

'Anyway, I thought it would be a great chance to catch up with you. Show you my appreciation. What say we get together? Swap a few war stories from the old days. Have a few quiet ones? I'm very grateful for what you did for me.'

'I didn't do anything for you,' I said. In my irritation with the man, my fingers flicked and fiddled with the paperweight. 'I simply did my job. Same as I'd do any day, any time for anyone. I gathered the evidence and the evidence fell in a certain direction.'

'But not in mine,' said Earl. 'Praise the Lord. You know, I wanted to get back with Tianna. Marriage is a sacred sacrament and yet she wanted to party all the time. I kept trying to interest her in going to Mass again and saying the rosary. She was raised a Catholic, you know. Had the faith and threw it away. Threw me out, too.'

The image of party girl Tianna saying the rosary with her estranged husband almost made me laugh out loud.

'You know,' Earl was saying, 'I read in the press that people with religious beliefs are much healthier than people who don't have faith. I've never been healthier in my life. Did you know that? Religious faith has the power to keep you healthy.'

I bit my tongue.

'I hear some scientist down your way went mad,' Earl continued. 'Ended up shooting a colleague.'

'He was a man of religion, Earl.' I couldn't resist.

'Not the true faith,' he said.

I could have recited a few facts about some luminaries in the IRA but decided it was better to just let Earl Richardson go away.

'So what do you say we meet up with a few of the fellers and knock over a couple of beers for Auld Lang Syne? Then we can have a good chat. You need God in your life, Jack.'

I managed to remain professional. 'Earl, I gave up the booze over twelve years ago. I don't drink at all these days. Can't make the piss-up.'

'Jack, I'm sorry to hear you can't hold your liquor. But I want to drop around while I'm down here and thank you in person. Without you, I could've been in all sorts of trouble. I'll swing by sometime.'

I hung up. Earl Richardson left a bad smell in the air, I thought. Then realised it was dog shit I could smell and it seemed to be coming from under my chair. I must have trekked some in by way of one of my pairs of shoes.

I pushed myself out from the desk and peered down. The smell was definitely stronger the closer I came to the floor. I was about to straighten up, intending to go and get disinfectant from the cleaning station, when something caught my eye.

Right there, in the place I'd been sitting, where my shoes would have been resting on the floor as I spoke on the phone, I could see greyish particles of coarse sand. I didn't need any microscopic examination. I'd seen this material so frequently recently that I knew straightaway what it was. But I had to be sure for the records so I pushed my chair right back, tape-lifted the grit from under my desk and took this and my bagged shoes into a nearby examination room.

It wasn't long before I had recorded that the greyish particles on my shoes were indistinguishable from those we'd collected from Damien Henshaw's workboots and the head wounds of both Tianna Richardson and Albert Vaughan. I straightened up from the stereo microscope, trying to recall how long it had been since the cleaners had done my office. Over a week, I realised. I wrote up my findings and padded back to my desk. Somewhere, in the last week, I'd come into contact with Universal Cement's defunct Roman White aggregate blocks. I was going to have to retrace every damn step I'd taken in this pair of shoes because, somewhere, I'd been at or very close to the primary crime scene where Tianna Richardson met her end.

I sat at my desk, walking through my recent days again. The crime scenes I'd visited could be eliminated because I'd been wearing protective gear or gumboots which I had never worn in this office. I'd worn these shoes every day to work and the only places I'd visited that couldn't be eliminated from my list of possible sites were the cottage where I lived, Wendy Chen's flat and Alana Richardson's house. It definitely wasn't the cottage because I knew the soil type round there.

I rang Brian and told him.

'Doesn't really make much difference to me,' he said. 'Wherever the crime scene is, Damien Henshaw's been there too. And smoked a joint there. And had sex with the victim. He left his DNA at the Blackspot Nightclub, Jack,' he reminded me. 'Not just the grey particles.'

He was right. The DNA results proved that Damien Henshaw had smoked the joint we found near Tianna Richardson's body. Bob had checked his house again and found a couple of joints in a tin rolled in the identical way, with little twists at both ends, like a Christmas cracker. I doubted, given all the other evidence, that the defence could raise a plausible 'reasonable doubt' in a jury's mind. I rang off. Despite all the evidence pointing to Henshaw, my suspicions about someone else would not go away. Regardless, I was going to check out the two other places. I couldn't imagine Wendy Chen being a murderer on the side, but it was possible that she might use or have lying around some of the disused blocks. But I *had* been to a house recently where a young man, Jason Richardson, had been labouring, laying blocks on a retaining wall. I wanted to check that out.

As I was thinking of this, the desk phone rang. It was Jerri Quill. 'I've decided,' she said, 'to come back and discuss my situation with the nuclear biology people.'

'I'm happy to hear that,' I said, and I was.

'I visited Wendy the other day, before you took the reconstruction away. That made me think of the re-enactment. Even though it was upsetting, it was a good example of the work you do—the work I hope to do one day. Take the facts and examine them. Put disconnected things back together again. See the pattern. Find the truth.' There was a silence on the line before she spoke again. 'I realised for the first time that this really is the work I want to do.'

I was about to compliment her on her choice when she was interrupted and I could hear Wendy's voice in the background.

'Wendy wants to know when will you be bringing La Incognita back again?'

'Very soon,' I said. 'Wendy can take her home after she delivers her talk to the Sydney police tomorrow. I won't need her after that.'

It had been a long day, I thought, as I closed my notebook.

As soon as I could get away tomorrow, I wanted to go back to Alana Richardson's place at Sparrows Ridge Road and take a closer look.

I swivelled round in my chair and stared back at the life-like head, thinking about women, especially the first woman in my life, just as Charlie had suggested I should. Sitting there, doing nothing, just *being*, as Charlie had also suggested I do. I allowed the restlessness to build. He'd asked me to watch what happened if I didn't take my usual habitual action, that was, get up and get *busy*. The restlessness grew and grew and changed into something much more unpleasant. I was aware of a creeping anxiety growing in my stomach and chest, an unpleasant shuddery feeling that lay hidden under the cover of always being busy. This is why I can't lie around on river banks idling, I thought, spending aimless time with a woman. Because if I did, this was exactly what would happen.

I sat there staring at the come-hither expression on the sweet three-quarter profile of the unknown female. No wonder I didn't want to spend time with a woman, because, out of the anxiety, the first part of the challenge Charlie had put to me was starting to form. *Why would you ever open up to a woman again*, it began.

I didn't let it finish. I had work to do.

Early the next morning, skipping the first sessions of the conference proper, I was back at Alana Richardson's cottage. This time, only the little blue hatchback was there. As she opened the door, I saw her expression change from polite surprise to puzzlement and then concern.

'If you've come to talk to Jason, he's not here,' she said.

'I noticed,' I said. 'But that will keep.' I smiled to ease her worry. 'What I'd really like to do is take a look around here. The grounds. The garden.'

Her slight frown betrayed her anxiety. She knew people like me didn't look around houses and gardens because of aesthetic interests.

'Of course. Please,' she said as she ushered me in. 'Whatever you need to do. I'll be here in the kitchen if you should need anything.' Before, in our brief dealings, there'd been just a hint of flirtatiousness underlying her manner. Now, however, she was all formal courtesy.

Alana led me through the house and out to the back garden—a wide, rambling area, with old fruit trees and various old-fashioned briar roses bordered by a photinia hedge. But it was the back fence I was interested in, the area where I'd seen Jason working, rebuilding a partly tumbled-down retaining wall. Behind this I couldn't see much, just the odd native scrubby bush.

I walked right down to the end of the long garden to inspect the building blocks. It was clear that the newer ones didn't quite match the old ones and it wasn't just a matter of the accretions and dulling of age. The first five or six courses had been built at a much earlier time. I squatted beside the wall, took a small tool and plastic bag from my pocket and scraped the sides of several of the original blocks. I would have to test them, but I had the same sense of sureness about these as I'd had back in my office when I'd collected the coarse sandy particles from under my desk. I was willing to bet my career that the lower courses had been made from Universal Cement's discontinued blocks.

I sealed the scrapings, pocketed them and stood up, looking around. Jason had been adding two new courses of a similar type of block along the top of what I saw now was quite a long retaining wall, sweeping around in a slight curve. The bushes just beyond obscured the valley view and I jumped up on top of the wall to get a better view of what lay beyond. The block I was on shifted a little, throwing me off balance. I teetered a moment then looked down on the other side of the wall. The shock made me swear out loud in terror as I realised I was swaying on the edge of a precipice. Less than a third of a metre of solid ground lay beyond the wall on the other side and the bushes had somehow curved their roots into fissures in a sheer cliff wall. If I hadn't regained my footing, I could have fallen to my death on the rocks many metres below.

Shaken, I stepped down and walked the length of the wall until I found a place where I could more safely climb up onto the old blocks and look down. The drop must have been around fifteen metres or so. I jumped down on the wrong side of the fence and, holding on tightly to an old acacia, took another look. From this angle, I could see the dusty fire trail that ran below, hugging the cliff side. I stared down thinking, yes, things are falling into place.

Climbing back over the retaining wall, I walked back up the garden.

'Did you see anything interesting?' Alana asked, trying to sound light-hearted.

'Hard to say,' I said. 'When will Jason be back?'

As if on cue, I heard the sound of a car slowing down out the front and wished I'd followed Adam Shiner's example of parking outside another house. I heard the car accelerate and, although I sprinted as fast as I could round to the front of the property, I only caught a glimpse of Jason's old panel van and his surfboard disappearing in an explosion of dust. I raced to my own vehicle and jumped in, gunning the motor and screeching off after him. But he'd had just enough time to take advantage of the T-intersection at the end of Sparrows Ridge Road. My guess was that he'd be heading right, driving north to Sydney, where the pond was bigger.

I took the south road and drove fast to Heronvale.

'They must know each other,' Brian said when I told him what I'd found. 'Damien Henshaw and Jason Richardson. They *must* have been in it together. Somehow got Tianna there and pushed her over.'

'It would take two of them,' I said. 'Then they dress her up in her party gear and dump her back at the Blackspot to make us think what we thought at first. That she'd met someone at the nightclub and been killed there in the car park.'

'It's a reasonable assumption,' said Brian. 'But they didn't bother with the skirt because it was too hard to get on. They used another, easier-fitting skirt. She must have been dead in the car—'

'We've no evidence of that from Henshaw's car,' I reminded him.

'Maybe she was wrapped in something. And the evidence is pointing that way,' said Brian.

'We just need to discover the connection,' I said, thinking of the unseen circuitry.

'Tianna's the connection,' said Brian. 'Stepmother to one, the other screwing her. I'll get some people together and we'll examine the area beneath Jason Richardson's grandmother's place. We'll also put the word out on Jason's vehicle. And I'm going to have another chat with young Damien and tell him that not only have we discovered that Jason Richardson was in it with him, but that Jason is now telling us everything, saying that *he* tried to stop Damien. But Damien did both killings. That should get him going.'

'I didn't hear that,' I said, in a hurry to leave. 'I've got some particles I want to analyse. I'm confident what I have here will lock in the physical evidence we got from the head injuries beyond dispute.'

Brian nodded, then frowned. 'But I still don't get how Albert Vaughan fits into this, how he comes to have the same coarse granite sand embedded in his head wound?'

I couldn't answer that one. There was a lot I still didn't get.

It didn't take me long to demonstrate to my own satisfaction that the particles I'd scraped from the old Roman White blocks at the end of Mrs Richardson's garden were indistinguishable from those found in the wounds of Tianna Richardson, Albert Vaughan and unknown female 17/2000. I'd arrived at certain conclusions about how the body of Tianna Richardson might have gathered these particles. As to the other two, I had not been able to form any conclusion. In short, I had no idea.

My head was aching and I needed a break. I walked down the corridor to the staff common room to make myself a coffee and have a look at the newspaper headlines. As I was stirring too much sugar into the cup, I became aware of a lot of traffic in the car-park area. I remembered the Sydney detectives were here for the conference lectures and guided tours of the labs and museum over the next couple of days. It would be a good idea, I thought, for people to stay out of town tonight, as carousing Sydney personnel would be piling into the Cat and Castle. For a split second I envied them. I couldn't go and join them in standard operating procedure—getting wasted to take my mind off what troubled me. All I could look forward to was another early, lonely night back at the cottage.

I finished my coffee and went back to my office but, before going to my desk, I stood a moment, studying Ms 17/2000's sweet face. How the hell, I asked her, did you get yourself mixed up with a rare orchid and granite sand particles?

And how did an old man living out on the Ginninderra Road get those particles in his head wounds too? In this game, there were always far more questions than answers.

In my absence, a whole lot of new mail had been dumped on my desk. I was about to make a start on the paperwork but the mess on the desktop was dispiriting. I put the Venetian glass ball safely away on top of the filing cabinet, next to Ms 17/2000. Inside its fragile mysterious world, frozen coloured spirals, energy immobilised in glass, shone. Somehow I knew something similar had happened deep within me a long time ago, caused me to freeze up when it came to intimate relations, and this had driven Iona away. But I couldn't just lose her like this. If I wanted to win her back, I knew I *must* find the way to change so that I could offer her what she wanted from me.

I made a start on the different trays, using my triage system of those that demanded immediate attention, those that could be left a while longer and those I could safely give to someone else to handle. I was making some headway, aware of all the noise in the building, of people moving around in the corridors and bursts of laughter. The Sydney boys were on their tour. Finally, I had cleared some space and could work with some dignity.

My desk phone rang and I grabbed it, relieved by the distraction.

'Bob,' I said. 'Where are you?'

'Sydney,' he said. 'I've just come away from a crime scene.'

'No way am I involved in this one,' I said. 'Keep this case all to yourself. From now on, I'm keeping my nose right out of other people's investigations. I'm way overdue for long service leave. Any news on young Shaz?'

'Sorry, Jack. Sharon Lockhart was found dead in the backyard of her boyfriend's flat.'

'Shaz,' I said, recognising the full name. 'What *happened*?'

'It's a horror show,' Bob said. 'She'd tried to get away from him, but he'd followed her through the house, down the stairs and out into the yard. I've been picking up pieces of her all morning.'

Jacinta, I thought. This is going to be very hard for her.

'We're still trying to trace her family to inform them,' said Bob.

'What about the boyfriend?'

'He's wandering around somewhere with a nine-inch blade. We're out hunting him right now.'

I rang off. I could feel the anger sweeping up my spine. Another young girl had died because nobody cared about her.

I called Charlie, grateful to hear his voice, and told him.

'Shit,' he said.

'Pick up Jacinta, wherever she is,' I said. 'Our address might be somewhere in Shaz's personal effects. Don't let her out of your sight till I get there.'

'She'd better stay at my place,' said Charlie. 'Or her boyfriend's.'

'I'll get going the minute I can get away,' I said. 'I hope they lock up Shaz's family too. For not loving her.'

'You'd have to lock up most of the world on that charge,' said Charlie.

I sat still, lost in my thoughts. It came as a shock when I realised I was part of such a family system and that Iona could reasonably charge me with the same offence. But this admission didn't quench my anger. I thought of my alcoholic mother, whose first and only love eventually was ethyl alcohol. I thought of Jason who shared the same birthday as my son Greg, and his absconding mother.

Armed with this information, I switched on my email system and found Interpol, London. Lily Richardson, née Meadowes, I decided, you're going to have to show up. I'm going to make sure you know that your son Jason, whom you dumped when he was just a baby, is facing the possibility of being charged with murder. I want you to *know* that. I want you to have to face that.

I filled in a Missing Person file, listing her name and the approximate year of her arrival in the UK. That amount of information faxed to Interpol would, I hoped, be sufficient for the authorities to track her down quite soon. Maybe my motivation for doing this was because of my own problems in this area, as Charlie reckoned. Maybe I was acting as fate in the life of an irresponsible woman. Whatever reason, I felt better after I'd done it.

The next thing was to be in Sydney with my daughter. I called her but the phone went straight to voicemail. I left a message saying I'd be at Malabar later that evening. It was unlikely that Docker would do anything more than try to hide. But I didn't like the idea, no matter how remote, of a man with a nine-inch blade, whose girlfriend had been spirited away from him with the support of my daughter, discovering where Jacinta lived.

THIRTY-TWO

When I switched off the ignition, the swinging surge of the Tasman filled my ears, louder because of the silence of the night. In the living room, the lemurs, embracing tightly, swung gently from the central light fitting. I rang Charlie and then Jacinta from the empty house but both mobiles were switched off, which didn't do anything to relieve my anxiety about my daughter.

I poured myself a drink of orange juice and rang Greg, who said he'd catch up sometime this week.

My phone rang and I pounced on it. 'She's here, and we're both fine,' Charlie said in answer to my questions.

'So she doesn't know about Shaz yet?' I asked.

'She just knows you're coming over,' Charlie said.

'I'm on my way,' I replied.

During the drive to my brother's place at Little Bay I was nervous about how I was going to tell Jacinta about Shaz. The ringing of my mobile made me jump. Bob.

'Have you got Docker?' was my first question.

'Not yet. But I've had a chance to talk to one of the girls who lives in the same building,' said Bob, his voice heavy, and I knew something was troubling him. 'Seems like Shaz got lonely at the motel. She rang Docker.'

'Jesus, no,' I said.

'Then she packed up and went back to his place,' Bob continued. 'And he sure was waiting for her.'

Now I understood the reason for the quiet despair in Bob's voice.

'We can only offer people limited protection from the predators, Bob,' I said. 'And there's no way on earth that we can protect people from themselves.'

There was a silence from the other end.

'Gotta go, Bob,' I said, ringing off, preparing myself in the few minutes I had in the drive to Charlie's place for what I had to tell my daughter.

My brother was opening the door as I walked up the path and behind him I could see my daughter's apprehensive face.

'Jass,' I said, putting my arm around her shoulders, pulling her to me and kissing the top of her head.

'Something's wrong!' she said, hurrying ahead of me, turning to study my face as we reached the light of the living room. 'What is it?'

'It's Shaz,' I said and her hand flew to her mouth to cover it, as if suppressing a scream.

I told her what had happened and she listened in silence until I'd finished. Then, with the tears running down her face, she sat slowly on Charlie's lounge, hugging a cushion to her. 'But why? Why did she do that? After everything we talked about. She knew what he was like! She *knew*!'

I shook my head. 'That's just it. She *didn't* know. She was living in a dream, a delusion. You explained it to me earlier. She didn't know what love looks like, feels like. She believed someone's words more than the evidence of his behaviour. Shaz mistook violent attachment for love.'

My daughter came over to me and I hugged her, holding her lightly, letting her sob, trying to comfort her, but she pulled away.

'We should have stopped it! Nobody did anything!' she said.

'Not true, Jass,' I said. 'You think about it. At least three or four people, including yourself, were so concerned they got together to remove her from a dangerous situation. Bob went out of his way. You did. I did. Bob's motel mate.'

'We should have stopped her! Locked her up!'

'I'll make a cup of tea,' offered Charlie, who'd been quietly standing near the entrance to his kitchen.

'I don't want bloody tea! I need something stronger!'

'Do you think that's really a good idea?' I didn't want to sound too censorious, but ex-heroin addicts were better staying away from alcohol—addiction to one substance seemed to automatically confer immediate addiction to another. I'd seen the way addicts 'weaned' themselves off one drug by taking on another.

My daughter didn't answer; instead, she was weeping, hands over her face. When she looked up there were tears running down her cheeks. I passed her my big handkerchief and she blew her nose and wiped her eyes, shaking hair out of her eyes.

'It's so damn sad,' she said. 'I thought she would make it. I thought that by leaving him she'd break the pattern and make it.'

I thought of beautiful Shaz and wanted to cry too.

'I want to know what happened,' Jacinta said. 'I want to know everything.'

I sat down beside her and put an arm around her, remembering not to pat her.

It was going to be a long night.

Before she went to bed, I did everything I could to convince Jacinta to come back to Canberra with me, but the best I could do was get her to promise she'd stay at Charlie's place until Docker was locked up.

I left her writing a letter to Shaz.

Charlie had heated up some of the soup he'd made earlier in the evening and I was happy to eat a bowl of it while he read and relaxed in his armchair, a man at peace with himself and his world.

'You look worried, bro,' he said, looking up from his reading. 'Not that you shouldn't be. You sure blew it with Iona.'

'Thanks a lot, Charlie,' I said. But he was right.

'I did,' I admitted. 'I find it hard to stop and just do nothing. Spend easy time with the woman I love.'

That wasn't quite what I meant and Charlie recognised it straightaway.

'You mean if you did such a thing, you'd have to talk to her about *yourself*—eventually,' he rephrased. 'About your hopes and fears, your feelings. And you don't really want to do that, do you? You don't want to have to examine why you feel obliged to work rather than enjoy the activities that bring pleasure and happiness into our lives.'

'Obliged?' I said. 'I've already explained that to Iona—that I have an obligation to the dead—'

'Which dead?' Charlie interrupted. 'Your mother whom you couldn't save? Rosie who you still somewhere believe was taken on your watch?'

I felt like I'd been kicked in the chest by a horse. 'Why are you saying these things to me?'

'Because they're questions you should be asking yourself and you're not!'

'Look, Charlie. You're way out of line. I can partly understand why you questioned me when I said I wanted to spend time with Iona—'

'—but you didn't really want to,' he interrupted with a smile. 'Did you?'

'I don't know,' I said, unsure.

'If you do ever get round to looking at some of these issues, what are you going to do? What changes *could* you make?'

'That's what I'm asking you,' I said.

Charlie smiled. 'You seem to have found the answers to my earlier questions yourself, bro,' he said. 'Keep working on these.'

'Just tell me what you think,' I persisted.

'It's not about what *I* think,' he said. 'You've got to find the answers for yourself. Jeez, Jack, you insist on doing that in every other area of your damn life. Why can't you do it in this one?'

Next morning, early, after a restless night on Charlie's lounge, where thoughts of what my brother had said to me circled my mind all night, I finally got up and put the coffee on. I checked on my daughter—a lump with tousled spiky hair under the doona in the spare bedroom.

After a quick breakfast, I knocked on Charlie's door to say goodbye and he grunted back.

Then I loaded myself and my briefcase back into my wagon, all the time wondering whether Charlie was right. That I felt obligated to 'save' these women because I hadn't been able to help those nearest to me. I wondered again why I turned to work instead of the pleasures of companionship and relating with Iona and my children more. What was I avoiding by doing so?

I'd failed Iona because of these hungry ghosts and the parts of my heart they'd eaten; it was these very missing parts that Iona wanted—and now it was too late. Hell, I thought as I turned the ignition. Here I was driving to Canberra. Again. I'd had enough of this.

Before I was clear of Sydney, I rang Bob. He wasn't at work but he hadn't heard any news about Docker, who was still out there with his nine-inch blade. I told him of my concern for Jacinta and that she'd be staying at Charlie's place.

Bob knew the address and, although agreeing that it was highly unlikely Jacinta was in any danger from Shaz's killer, promised to keep an eye on her.

First thing I did when I walked into my office at Forensic Services was nod a greeting to Ms 17/2000. From her position in the corner, she gave me her customary sideways glance. I stood a moment, admiring her, and noticing that if I moved just a little out of her direct gaze, the position of her lifelike eyes gave the illusion that she was looking sideways at me. I came up close and studied the face of the unknown woman. Again, I was sure she wasn't unknown to me. In fact, the sense that I knew her was growing stronger every time I looked at her.

I called Brian. Jason Richardson had not been found, but he was confident the youth was still in the area and that it was only a matter of time before he showed up. Brian had someone keeping a discreet eye on Alana Richardson's house on Sparrows Ridge Road and it was fine with him, he said, if I wanted to go and check out the bottom of the ravine. The crime scene people had finished with the area. 'The samples we took are probably with you already,' he said. 'Or they'll be arriving today.'

'Did the Kiwi Krait turn up?' I asked, smiling as I used his term.

'She was there. And she was much less officious today. You know,' he added after a pause, 'she's not a bad-looking woman.'

I set about tackling another pile of paper that had somehow found its way onto my desk in my absence.

Some time later, while I was immersed in trying to make the next month's roster work, a knock at the door caused me to swing round.

'Come in,' I said.

Before I'd finished speaking, the door was flung open to reveal Earl Richardson. Of all the people I didn't want to see, he headed the list.

'Jack! God bless you! It was so good knowing you were on the job at such a dreadful time!' said Earl, looking very dapper in an expensive Italian suit. 'So this is where you hide away, eh?'

Moving fast, as if I'd been on the way out as he knocked, I grabbed my briefcase, intending to head him off at the pass, make him a coffee and abandon him as quickly as I could. I extended my hand to match his, trying hard to smile, about to make some comment about the pressure of work when a loud burst of laughter made us pause in the doorway where we were standing. A noisy group had turned the corner and immediately I recognised one of them—Adam Shiner—flanked by two laughing women.

'Come on, Earl,' I said, nodding to the group, closing my office door behind me so that Earl

Richardson couldn't go in any further. 'Tea or coffee?'

Then I noticed the expressions of the three people in the group.

'Earl?' I looked back, wondering at his silence.

Earl Richardson was turning like a robot and staring, open-mouthed, at them. The hand that he'd suddenly withdrawn from my greeting was flailing around near his throat. His colour was terrible, a dark purple red. He clawed the front of his expensive shirt, his eyes shocked and staring. I grabbed for him as he began to keel over but he would have hit the floor, except that Adam Shiner had darted forward and grabbed him first.

'Undo his collar!'

'Airways clear?'

'Anyone here good with CPR?'

'It's a coronary.'

'Roll him onto his side.'

I had the ambulance on its way in minutes. I didn't hang round but I heard them arriving and dealing with the collapsed man.

As they stretchered him, I couldn't help thinking: so much for the health-giving powers of religious faith.

The shock of Earl Richardson's heart attack had permeated the building. It didn't take long for everyone to hear about it and the predictable appalling jokes were circulating within a few hours. Even though I didn't like the guy, his collapse at my office door had connected me to him and, later,

I phoned Woden Hospital. He was out of intensive care, I was told, in a stable condition and although medical staff were surprised at the speed of his recovery, they wanted him to stay until the test results came back.

It was a sobering thought that Earl Richardson was my age and that the stress he'd been through with his marital problems was similar to my own just a few years back. I became aware of my heart and its measured beats. Measured was the right word; an allocation was given each of us. Nine o'clock on a Monday morning was the time most heart attacks occurred, I thought, and I'd been working non-stop for too long. Men died because of this. More importantly, I had to build a life for myself that wasn't just work. Until Iona, my emotional life over the last few years had been a barren landscape. And what had I done when I'd been offered the wonderful chance that Iona brought to me? I'd failed to grow into a mature relationship with her. I hadn't been able to change. I was a scientist and I knew that species that couldn't adapt to changed circumstances simply don't make it in the evolutionary stakes. No wonder Iona had walked out. Who wanted to live with a man who still believed somewhere that his first duty was to the dead rather than the living?

I stood up and walked to the window, watching the movements in the autumn-flowering grevillea bushes as the honeyeaters probed their blossoms before winter stopped the nectar flow. The dark gunmetal sky with its threatening clouds that never rained was suddenly pierced by a ray of sunlight, making the whole world outside my window fill with a menacing brilliance. Do something, Jack, I told myself.

I called my boss in Sydney, outlining my situation and pointing out that I had far too much accrued leave and needed to take some. He agreed and said he'd approve my application as long as I could organise someone else who'd be willing to take over my position for a month. I thanked him and rang off, opened my bottom drawer and took out a leave form. I rang Florence and made her an offer, which she was happy to accept, then I filled out the form, starting with next Monday's date and taking a whole calendar month. Then—and this was about the only good thing I could say right this minute about being acting chief—I signed my approval of leave at the local area level with a flourish.

Pen down, I found myself wondering why Richardson's heart had attacked at the moment it had, with the three Sydney detectives coming into view. I wondered if there was unknown business between Earl Richardson and Adam Shiner. Maybe Earl *had* known that Shiner was shafting his missus and this had resulted in a sudden surge of angry blood. I found I was looking again into the serenely sideways gaze of 17/2000. *I know you,* my memory insisted. I've seen you recently.

My mobile rang. It was Bob. 'Docker's been arrested,' he said. 'He'll be charged today sometime. You can relax. Your daughter's fine, I've just spoken to her.'

I went down to Sofia Verstoek's office, feeling lighter, knowing that Shaz's murderer had been caught and I hadn't had to do a damn thing about it.

When I got to Sofia's office and knocked on her door, there was no answer so I walked further to the dedicated palynology lab and looked through the glass window of the door. I heard her call my name and turned. She'd come out the other end of the lab, shaking her hair free from its protective cover.

'Jack,' she repeated. 'I was just about to come looking for you. The pollen assemblage isn't finished yet, but I found traces of that rare orchid pollen from the gully. I'll have it all printed up and ready for you by tomorrow.'

'Great work,' I said. 'I want to go there and have a look for myself. I want to see how they did it.'

'They?' She looked puzzled.

'We believe now there were two offenders involved,' I said. 'As soon as we get hold of the second man, we'll be taking samples to see if he shows up.'

We stood there together, a little awkwardly. 'I'd like to have another look there myself,' she said. 'Could I come with you? I'd like to do a wider search up higher.' She flashed a smile at me, the first real one I'd ever seen from her. 'See if I can find that orchid.'

'Let's go first thing tomorrow,' I said. 'I'll pick you up at first light.'

THIRTY-THREE

With Sofia in the passenger seat, issuing directions, I drove past Mrs Richardson's place, now all quiet. No doubt she was keeping a vigil. I wondered what her attitude might be towards her grandson. I didn't know what she believed, whether or not she would defend him through thick or thin. By the time I'd driven to the end of the ridge and started the steep descent through the thick scrub of a state forest and found the fire trail, I was no longer thinking of Jason or his grandmother. Once I'd prised open the old steel gates to the trail and closed them again behind me, I was right back on the job.

We bumped along for a few kilometres until the land fell away even more and we were on the valley floor, driving back in the opposite direction along the dusty track, peering up for signs of houses on the ridge above.

It wasn't hard to find the bottom of the gully directly beneath Sparrows Ridge Road. Some householders had used the steep ravine as an ad hoc rubbish tip. We stopped just off the fire trail and got out, craning our necks to see the dull white retaining wall right at the top of the ridge above, noticing the tumbled spill of several blocks that had fallen away over the years to lodge halfway up the drop and were now partly covered in growth.

We both went to the back of my wagon and pulled on Tyvek suits and shoe protectors. I shoved some gloves and a magnifying glass in my pocket and we discussed how best to proceed. It was a relief knowing that the official team had been there and done their job. I was here to see where Tianna had fallen before being dumped at the nightclub car park. Some part of me insisted that I see this primary crime scene for myself. Despite the advances in video recording, for me there was no real alternative to life experience—to being there.

It didn't take us long to find the points of impact. Once we'd climbed up to the area where the fallen blocks lay half-buried in soil and vegetation, I could see with the naked eye an area that had been recently disturbed. Samples had clearly been taken and there was even still a smear of something dark along the side of one of the blocks. I straightened up and looked around. A couple of young saplings had been snapped in half, knocked down by something heavy hitting them.

Sofia climbed higher until she could go no further because of an arching overhang. Without proper climbing equipment, there was no way she'd be getting up and over that.

'How do you think it happened?' she asked, standing some way above me, hands on hips.

I considered, looking around at the fire trail a little distance beneath us and the ridge high above. 'I believe they somehow got her here—Damien might have suggested they go to a friend's place for more dope, for a threesome—I don't know. Maybe for baked beans on toast. He couldn't take her back to his place because of Kylie. Then, with Jason's help, he threw her over the wall, drove like we did just then along to the end of the ridge and down the hill, along the fire trail until they found her and collected her body. Took her home, dressed her up in her disco gear and drove the body back to the Blackspot to make it look like she'd come to grief there.'

'But why?'

I looked up at her, standing there on the hillside, a frown on her face.

'Make it look like she went out and picked up the wrong man,' I said. 'Throw the investigation onto the wrong track. And it worked—for a while.'

'Jason Richardson is still on the loose. And Damien Henshaw is still denying he knows him.'

'Wouldn't you? Under the circumstances?'

'But how come the techs found no trace of her in either of their vehicles?'

'That's not true,' I said. 'I found a necklace that matches the earrings she was wearing that night in Jason Richardson's glove box.'

'*And* Vic still has a packet of fibres from a car that don't fit anywhere,' she insisted.

'They could have come from anywhere,' I said. 'We can't join all the dots all the time. They could have pinched a car for the occasion. Until we get a confession, we'll never know. And that day may never come.'

'Brian Kruger told me you've never been happy with charging Damien Henshaw.'

'You're talking to Brian?' I asked.

'Well, you've never been happy about it, have you?' she repeated, ignoring my question.

It was true. 'I wasn't. But in view of the evidence I have to change my mind.'

'And you're not even a blond,' she joked.

'You're going to need climbing equipment if you want to go higher than that overhang,' I said.

But she wasn't listening and had almost disappeared beyond the overhang.

'Hey!' she called back, her voice edged with excitement. 'I've found the orchid! Most of the flowerets are gone but I can still get the idea.'

She was pointing to a dark-green-leafed plant attached to some rocks in the shelter of a small hollow formed under the bole of one of the larger eucalypts. I waited while she took shot after shot of it with her digital camera. Then she took a container and brushed the tiny orchids into its mouth, quickly capping it, capturing pollen.

Pollen, I remembered, that wasn't windblown. That must be brushed against to leave its mark.

'Sofia,' I said as we drove back to Forensic Services. 'Surely we'd expect to find some traces of that pollen on Damien Henshaw and Jason Richardson?'

A few moments passed before she responded. 'Not necessarily. Not with this particular species. It doesn't produce a great deal. Unless they touched the body in the place Tianna had collected it, they could be home free.'

It made sense, I thought. No traces on the killers unless they'd touched the wounds on the back of Tianna's head.

We bought some fish and chips for lunch and ate them in the gardens near the lake. As I lay back on the grass with Sofia in the distance checking out an unusually bright pink callistemon, I realised this was the sort of pleasant break I never thought to take. My heart was heavy as I gathered up the empty containers and dumped them in a garbage bin.

Later, as we arrived in the car park at Forensic Services and I was backing into my usual spot, there was Vic Agnew again, about to climb into his car. He watched as Sofia swung out of the passenger seat.

'We've been out looking at a rare orchid,' I said, goaded into defensiveness by his wordless leer. Sofia gave me a look.

'Okay,' I said. 'I could have phrased that differently.'

I heard him laugh as he drove away.

•

We disposed of our used gear and walked up the stairs together, preparing to separate at the entrance to the floor.

'Sofia,' I said. 'I'm speaking as someone who's been in this game a very long time. Next time there's a crime scene you need to attend, ring Brian and ask if you can be included. Speak to him nicely. Say, please can you have first go at the pollen traps.'

She frowned, transferring her carry case to the other hand, about to push the door to the floor level open.

'Brian is an overworked crime scene examiner, like I used to be once,' I continued. 'On call twenty-four hours a day, often dragged away from trying to get his cases ready for court by yet another crime scene demanding his attention. Always behind in his work. Always being loaded up with more. You'll be working with lots of young police like that. The fact that he makes so few errors given the huge pressures he's under, which he's constantly struggling to manage, is a tribute to him. Do you think you can give him a break?'

I waited with some trepidation. But she gave me the beginning of her rare smile.

'Okay,' she said. 'I'll try. After all, I owe you one.'

I shook my head. 'It's not me you owe. It's *you*. In this job, you need other people. Alienate too many people and you'll end up completely isolated. And maybe even out of a job.'

She cocked her head on one side, and the large brown eyes regarded me, appraised me. With a swift movement, she leaned forward and kissed me fast and hard on the lips, then turned and hurried away.

I watched after her as she turned the corner of the corridor, vanishing towards her end of the building.

I spent the rest of the afternoon getting on top of a stack of invoices and it wasn't until I was on my way out of the building, bracing myself to finally face the loneliness of the cottage, that my mobile rang.

'Jack McCain? It's Alana Richardson,' said the voice on the line. 'I probably should be ringing the police. But seeing as I know you…'

'What is it?' I asked.

'Jack, I've just come back from the hospital. Earl discharged himself a while ago. But that's not why I'm ringing. While I was out, my house has been burgled! Someone's taken every cent from the place!'

'Don't touch a thing. Ring the local police,' I said.

'I don't know where my grandson's gone and then I come home to this!… Oh God,' she said, her voice dropping to a whisper, 'I just heard something. I think someone's in the house!'

'Call the local cops,' I said. 'I'll alert them too. I'm on my way. Either lock yourself in a room or get out of the house. Now!'

I hurried back up the stairs and ducked into my office, intent on grabbing an old baton that I'd stashed away ages ago and a hand gun I had locked in my bottom filing cabinet drawer. It had been a long time since I'd handled the prohibited item and I didn't want to introduce it into a domestic scene unless lethal force was required.

I snatched up the baton, hid the gun inside my jacket and hurried back downstairs, letting myself out of the building, my brain going as fast as it could, trying to put things together.

I jumped back in the car, placed the gun under my seat and tried getting through to Brian again as I drove to Sparrows Ridge Road, but failed so I left a message. As the kilometres clicked by, I wondered what I would find. Images of how I'd tried to stack the vertebrae of 17/2000 the very first time I'd seen them came to mind. Making structural sense from disordered array. The unknown male had turned into a woman and swung the investigation around 360 degrees.

Just as I'd done with Claire Dimitriou's murder, I started again with the Tianna Richardson investigation. I was rerunning the case from my first glimpse of her lying on the asphalt to the last time I'd seen her, when Harry and I laboriously dragged her perfectly fitting skirt onto her cold corpse. I examined all the disparate pieces of information, the way an intelligence group interpreted seemingly unrelated incidents and responses. My mind reached desperately to find the subterranean connectors whose invisible conduits linked all the pieces, perfectly. But they remained out of view.

I considered everything that had happened, right up to the events of the last few days—the carefully pegged-out muscle and skin measurements that Wendy had crafted over her cast of 17/2000's skull. Locard's caveat about physical evidence jumped into my mind. 'Only human failure to find it, study it and understand it can diminish its value.'

I was getting closer to Sparrows Ridge Road for the second time that day and I glanced at the strong steel baton lying across the passenger seat, street lighting slipping strobe-like over its shiny black surface. And I knew in that moment why I'd been so sure that 17/2000's face was familiar to me. Because now I knew who she was. This afternoon's incident in the corridor with Adam Shiner and Earl Richardson and the group of visiting detectives now became perfectly clear. It had been there all the time, right in front of me. Bob had first drawn these facts to my attention. And Rosalie, the young pathologist, and Harry Marshall had pushed them even closer to me. But I hadn't been able to see then. I had failed to understand—I'd looked straight at the features of 17/2000 and *knew* I recognised her, yet failed to make the right connection. In that instant, the truth stood clean and clear in my mind: I knew who 17/2000 was and I knew who'd killed her.

Speeding towards the rising country where Tianna Richardson had been murdered, I berated myself. Now it was becoming abundantly clear why Tianna Richardson had been wearing a daggy woollen skirt and pearl and peridot earrings that did not match anything else she was wearing. It became easy to understand why the Stewart Chambray skirt still lay on top of its wrappings, still unworn, the label still attached.

Switching off the headlights, I swung round the curve in the road and approached the dozen or so households before Alana Richardson's cottage. I parked and got out, closing the door silently, gripping the steel baton. The streetlights here were dim and a light drizzle had started, chilling the air further. Someone nearby was playing very loud rock music and I moved as quickly and lightly as I could, grateful for the cover of the music. Peering over the hedges that constituted the front borders of Alana's place, I looked around in vain for Jason's car. The front garden was easy to see from the light shining out of the open front door.

The music stopped and, in the sudden silence, I heard a car idling. I ducked down the side of the house and found Alana's car in the driveway, rear door raised, and in the dim interior light I glimpsed the tartan rug, dusty with masonry particles and tools—remembered the fibres with unknown origin that had shown up in Tianna's case.

He hadn't left yet.

The music started up again and I stole towards the front door of the cottage, baton at the ready, using my other hand to open the door a little more. But something was blocking it. I pushed it a little harder then looked down to see what the problem was; Alana Richardson lying in the hallway.

I edged around the door, came in and was bending over, about to check her vital signs, when a sound from behind made me swing round, too late. The hall light clicked off, but in the shadows I could still make out his face.

And just before whatever he was swinging connected with my head, I had time to say his name.

THIRTY-FOUR

I woke up swaying from a nightmare blackout where I'd been trying to swim up through pitch-dark water to a surface that forever eluded me, reduced to a graph spike of consciousness on a broad black ground: no past, no future, just this awful moment of pain and confusion.

I struggled towards consciousness and reality. It was hard to do, like coming out of anaesthetic, with everything garbled and a long way away.

'You've got a nasty head wound, mate,' said my companion.

I was in the back of an ambulance. 'Brian? Is that you?' That was what I intended to say, but when I tried to make the words, all I could hear were peculiar noises.

'You're alive. Welcome back to life.'

'What happened?' I tried. 'After he hit me?' But again, although I knew what I was meaning to say, the way it came out was another series of groaning noises.

'He pissed off in your car, we think,' said Brian, trying to second guess my concerns.

'Probably passed him coming down on the way up here. He could be in Sydney by the time we get you sorted out.'

But that wasn't right. In vain, I tried to formulate the words. The prohibited item.

'His grandmother's okay,' said Brian, thinking that was my concern. 'She's in another ambulance on her way to hospital. He'd whacked her hard too. Little bastard.'

Little bastard. That's what his father had called him when we spoke in another world, another time.

'No,' I tried to say. 'No, that's not right. He's got my baton. And the handgun if he finds it.'

'Take it easy, Jack. You're not making much sense.'

Then my line to the world dropped out again and the fear in my mind and the strange sounds I was trying to make swirled away.

Next, I was being hauled upright to sit swaying on the edge of one of those green fake leather examination tables in Casualty at Woden Hospital. 'Just a couple of stitches,' said the young resident, who looked younger than Jacinta. 'You'll feel a little prick—from the local.' She smiled at her wordplay.

I looked around. 'The police officer who was here. The one in the ambulance. Where is he?' Relief. I could speak again and the words came out reasonably well.

'Hold still, please,' she said. 'You'll have to ask someone at the desk.'

I blinked. I couldn't really leave right now, dragging this young woman and her sewing kit behind me, leading her with my stitches. I fumbled for my mobile.

'Please,' she said, quite sharply. 'You can't be seriously trying to make a phone call while I'm attending to a bad laceration on your scalp.'

'They're after the wrong man,' I said. 'I've got to tell someone.'

Then the local anaesthetic must have hit the spot, and the young resident must have misjudged the dosage given my frail state, because I heard her yell for someone to come and help hold me and her voice came from a long distance while I vanished down the wrong end of a black vortex.

'I want to keep you here for observation,' she was saying as I came back. This time, I was flat on my back. 'Just overnight. We need to watch injuries like these. You could have a slow bleed in there, between your brain and your skull. I want to send you down to X-ray if you can walk.'

'I've got to get out,' I said. 'I've got to make a phone call.'

This time, I was able to sit up and dig my mobile out. I called Brian.

'Listen,' I said. 'It wasn't Damien who killed Tianna. And I know who 17/2000 is.'

'What the hell are you talking about?' Brian's voice. 'You're not making any sense, mate.'

'Come and pick me up. But first, go to my office and bring the reconstructed skull from the top of my filing cabinet. Take great care of her. She's very precious.'

'Jack. Take it easy. You've got a head injury.'

'So did she. So did Tianna. Listen to me. This is what happened.'

I told him about the break-in at Alana's place and the tartan rug in her car with its dusty particles and tools. 'If you test them, particularly the tyre brace,' I suggested, 'you might find it has granite particles on it. As well as trace blood residue.' I told him that my car could provide a mini-armoury. I told him about the baton and fudged a bit about the prohibited item. And most of all, I told him about the moment when the three noisy Sydney cops had turned the corner and started walking past us while Earl Richardson and I stood in the doorway of my office.

I talked fast, despite my condition, and after a while Brian stopped interrupting. By the end of it, he was listening.

Half an hour later we were speeding towards Sydney, my bandaged head feeling several sizes too big for me, despite or because of the painkillers I'd taken.

'He needs help if he wants to get out of the country,' I said.

'We've got people watching his house,' Brian said. 'He can't get far on the money he took from Alana's place. He's finished.' He turned the police radio down. 'But how did you get onto him? How did you work it out?'

'I didn't have to do it at all,' I said. 'Lily Meadowes did it for me.'

'Who?'

'Earl Richardson's first wife. All I had to do was join the dots and suddenly the evidence all made perfect sense. The skirt, the earrings. My sense of recognition.'

Brian shook his head. 'Will you for Christ's sake tell me what's going on?'

And so I did. It was always nice to impress people, even nicer to impress a young colleague like Brian Kruger. I watched sideways by the glow of the dashboard lights as he kept nodding his head slowly, taking it in and savouring it, bit by bit.

When I'd finished he glanced across at me, while the small computer screen came to life at his touch.

'Jack,' he said. 'I don't know what to say. The facts were there all the time.'

'Do you know where Jason is?' I asked.

'We'll find him,' said Brian, reaching for the radio. When he'd finished speaking, he rehoused it. 'All those clever Sydney types who are in town for the conference,' he said. 'Those guys who call us "plastics"? They should hear about this. From you.'

'I don't know if my head could manage getting around it all just now,' I said.

'And there could be a commissioner's commendation in it for you, too.'

'You know it wasn't just me,' I said. 'It was a team effort. He had every base covered. He thought.'

'That's what you should say,' said Brian. 'In your presentation.'

'I don't think I should say that. Not until he's arrested.'

'He won't be able to access any of his bank accounts. He's got to have money to do anything.' He considered. 'We might be able to track him via his mobile.'

'Which he won't use,' I said.

'Not if he's got half a brain.'

'He's got considerably more than that,' I said. 'Plus crime scene experience. And a helpful bereavement counsellor. All that bullshit about wanting to get back with Tianna was just smoke in our eyes. He wanted to be rid of her, keep all the property, and he'd found what he thought was a perfect unwanted wife disposal method.'

I told him about the information Bob had passed on and remembered the intimate moment when Deirdre Delaney brushed something from Earl Richardson's black jacket.

Brian put his foot down while I rang Bob. We were driving northeast, angled into the rising sun.

When we arrived at the Police Centre, Bob was waiting for me and came down to the basement car park to meet us. 'Your wagon turned up,' he said. 'Dumped near Central. I went over and picked it up for you.' He handed me the keys.

'Central,' said Brian. 'He could be on a train to anywhere.'

Somehow, I didn't think so. No point in using the little money he had to arrive broke in a country town. 'He'd stick out like dogs' balls,' I said. 'He'll stay in the big city. Till he can get organised and out. He could be with Deirdre Delaney.'

'The woman with the interesting underwear? Your car's over here,' said Bob, leading us to it.

I noticed immediately that the baton had gone. I opened the door and when I felt under the seat, I cursed.

'He's armed,' I said.

Brian and I left his car and continued in my wagon to Earl Richardson's address, leaving Bob, who was officer in charge, to organise the search team from Sydney. As I took a turn too fast, the bag with 17/2000's rebuilt face rolled towards the window.

'What's that on the back seat?' Brian asked. 'More of your armoury?'

I reminded him that it was the skull reconstruction he'd brought from my office.

We parked in the back lane of the semi in Glebe and met up with the Sydney crime scene team. A door-knock around the neighbours turned up a spare key. Don, a sergeant I'd worked with fifteen years before was among them and even remembered me.

I climbed into a Tyvek suit, wincing as I cautiously pulled the hood over my stitched head, and went inside with the Sydney guys, putting my gloves on, hoping that the pain in my head wouldn't interfere too badly.

The search team went methodically through each room, dividing the space systematically so that not one inch was overlooked. In the back bedroom I saw an unrolled sleeping bag and an old army duffle bag and watched while they sorted through the clothes in it—mostly boardies, faded T-shirts and worn underpants. And an old colour photograph. The exhibit list grew: a small stash of leafy heads and a packet of cigarette papers.

I took the photograph from Brian and recognised it. A baby and a young mother with her face turned away from the camera, her soft dark hair with blonded tips shining in the Australian sunshine—the photo I'd briefly seen at Alana Richardson's place. I looked into the main bedroom. It was dark, facing south, and the drawers beside the bed yielded some very recent photographs of Earl Richardson with Deirdre Delaney. I noticed, too, that the bedspread was missing from the bed and another small question was answered.

The search of the premises took a long time, but, finally, in an outside drain near the laundry, Elisabeth from the Surry Hills physical evidence unit found a set of old dentures. With my gloved fingers I picked them up.

'Granny's dentures,' I said, turning the combined upper and lower set over in their bag, remembering what Alana had told me. 'He used these to make those so-called bite marks on Tianna's body. He was trying to make it look like some mad sex- and violence-killer. But the pressures were all wrong and the marks didn't even look authentic.'

'He was trying to muddy the waters,' said Brian as he labelled them.

'Send them down to Harry Marshall,' I said. 'Ask him to check these against the photographs of those so-called bite marks on Tianna Richardson's body.'

'We can't find much in the way of official documents,' said one of the team, who was going through all the drawers. 'Looks like he's already been here—taken his passport and other documents.'

A loud commotion near the front door made me turn injudiciously, hurting my head. In came Jason Richardson, half off the floor, struggling in the hands of Don from Maroubra police. 'Look who we've got here! He conveniently ran into a car at the end of the street.'

'Jason,' I said, 'why did you come here?'

'He was driving past the house but when he saw the police presence he took off. Didn't you?' said Don.

'Leave me alone! Get your bloody hands off me!' Jason struggled to free himself.

Pulling the hood of my spacesuit off my injured head, I stepped forward. 'He's okay, Don,' I said. 'I know him.'

And I did. Intimately. Abandoned by his mother, unloved by his father. And now in big trouble. The stitched injury on my head throbbed in time with the beating of my pulse.

'Where's your father, Jason?' I asked. 'We really need to know before things get worse.'

'I don't know,' he said.

The defiance was real, the denial was false and he knew that I knew he was lying.

'Your father's on the run,' I said. 'He needs to get away urgently. He's already contacted you, hasn't he? You were on your way here to pick up his gear. But we got here much faster than he'd imagined. Has he told you where to find his passport and his emergency stash?'

Jason remained silent.

'We'll find them, Jason. Even if we have to take this place apart, brick by brick. And we'll charge you with aiding and abetting. Not to mention obstruction. You wouldn't last five minutes in prison, son.'

I could see the kid was almost in tears. But his mouth was set in a hard line.

He turned away, refusing to look at me.

'He needs someone to get him money, to act as a go-between. Someone who will help him escape. Suddenly, after all these years of pissing you off and calling you a dole bludger, he needs you. He can't really rely on his girlfriend. She might start asking too many questions and get suspicious herself. But a son is different. Especially when your father *needs* you.'

I saw the lower part of his face start to slide.

'That must feel good, real good,' I said. 'But the sad fact is that he's using you, Jason. The minute he gets what he wants, he'll piss you right off again.

He'll be on the next aeroplane, ship, yacht, whatever, out of the country. Just like your absconding mother.'

I thought that might break him, but he held firm.

'You know where he's hiding, don't you?'

Jason struggled again but he was no match for the big man who held him with one of the mean wristlocks I'd used on Greg.

Where would he hide, I wondered, as my head throbbed even harder and hotter. Where would he lie low, waiting for the necessary documents to be delivered to him? It came to me in a flash. I suddenly knew where Earl Richardson would be.

'Father Basil,' I said.

THIRTY-FIVE

We decided to do it quietly rather than the weapons-drawn, sirens-screaming business and an hour later, once we'd tracked down Father Basil's whereabouts, Bob, Brian and I drove there in my wagon. We parked in the back lane behind St Aloysius's in the inner city, waiting for the rest of the troops to arrive. Bob got out and did a quick survey of the back of the church and the small attached rectory and its tiny cement garden.

'I don't like this,' he said as he climbed back into the car. 'It's too quiet.'

We decided to move then and check the grounds more thoroughly. As Brian got out of the car, I called after him, 'When all this is over, I'll buy you and your girlfriend a cocktail.'

Brian ducked through the backyard to disappear around the front of the church; Bob and I made sure the small cemented area around the entrance to the rectory was clear. A sign next to the buzzer invited visitors to press for attention.

I tried the door and found it wasn't locked.

'I'll go first,' Bob said in a low voice. He already had his weapon drawn and I was glad of that. 'Let's go.'

'Be careful, Bob,' I said. 'This man has nothing to lose.'

He pushed the door open and the squad car suddenly arrived in the back lane, its hotted-up engine roaring a warning. I swore and moved in fast behind Bob only to see Father Basil racing towards us, almost knocking Bob over. I grabbed him before he hit the ground. The Franciscan almost followed him. 'Where is he?' I shouted.

'Jesus, Mary and Joseph!' Father Basil's face was drained, his words hoarse. 'I thought he was going to kill me!'

'Where *is he*?' My voice was almost a scream.

'He's gone through into the church! As soon as he heard the car outside!' I knew the front entrance of the church opened onto a busy road. We had to contain him.

'Brian!' Bob yelled, disappearing round the front after our colleague. The place was seething with cops as squad cars from all over arrived and I hurried back to my wagon and jumped in, intending to drive round to the front of the church. Reversing, I turned and revved my car down the alley that ran parallel to the church grounds, linking the back lane with the main street frontage. I braked suddenly. At the end of the lane I saw Earl Richardson struggling in the hands of several police.

As the relief surged through my body, the throbbing in my head became worse. The bastard owed me one.

The search team was still busy wrecking large sections of the walls and flooring in the Glebe semi when Earl Richardson was led in handcuffs towards the dejected figure of his son slumped against the wall.

'Useless little prick,' his father snarled.

'Is that any way for a daily communicant to talk?' I said, aware of the throbbing in my head. 'What were you doing at Father Basil's? Confessing?'

The search team counted the money in the cashbox they'd uncovered and entered it in the exhibits' book, doing the same with the passport.

'I'll get off this, McCain,' Earl said. 'I'll say that I asked you to do me a favour but you had it in for me, that you maliciously fixed evidence against me. I'll tell them how you did it, too. I'll tell them how you threatened me. How you tried to extract money from me. Why do you think I called you in the first place? Just to cover every base, that's why. Just in case this happened. There are a lot of phone calls between you and me. Any court will want to know why the crime scene examiner and the alleged killer were in daily communication with each other during the time of the crime scene examination. You know the code of ethics. I'll walk free and you'll be out of a job.'

'Shut up, Earl,' I said, though I didn't like what he was saying. I remembered how he'd described us as 'friends'. My findings as a scientist would fall under suspicion. Questions would be raised as to why I'd taken on the role of crime scene examiner when it clearly wasn't my place to act in this way. I couldn't remember any other chief scientist who'd done what I'd done. Suddenly, I felt sick.

I went outside to my wagon. My head was getting worse. I wanted to lie down for a minute, relieve the throbbing in my head. I looked through the glove box for some aspirin. As I straightened up, I saw the bag with Wendy's reconstruction in it. Through the haze of pain and fear, an idea suggested itself and I snatched up the bag, hurrying back towards the door.

Just before arriving at the room where the others were, I took the reconstruction out of its bag and, holding it in front of me, approached the doorway, pointing 17/2000's head so that her serene, sideways glance was directed straight at Earl Richardson. I stood there in the doorway, like he'd done at my office, holding the head up in front of me, looking past her soft, dark, blonde-tipped hair.

'Talk your way out of this one, Richardson!' I yelled. 'Look who's here!'

He started to rise to his feet, his face shocked. I heard his sudden intake of breath, saw his face go red, then purple, saw the spasm of agony as his heart went crazy. I watched, hard and cold, while he gasped and staggered, unable to stand up.

'Come on, Earl,' I said. 'Talk your way out of her!'

He'd slid to his knees, his face a ghastly grey.

'Dad!' Jason cried, running to support him while I stood there, pointing her head, her youthful face, at him.

'Call the ambulance!' someone screamed.

Jason turned to me with stricken eyes. I saw how like her he was, with the same narrow face, fine, long nose, the same high cheekbones.

'Stop doing that!' Jason screamed at me. Then, in a softer voice, 'Who is she? What's happening? Dad!'

'The spitting image,' Alana had said. Jason was the spitting image of his mother.

I rested up at Charlie's, visiting my doctor later that day, who changed the dressing on my head and made noises about how I should be concentrating more on clerical work and less on tactical operations. I could only agree with her.

Jacinta, still very teary about Shaz, nevertheless did a great job with the tea tray and even made a cake as a special cheer-up treat for us all.

'How are the lemurs?' I asked her, sitting up from the spare bed, deciding it was time, at 3 p.m., to start the day.

'The lemurs are fine,' she said, laughing. 'Me and Andy wanted to know if it's okay to come down and spend a few days at the cottage with you. I'll see if Greg and Ellie can make it too.'

My spirits lifted immediately. 'I'd like that a lot,' I said. 'I've taken a month's leave.'

'That is so cool, Dad,' she said, coming over to kiss me. 'I'll need cheering up. We'll probably drive straight down after Shaz's funeral.' She drew back and looked at me with her mother's eyes.

'What is it?' I asked, sensing her hesitation.

'I want to see Iona, Dad. I don't want to lose her just because you're hopeless. Where is she?'

I gave her the address of Anne-Marie's Ainslie apartment and then I lay back and planned my next move to win Iona Seymour back into my life. She'd never left my heart, not for a second.

But I still felt sick whenever I thought of Earl Richardson's threat. Combined with the disciplinary action I could face for not merely having an unlicensed handgun, but permitting it to fall into criminal hands, his threats could mean the end of my life as a jobbing scientist.

'He came knocking on my door,' I said, as I sat on Charlie's garden deck, after telling him what had happened. 'Wanting to thank me for all I'd done for him. I'll bet the prick was laughing all the way. He'd set things up so well that we went for it.' I paused. '*I* went for it. He had another woman lined up and Tianna was a nuisance and he didn't want all the fuss of a divorce. Not to mention the financial loss. He planned this well. Even brought an extra bedspread with him, just in case.'

Charlie gave me a look.

'I'll explain sometime.' I shook my head. 'You're right, Charlie. I am heading for burnout if I don't take some time off.'

Charlie nodded slowly. 'But then, when he did come knocking on your door,' he said, 'he saw what looked like someone standing in the corner of your office.'

I nodded. 'He found himself staring straight at his first wife, looking like she did all those years ago when he murdered her. He had the first heart attack.' I paused and drank some coffee. 'At the time, I'd thought he'd got into a state seeing Adam Shiner turn the corner. But it had nothing to do with Shiner and everything to do with Lily Meadowes' eyes staring straight out at him.'

'No wonder he can't bear Jason, if he's like his mother,' said Charlie. 'I feel sorry for the poor kid.'

'Not only was he staring straight at his young bride again,' I said, 'but he was also realising that it was just a matter of time before that pretty face would be all over the newspapers. And no time at all before someone—probably Alana Richardson—said, "Hey, that's my first daughter-in-law, Lily Meadowes!" Then the inference would be drawn about Tianna. And Earl Richardson, conman, pantsman and wife-killer, who up until that minute believed he'd got away with everything, would be fucked good and proper.' I felt I wanted to spit.

'All that religious crap,' I added. 'What was he thinking?'

Dusk was falling and Charlie's garden was suffused with a soft light that made the greens glow with an intense brilliance.

'Charlie,' I said, 'I've got a confession. I hope Earl Richardson doesn't survive this second coronary.'

'You're saying you wish him dead?' said Charlie as he got up from the table and went into the kitchen. 'It would be a great deal easier for you if he would just go away,' he called back.

I thought about that. That was what Earl Richardson must have thought, about first one woman, then, twenty years later, another one, and here I was, having the same thought. So what did that make me?

Charlie had returned with the percolator and I held my cup up. 'He's got nothing to lose if he tries to bring you down with him,' Charlie said, filling my cup. 'All he has left to avenge himself is malice.'

The soft dusk light darkened. Maybe I was being too gloomy. Maybe no one would believe Earl Richardson, no mud would stick. I had done some good work. In discovering the murderer of Tianna Richardson, I'd also solved another murder, one that had gone unnoticed for nearly twenty years.

'You know,' I said, thinking of this, 'whenever I think of Jason Richardson, I feel sad. What will he do now?'

'There're a lot of kids like him around, one parent murdered, the other in gaol for the murder.'

I made a silent promise that I'd look in on the youth—I needed to connect more with the living, much more. Even if it was too late for me and Iona and the plan I was making to win her back, she'd taught me this much.

'I'd still like to know why Earl killed Albert Vaughan,' I said, voicing another concern.

'Sometimes you just don't get to join up all the dots,' Charlie observed.

Noisy miners squabbled in the trees around us as they jostled for night roosts.

'So, bro,' Charlie said after a silence. 'How did he do it?'

THIRTY-SIX

'I've heard from old crims,' I said, standing at the lectern, the bright overhead spotlights making my eyes ache, 'that after the first killing, the rest are easy.'

Hundreds of people had attended this special presentation at the Weston Federal Police complex. Wendy Chen had taken them through the process of forensic sculpture and behind me, taking up the full dimensions of the screen, 17/2000's face shimmered.

I'd almost finished my address in the AFP theatre and on the lectern in front of me, with my rough notes, was a letter that Sofia had found in Albert Vaughan's personal items and handed to me just before I was due to start my talk. I'd stared at it a few minutes, not understanding the significance of the re-addressed envelope, until the full implication of it hit me like an electric shock and the last part of the puzzle fell into place. Of course, I thought to myself, and the mystery of Albert Vaughan's connection to the granite particles became clear.

Outside, a roll of thunder sounded—still distant but heralding the slow-moving weather system that we were all praying would bring desperately needed rain—and I waited until it had stopped before continuing.

'No one doubted that Lily had run away and when the postcards arrived, the in-laws in Australia wiped their hands of her. Her mother-in-law raised the baby she'd left. With some intermittent support from her son.'

If I hadn't been so angry about Lily Meadowes abandoning her son, an anger that came from my own old childhood suffering, I never would have contacted Interpol to track her. The fact that there were no records of her ever arriving in the UK might never have surfaced. The muscles in my face were aching and the throbbing in my head, legacy of the man about whom I'd been speaking, was beginning to interfere with my thought processes.

'Postcards are often scrawled in a hurry,' I continued, 'and no one suspected anything. A flighty young thing had found family responsibilities too much for her and had run away back to the old country. It's not an uncommon event.'

I'd referred to Earl Richardson as 'the alleged killer' all through my address. I didn't want a contempt charge on top of all the others I could be facing.

'When I first looked into the cold case of 17/2000, it was because I'd remembered the rare native pollen trace found in the hair of what were only skeletal remains. I had no idea that this case would eventually fuse itself with that of a present-day murder investigation.'

I paused and took a sip of water from the glass on the lectern.

'I believe that the alleged offender, remembering how easily and simply he'd removed his first wife,' I continued, 'lured the second victim, his next wife, to his mother's property by telling her that she could pick up some jewellery that she desired very much. I don't know exactly what happened next, but I imagine he attacked her. Perhaps he knocked her down, perhaps he just lifted her and threw her over. She fell to her death in the same place as his first wife had—into a ravine at the end of the garden where there's almost no ground beyond the retaining wall.'

I suddenly remembered the reason for the blue I'd had with Richardson all those years ago—a crude remark he'd made about a policewoman we both knew who'd been sexually assaulted; 'asking for it', according to him.

I looked around the theatre. The audience was riveted but I knew I had to finish up soon and I tried blinking away the pain across my forehead.

'Just as he'd done in the first case,' I continued, 'he drove along the ridge, down the fire trail and into the valley, where he picked up the body and put her in the passenger seat. He must have had a body bag with him to contain any leakages, and a dead body doesn't bleed. He drove her back to what had once been their mutual home, took his car into the city centre and left it there, got himself back to the marital house, knowing that if he covered up well—this man has had a fair amount of forensic science experience—any DNA traces he left could easily be explained as historical and therefore be eliminated. He would make it look as if his wife had gone dancing and picked up the wrong man. But he had only limited time. He needed to dispose of her and get himself back to Sydney—a drive of some three hours or so—so that he could be suitably shocked and horrified, and of course *innocent*, when the police came knocking on his door with the death message.'

And so that he could ring me shortly afterwards, I thought. And set me right up.

'Time was running out,' I continued. 'He had to work fast. He carried her into the bedroom, unbagged her, laid her out somewhere on a big plastic sheet, cleaned her up, saw the new outfit she'd bought herself and started to dress her up. But when it came to the skirt, he just found it too difficult and time was slipping away.'

I remembered what a struggle it had been for the two of us, Harry and me, with that dead weight, pulling the tight skirt up, zipping it.

'So he grabbed an easy, slip-on skirt with an elastic band, put that on her, and the new sandals, but, being a man in a hurry, didn't bother with the matching jewellery she'd bought. In spite of all his care, he must have noticed some blood on the bedspread in his victim's room so, from among the things he'd brought with him, he replaced it with one of his own. He found her young lover's boots and wore them. He found a half-smoked joint somewhere in the house and took that with him too. So off she went to the Blackspot Nightclub, still wearing the peridot and pearl earrings. He parked briefly at the rear edge of the nightclub's parking area, away from the central, lit area, tipped her out and locked her car, wearing gloves all the while.

'Next, he picked up his own car in the city centre, returned the boots to the house and was heading back to Sydney—and that's when he had the very bad luck of being seen by someone,' I referred to the re-addressed envelope. 'An elderly man, on his way to the pharmacy from out of town because of an asthma attack, pulled up beside another car at a red light—and no doubt was surprised to see someone he knew waiting at the lights beside him. This person turned to the alleged killer and saw him, maybe even waved at him. Until he moved a couple of years ago, this old man Albert Vaughan, used to live in Kincaid Street, Deakin, not far from the house where the alleged killer and his wife also lived. This was appalling bad luck—a terrible fluke. The alleged killer realised the old man, once the murder became known, would definitely remember this chance encounter late at night with his ex-neighbour who was supposed to be in Sydney. He knew he had to silence the old man so he quietly followed him out along the Ginninderra Road to his house and, as he was opening the door, slipped in behind him and killed him. Then he continued on his way to Sydney.'

I changed the image on the screen to the highly magnified grey granite particles.

'What the alleged killer didn't know was that traces of *this* material,' I pointed the red laser dot '—from the retaining wall from where both female victims fell had transferred themselves from his car boot, in which in the past he'd carried retaining wall blocks—onto the wheelbrace which he'd pinched from his mother's car to use as a weapon, and from there into the wounds on the head of his third victim.'

I wanted to talk about the pollen evidence, but Sofia could do that on another occasion. It was, after all, her discovery that had helped bring these two cases together. Also, my headache was causing me to blink and the pain now extended right around my head. I would have to leave early if I wanted to make it to my planned meeting and get home by a reasonable hour.

'Thank you,' I said to the audience, explaining why I wouldn't be available after the closing speech to take further questions. I said goodnight to Wendy Chen and then walked outside into a cold Canberra night, the sky black and low above me, leaving the audience to crowd around Wendy and other speakers.

Lightning zig-zagged through the sky and accompanying thunder cracked almost overhead as I drove to the youth hostel where Jason Richardson was staying, picking up some fried chicken and some heavy-duty painkillers on the way.

•

We met in the cramped lounge room of the hostel with its odd furniture, piles of magazines, empty takeaway food cartons and a television that no one seemed to be watching, flashing away in a corner near the drinks dispenser.

Jason looked up from the table he was sitting at as I came into the room. A few of the others glanced my way before returning to their conversations or eating. I sat down opposite him and passed over the container of fried chicken. I knew from my experience with Greg that you could never go wrong offering food to young males. He took it silently and stood up.

'Let's go upstairs where it's quiet,' he said. 'My roommate won't be in till really late.'

We went upstairs to a room where two double bunks took up most of the area and sat down on opposite lower bunks. Jason opened the container of chicken. He pounced on it without offering me any while I asked him about the health of his grandmother who was recovering in hospital. She'd be home in a day or two, he said. An awkward silence followed.

'I'm not going to stay long, Jason,' I said. 'But I wanted to let you know I'm sorry about what I had to do and say the other night when your father was arrested.'

He looked away, sorrowfully embarrassed at the memory.

'And what your father said isn't true. You're not hopeless and you're not a loser. You've had a very difficult life.'

He reminded me of my own youth, the same lostness, aimlessness, and so I told him about my little sister Rosie and what had happened to her and how that had driven me until I found out the truth and how I was now in love with a woman whose family, too, was filled with suffering and homicide like his was, but that this hadn't prevented her from eventually having a good life. I even told him I'd stuffed up my relationship with this woman because of my own personal failings. 'What I'm trying to say in my not very expert way is, you're not alone. I used to think I was the only person in the world who had problems like mine but, as I've gathered more experience, I've discovered this isn't so.'

I was aware of his interest by the way he'd stopped chewing so I pulled out my card. 'The question—for both of us—is this: are we willing to do something to make our future different from the past?'

You have problems? said his disbelieving look as he took my card.

'If you want to do something to change the way you live, come and see me and I'll introduce you to a few people who might be helpful. That is, if you haven't given up on adults completely.'

His downcast eyes flashed upwards to meet mine and I held them. I saw the pain in him caused by the hollow in his heart that should have been filled with a father's love and I felt that same absence in my own heart.

'I don't know what to do, where to go. I feel I've lost everyone,' he said, his eyes filling. He bowed his head, silent sobs shaking his narrow frame. Hesitantly, I put my hand on his shoulder, like Charlie sometimes did to me. Now wasn't the time for soothing words. Sometimes grief had to be honoured and allowed to do its job.

There were tears in my eyes, too.

As I left the hostel, the rain started. Moderate at first, then heavy; the small group of addicts who sometimes hung around this corner waiting for the dealer were already sodden. That reminded me to tell Jacinta about Cheryl Tobin. Jass might talk to the girl when she surfaced, addict to addict, and show her that there *is* life after the living death of addiction—if a person has just a little willingness and the courage to change.

The question for me was the same as the one I'd put to Jason Richardson.

And I *was* willing to make the changes. But I would need a patient and gentle teacher and, at my age, I had no reason to expect this.

In the car, the rain was so heavy that I had to put the wipers on the highest speed and sit in second gear a lot of the time for the drive to Weston.

I dropped into my office and made a photocopy of my leave application, tucking it in an envelope before driving back to the cottage.

Some mail was sticking out of the painted four-gallon drum on the fence and I grabbed it as I drove through the gate and up the driveway. I smiled when I saw Jacinta's car parked near the house.

I tiptoed through the sleeping household, threw the damp mail on the coffee table near the fire, saw Greg's backpack tossed on the lounge next to the cuddling lemurs, took a couple of painkillers and collapsed onto a lounge chair, the sound of the heavy rain soothing. Half of my little family was here.

The sodden sound of heavy dripping made me swear and I looked up to see water coming through the ceiling onto a darker patch on the old carpet. I dug out a bucket, thinking that as soon as the rain stopped, I was going to have to get on the roof and fix that leak.

Next morning, my head had improved considerably and the rain was still falling. I looked in on the spare bedroom to see Jacinta snuggled down and gently closed the door again. Greg's snores from the little back room across the hall were a comforting sound.

Leaving the youngsters to sleep in, I ate my toast and scrambled eggs in the lounge room, in front of the fire which I'd rebuilt from the coals. The water feature in the middle of the room splashed away—the bucket was almost full. I emptied it, then cleared the table near the window and sat to compose my letter to Iona. Short and to the point, I wrote that I'd seen enough of—*lived* in—the terrible silence that permeates the lives of unhappy families to know that it was essential that I learn how to spend time with her as she wanted, my son and daughter as well. I'd come to see that my obligations were to her and my kids, not to the dead, the job or anything else. To this end, I'd taken a month's leave from work to take stock of my situation and to start changing—if she would give me one more chance. I signed it with love and enclosed the photocopy of my leave application. Then I added a P.S. asking her to ring me if there was still a chance.

I stood up and went to the window, staring out at the blessed rain spreading the falling petals of the last roses, gurgling into the tanks, beating on the roof, steady and constant. Brown rivulets ran down either side of the cambered gravel driveway onto the road; the paddocks opposite were already misted with sharper gold, as if an artist had touched a wet yellow ground with one camel hair of blue from his brush and hinted green; the hills beyond them seemed already softer, more fully rounded, swelling under the flow of rain.

I'd deal with the unlicensed handgun. I'd find some way round it. And anything Earl Richardson said about me—if he survived his second coronary—I'd simply deny. It would be his word against mine and I had a certain amount of confidence that I'd win that fight.

I turned my attention to the pile of mail on the table. A couple of damp bills and a pink envelope. When I opened it, out fell a pale pink business card depicting a reclining nude, in tones so pale as to be almost invisible. *The pleasure of a life-time*, read the dark gold overprinting. *Demi of Bondi will take you to heaven and back. Erotic body-slides, full massage, full service available.*

I turned it over. On the back she'd scrawled, *Like I said, Jack, I owe you one.* And signed it with a graceful 'S'. I couldn't help smiling.

I put down both the bills and the business card, sealed my letter and, grabbing an old raincoat, hurried out to my car.

The drive back into town was slow through the slanting rain and when I came to the apartment block in Ainslie, I wondered if I was doing the right thing. Hell, I thought, the worst she can do is throw my letter away.

I scuttled across the road and shoved it in Anne-Marie's mailbox and returned to the car. As I was climbing in, I saw someone at the window of the apartment but couldn't discern who it was.

I drove away, swishing through water. There were a dozen jobs that needed doing at work but I didn't stop at Weston. I drove straight back to the cottage, praying Iona would call soon and, as I pulled up outside the house, I could hear the phone ringing inside.

I raced to unlock the front door, ran down the hall and grabbed it, my heart pounding.

'Jack?' she said.

Outside, the rain grew steadily heavier, teeming, the sound deafening on the tin roof.

'Yes,' I said, my heart skipping. 'Yes, yes, yes.'